Praise for Ward Carroll's "Punk" novels

"This superb novel of contemporary naval aviation by former fighter pilot Carroll . . . will set readers' adrenaline and testosterone racing." —*Publishers Weekly*

"Tom Clancy meets Joseph Heller in this riveting, irreverent portrait of the fighter pilots of today's Navy. At last somebody got it right. I couldn't put it down."
—Stephen Coonts

"A rousing debut tale about the jet-flying set in which heroism, high-tech expertise, and a warts-and-all look at the Navy get equal measure. . . . Written by a man who spent fifteen years flying Tomcats, and who has served as a consultant on such films as *The Hunt for Red October*: a convincing, often amusing, surprisingly unflinching account." —*Kirkus Reviews*

"An exciting tale of a young lieutenant's tour of duty as a fighter pilot on an aircraft carrier stationed near Iraq. . . . An intriguing look at the modern military, this novel honors the men and women who serve . . . a fast and worthwhile debut." —*Library Journal*

"A thoughtful rumination on the ethics of war fighters and the notions of duty, loyalty, and honor. . . . This is a compelling picture of the harsh realities of professional life for some of the most intelligent, able, and courageous young people in our society." —*Booklist*

"For your bookshelf to rest alongside *The Caine Mutiny, The Bridges at Toko Ri,* and *Run Silent, Run Deep*."
—*The Hook*, official journal of the Tailhook Association

continued . . .

PUNK'S FIGHT

······························

WARD CARROLL

A SIGNET BOOK

SIGNET
Published by New American Library, a division of
Penguin Group (USA) Inc., 375 Hudson Street,
New York, New York 10014, U.S.A.
Penguin Books Ltd, 80 Strand,
London WC2R 0RL, England
Penguin Books Australia Ltd, 250 Camberwell Road,
Camberwell, Victoria 3124, Australia
Penguin Books Canada Ltd, 10 Alcorn Avenue,
Toronto, Ontario, Canada M4V 3B2
Penguin Books (N.Z.) Ltd, Cnr Rosedale and Airborne Roads,
Albany, Auckland 1310, New Zealand

Penguin Books Ltd, Registered Offices:
80 Strand, London WC2R 0RL, England

First published by Signet, an imprint of New American Library,
a division of Penguin Group (USA) Inc.

First Printing, March 2004
10 9 8 7 6 5 4 3 2 1

PUBLISHER'S NOTE
This is a work of fiction. Names, characters, places, and incidents either are
the product of the author's imagination or are used fictitiously, and any resem-
blance to actual persons, living or dead, business establishments, events, or
locales is entirely coincidental.

For those on the ground

PUNK'S
FIGHT

· ·

CHAPTER ONE

Closing the steel hatch behind him, Lieutenant Rick "Punk" Reichert realized that over the course of the last week he had become a stranger to the sun. He moved across Vultures' Row, the aircraft carrier's observation deck, adjusted his sunglasses, and pushed the foamies a bit deeper into his ears. At the base of the island, sixty feet below, a Tomcat roared to life, joining the shrill chorus of airplanes readying for the launch. Punk had a few hours to kill, the first discretionary time he had been afforded in some time, so he had ventured to Vultures' Row to enjoy the outdoors, as exhaust tinged as it might be at the moment.

Punk leaned his wiry frame against the ledge that ringed Vultures' Row. During his years at sea he had learned the therapeutic value of simple pleasures. Fresh from the luxury of six hours of postmission uninterrupted sleep, he tilted his head back and let the midafternoon sun above the Northern Arabian Sea beat against his angular face. He thought back to his flight-school days in Florida when the beach was only a step out the back door of the cinder-block rambler he'd rented with three fellow students. None of them would have been caught dead without a tan, and whatever studying had to be done during daylight hours was done from the comfort of a beach chair parked in the sand. The lieutenant pushed a khaki-colored flight suit sleeve up his arm and considered his skin pale from having been bathed for days in nothing but the fluorescent light of the carrier's bowels or the artificial glow of his cockpit, and wondered if he'd ever again have time for pursuits as frivolous as tan maintenance.

"Excuse me, sir," a reedy voice called through the noise. "How long do you think it'll take us to win this war?"

Punk looked to his left where a young black sailor wearing mouse ears (bulkier but more effective than the foamies) stood, an earnest expression behind his thick Navy-issue glasses. The question snapped Punk's mind briefly back to the mission over Afghanistan he'd flown during the first hours of the day, a strike against a fuel farm in the heart of Taliban-controlled territory just north of Kandahar. With the exception of a bit of jousting behind the heavy tanker by his wingman, Muddy, a female pilot on her first deployment, the mission had gone well. Save the occasional flash of ineffective small-arms fire from the ground, the two Tomcats had been unopposed in the course of dropping one-thousand-pound bombs on the assigned geographic coordinates. The first explosions had ignited the stored fuel, and the resultant mushroom cloud was captured on their mission recorders much to the glee of those gathered around the monitor during the debrief in the carrier's intelligence center.

The wind howled down the flight deck as the carrier

reached the proper course for flight operations, and Punk tugged the front zipper of his flight suit to its upper limit.

"It'll be over very soon, I think," he answered the sailor.

"That's good," the sailor said, working even harder to be heard over the breeze and the growing din from the flight deck below. "How many missions have you flown?"

Punk started to speak but paused to watch the first aircraft, an S-3 Viking, race down one of the waist catapults. "Twelve," he said with a stretch of his still-waking body.

"Is that a lot?"

"About average, I guess."

"Have you been shot at?"

"Some, yeah."

"But you guys are flying too high to get hit, right?"

"Pretty much."

The sailor whistled sharply, cutting through the whine of engines below. "Man, it must be great to drop bombs on the bad guys while knowing there's no way they can get you. And you got computers figuring everything out for you, too, right?"

Punk sensed the light of adoration had dimmed suddenly and without warning. "It's not *all* computers," he tried to explain over a Hornet roaring down the outboard waist catapult.

The noise briefly dropped back to the baseline cacophony of twenty-some airplanes at idle power.

"I was watching television in aft berthing and saw a special report on the news about the strikes on Afghanistan," the sailor said. "They called it 'video game warfare.'"

"Video game warfare, huh?"

"Yeah." The sailor briefly appeared deep in thought.

Another Hornet went to full power on the inboard waist cat. "Where do you work?" Punk shouted.

"Down in the aft galley on the second deck," the sailor yelled back. "It sucks—I think I'd rather be in the air."

The F/A-18 roared into the air and drowned Punk's chuckle out. He waited for the sound to die off a bit as the jet sped away and then paternally said, "Mess cranking's not glorious, but I'm sure your shipmates appreciate your efforts."

"I'm not mess cranking. I'm cleaning shitters."

"Oh . . . then, I *guarantee* your shipmates appreciate your efforts."

The sailor puffed a laugh and checked his watch. "Damn, I'm late," he said. "My shift supervisor's gonna have my ass again."

"Stay out of trouble, now," Punk said and extended his hand toward the sailor. "If you ever want to talk about flying, stop by the *Arrowslingers'* ready room and ask for Lieutenant Reichert."

"Lieutenant Reichert, huh?" the sailor said, pumping the officer's arm. "I just might do that, sir."

"I look forward to it," Punk said. "Here, this will remind you." He fished into the left breast pocket of his flight suit, found his wallet, and produced a half-dollar-sized sticker adorned with the *Arrowslingers'* emblem.

The sailor studied the sticker and nodded to himself. Things like patches and stickers, especially those tendered by the aviators themselves, were wampum of sorts among many of the junior enlisted who treated the squadrons in the carrier's air wing like fans treated teams in the NFL, developing a strong bias toward their favorites. For their part, the aviators cultivated the proclivities with the cunning of so many ad men.

"I'll put it on my mop handle," the sailor said with an air of self-deprecation as he pulled up on the long bar across the hatch that led back into the island.

"A place of honor," Punk said. "I feel your pain. I cleaned heads for a couple of summers when I was in high school." Actually, he'd worked as a summer camp counselor and endured the task of commode duty only a handful of times, but the sailor's smile just before he disappeared into the island told the lieutenant his half-truth was justified.

Punk watched the bar translate back to the closed position as the sailor secured the hatch from the other side and then realized he was now alone on Vultures' Row. *Alone*—a relative phenomenon on a vessel populated by fifty-five hundred people. He felt alone when he occupied his rack even though his roommate, Lieutenant "Flex" Golightly, was just feet above him in the upper bunk. He felt alone when he sat on the can in spite of the adjacent pair of legs to either side of him. And in a life dominated by the kind of brainpower required while planning wars or dropping bombs or landing on an aircraft carrier at night, a mind readily broke free when demands waned.

And so his did. Punk blankly looked down on the puzzle that was movement across the flight deck during a launch. How many hours had he spent down there behind the controls of an F-14 Tomcat, and how many more would he spend before he hung up his G suit for good?

A sea of faces passed in front of his mind's eye— flight leads, wingmen, and backseaters he'd flown with. In spite of promises to the contrary, he'd lost touch with most of them over the nine years he'd been strapping himself into an ejection seat. He reached back to even earlier days, to his time at the Naval Academy and reviewed the more memorable of the coming-of-age milestones he'd shared with classmates and wondered where those guys were now. Had a decade really gone by since they'd thrown their hats in the air at graduation and exchanged teary-eyed hugs and sworn that they'd be godparents to each others' kids?

The last of the bomb-laden Hornets of this launch was shot down catapult four and the deck hands began to button up the waist catapults so that the recovery of the fuel-critical jets and mission-weary pilots could begin. It was part of the endless cycle on the Boat: Jets launch, jets land . . . repeat, fourteen hours on, ten off, until relieved by another boat.

The noise momentarily subsided as the four airplanes yet to take off waited at idle power behind the bow catapults forward of the island. An ordnance team pushed a rack of precision-guided bombs along the right side of the landing area, reminding Punk that there was a war on.

War. How naive he'd been at graduation in spite of the lectures, sea stories, videos, and readings the Academy faculty had bombarded him with during his four years there. But that was life. There had been no way to know. Young men could wrestle with what the future held only so long before innocence and libidos pushed those concerns aside.

And who could predict the future, anyway? The changes that defined a life always came out of left field. If Punk's conception ten years ago of where he thought he'd be now had been accurate, he'd be married with two kids and flying for the airlines. But he was single in the North Arabian Sea with more than two months left in theater before the Boat was scheduled to start the journey home—assuming the current schedule was accurate.

How long do you think it'll take us to win this war, sir?

Punk hated to consider any more days on the Boat than the plan had originally called for, but war did require sacrifice, and he was fighting a war. A video game war . . .

The first Hornet crossed the ramp and slammed onto the deck in the controlled crash that was a twenty-ton fighter landing on an aircraft carrier. The jet roared at military power until the arresting wire completely halted its forward movement. The pilot pulled the throttles to idle and, on the director's signal, raised the tail hook, folded the wings, and quickly taxied out of the landing area to clear the way for his wingman, who would perform the same drill about fifty seconds later.

Punk noted that the Hornet still had a Sidewinder air-to-air missile on each wingtip but that its bomb racks were empty—no surprise, really. The enemy's air force had been destroyed on the ground within hours of the first strike of the war. The American fighter pilots had entered the conflict with the hope that their opponent of little ability but vehement zealotry would choose to confront them in the skies over Afghanistan. But the other airplanes had shown up only as infrared-generated objects on cockpit screens, and immobile objects at that.

Forward of the newly recovered Hornet now being de-armed by the ordies, a Tomcat launched off the bow and the deckhands disappeared into the resultant cloud of steam billowing out of the catapult track. The next Hornet trapped, and the "Hook Runner"—the deckhand charged with ensuring the arresting wire was clear before the pilot raised the tail hook—ran toward the aft of the fighter even as the wire was paying out. The action across the flight deck, to the untrained eye a chaotic rush of bodies maniacally signaling each other or tending to the airplanes like remoras on sharks, was a miracle of coordination, and regardless of how many times Punk took the time to consider the operation he was always struck by the working-man's beauty of it.

Punk returned his attention to the bow, where one of the last two F-14 Tomcats was about to launch. Exhaust violently washed off the raised jet blast deflector behind the fighter, and the view from Vultures' Row was distorted by the waves of heat and obscured by a veil of soot. Punk saw the airplane's rudders swish from side to side and the spoilers pop up on each wing as the pilot stirred the stick about the cockpit in a final check of the controls. The catapult officer returned the pilot's salute and then touched the deck.

Sixty-eight-thousand pounds of fighter lurched and started the quick trip down the catapult track. Punk knew the pilot was fighting the acceleration now, the force of it cutting through his midsection while he simultaneously synthesized sensory cues and absorbed the host of readings from the needles and tapes and digits and dials before him.

But halfway down the stroke something went wrong. The Tomcat suddenly stopped accelerating. A long and thin object awkwardly flung off the bow like a poorly thrown javelin—the force of the cat shot had sheared the F-14's nose gear clean off. The fighter fell against its nose and agonizingly slid toward the bow at a slowing but deliberate pace. The tires on the mainmounts transformed into white clouds as the pilot stomped the brakes in a desperate attempt to stop. The Tomcat kept going.

Punk watched, horrified, as the fighter teetered on the forward edge of the flight deck. "Eject!" he cried into the thirty knots of wind across the deck, but neither of the two seats under the canopy fired. For another heartbeat the F-14 balanced in place, and it appeared the jet might stay on the flight deck after all.

But it didn't. Instead, bomb-laden belly flashing back toward the island, the fighter pitched toward the water and disappeared over the bow. A second later an unceremonious splash crested into view, dousing the deckhands who'd run forward in a futile effort to offer assistance.

The ship heeled as it went into a hard port turn in an attempt to miss the F-14 in its path. The crash claxon clanged and the intercom began to saturate with calls for emergency personnel. The landing signal officers waved off the Hornet on the final part of its approach as the ship continued to turn and the relative wind clocked out of limits for a safe airplane recovery.

A sixty-thousand-ton aircraft carrier moving through the water at twenty knots didn't readily stop even with all four screws churning fully against its forward progress, and soon the crash site was in its wake. Punk rushed to the aft-most part of Vultures' Row and watched the plane guard helicopter hover over the spot where the North Arabian Sea had swallowed both the jet and its crew. No debris was floating on the surface. Nothing was dropped from the helo.

Only then did Punk wonder who was in the ill-fated jet. He'd reviewed the day's flight schedule just before he'd left his stateroom on his way to Vultures' Row, but in searching for his name among the twenty-four sorties, he'd failed to notice who was about to launch on the next event. He continued to watch the sea under the helicopter, willing the appearance of a helmet or a waving arm. Another helicopter hovered near the first, and both of them fell farther behind the carrier as it turned back into the wind and resumed the proper speed to recover airplanes and to launch the spare Tomcat that would take the place of the lost jet in the strike package now headed for Afghanistan.

Punk had to get to the ready room. He torqued the handle on the hatch and passed into the island. He had to wait for several sailors to pass before taking his place among the procession rushing down the ladder. His long legs were a blur as he negotiated the steps, hurrying to keep up with the pace of the others, fearing that if he lost too much distance on the man in front and below the man behind and above might climb right over him.

Punk's mind raced along with his body. Two of his squadronmates had died before his eyes. The air wing had spent three weeks bombing the enemy without a single loss, and now aviators had been killed in the routine process of launching from the deck of the aircraft carrier.

Who were they?

Spud? He couldn't have been scheduled so soon after last night's mission, but plans often changed on the Boat, and Punk knew the veteran radar intercept officer or "RIO"—*ree-oh,* as backseaters were known in the Tomcat community—would never turn down an opportunity to jump into a jet bound for the war. Reckless volunteerism, it was . . . the kind that got a man killed.

Spud was the *Arrowslingers'* executive officer, the number two man in the squadron, and the guy who'd convinced Punk to join him on this deployment with

a timely appeal to the younger pilot's patriotic sense
in the wake of the terrorist attacks of 9-11. After two
squadron tours together—one at sea and one ashore—
and too many sorties under the same canopy to count
without pulling out the log books, Spud knew exactly
how to draw the desired response out of Punk, although the emotions of that infamous day didn't make
the job of finding qualified volunteers very tough.

After working his way aft on the 0-3 level, Punk
burst through the back entrance to the *Arrowslingers'*
ready room and was immediately relieved to see
Spud's bald pate cresting above the heads of the others who'd gathered around the duty desk near the
front of the room.

Too many times in his flying life he'd waited that
eternity between the question, "Who was it?" and the
answer. He'd lost six good friends to aviation mishaps
since he'd first started taking to the air as a military
man. Beyond that figure were a dozen or so ill-fated
aviators he hadn't known as well—strike planning
teammates or guys who'd struck up conversations on
a late-night barge ride after a big night in port, just
call signs or faces—but still he'd felt each loss.

In spite of the large number of people gathered, the
ready room was draped in a public library–like quiet,
broken only by the occasional roar of a jet catching
an arresting wire just feet above them. Spud leaned
against the chest-high railing around the elevated duty
desk, talking into a phone in clipped phrases and scribbling on a notepad. Lieutenant commanders stood to
either side of him with dour countenances. The duty
officer, Lieutenant "Helmet" Villacone, a burly first-
tour pilot from Philly who'd earned his call sign for
the way he styled his thick hair, was seated behind
the desk and talking on the other line. Helmet, work-

ing hard to keep his voice down, repeated, "I don't have that information, yet," a half-dozen times, his unibrow in deep furrow, fingers fitfully working through his jet-black pompadour. Duty days were bad enough on any day at sea, but losing a jet on your watch was like winning the lottery from hell.

"I've told you everything I know, sir," Spud said curtly into the other phone. "I'll keep you posted as we go along here." After a few yessirs he hung up. The phone immediately rang again, and the XO looked to the thin and balding squadron safety officer, Lieutenant Commander "Slick" Floatney, and said, "You get it."

Slick didn't appear very eager to answer the phone but did, and as he listened intently to the voice on the other end of the line, Spud pushed through the small crowd and fell back into his ready room chair at the front of the room, cradling his chin in one hand while running the other across the full surface of his pate. Another tail hook hit the deck and the crack of steel on steel split through the ready room, followed by the whoosh of jet engines and the deafening whine of the arresting gear machinery in the adjacent space.

Once the wire was done paying out, Punk pulled his fingers out of his ears and looked up at the dry erase board behind the duty desk upon which the day's flight schedule was scribed. He noted that the only jet from the last event without a diagonal line next to it—an "airborne" indication—was the one piloted by the commanding officer.

"That was the skipper's jet that went down?" Punk asked. Several irritated grimaces, stern petitions for silence, gave the reply. He refocused on the board to see who was in the rear cockpit of the lost Tomcat and was shocked to see "CAG" written in the RIO

column next to the skipper's name. "CAG," short for
the archaic designation of "carrier air group," remained the traditional label for the air wing commander, the senior flying officer on the carrier.

"And CAG—" The end of Punk's emphatic whisper
was cut off by the sound of the last airplane, an S-3
Viking, recovering.

Lieutenant "Einstein" Francis, a first-tour RIO and
one of the handful of officers remaining on the *Arrowslingers'* roster from Punk's previous tour with the
squadron a couple of years before caught his eye.
Even after several weeks Punk still wasn't used to
seeing him with a shaved head, a haircut that seemed
out of character for a guy who'd descended upon the
squadron three years ago with a full head of proudly
combed brown hair. The haircut put a militant spin
on an otherwise conforming package, and Punk had
kept a keen eye out for other signs of how Einstein's
tour with the *Arrowslingers* had changed him. He was
definitely heavier—Punk would've guessed as much as
twenty pounds had been added to his previously svelte
frame—but that was probably just a result of his diet
at sea. Einstein wasn't the first guy to bulk up a bit
after a cruise or two.

Einstein noticed Punk in return, waited a few beats,
and then leaned over and quietly said, "They had a
bad cat shot. It looks like the nose gear ripped off
halfway down the track."

"I know," Punk replied, matching the volume of
Einstein's voice. "I saw it happen from Vultures'
Row."

Einstein glanced over each shoulder and then led
Punk by the biceps to the second row of ready room
chairs. "What did you see?" Einstein asked in a voice
just louder than a whisper as he sat down.

"Just like you said," Punk replied from the adjacent chair. "The shot started out all right, but in the middle of it the nose gear came off somehow." He raised a hand to illustrate his explanation. "I saw the jet flop down and then the shuttle chucked the nose gear off the bow. I kept waiting for them to eject . . ." His voice trailed off.

They sat silently for a time, each staring at the back of the headrest of the chair directly in front of him, listening to the local side of the phone conversations going on around the duty desk.

"Did you ever fly with CAG Bernard out here?" Einstein muttered.

"Once," Punk said. "Early on."

"What did you think?"

"Friendly. Quiet. Competent enough for a Prowler guy with limited time in the back of the Tomcat."

Einstein sighed and shook his head. "He'd just decided to fly with us more often since CENTCOM had left the jammers off the air tasking order after the second night of the war," he said. "Not enough tankers and too few radar sites in Afghanistan for them to jam, so CAG decided to stay in the game by putting on his RIO hat. Must be nice to be in charge and fly whatever you want . . . except in this case, of course."

Another silence followed. Punk tried to recall the details of the flight with Captain Bernard. It had been a simple mission: combat air patrol fifty miles north of the Boat. A perfect hop for a senior officer with limited time in the F-14.

Einstein's thoughts drifted to the other man. "I always liked the skipper," he said. "The rumors about him were mostly bogus, you know? He wasn't that much of a politician. Sure, he knew the system, but Smooth was a junior officer at heart."

"I knew him for only a few weeks," Punk said, "but I never had any problem with him."

"Did you ever hear him tell the story from his lieutenant days about the admin in Rio de Janeiro?"

"No, I don't think so."

Einstein leaned toward Punk and said, "Put it this way: blow jobs and dysentery are generally a bad combination." They momentarily lost themselves in a snicker, suppressed before drawing more icy stares.

"But just like that he's gone, huh?" Einstein wondered aloud as he rubbed his eyes with his fists. "I never figured he'd be the guy to die like this. He had that aura, you know? I thought he was bulletproof."

"I'm afraid none of us are," Punk said.

Punk saw Einstein blink as if coming out of a trance. "You need to talk to the safety officer, Punk," Einstein said, pointing toward Slick, who remained on the phone. "He'll want you to write down a witness statement."

Slick hung up and took a seat next to Spud. The two of them conferred for a few minutes, and then Slick pushed through the crowd and headed for the back of the ready room, presumably to recharge the empty coffee mug he balanced on a folder he was holding with both hands. Punk rose out of his seat and moved silently behind the lieutenant commander as the senior man added packets of cream and sugar to his coffee. Slick whirled around and jerked a bit in surprise, nearly spilling his newly filled mug over the folder.

"I saw the mishap happen," Punk said as Slick steadied his burden.

"On the PLAT?" Slick asked, referring to the pilot landing assist television, the closed-circuit system that continuously broadcast flight operations to monitors throughout the carrier.

"No, I was up on Vultures' Row."

"You saw the whole thing, the cat shot from beginning to end?"

"Yeah."

"That makes you a witness." Slick set the mug down on the counter next to the coffeepot and removed a sheet of paper from the inside of the folder. "Fill this out and spare no details." He pointed toward the last row of ready room chairs. "Take a seat with those guys, but leave the chair next to you empty and don't talk to anyone while you're writing your statement."

Punk took the piece of paper and moved toward the last row.

"You're lucky," Slick said to his back. "Witnesses can't be on the mishap board."

Punk considered that fact as he sat down again and felt guilty for allowing himself even the briefest sense of relief.

Standing at attention in the third rank of the formation of squadron officers and chiefs, Punk furtively cut his eyes toward the podium and watched Rear Admiral Reginald "Dutch" Dykstra, the aircraft carrier's battle group commander, rise out of his chair and move behind the podium on the modest dais towering all of a foot over the hangar bay's nonskid surface. The admiral removed his cover before starting his remarks, which allowed several locks of brilliant white hair to cascade across his weathered forehead, and stared above the heads of those mustered as if searching for inspiration on the far bulkhead. He held the pose, aged but still chiseled lines of his face fixed, working the tension the silence created.

After a few moments the admiral shifted his attention to the officers and enlisted men lined up before him and began his eulogy. His voice projected through the speakers on the corners of the dais and echoed around the stricken jets between which the ceremony had been shoehorned. He delivered his remarks with a statesman's polish, calling the fallen "lamplighters for the town that is the air wing" and relating that the way to tell a true hero was that "he or she doesn't come back." On the hangar bay floor each superlative was met by Punk's roommate, Flex, who stood in the ranks repeatedly muttering under his breath, "So what? They're dead."

Punk's eyes followed the admiral back to his seat, and he considered what the old man had been like in his days as a lieutenant. It seemed unlikely that he'd ever been simply one of the boys trying to light his farts in the eight-man stateroom. Then Punk tried to picture any one of the squadron lieutenants who surrounded him as an admiral twenty-five years down the line, but no images would form.

The memorial service went on and Punk wrestled with whether to be amazed or put off by the efficiency with which it had been arranged. The supporting players unflinchingly went through the motions. The color guard marched smartly. The band played. The chaplain prayed. Seven Marines perched on the lowered elevator repeatedly fired in unison toward the sea. All of these people had seemingly laid in wait for this sort of tragedy to descend on the ship. In less than twenty-four hours the two leaders had been transformed from flesh and blood into dry-mounted posters resting on easels to either side of the podium. Now a squadron without a skipper and an air wing without a CAG stood before the large portraits in silence. The chaplain gave the benediction, bridging from scripture to the definition of a patriot as the band played the sad strains of the Navy Hymn in the background, and Punk, as he had when previously studying pictures of the deceased at memorial services, looked into the eyes of the two-dimensional faces beaming down from the dais and wondered what they might be seeing now.

CHAPTER TWO

No speeches, no band, no reception, no fanfare, not at all the assumption of command Spud had repeatedly imagined from the moment nearly two years ago when the Chief of Naval Operations had informed him that he'd screened for his own squadron. Instead, Rear Admiral Dykstra had approached him after the memorial service and casually announced: "I guess you're the skipper now. Good luck with it."

At dinner hours later Punk herded the baked beans on his plate into a circle and stole glances across the wardroom table at the squadron's new commanding officer. He'd seen Spud down before, but not like this. His face was still except for the slow movement of his jaw as he chewed. His eyes were distant, unfocused.

Punk took a bite of stale roll and thought back to the flight he'd flown with Spud in his backseat earlier in the day. The skipper had been uncharacteristically withdrawn in the airplane in spite of the fact that the mission was only a postmaintenance check flight, a relatively low-stress event compared to dropping bombs on Afghanistan. As the two of them had manned up on the flight deck, Punk had been sure the hop would be just the sort of therapy Spud needed to clear the funk that shrouded him. But he'd barely uttered a word during the two hours they'd shared under the F-14's canopy.

The catapult fired above the heads of the officers in Wardroom One, the air wings' dining area in the bow, drowning out the clatter of silverware against plates and shaking everything that wasn't bolted down. Spud cut his eyes toward the PLAT monitor in the near corner of the room as he removed a folded paper copy of the day's flight schedule from one of the chest pockets of his flight suit. He concentrated on the screen: a black-and-white presentation showing the twin white glows of the engines eventually disappearing into the night. Punk then shifted his attention to the flight schedule.

"Was that one of ours?" Spud asked, attempting to take in all of the faces around him at once. "Did anyone see?" No one answered, and he seethed a bit as he refolded the paper and returned it to his pocket. He stared at his plate a bit longer and then quietly excused himself and walked out of the wardroom.

Peeler, one of the midgrade lieutenants, waited until Spud disappeared before wondering aloud, "Is it just me, or does the skipper seem exceptionally bummed out?" Peeler suffered from eczema flare-ups when he was stressed, and combat sorties over Afghanistan had covered his hands, face, and neck in red, flaky blotches that were poorly hidden by a white cream the flight surgeon had prescribed with the warning that if the condition grew any worse he'd be grounded. Punk tried not to look at him, fearing the sight of his molting might completely ruin his already meager appetite.

"Does anyone know who our new XO is going to be?" Einstein asked.

"Won't have one right away," Lieutenant Commander "Monster" Meyers said, his wide mouth stuffed full of hamburger and framed above with a thick black mustache. "They're scrambling stateside. May wind up shifting in-house." Monster was a large man, Mutt to his roommate Slick's Jeff. Like Einstein, he had shaved his head to the skin once the Boat passed through the Suez Canal and had been satisfied enough with the result to preserve the look since then—an even more imposing presentation for the former college football standout. He held the collateral billet of operations officer, and with Smooth's passing he had become the squadron's senior pilot. He was also the junior officers' most prolific, if not accurate, news source.

"So, is Captain Sutcliffe fleeting up from Deputy CAG to CAG?"

"Yes."

The form of Captain "Penguin" Sutcliffe briefly flashed into Punk's mind: Even when dressed in full flight gear Penguin couldn't hide that his hips were nearly twice as wide as his shoulders. And that, along with the fact that the captain was an S-3 tanker pilot, was basically all Punk knew about the man.

"Who's going to be the new deputy?"

"Some guy coming in from the Pentagon," Monster said. "A Captain Campbell, I think. I'm not sure I know him, although I guess I should. Supposedly he's a Tomcat pilot."

"Not Soup Campbell," Punk said with a wince.

"You know, now that you mention it," Monster replied, expression brightening with the clarity, "I'll bet it *is* Soup Campbell." He considered his words and his joy quickly faded. "Oh, Christ. Soup Campbell . . ." He looked over at Punk. "Weren't you in the *Arrowslingers* when he was the skipper? Is he really as bad as they say?"

Punk didn't reply but focused on Einstein, whose face had now lost all color. Without a word the two of them dropped their forks and rushed out of the wardroom. Punk led the way with Einstein in close trail chanting "Soup Campbell" over and over in a zombielike monotone as they hustled down the port main passageway on the 0-3 level with the intensity of sailors headed for their battle stations, nearly bowling over the less harried along the way.

Punk banged on the door to Spud's stateroom like a revolutionary pounding on the palace gate. Spud threw the door open, ready to jump down their throats until he realized who'd summoned him. His posture relaxed. He read their eyes and knew why they were there.

"Yes," the skipper said with a sigh. "He's coming."

Punk and Einstein looked down on the flight deck from primary flight control, the lofty perch six stories up, the uppermost enclosed vantage point on the aircraft carrier's island. They watched the C-2 carrier on-board delivery airplane—the COD—trap and then park behind the bow catapults. The propellers came to a halt, and the passengers filed down the COD's aft ramp.

"There he is," Einstein said, pressing an index finger against the thick glass that surrounded pri-fly. There was no mistaking him: Soup Campbell, abusive, self-centered, obtuse, connected, polished, and disarmingly charismatic when he wanted or needed to be; he of admirable aviation pedigree, including tours as a Top Gun instructor and Opposing Solo on the Blue Angels. He strode among the procession of sailors in blue dungarees and officers in khakis, all wearing "cranials," the inelegant headgear that integrated sound attenuators and goggles, wholly distinct in a green flight suit and aviator's helmet topped with a gold visor.

"Looks like he's still got his crown," Punk said. "Of course, he'd never be caught dead in a cranial. Those are for the commoners."

"I really hoped I'd never see him again," Einstein said wistfully. He concentrated on the helmeted figure now separated from the single-file line of new arrivals making their way across the flight deck toward the air transport office where they'd be reunited with their baggage, and as he did, he unconsciously and very slowly shook his head. "Do you think about it?"

"Of course," Punk replied.

"Sometimes I wonder if I think about it too much."

"What part?"

"The ejection, mostly. How Iraq looked during the parachute ride down." Einstein nervously scratched his scalp and faced Punk. "Did you ever stop and consider that you and I ejected several weeks apart and both of those events could have been attributed to command decisions made by Soup Campbell?"

"Countless times."

"Then why weren't they?"

"Mine was, more or less," Punk said. "Yours . . . I don't know. I guess it got lost along the way to Soup Campbell becoming a national hero."

Einstein leaned his forehead against the glass and cast his eyes back downward. Punk reached over and gave the back of his neck a paternal squeeze. "You've already outlasted him," he said with a smile. "We both have."

Einstein tapped the glass and said, "But he's back now." Punk refocused on the flight deck. His smile faded.

Just before Captain Campbell reached the base of the island and disappeared from the two junior officers' view, he stopped and removed his helmet. Both of the lieutenants pressed their foreheads against the thick glass of pri-fly and rose up on their tiptoes to keep him in sight. They watched him intently, absorbing clues, hoping for something that would diminish their anxiety.

Soup used his free hand to smooth his thick hair. Was it completely gray now? He was really too far away for them to tell. The captain paused for another beat, looked down at his flight boots, and then, without warning, raised his face to pri-fly and the junior officers therein. They froze, trapped by Soup's cold blue eyes. And despite the distance between pri-fly and the flight deck, each of the lieutenants was convinced that he was the target.

Spud sat on the small couch in CAG's stateroom and waited with the other eight air wing commanding officers for the new Deputy CAG to show up. In an adjacent corner were three cardboard boxes stacked nearly to the acoustic tiled ceiling, and after a moment's curiosity Spud spotted "Captain Bernard" scribbled in black ink on the top line of the form taped to the side of each box. Personal effects of the deceased CAG. Twenty-some years at sea reduced to three cardboard boxes. Who'd had the macabre task of packing, and what would Mrs. Bernard do when she received them?

Unlike the squadron CO and XO staterooms, which were mix and match, the air wing commander's stateroom was bigger and more functional than the Deputy CAG's glorified version of the squadron staterooms. The CAG stateroom was near the battle group commander's spaces and included an adjoining office with a desk and enough furniture for most of the commanding officers to sit down at once. Regardless of how Captain Sutcliffe had felt about the move, he'd had to make it. He was the CAG now, and the CAG worked out of the CAG's stateroom.

The door opened, and the commanding officers instinctively came to attention. They waited. And waited. They could hear a conversation in the passageway. Then laughter. In the time spent anticipating a body materializing in the doorway, Spud's mind raced with the possible scenarios the meeting might hold, none of them good.

Then Captain "Soup" Campbell appeared, beaming with an air of celebrity, a swagger that said "of course you've heard of me and read my book." His attitude was just short of arrogant, and he was too well bred to come off as affected. Spud noted that he had allowed his hair to turn completely gray and was as perma-tanned as ever. He looked fit, distinguished, and statesmanlike.

CAG Sutcliffe, a head shorter and several strings less athletic in appearance, followed Captain Campbell into the stateroom and shut the door. Before Sutcliffe could manage an introduction, Soup began to work the room in a counterclockwise circle, shaking hands with each commander, disarming them along the way

with the illusion that they were all old friends, even
the officers he'd never met before:

"Frosty, good to see you, shipmate."

"J-Dog, the best damn helicopter pilot in the fleet."

"And Paulie Perilio, the Italian stallion, you war-
fighting sonofagun. You're always where the action is,
aren't you?"

Spud looked to either side of him and realized he
would be last in the de facto receiving line. He tried
to suppress his thoughts, tried to forget that Soup was
the man who'd attempted to keep him from ever getting his own fighter squadron by laying the blame on
Punk and him for flaming out one night on their last
deployment while diverting to a base in Kuwait they
were told was open but was really closed. He fought
to quiet his heart as it increasingly pounded in his
chest and throat. He surreptitiously rubbed his palms
against his flight suit in an attempt to keep them dry.

An eternity and eight commanding officers later,
Soup stood before Spud. The captain was silent, his
expression stern. Spud tried to remain impassive as
they locked eyes. He tried not to blink. The contest
of wills went on for several seconds. Spud thought he
heard a nervous titter from across the circle.

Soup's stern countenance slowly broke into a smile.
"Skipper, huh?" he said and extended his hand. As
Spud reached for it, Soup instead threw both arms
around Spud's biceps in a chummy hug, pinning his
arms against his sides. Across Deputy CAG's shoulder
Spud saw a few smiles, but he was too shocked by the
gesture to think about interpreting them. Soup shook
him a few times and then pushed back to arm's length.

"It is really good to see you, Spud," Soup gushed
before turning around to Captain Sutcliffe. "I go way
back with this guy, CAG." He shook Spud a few more

times and then moved back toward the desk. "You certainly have an all-star team here."

"I do, indeed," CAG replied as he gestured for the deputy to take a seat behind the desk in a leather executive chair. The Deputy CAG stepped across the office and sat down, and Sutcliffe stood behind him and began to address the skippers: "I wanted all of you to have a chance to—"

"Sorry, CAG," Soup said with a half turn behind him, throwing a hand up like he expected CAG to pass him something, "but would you mind if I said a few things first?" Sutcliffe flinched slightly, surprised by the request, but then shrugged. Soup returned a single sharp nod and turned back to the commanders. He saw they were still standing and directed them to sit down, which left CAG without a chair. A few of the COs feigned getting out of their seats, but Sutcliffe waved them back down and wound up sitting on an arm of the couch opposite the desk, which forced the three skippers seated there, including Spud, to scrunch uncomfortably close to each other.

"First, let me say I'm very sorry for the loss of CAG Bernard and Skipper Renforth," Captain Campbell said. "They were both great leaders and this wing has suffered a terrible blow because of this tragedy. I'm sure CAG has already talked to you about moving on emotionally, so I won't belabor that point except to second that motion. We do have to move on, and quickly."

Spud shot a furtive glance at the sheet of paper on Sutcliffe's lap and noticed the first bullet of the talking points he'd intended to go over with the group: *1. Need to get past grief.*

"I'm not here to change anything," Soup continued. "I'm just here to help. Like I said, this is an all-star

team. I'd be a fool to try and mess with a good thing."
He faced CAG. "Are you flying anything other than
the S-3 out here, Penguin?" CAG shook his head.
"All right," Soup said, leering into each face of the
three Hornet skippers and Spud. "When the bubble
went up I took the time to get dual qualified, so I
guess I'll be flying with you boys on CAG's behalf
then. Here are my general guidelines . . ." He leaned
against the desk, raised a fist, and added a finger to it
with each one of his points. "I'd like to fly day strikes
in both types of jet but keep only my night currency
in the Hornet." It was common knowledge that the
Hornet was easier to bring aboard the carrier than the
Tomcat, especially at night. "I don't want to lead any
events at first, so tell your operations officers to schedule me as a wingman. That's the best way for me to
gauge for myself the proficiency of the air wing's strike
leads. If your stateside reputation is any indication,
I'm sure I'll be impressed." He smiled, and as his eyes
danced around several of the COs each of them offered an obligatory smile back. "And no graduation
runs right out of the chute, please."

"Do you want to fly a FAM hop or two before you
go feet dry?" CAG asked.

"No, I'm ready," Soup insisted, but then paused for
a few moments. "Let's do it this way: Make the first
hop a straightforward day strike in the Tomcat."

CAG shrugged again and pointed at the ranking
Arrowslinger. Spud nodded while scribbling a note
against the screen of his PDA and asked, "Day after
tomorrow?"

The new Deputy glanced at CAG, who shrugged
once again. "Fine," Soup said after waiting one more
beat for Sutcliffe to offer an objection. "Have your

ops officer come brief me on the high points once the flight schedule for that day is finalized."

"Roger," Spud replied without looking up, still intently scribbling on the handheld.

"All right," CAG said, "as I was saying before, I just wanted to give you a chance—"

"Oh, one more thing," Soup said. "Is there a press pool out here?"

Captain Sutcliffe winced in confusion. "Press pool?"

"Yeah, you know, media types."

CAG looked around the room to make sure he wasn't being put on, and said, "They come and go, I guess."

"Let me handle them." Soup's lips curled in a wry grin as he looked across the faces of the others. "I've had a bit of experience with that."

"Whatever."

"All questions from the onboard press corps should be directed to me first."

"Fine."

Commander "J-Dog" Miller, one of the wing's three Hornet squadron COs, coyly leaned over and whispered into Spud's ear: "The secret to Soup's success."

Soup pushed away from the desk. "Like I said, I'm here to help."

Spud could see in CAG Sutcliffe's expression that he'd either lost interest in this particular meeting or the endurance required to keep it going in the direction he'd originally intended. Without another attempt at fanfare or even a formal introduction, he stood and said, "That's it, fellas. Thanks for coming by."

After the last jet recovered and the flight deck crew put the airplanes in place for the few hours they'd be

idle during the night, the *Arrowslinger* officers, save
those who were debriefing the strike they'd just flown
or those who were planning strikes for the next day,
gathered in the ready room at the skipper's behest.
Normally at this point in an evening, the duty officer
would have pulled down the screen mounted above
the dry erase boards, turned on the projector hanging
above the skipper's chair, and slipped a DVD into the
player. The nightly movie, or "roll 'em" as it was better known, had been poorly attended since the strikes
had begun—officers were either too tired or too busy
for the diversion—but Skipper Renforth had insisted
the ritual continue all the same. So duty officers, as
they always had during the course of their duty day,
scribed elaborate, perhaps garish, marquees with dry
erase marker on the boards like theater managers attempting to up their gate, and the aviators smiled and
took brief solace in the insouciance of the routine as
they hurried off to fashion or fight a war.

But not tonight. As he stood at the front of the
ready room, Spud could see in the hollow stares before him that his charges were dragging, so he got
right to the point.

"We have a new Deputy CAG," Spud said, attempting to be stoic about the fact. "You may know
Captain Campbell was the commanding officer of this
squadron a few years back." He paused for a moment,
searching the floor at his feet. He cleared his throat
and continued. "He's a Tomcat pilot and will be flying
with us occasionally."

Spud ignored the few groans uttered from the seats.
"But that news is not the primary reason behind my
calling this meeting. It's become obvious to me over
the last two days that the squadron cannot function
without an executive officer. Now we've all heard the

bureau isn't sending us one right away, so I'm making Monster the acting XO."

Monster's head jerked back with the news. He shrugged and smiled sheepishly and warded off the backslaps that were thrown at him across his seat in the second row. "Although this increase in responsibility doesn't come with a promotion," Spud said, "I expect everyone to treat him just like you treated me when I was the XO." He caught himself. "Amend that: Treat him *better* than you treated me."

The skipper raised his arms to quiet the cross talk, although pleased by the animation considering that everyone had worn hangdog expressions on the way in. "Obviously, if we fleet Monster up to XO that leaves us in need of an operations officer." He scanned the room as if he were about to announce the winner of a raffle. "It strikes me that the least disruptive way to fill the bill is give the job to the *assistant* operations officer."

Punk flinched. *He* was the assistant operations officer. "The change is effective immediately, Punk," Spud said.

The rumble of side conversations increased again. Flex waved his hand in an attempt to get the skipper's attention, and when that didn't work he stood up. "Shouldn't the operations officer be a lieutenant commander, skipper?" the muscular RIO asked, one hand working his blond hair off of his forehead as he spoke.

Spud gestured toward Monster and said, "You mean the same way the XO should be a commander?"

Flex's eyes narrowed and he slumped back into his high-backed, faux-leather ready room chair. In a world of change was *everything* subject to change?

Spud nodded and said, "You're right, Flex. The op-

erations officer should be a lieutenant commander."
He removed a sheet of paper from the lower leg
pocket of his flight suit. "Punk, front and center."

Punk furrowed his brow and moved warily out of
his chair and stood next to the skipper. "I've been
distracted today, but I did manage to see this," Spud
said as he studied the paper at close range. He turned
to Punk and asked, "Is your name Richard J.
Reichert?"

"Yes, sir," Punk replied.

"Are the last four digits of your social security number zero-five-five-seven?"

"Yes."

"In that case, congratulations. You've been promoted to lieutenant commander."

Spud fished into a chest pocket and produced two
gold oak leaf collar devices as the officers applauded
with various degrees of enthusiasm. A few of them
cheered. The skipper gestured for Monster to come
up, and the two of them split the duty of pinning the
insignia to the collar of Punk's flight suit, which looked
strange but appropriately ceremonial.

Spud shook Punk's hand as the others filed out of
their chairs and formed a line down the center aisle.
As they greeted him, the handful of lieutenant commanders welcomed Punk to the ranks of middle man-
agement, some halfheartedly, and the twenty-some
lieutenants and lieutenants (junior grade) asked when
the lobotomy was scheduled to take place.

But the celebration died off as quickly as it ramped
up with the realization that the war hadn't ended with
these changes in rank and status. Monster and several
other lieutenant commanders beseeched the skipper
to hold a department head meeting, no doubt to run

the new changes to absolute ground before too much
time passed, but Spud balked at the idea and instead
attempted to keep the party going with an announce-
ment that the roll 'em would be his favorite movie,
Cheers for Reggie. The skipper's morale-building efforts were in vain; by the end of the opening credits
the only officers left in the ready room were Spud,
Punk, and the duty officer, Lieutenant "Frisco" Fran-
cisco, a fiery Hispanic pilot who'd fretted that his
choice for the roll 'em had not been *Cheers for Reggie.*

For Punk, watching *Cheers for Reggie* in the presence of Spud was like listening to classic rock on the
radio. Sitting in the dark, as Spud spouted each line
of dialogue a split second before the actor on the
screen, Punk reflected on the last deployment and the
innocence lost across the spectrum of his life over
those six months. He thought of his former girlfriend,
Jordan, and the bad phone call they'd had while he
was on liberty in Bahrain, and of her final "Dear
Rick" e-mail. And he thought of Soup Campbell.

"Does he seem any different?" Punk asked in one
of the film's few quiet moments.

"It's hard to tell," Spud replied without questioning
the pronoun's antecedent. His mind had obviously
been similarly occupied. "I expect we'll know soon."
He lolled his head across the headrest toward Punk.
"Speaking of that: I just made you the operations officer, didn't I, Lieutenant Commander Reichert?"

"You did. It's not too late to change your mind."

"I have a task for you: You need to stick the new
Deputy CAG on the flight schedule for the day after
tomorrow."

"Already, huh? What kind of hop?"

"Day strike."

"Into Afghanistan?"

"Are we dropping bombs on another country I don't know about?"

"Is he leading this flight?"

"No. He gave explicit instructions that he only wanted to be a wingman."

"So, whose wing should I put him on?" Punk had his answer as a sardonic grin grew across Spud's face, highlighted by the glow from the screen. "You've got to be shitting me."

"I'll be right there with you, buddy," Spud said. "You know I don't like this root canal any more than you, but who else in the squadron could handle this if we don't?"

"Who's going to be his RIO?"

Spud repeated the expression he'd used to answer the previous question and said, "The Deputy CAG has requested a brief on the details of the mission as soon as they're known."

The door to the eight-man stateroom jarred more memories loose as he approached. It had been re-painted since the last deployment, changed to a bright glossy red from flat black, and although the lettering was a different style, it still read, THE CHEESEQUART-ERS. This was where Punk had lived during his first cruise, the center of his universe, the home of truth, justice, and the junior officers' way.

Their faces came to him, his roommates from those days that seemed like decades ago and just yesterday all at the same time: Biff, husky, pink, blond, always complaining. He'd left the Navy to fly for the airlines, been furloughed in the wake of 9-11, and was now working as a Realtor. Trash, the porn king, the exhibitionist, had taken a job as a car salesman. Scooter, "the most handsome man in naval aviation," had married well, his wife a successful boutique owner. On last report Scooter was spending his days poolside in Miami. Monk, the puritan, the anti-Trash, had resigned his commission to pursue an advanced theology degree. Fuzzy, the fighter pilot who had pushed the lower limit of the lowest common denominator in terms of flying ability every time he'd strapped into a Tomcat, had earned a helicopter type rating and was working in Los Angeles as "Chopper Dave" for a local radio shock jock where the irreverent outlook he'd honed in the *Arrowslingers* was given full play. The others, Weezer and Chum, had stayed in the Navy but several tours later Punk had lost track of them.

Punk knocked quietly, hoping not to disturb those who might have hit the rack in the half hour that had passed since the meeting in the ready room ended. He waited and then knocked a little harder.

The door cracked and Peeler's cream-slathered face appeared. "What?" he asked curtly.

"Is Einstein around?"

Peeler looked over his shoulder. "Yeah, he's here."

Punk waited for Peeler to open the door, but he didn't. "Can I talk to him?"

"Hold on for a second." Peeler pulled his face back and shut the door. Punk was left standing out in the passageway, awkwardly nodding to passersby, who gave him quizzical looks.

After a minute Punk grew impatient, and just as he raised his fist to knock again the door opened and Einstein materialized. "You need to talk to me?" he asked.

"Yeah," Punk said. "It's about an upcoming strike."

"Can we talk in the room?"

Punk shrugged, and the door was pulled fully open.

He stepped in and was hit by the familiar musk of deodorant-veiled masculinity, a smell offensive to all but those who've dwelled in it for months on end. The odor caused Punk another brief wave of nostalgia, and the feeling was heightened when he saw that the occupants of the eight-man had gathered their chairs around the center of the living area of the stateroom. The circle had been formed, the ritualistic coming together of the Cheesequarters occupants like braves around a fire. Punk smiled; he'd solved many problems around the circle. But as he approached them he was greeted with nothing but derisive stares.

"No hinge-heads allowed in the Cheesequarters," Lieutenant "Elf" Donahue said over his shoulder, tilt of his head and fluorescent backlighting from one of the desk lights framing the strange shape of his ears.

"Yeah," Peeler followed, "no lieutenant commanders."

Punk obliged them with a "you got me" stance and then began to knead Elf's shoulders in a playful massage. "Remember, I'm a Cheesequarters resident emeritus," Punk offered.

The expressions of the seven seated lieutenants didn't soften. "That only works for lieutenants," Elf said as he pulled Punk's hands off of him.

"Can we help you with something?" Lieutenant "Yoda" Connors asked in the halting high-pitched voice that earned him his call sign.

Punk attempted to hide his surprise at the rate and depth of their ire. At dinner he'd been one of them. He felt a bristling with the showdown, and then shocked himself with a thought: *I'm a lieutenant commander, and these lieutenants should respect that.*

He'd been a lieutenant commander for only thirty minutes and was already petitioning rank, the one fork in the logic matrix he swore he'd never take if he stayed around long enough to be promoted beyond the rank of lieutenant. But at the same time, he *was* a lieutenant commander. Punk cast a finger at Yoda and said, "I hope you're—"

"Let's talk, Punk," Einstein said from behind. "I'd like to hit the rack pretty soon."

Punk glanced over his shoulder at Einstein and then ran a wary eye across the circle, nodding slightly. "We've got a busy day tomorrow, boys. Let's not stay up too late solving the world's problems, okay?" He smiled and waited a beat for them to do the same, but they only glared back.

Einstein led Punk around the corner through the curtain to the other half of the stateroom where the bunks were. "What about a strike?"

"Let me say up front that you don't have to do this," Punk said, palms out. "The skipper is not ordering you to do this."

"You're making me fly with Soup," Einstein intoned.

"No, we're not *making* you. We wanted to see what you thought."

Einstein laughed sarcastically and stepped to the bulkhead between the second pair of bunk beds. He ran a hand along the smooth surface of the wall. "I think this pilot almost killed me the last time we flew together. I think this pilot, this fucking glory hound, wasn't scheduled for that flight but decided to jump in—even though he missed the brief—after he heard MiGs were flying over the no-fly zone in southern Iraq. I think this pilot drove into a SAM trap in spite of my protests over the intercom and got us shot down." He looked back at Punk. "Do these seem like reasonable thoughts, ops officer?"

Punk shrugged and said, "Sure. The skipper just wanted to get your take. I'll let you hit the rack now." He started around the corner for the stateroom door.

"Punk, wait a second," Einstein called to him. He waited for the pilot to reappear and then asked, "Are you leading this hop?"

Punk nodded.

"Spud flying with you?"

Punk nodded again and, after a brief pause to consider Einstein's expression, hurried out of the stateroom before drawing any more fire from the circle.

Einstein heard the door shutting behind Punk and then peeled off his flight suit and lay on his bunk. He stared at the gray sheet-metal bottom of the upper rack and listened to the conversation between his seven roommates still formed around the circle, knowing exactly why he was chosen to fly with Soup Campbell again.

"Of course the skipper makes his boy the ops officer," Elf said. "I'm sure there are two lieutenant commanders sitting in their staterooms right now pissed off that they didn't get the nod."

Einstein had grown to like Elf despite that he'd come off as too much of a wiseass—a fine line in a fighter squadron—during his first days in the outfit a year ago. Over time Elf had emerged as a good roommate, skilled in keeping things light with his rapier wit. But his performance in the airplane was suspect. Einstein had heard several pilots complain that he had a tendency to lose the bubble when the pace of a flight picked up beyond routine tasks. That would never work with Soup Campbell. Not even reviewing the take-off checklist was routine with him.

"I love it when lieutenant commanders fight," Lieutenant "Hog" Pearson said. Spit and polish was anathema to the corpulent Hog, whose pig-nosed visage was as often dirty as ruddy. Einstein knew Soup would be repulsed as soon as he laid eyes on him and things would go downhill from there.

"I love it when supermodels fight and then kiss"—pronounced as *zen keez*—"don't you know," Lieutenant Pierre "Cracker" Croiquier added in his distinct accent. Cracker was a very French-looking French Canadian, with a long nose and a weak chin who'd become a naturalized American citizen during his college days in Ohio. In spite of that, his presence would ignite every proclivity of the oft-xenophobic Captain Campbell.

Einstein exhaled deeply and ran both hands across his face. He wasn't beyond judgment. Soup would notice he'd gained some weight and was definitely going to view something as radical as a shaved head with a disapproving eye. But he had no choice but to weather it.

And why not? What was this thing within that drove him headlong toward situations more rational sorts would avoid without a second thought? Why hadn't he taken the hint and turned in his naval flight officer's wings after getting haplessly blown out of the sky three years ago? Who would've blamed him for choosing another career?

Yet here he was. And while he'd couched his decision in the idea that he'd been a victim of nothing more than bad timing, the sort of plucky stance he'd learned from his naval aviator father, deep down he feared he'd simply been too lazy to attempt another path. For the sin of that sloth, he was cursed with the return of Soup Campbell.

Einstein fluffed the pillow and laughed about the illusion he'd built for himself over the last few years.

Between deployments he'd arrived at the hangar earlier and stayed later than his peers; he'd worked more weekends and volunteered for more of the shitty little jobs that popped up. He'd gone to schools, rewritten tactical notes, trained new arrivals, and reached the 1,000-F-14-flight-hour milestone in record time. He'd be rolling out of the *Arrowslingers* soon, and his detailer had hinted that his fitness reports were good enough for him to write his own shore duty ticket.

But now Einstein knew the truth: He wasn't the second coming of Chester Nimitz. He was Soup Campbell's bitch.

The discussion beaming over the television in the corner of the mission planning area of the carrier's intelligence center pulled Punk's attention from the air tasking order on the table in front of him. After spending twenty minutes poring through the ATO's pages just to find his mission from among the hundreds assigned by CENTCOM, he welcomed the diversion. He drew up a stool closer to the screen, turned the volume with the remote, and momentarily lost himself in the world of twenty-four-hour news coverage.

"We're caught up in a stalemate," said a retired Army general with snow-white hair, a dark suit, and a bright red power tie. His lined face twisted in a terminal grimace as he spoke from a Washington studio with the Capitol dome out of focus through the smoked picture window behind him. "Our strategy is flawed."

"What is our strategy?" asked an attractive blond anchor from the studio in Times Square. "It seems like we're trying to soften them up and then get the Northern Alliance to do the heavy lifting. Is that the case?"

"She's not real, you know," said Einstein, standing behind Punk. "She's computer generated." Punk silenced him with a quick wave of his hand.

"If that's our strategy," the general said, "then we're in for a very long war."

"What about the air war, General?" the anchor said. "How do you think it's going on that front?"

"It's going to take more than air power to unseat the enemy," the general said as the view shifted from him seated in the studio to a montage of forward-looking infrared footage. Punk could see from the symbols superimposed over the explosions that all of the footage had been obtained from either Hornet or Tomcat missions. "We're going to have to get boots on the ground, American boots, and soon."

"So, would you say the air strikes have been ineffective, General?" the anchor asked as the strike highlights continued to roll.

"Not *totally* ineffective, no," the general replied. "I see a lot of explosions on these mission tapes. I'm sure these attacks are having some effect, but probably not as much as most people think. We're enamored with technology, but you can't win a war staring at a video screen. Victory takes more guts than that."

The television suddenly cut off, and Punk looked down at the remote in his hands and realized he'd been squeezing it and inadvertently hit the power button. He sat in place for a time, pensively staring at his reflection in the blank screen before joining Einstein back at the planning table.

The Deputy CAG's focus on the pages as he attempted to make sense of the information in the air tasking order allowed the newly pinned lieutenant commander to study him with impunity. Soup Campbell hadn't aged much in the years since Punk had seen him last. In fact, Punk thought he might have looked a little younger now, even with more gray in his hair. Seated at the desk in his stateroom, Soup remained a model of military bearing even in his flight suit, which appeared brand-new and custom tailored.

"I can't figure out these numbers," the captain said, drawing his face closer to the pages. "What are the coordinates of our target?"

"We don't have a preassigned target, sir," Punk explained.

Captain Campbell winced. "How can we fly a strike without a target?"

Punk leaned over the desk and used a finger to focus the captain's attention on the ATO. "It's an on-call interdiction mission, DCAG"—*dee-cag*—"we wait for the forward air controllers to assign us a target."

"Wait? How long?"

"As long as it takes, or until it's time to get back to the Boat for our recovery."

"We might bring our bombs back?"

"In theory . . ."

"I don't want to fly a mission where I bring my bombs back," Captain Campbell said, tapping a finger against the chart of Afghanistan Punk had spread out before him.

"Most likely, you won't, DCAG," Punk offered. "I've flown six of these missions and dropped on every one of them."

Captain Campbell looked up from the chart. "You're guaranteeing that we'll drop on this strike?"

"All I'm saying, sir, is that I've dropped on every one of these missions I've flown."

Soup smiled slyly. "That sounds like a guarantee to me," he said. He waited a few seconds for a response from Punk, and when he didn't get one he swung an arm in the air. "Whatever. Based on what you say, it sounds like the odds are pretty good. What kind of ordnance are we carrying?"

Punk flipped to the second-to-last page of the ATO and ran his finger along another line. "We're each carrying one GBU-sixteen and one Mark-eighty-three. The combination of smart and dumb bombs gives us good flexibility—"

"I've got it," Captain Campbell said with another wave of his hand, like royalty suddenly bored with the court jester. He pushed the ATO and chart across his desk toward Punk. "Now, if everything else can wait until the brief tomorrow morning, I'd like to get back to work."

Punk seized the materials off the desk and, with a mumble of a respectful salutation on the way out, made for the door.

"Those gold leaves look good on your shoulders," Captain Campbell said to Punk's back. "You're welcome."

Punk momentarily wrestled with the idea of ignoring the remark and continuing out of the stateroom, something a more tolerant, perhaps wiser officer would have done, but instead he released the doorknob. "I'm welcome? For what?"

"Obviously the two fitness reports I submitted on you during my time as your commanding officer carried the day in your promotion board. In fact, if I'm not mistaken, you were promoted a year ahead of your peers. So, *you're welcome.*"

Punk swallowed hard. The gall was unbelievable, even for Soup Campbell. Punk couldn't remember any glowing fitness reports by Soup's hand; in fact, as he stood briefly considering the notion, all he could recall was that then-Commander Campbell had more than once threatened to pull his wings.

Punk took a cleansing breath. "Perhaps it would be best if we ignored our previous experiences together," he said. "Otherwise I might be inclined to counter your assertion, sir."

Soup smiled wryly, leaning against his palms with his elbows on the desk and raised his eyebrows. "How *might* you do that?"

Punk's mind flashed with an image of the Chief of Naval Operations pinning the Distinguished Flying Cross to his chest as a result of his actions over southern Iraq the day Soup got himself shot down. That award had certainly eclipsed any professional damage Soup Campbell had wrought, intentional or otherwise. He started to speak but stopped himself and changed his tack saying, "Why don't I let you get back to work, DCAG?" before turning back for the door.

"Good idea," Soup chided, a taunt of sorts. Punk gritted his teeth and pulled the door open.

"One more thing," the captain said just before Punk slipped down the passageway. "Who's my RIO?"

"Einstein," Punk replied.

Soup chewed on the answer for a time, head nodding slightly. "Einstein, huh?" He chuckled. "Just like old times."

As the door to Captain Campbell's stateroom shut, Punk hoped that wasn't true.

CHAPTER THREE

"Shamrock seven-oh-three is steadying up north-bound," the S-3 pilot transmitted as Soup stabilized his Tomcat on the tanker's left wing. Punk, already plugged into the Viking's refueling basket, shot a glance at his fuel totalizer and noted that he'd taken on nearly half of the four thousand pounds he was slated for. Gas was a precious commodity on these long missions, and he was going to make sure he received every drop the air plan had assigned to him.

And so he did, even cheating a couple hundred extra pounds from the hose before backing out, retracting his probe, and positioning himself on the tanker's right wing to wait for the Deputy CAG to take on his gas. Punk retrimmed the Tomcat to its post-tanking configuration and watched Soup attempt his first plug in several years.

"This ought to be good," Punk said over the intercom.

Spud looked up from punching coordinates into his mission computer and saw that Punk was focused out the left side of the jet. "I doubt it. Soup has always been a natural with the by-the-numbers stuff. I'll bet you he gets in the basket on the first try."

"How much?"

"You're a lieutenant commander now, a single successful guy making the big bucks. A dollar?"

"You're on."

Punk had barely finished agreeing to the bet when Soup slid his probe into the drogue with nary a noticeable adjustment to his flight path. "Fuck you," Punk said, attempting to preempt Spud's crowing.

"You'd have just wasted your money on beer or porn anyway," Spud said. "Better you give it to me, your humble commanding officer."

"Oh, that's right, you're my commanding officer now; sorry about the disrespect. Fuck you, *skipper*."

A few minutes later Captain Campbell had taken on his gas and moved outside of Punk on the S-3's right wing. Once Soup appeared situated, the tanker's crew waved to the fighters and started their sixty-mile journey back to the Boat, banking to the left as quickly as the Viking's boxy air frame would allow.

Punk sighted over the left canopy rail, watching the S-3 fall away from the section of fighters like a jettisoned stage of a Saturn rocket. Spud spoke over the backseat radio: "Seabird six-oh-three, Slinger one-zero-one is a flight of two. Organic tanking complete. Heading north, currently thirty miles south of feet dry."

"Roger, Slinger," one of the three controllers in the tube of the E-2 replied. "Standby for words."

The frequency went silent for a time as the controller switched to satellite communications to get a fighter mission update from the Current Operations Cell at the Joint Task Force—Southwest Asia in Riy-

adh, Saudi Arabia. Just as Punk feared that they might
have had a radio failure talking to the E-2, the controller came back with, "Slinger, your tasking is as
fragged. Proceed to OP-one after second mission tanking complete. You'll be working with Tiger zero-three
on frequency Beige four."

"Copy Tiger zero-three on frequency Beige four,"
Spud replied.

"Switch Bossman on Red one for en route advisories."

"Slinger's switching."

Spud looked over at Einstein in Soup's backseat,
and they exchanged a thumbs-up. Each buried his
head in the cockpit for a few seconds, checking the
Red one frequency on his kneeboard card and manipulating the switches on the UHF radio. Once both
were satisfied they'd entered the digits correctly, they
traded another thumbs-up.

"Bossman, Thor two-five is checking in," Spud
transmitted, switching from "Slinger," his squadron's
tactical call sign, to "Thor," his ATO-assigned label
for this mission. "Proceeding to Duke track for
Texaco."

"Bossman reads you loud and clear," a female voice
replied, that of the controller in the AWACS, the massive Air Force command-and-control aircraft with a
radar unit that looked like a giant black Frisbee
mounted to the top of it. "Lion one-three is currently
on station at Duke. Initial steer is three-five-five degrees for three hundred and eleven miles."

"Roger."

Although the ranges that the flights were covering
had become somewhat routine over the last weeks in
theater, Punk was still taken aback by the numbers
they were kicking around. Three hundred and eleven

miles was like flying from Oceana to Atlanta. And that was just to tank before continuing another one hundred–plus miles to an orbit point, then flying around some more as a precursor to retracing their steps back to the Boat. Six hours in the sky. Six hours of riding a man-made contraption—and an old one at that, a collection of composite fibers, spinning metal, controlled explosions, electrical currents, and hydraulic fluids.

"Diego Garcia," Spud said over the intercom.

"What?"

"Diego Garcia. It's an island in the middle of the Indian Ocean. The Air Force is flying sorties from the airfield there. It's really far away, much farther than we have to fly."

"Thanks for that," Punk said.

"Don't mention it. A good leader knows how to keep morale high among his troops."

"And you would know that how?" Punk deadpanned.

Under the canopy of the other Tomcat the atmosphere was less jovial. Einstein looked over and saw Spud's hands waving and both helmets moving, and he longed to be sitting behind Yoda, the pilot he was normally crewed with. He also wondered when Soup was going to make some mention of their past shared flying experiences, at once relieved and insulted that the captain had spent the last hours treating him as if they'd never met before today's brief.

"Have you checked the weapons stations yet?" Captain Campbell shot over the intercom.

"Yes, sir," Einstein replied. "They checked out fine."

"I'll be pissed if we fly all this way and can't drop anything."

Einstein remained wary of how Soup's demeanor vacillated once he slipped between the canopy rails. The young RIO had quickly been reminded of the drill even before the catapult shot: As sure as Soup radiated calm and the cocksure bravado of one born strapped to an ejection seat, he'd mercurially morph into a guy who loathed flying and then back again. Einstein thought about the thousands of flight hours and the numbers of sorties the captain had flown, and he wondered why the man had tortured himself for so many years. What demons had he hoped to exorcise along the way, and would he ever be rid of them?

The two fighters continued north at thirty-five thousand feet, straight and level through a cerulean sky. The transits seldom felt like war to Punk, especially when the radios fell silent for extended periods. He monitored the profusion of information on the gauges around him and, like Einstein, his thoughts drifted.

To Suzanne. Over the last six months she'd gone from best friend's wife to best friend's widow to girlfriend, although she had just attained the latter status when he was called away to fight. He conjured up a vision of her, just after two o'clock in the morning on the day he flew out, backlit by the bathroom light as she approached the bed and allowed the towel to fall away. Their lovemaking had been a brief celebration of living following a day of unspeakable horrors, a day that had prematurely driven him back to the Boat.

And now he'd returned to the world of reading between the lines of letters and, more often, e-mails. He repeatedly scrolled the last sentence of her latest cyber dispatch through his head: "It's starting to be too long," and wrestled with the hidden meanings and cursed himself for violating his rule about checking e-mail right before a flight.

The fighters crossed from Pakistan into Afghanistan with less chatter over the frequency than a flight might hear passing from Nevada into California. Punk noted the digits on his handheld GPS and peered over the right canopy rail in an attempt to verify their position, but their lofty perch made it tough to discriminate where the border might run along the mountain ranges that loosely divided the two countries.

"Bossman, Thor lead has a contact," Spud transmitted, "north for fifty-three miles, angels medium."

"That's your Texaco, Thor," the female controller replied. "Contact Lion one-three on Orange six. Come back to me after you're complete."

"Oh, I'll come back to you all right, you blue-suited minx," Spud salaciously quipped over the intercom before clearing his throat and keying the radio again: "Roger, Bossman. Thor flight is switching." A thumbs-up between RIOs was followed by a flurry of fingers on consoles and another exchange of a thumbs-up. "Lion one-three, Thor two-five is twenty miles away. Got you on radar."

"Roger, Thor," the RAF tanker pilot replied in an accent an Anglophile would've tagged to an affluent, well-educated caste. "We'll be ready for you on arrival."

The clear, cloudless sky was tuned to a fighter pilot's eye, and Punk sighted through the diamond on his HUD that Spud's radar lock had generated, having spotted the British VC-10 at twenty miles out. "Punk's tally the tanker," he passed over the front seat radio, dialed to the squadron's common frequency.

"I'm blind," Soup returned, a twinge of anxiety evident in his voice.

"Twelve-thirty, slightly low," Punk said, attempting to direct his wingman's eye to the correct piece of sky. "He's eastbound at this time."

"No joy," Soup shot back.

Punk urged the stick forward to effect his descent to the tanker's altitude and muttered a dammit into his mask before keying the radio again: "Cross under me to the left side and stay in loose cruise, DCAG. I'll get you there."

Spud worked the intercom for a few seconds in an effort to keep his pilot cool (and respectful) while in the other jet, Einstein weathered another blast of airborne Captain Campbell's choleric self: "That guy had better watch himself," Soup said.

Einstein felt the captain's anger growing with each rant. He checked his watch: Just about two and a half hours had passed since they'd catapulted off the Boat's flight deck, and they had roughly three and a half hours to go until they recovered back aboard. He fought off a wave of apprehension with the notion that even Soup Campbell had learned from his mistakes and wouldn't be in a big hurry to repeat them.

Based on the earlier exchange with the tanker, Punk bypassed the normal stop on the left wing and moved right to its business end, throwing his probe into the air stream just seconds before mating it with the drogue. Soup stationed his Tomcat down the VC-10's left wing just as the tanker started a right-hand turn.

"Which way are we headed?" the British pilot asked.

Spud took a quick look down at his tactical display to get a bearing to OP-1 and passed, "Zero-two-five."

"Copy, zero-two-five."

The VC-10s had become the naval aviators' strategic tankers of choice because of their big baskets, docile hoses, high gas-flow rates, and the balls-out attitude of the crews. Of the organizations offering heavy tanker support to the war effort, including those of the United States Air Force, only the Royal Air Force consistently demonstrated the willingness to leave the constraints of their assigned tanker track to get the fighters closer to their destinations. That willingness, reckless and anarchic in the minds of the planners at CENTCOM, translated into more gas and thereby more speed for the fighters when it might be required over their targets and for that the carrier-based crews were not only grateful but, when it came to prolonged use of afterburner to dodge missiles deep over enemy territory, also in the Brits' debt.

Both F-14s were topped off in short order, and with a palms'-out salute and a "Cheers, mates," the VC-10 lumbered into a left-hand turn back to the Duke track. The fighters continued northbound as Spud checked back in with the AWACS controller and received a succinct "Roger" in response.

They closed within twenty-five miles of OP-1, nearly one hundred miles due west of Kandahar, and at that point Spud grew tired of waiting for the controller's guidance: "Bossman, Thor is ready for the switch to Tiger zero-three."

"Copy, Thor," the controller replied. "Standby, please." As she keyed the radio, Punk thought he heard the shuffling of papers in the background. The radio was silent for another minute, and then the controller came back with, "New tasking, Thor. Contact Jaguar five-two on Yellow two."

"Thor flight copies," Spud said. "Understand we should continue toward OP-one?"

There was a slight delay in the response before she passed, "Ah . . . sure, why not?"

"Why not?" Spud mused over the intercom. "Gee, because it's nowhere near where Jaguar five-two needs us, maybe?"

"I think you flummoxed her," Punk said. "Hell of a way to run a war, ain't it?"

"Thor's switching Jaguar five-two," Spud transmitted before going through the thumb drill with Einstein and then checking in with the FAC. "Jaguar five-two, Thor two-five is checking in."

"Roger," a just-audible voice replied over what sounded like machine-gun fire. "Say your posit."

"Approaching OP-one."

The FAC keyed the radio but didn't speak while the sound of guns erupted around him, firing several semiautomatic bursts. At the first break he said, "Copy. Hold for tasking."

Captain Campbell keyed the intercom: "Did you hear that? There's a firefight going on down there."

"Sounds like it," Einstein replied. "We'll just have to wait and see."

"Wait? Why wait? Those guys are under fire." Soup paused for a moment and then asked, "How many of these missions have you done?"

"On-call interdiction? Six."

"And during how many of those did you drop bombs?"

"Five."

"Okay, then. Let's do it. That's why I hauled ass over here from the Pentagon, for crissakes."

The Tomcats reached the coordinates that defined OP-1, and Punk picked up a slow orbit while the RIOs in both airplanes stirred the joysticks on their left consoles, combing the ground around them with their forward-looking infrared pods, looking for clues that would help them figure out what they might be up against.

"Anything down there?" Punk asked.

"Negative," Spud replied. "Of course, I have no idea where that FAC was calling us from. I'm just biding my time swinging at a piñata here."

The radios remained silent as Punk led the flight in circles around the orbit point. He studied the terrain beneath them, again struck by how much the landscape resembled the Navy's training areas in the High Sierras. "Train like you fight," was the oft-repeated mantra of the commands charged with preparing units for deployment, and while those who'd fought the Cold War might have disagreed, from Punk's point of view whoever had picked Fallon, Nevada, as the venue for air-wing-strike warfare training decades before this particular war had shown laudable prescience.

The two fighters started the fourth trip around the holding pattern. "This is bullshit," Soup said to Einstein. "Why hasn't that guy called us back?"

"I'm sure he'll call us if he needs us, DCAG," Einstein said. "Sometimes these hops are a waiting game."

Soup returned a grunt over the intercom and then keyed the front seat radio: "Are we going to get into this war, or not?"

Punk's reply was interrupted by a burst of static over the other radio followed by two more in rapid succession.

"Jaguar, this is Thor," Spud transmitted. "Were you just calling us?"

No response. In the wing Tomcat, Einstein looked down the right side of the ejection seat headrest in front of him and saw the Deputy CAG smack the

canopy with his fist. "They're being overrun," Soup
carped over the squadron common frequency. "We
need to get down there and help them."

"Overrun?" Punk returned, trying to mute his own
growing frustration. "We don't even know where they
are let alone what's going on down there."

"Give me the lead," Soup said.

"What?"

"Pass me the flight lead. I'll find them if you won't."

Punk looked into one of his mirrors at Spud: "He's
kidding, right?"

"Let's keep our heads here, DCAG," Spud beseeched over squadron common. "Give this thing a
minute to sort itself out."

"Give me the lead, I said!" Soup snapped. "That's
an order."

"There it is," Punk said over the intercom. "I knew
it. He hasn't changed a fucking bit."

Spud just shook his head.

"All right, Captain," Punk said without any effort
to mute his ire. "You want the lead, you've got it."

"Stay with me," Captain Campbell said. "That's another order."

In the rear cockpit, Einstein fought an ugly sense
of déjà vu and said, "Punk's right, sir. We don't know
where that FAC is. If we wait a bit, I'm sure he'll tell
us—"

"Pipe down back there," Soup railed. "Concentrate
on finding something with that damn pod."

Einstein perfunctorily wiggled the pod back and
forth while he made another, more desperate, attempt
to talk to the FAC: "Jaguar five-two, this is Thor two-
five; how do you read?" Silence. "Jaguar, this is Thor;
how do you read?"

Soup jumped on the radio as if Einstein simply

wasn't trying hard enough: "Jaguar this is Thor lead; how do you read?"

"Watch the altitude," Punk advised over squadron common.

"I've got it," Soup returned, reefing the stick into his lap and fighting the onset of four Gs before giving Einstein another command: "Switch back to the AWACS freq . . . and figure out . . . what the hell is going on."

Einstein hadn't expected the sudden rush of several times the normal pull of gravity, and he searched for the other Tomcat while warding off stars in his eyes. After a few beats the transient cosmos had cleared enough for him to determine that Spud was too far away to see hand signals, so he passed, "Thor flight is switching back to Bossman."

"Two," Spud replied.

Einstein manipulated his radio, waited a few seconds for Spud to do the same, and then transmitted, "Bossman, Thor two-five is back up your frequency. We lost comms with Jaguar five-two."

"Standby, Thor," the AWACS controller said. "Let me check with Zeus."

" 'Zeus'?" Soup asked.

"The current operations cell in Saudi," Einstein explained, further disquieted that his pilot wasn't familiar with the standard theater call signs.

They had waited nearly two minutes for the controller to come back on the line when a male voice crackled over the freq: "Bossman, this is Jaguar five-two. I lost comms with Thor two-five on Yellow two. Do you know where they went?"

"We were up Yellow two, Jaguar," Soup interjected. "We couldn't get you to talk to us."

"Who's that talking?" the FAC said.

"Thor lead."

"Well, Thor, it gets noisy down here from time to time. Kick back to Yellow two."

"Roger," Einstein replied, deftly seizing the radios back from his pilot, preventing an exchange that he feared would not help the war effort. "Switching Yellow two."

"It gets noisy down here," Soup mimicked. "That guy needs an attitude check."

The fighters tuned back into the FAC's working frequency and were greeted by another burst of machine-gun fire over the net. "Thor, are you up yet?" the FAC asked.

"Thor's up," Einstein replied.

"Say ordnance."

"Two thousand pounders each: one precision, one dumb."

"Copy. Standby. And don't leave this freq again, please."

Einstein started to key the radio but Soup beat him to the draw: "Just talk to us when we call and everything will be fine, Jaguar."

A click followed by static and then another click gave the reply, a sequence that sounded to Einstein as if the FAC had something he wanted to say but had thought better of it.

As the two F-14s waited for tasking, Soup drove the flight north, making sharp S turns through the clear sky and visually scouring the ground for any signs of a skirmish below.

"Recommend we stay in the vicinity of OP-one," Punk said on squadron common. "That's where the FAC thinks we are."

"When are we going to do something here?" Soup said.

"Easy, DCAG," Spud said. "No sense in getting—"

"Thor, this is Jaguar," the FAC transmitted over Yellow two. "Understand you're at OP-one at this time?"

"Just north of it," Einstein said.

"How far north?"

"Thirty miles."

Another series of clicks and static followed, and shortly thereafter the FAC said, "Come south immediately."

"Thor flight coming south."

Soup wrapped the jet into a hard left turn as the FAC kept his instructions coming: "There's a hardball that runs east-west through OP-one. Are you contact that hardball?"

"Hardball?" Soup asked over the intercom.

"Paved road," Einstein explained. "Maybe you should hand the lead back to Punk, DCAG."

"No, I've got it. Answer the FAC."

"Are you contact the hardball he's talking about?" Einstein fired back at his pilot.

Captain Campbell was silent for a moment, and Einstein saw him crane his head from side to side a couple of times and then lock on something across his right shoulder.

"I think I see it," the captain said. "You see what I'm talking about?"

Einstein focused his contact-corrected eyes across the canopy rail and to the ground. The road was hard to make out at first but eventually appeared—not wide and black like a stateside interstate but a sliver just slightly darker than the surrounding tan wasteland. Einstein keyed the radio: "Jaguar, Thor is contact the road."

"If you work your way from OP-one westbound

down the hardball," the FAC continued, "you'll see a small bridge that crosses a river that runs northeast-southwest."

"I've got it, er . . . *contact,*" Soup said over Yellow two.

"We have an armor column east of the bridge moving east along the hardball. Find them and take them out." The sound of another burst of gunfire was cut off as the FAC unkeyed the radio.

"Thor copies," Einstein said. "Looking for tanks moving eastbound east of bridge."

"Jaguar, say your position," Spud thought to ask.

"Standby," the FAC said over the firing. A second later his surroundings were momentarily quieter. "Say again for Jaguar?"

"Say your position," Spud repeated.

"We're roughly at thirty-two north, sixty-five east, on the western face of the first ridge line. We're engaged with the forces those tanks are moving to reinforce. Stick to the hardball and we'll be out of your way."

Captain Campbell threw the stick against his left thigh without warning, smashing Einstein's helmet against the right side of the canopy, and several seconds later rolled back to the right. Through another set of stars Einstein joined the DCAG in looking down, but neither could make out any movement along the road that meekly split the parched earth.

"I can't see anything from up here," Soup said. "We need to get lower."

Einstein checked the altimeter. "Any lower and we'll be within Stinger range of those guys," he said. "Recommend we level off here and fly down the axis of the hardball with our FLIR pods in snowplow. If the tanks are there, we'll find them."

"Tell me where to go, then," Soup replied.

The young RIO keyed the intercom and said, "Let's set up to the west with enough straightaway to start the pods at the bridge."

"Coming west."

Einstein met the oncoming G forces buoyed by a sense of optimism. Perhaps he'd been mistaken: Could it be that he wasn't Soup Campbell's bitch but rather one of the few RIOs Soup Campbell would listen to? He wanted to believe it but balanced that eternal hope with thoughts of how he'd been burned in the wake of brief bonhomie with this man before.

Introspection was again eclipsed by the tasks at hand. Einstein passed, "Going snowplow," over squadron common, and with those words both Punk and Spud understood the game plan. Captain Campbell scribed a tight arc mirrored by Punk and soon the F-14s bracketed the road from just over ten thousand feet above it.

"Check mission recorders on," Spud said, which prompted Einstein to flip the appropriate switch on his right console and stare at the counter for a few seconds to confirm the system was working. It was. He breathed a sigh of relief. No tape, no glory. DCAG wouldn't have been pleased.

The RIOs stared intently at their screens while the pilots shared their attention between their smaller screens, the ground, and the other Tomcat. The bridge was easily recognized in the black-and-white FLIR presentation, but beyond that the first tanklike shapes turned out to be gaping holes in the road. Each RIO alternated his pod's field of view but came up empty, and after another minute the jets had flown past the southern tip of the first ridgeline—too far to the east, they feared.

"No joy, Jaguar," Einstein said on Yellow two. "Any chance they passed south of you toward Kandahar?"

"Negative, Thor," the FAC said, this time joined by both the chattering of the machine gun and the crack of rifle shots. "We had big eyes on them a short time ago as they crossed the bridge. They couldn't have gone that far yet." The pitch of FAC's voice was notably higher. The battle was intensifying down there.

"We'll take another look," Einstein said.

"We could save time by backtracking down the road from here," Punk recommended on squadron common.

"Thor, try looking for the tanks on the side of the hardball," the FAC said. Jets shrieked in the distance as he continued to speak, and one by one the aviators realized they were hearing their own noise over the radio: "When jets fly overhead they sometimes pull off and stop."

The RIO expanded their search to either side of the road as the fighters came out of the turn, and no sooner had the Tomcats steadied up to the west than Spud called, "I've got three tanks along the right side of the hardball."

Einstein fished for a few more seconds before capturing the tanks on his screen. "Got 'em."

"Designated on the easternmost tank," Spud said. "Standby for release."

"They're bombing already?" Soup asked over the intercom.

"Check master arm on, DCAG," Einstein instructed. "We'll take the western guy."

"Pickle, pickle, pickle," Spud said. The first bomb fell away from the wing Tomcat.

"Master arm's on," Soup said.

"Standby," Einstein said, focusing on the "time to

release" counter on the right side of his FLIR screen. "Three, two, one . . . pickle, pickle, pickle."

They felt the thump as the rack under them released the bomb. A moment later, enough time for the weapon to drop clear of the fighter, Einstein pulled the trigger on his FLIR pod controller, and the laser in the pod fired, which, in turn, caused the fins on the bomb to move, steering the GBU-16 toward the tank. He increased the FLIR magnification one more click and held the dot between the crosshairs squarely on the turret. Seven seconds to impact, enough time to wonder if the enemy had any sense of what was about to happen.

"How much time left?" Soup asked. The explosion from Punk and Spud's bomb gave the answer and washed out the bottom right corner of Einstein's FLIR picture. Einstein fought the distraction and held the aim point rock steady over the westernmost tank.

The flash from the first explosion had just fully blossomed on the screen when the second bomb hit. Einstein decreased the FLIR's magnification and shot a quick look at the ground. One thousand pounders could do the trick—even from ten thousand feet the size of each of the still-growing frag patterns was eye-opening.

Captain Campbell whooped over the intercom and cheered, "Beats pushing papers!"

"Beautiful, Thor," the FAC said on Yellow two, explosions rolling like thunder in the background. "Can you mop up the third one? Looks like he's on the move."

"You want him or do you want Punk to take him, DCAG?" Einstein asked.

"I want him," Soup replied. "He's mine."

"Computer pilot or computer target?"

"Huh?"

"All we've got left is a dumb bomb," Einstein explained. "We're going to have to roll in on this guy. What sort of bomb sight do you want in your HUD?"

Captain Campbell didn't answer. Einstein glanced at the back of his helmet and could see the wheels turning.

In the other airplane, Punk looked over at the lead F-14 a mile abeam and then down at the ground. He was in a perfect position to make a dive on the tank now rolling at full speed down the road to Kandahar—but so was Soup.

"What's he doing?" Punk asked Spud over the intercom.

"Give him a second, lad," Spud counseled. "The tank isn't going anywhere, not very fast anyway."

"Your honor, DCAG," Punk prompted over squadron common.

"Remaining tank is now due south of us on the hardball, Thor," the FAC passed.

"We've got him, Jaguar," Einstein replied before keying the intercom: "DCAG, I've got Station Four selected and the fusing set. Do you want computer pilot or—"

"All right, all right," the captain irately returned, cutting the RIO off. "Give me computer pilot. Let's get it done already."

"Check master arm on, sir," Einstein said.

"It's on. Here we go."

Unlike the task sharing between cockpits inherent to precision-guided attacks in the Tomcat, conventional bombing was a pilot's game. Soup commanded a sharp roll and buried the jet's nose below the horizon while Einstein, blind to the target, backed him up with airspeeds and altitudes: "Nine thousand feet, three hundred and fifty knots." The RIO felt the airplane roll abruptly back and forth several times and figured that Soup was trying to align the bomb fall line in his HUD with the tank. Einstein had educated himself on the symbology flying the pilot simulator at NAS Oceana and fully appreciated what a juggling act successfully delivering a dumb bomb was in the Tomcat. Doing it took practice, and the new Deputy CAG probably hadn't had much while rushing from the Pentagon to join the war in progress. "Eight thousand feet, four hundred knots." One more instant and they'd be too low; even if the bomb hit, it wouldn't have had enough time to fuse. "Recommend abort."

Einstein fought the crush of the G forces and fielded a "goddam it" from Soup over the intercom as the fighter started climbing again.

"Lead's off, no drop," Einstein said on Yellow two.

"Well, happy birthday to me," Punk quipped to Spud before keying the radio: "Wing's in hot."

Arcing overhead, the crew in the lead F-14 had a balcony seat for the show. Einstein studied the tank with his FLIR and noticed flashes across the top of it. "I think they're shooting at you, Punk."

"I'd expect they would be," Punk replied, sweetening the solution in his HUD. Spud called, "Eight thousand feet, three hundred and fifty knots," over the intercom just as the pipper—the aiming cue in the HUD—started to walk up the glass. Punk waited until the aim point was superimposed on the tank and then let it travel another potato ahead of the target to account for the tank's speed down the hardball. He mashed the bomb button, waited for the thump, and started the nose back above the horizon while rolling the jet to the left. As the fighter gained altitude, he looked over his left shoulder and waited for the result like a bowler hoping for a spare.

The bomb hadn't been precision guided, but the effect of the explosion on the third tank was just as devastating as the GBU-16s had been. Einstein watched the Mark-83 go high order, seeing the turret sail straight up, and winced under his oxygen mask as the fireball swallowed the rest of the tank.

"That did it, Thor," the FAC said, fighting to talk between breaths as if he were on the run. "We've got the gomers turning tail." The aviators heard cheering around the FAC, and Einstein pictured a scene from a Civil War movie showing a line of troops waving their hats in the air at the retreating enemy.

Einstein checked his watch: time to head for the tanker and then back to the Boat. He switched the steering cue to the waypoint he'd placed at the center of the Duke track and passed the information over the intercom: "Refueling point is one-nine-three for one hundred and twenty miles."

Instead of starting a smooth, climbing turn to the south, Soup threw the jet onto its back. Einstein, startled, looked through the top of the canopy and was greeted by nothing but the earth below. "Got something, DCAG?"

"Reselect Station Four," Soup ordered as he put the Tomcat into another dive. "There's a fast mover on the hardball."

Einstein worked to see around his pilot's head but couldn't. "What is it?"

"A vehicle. I'm sure we stirred up a hornet's nest down there. Is the mission recorder still on?"

"Yes, sir. Where is it?"

"On the other side of the bridge, going away."

Going away? "Westbound?" Einstein asked.

"Altitude?" Soup asked back.

"Where are you guys going?" Spud asked over squadron common.

"I just got a glint," Soup reported over the intercom. "He's firing at us. What's our altitude?"

"Passing eight thousand feet," Einstein replied. A half second later he felt a thump as their final bomb came off.

"It's a pickup truck," Spud said on squadron common. "I've got FLIR on him."

"DCAG, recommend getting Jaguar to help sort this out," Punk added.

"Our bomb's away," Einstein said.

"He's *got* to be hostile," Soup insisted between G-force-induced grunts as the fighter bottomed out of its dive. "He was firing at us . . . had to be with the tanks . . . and now he's on the run."

"The FAC would know," Einstein said, trying to get his own FLIR on target with a momentarily heavy left arm working the pod's control stick. "And if not . . ."

Soup eased the pull once the Tomcat began to climb. "Jaguar, confirm enemy on the hardball," he demanded on Yellow two while looking back to the ground over his left shoulder. "Headed west—"

He cut himself off as the bomb hit. Spud focused on the FLIR and saw that the Mark-83 had exploded several hundred yards behind the pickup. In turn, the pickup swerved and flipped over, spilling what looked to be people and possessions along the road.

"Jaguar's got an explosion west of the bridge," the FAC reported. "Was that yours, Thor?"

"Affirmative," Einstein replied.

"Man, you scared us," the FAC said, voice evincing relief. "What do you have there?"

"A vehicle. Can you confirm that it was hostile?" The radio was silent.

"Thor, can you confirm the vehicle was hostile?" Soup echoed, tone more desperate than he'd intended.

"Negative," the FAC replied. "Cannot confirm."

CHAPTER FOUR

In the Flag Wardroom, the mess specialists were prepping for the dinner sitting. Two white-coated enlisted men robotically placed silverware and china on long tables covered with blue linen, while another made a pot of coffee using the industrial-sized machine perched on top of big cabinets that also hosted an ice maker and a soda dispenser. The space was warmed with the scent of fried onions. Soon officers assigned to the battle group commander's staff would be wandering in from their desks or watch stations, hungry and ready to spend a cherished half hour sharing tales conjured up since lunch.

Across from the dining area in the adjacent lounge, three aviators sat on overstuffed leather couches along the rice paper–lined walls and stared at the news coming over the wide-screen television tucked into an opposite corner. They watched the report, a rebroadcast of a video phone feed that had aired live a few hours earlier, with great interest since it dealt with the mission they'd just flown. The correspondent, a thirty-something man with a narrow face, long black hair, and an English accent, stood close to the camera, face blurred and movement clunky by digital standards, like a series of impressionist paintings presented as flip cards. His voice had the modulation of a long-distance phone call.

"In spite of the coalition's claims to fighting a precision-guided war," the correspondent said, "things can still go horribly wrong." He stepped out of the frame and the camera revealed a flatbed pickup truck flipped onto its side in the middle of the dusty road. Around it several bundles were being loaded onto a cart pulled by a mule. "This truckload of refugees was targeted while trying to flee the violence that continues to descend on the area surrounding Kandahar."

The view switched to a close-up of a weathered Afghan man whose head was covered with a loosely wrapped cloth. The words from his toothless mouth were overdubbed by a female interpreter's voice: "We heard the noise of the aircraft and the next we knew a bomb exploded behind us. My brother was driving. The truck flipped and his leg was cut off. All of us in the back fell onto the road. Our baby was killed after her mother lost hold during the fall. Others were crushed and injured. I don't know why they attacked us. We are not their enemy."

The correspondent reappeared, closer to the camera now. "These sorts of mistakes threaten to destroy the hope of innocent locals who had hoped to be liberated from the evil that has gripped their lives for years," he said, free hand fighting to keep his windblown locks off his face. "And with each death, accidental or otherwise, they fear that the Americans are at war with all of Afghanistan or even all things Islam, and not just the Taliban or al Qaeda."

"Whose side is that fucker on?" Spud said, jabbing the remote at the television as if he were fencing with it instead of turning it off.

"How did that news crew get out there so fast?" Punk asked. "He couldn't have been very far away from the tanks when we hit them."

"Tanks?" Spud said sarcastically, throwing his hands up. "There were tanks out there? I didn't see anything about those on the news."

"That crew's lucky Soup didn't take them out instead," Punk said. He shot a furtive glance at Einstein, whose own focus was squarely on the coffee table in front of them. "I'm not pointing any fingers at you, of course." Einstein said nothing in return.

Rear Admiral Dykstra's voice suddenly boomed from behind the closed door to his stateroom. The three officers in the lounge exchanged wide-eyed looks while the admiral continued his rant. "And now it's all over the news!" he shouted more than once. The framed painting of the Boat shook above Spud's head as something—a fist, perhaps—slammed into the wall behind it.

The ream session went on for a painfully long time, and at one point Punk thought he heard poorly stifled sobbing. He cut his eyes over toward the dining room and was relieved that the enlisted men had exercised the sense to dismiss themselves for the time being. Without warning, the stateroom door flew open, and Spud, Punk, and Einstein got to their feet, feigning nonchalance.

The admiral appeared and asked Spud, "Where's Wheedle!"

"Wheedle, sir?"

"Yeah, Wheedle. The ship's public affairs guy."

Before Spud could answer, a tall, skinny black lieutenant with a medium-sized Afro poked his head through the door along the side that lead to Flag Briefing and Analysis and asked, "Are you looking for me, Admiral?"

"You're damn right I'm looking for you," the admiral snapped. "Get in here!"

Punk watched Lieutenant Ronnie Wheedle rush past and remembered their first encounter when Wheedle had made it a point to state that he'd voluntarily stopped flying helicopters because he'd *wanted* to be a public affairs officer, not because of the sort of dubious circumstance that often caused line officers to migrate to support ratings. Punk had never bought the explanation. He could see forgoing flying airplanes to go through medical or law school on the Navy's dime, but why would anyone *want* to baby-sit the press and explain away the occasional steaming turd left at the doorstep?

Wheedle disappeared into the stateroom, and the door slammed shut. The three aviators plopped back into the couches and continued to wait for further guidance, eavesdropping while pretending not to hear the proceedings within.

A hush fell over the press corps seated in Flag Briefing and Analysis as Rear Admiral Dykstra entered from the mess, closely followed by Captain Sutcliffe and Lieutenant Wheedle. At the back of the room Spud, Punk, and Einstein stood dressed in their long-sleeved wash khakis, indistinguishable at a glance from the flag staffers lining the walls around them, as Wheedle had hoped they'd be when he'd recommended the uniform change from their flight suits just over an hour before.

The principals made their way to the half podium

that had been placed at the far end of the "situation table," the huge slab of oak covered in blue Naugahyde that was the centerpiece of Flag Briefing and Analysis. Punk shifted his focus between the three-officer party and the door they'd just come through, and he wondered if Captain Campbell was going to join them. The door didn't open again.

The admiral cleared his throat, tapped a small stack of papers on the podium, and began to speak in measured tones: "This afternoon a flight of two F-14 Tomcats based aboard this aircraft carrier were called in to support friendly Afghan forces and U.S. Army advisors pinned down by hostile forces along a mountain range approximately fifty miles west of Kandahar. During the course of the mission the F-14s neutralized three enemy tanks moving along the road just south of the engagement, an action that turned the tide of the battle."

Rear Admiral Dykstra paused, running his gray eagle's stare across the media reps around the situation table. Punk scanned the faces he could see and got nothing in return. He then noticed a female reporter across the table—a brunette with high cheekbones, delightfully sad brown eyes, and pouty lips. He wondered how he'd missed her before.

"Let me walk you through the lead aircraft's mission tape," the admiral continued, gesturing over his shoulder toward a large monitor with a built-in tape player perched on a rolling stand. He nodded at Lieutenant Wheedle and the tape began running on the screen.

"The first two bombs hit one right after the other," the admiral narrated just before the FLIR view obliged. The explosions looked more violent on the big screen than they'd looked in the cockpit, and again

Punk scanned the faces of the correspondents. None of them seemed terribly impressed, and he figured they were probably numb to this sort of footage after nearly a month of watching variations on this theme. "After the wingman takes out the third tank," the admiral said, "the flight lead spots a vehicle moving rapidly from the impact area and reasoned it was part of the tank convoy. Okay, slow the tape down here, please. Now, you can see something flashing from the bed of the vehicle, and at this point the pilot assumes they're shooting at him. He commits a one thousand pound bomb." The picture switched from Einstein's FLIR to Soup's HUD. "You'll see that the bomb hits a good distance behind the vehicle, which turned out to be, as most of you now know, a civilian pickup. As you can also see, the driver loses control and the pickup flips over, which causes the subsequent injuries and one fatality. Note that the bomb does not hit the pickup. In fact, our analysis shows that what few fragments reached the vehicle did so after it had already flipped." The tape stopped and the monitor went black.

"We deeply regret the inadvertent loss of life and injury to civilians," the admiral said, once again reading from his notes. "We want to remind the international community that we are doing everything in our power to avoid collateral damage of any kind." He looked up from the podium. "I'll now answer questions."

A flurry of hands flew up and cries of "Admiral" filled the room. Dykstra pointed to a mousy female with big glasses at the end of the table.

"Admiral, you say you're doing everything in your power to avoid this sort of thing," she said. "How exactly do you intend to avoid this sort of mistake in the future?"

"We're having our pilots review proper procedures," the rear admiral replied.

"Did the pilot in question not follow proper procedures?" a portly man with a close-cropped beard asked from next to the woman without waiting to be recognized.

"I didn't say that," the admiral said.

"Were you able to confirm that they were actually shooting at the pilot?" the attractive brunette asked in a smoky Southern accent.

"I don't know," the admiral said.

"I ask only because reporters there found a smashed mirror among the refugees' possessions," she explained. "Do you think the pilot could've mistaken a reflection for gunshots?"

"I have no details about a mirror. You can see from the tape it was reasonable for the pilot to assume he was being fired upon in this situation."

"We heard word that the pilot was a fairly senior officer," a bushy red-haired man said from across the table. "Can you confirm this for us and if so, can you identify him?"

"Our policy of not identifying combatants involved in ongoing operations is still in place, as you know and certainly understand."

"I'd like to get back to the procedures, if I may," the portly man said. "Didn't you say the F-14s were working with a forward air controller, sir?"

"Yes, they were."

"Doesn't the forward air controller usually clear the jets he's working with for the attack?"

"Yes." The admiral looked over to CAG Sutcliffe, who nodded in return.

"So, is the pilot or the forward air controller at fault in this case?"

Rear Admiral Dykstra looked down at the podium,

and Punk could see his face turning red. The admiral suddenly glared at the fat, bearded reporter, raised a finger, and started to speak, but stopped himself with a long, cleansing breath and then shifted to another tack. "We're at war, ladies and gentlemen, a war not of our choosing. Now, war can be an ugly business with unintended consequences, but make no mistake: The military personnel going into harm's way are heroes all. To suggest otherwise or to point fingers is reckless and unpatriotic." With that sentiment the new tack became the old one, but instead of losing his temper he summarily strode toward the door to the Flag Mess as the press corps continued to shout questions at him. The admiral disappeared without another word.

Lieutenant Wheedle attempted to mollify the now-irate press corps by rerunning the mission tape. Spud and Einstein mentioned business in the ready room and quickly made their exit, while Punk migrated toward the periphery of the questions and answers being tossed around the monitor. CAG Sutcliffe tried his best to explain the symbols on the FLIR and HUD as they danced across the screen, but Punk could see the air wing commander was uncomfortable talking about systems with which he was not well practiced.

Punk turned to go, and when he did he bumped into the brunette who'd quietly saddled up behind him. He smiled and tried to excuse himself around her, but she blocked his way.

"Are you a pilot?" she asked, accompanied by a subtle waft of perfume. She was shorter than he'd imagined her to be when he'd first spotted her seated at the situation table.

"Yes," he said with an irrepressible glance past the line of her jaw to where her denim shirt bulged.

"What do you think about this?" she asked, pointing toward the monitor.

"It's terrible when innocents are hurt, of course," he offered, forcing himself to focus on the tip of her nose. "But, right or wrong, decisions have to be made very quickly in those situations."

"Why?"

He winced involuntarily, echoing the question back to her: "Why?"

"Yes, why?" she prodded. Her gestures became more emphatic as she continued to speak. "You're flying too high for the gunfire to hit you, right? Look at the tape: big bombs to little guns, if there are any guns at all. They posed no direct threat to you. You put the little cross over the tank on your screen, and it's destroyed. You can kill anyone at any time with no worries for you. So, why very quickly?"

No threat? Punk's mind spun in neutral, and before he could fashion a reply Lieutenant Wheedle shut the monitor off and herded the press corps into the far end of Flag Briefing and Analysis. The brunette turned on her heel and queued up behind the fat man as the group filed out one at a time.

Punk watched her walk away and fought off her sting, feeling not at all the valiant knight or doer of good deeds. He studied her from behind, noting her curves, telling himself that her butt was a couple of sizes too big for her short frame.

But even Punk's broadest extrapolations of that inclination failed to deaden her barb. A phrase popped into his head now, an ever-louder growing refrain, he feared: *Video game war.*

The conversation stopped to allow another jet to slam into the overhead. As the F/A-18 was pulled to a quick halt, all attention in the *Arrowslingers* ready room was momentarily on the PLAT monitor mounted in the front corner under the "regular" television. The TV had just finished showing the refugees strewn across the road yet again and was now informing viewers that the talk show coming up would deal with the topic of friendly fire and what should be done about it.

"This was different than the last time," Einstein said, seated in front of the skipper's chair on a hydraulic fluid can that had been covered with Naugahyde and reborn as an ottoman. "Soup may not have been entirely rational, but he wasn't temporarily insane either."

"Crazy or not, I'm afraid the admiral's press conference didn't do much to stop the media from trying to make a big deal out of it," Spud said.

"I shouldn't have let Soup take the lead," Punk muttered, seated in the XO's chair next to Spud.

"You were promoted to lieutenant commander, Punk," Spud said, "not captain."

"Still . . ."

Cheers erupted from a small gathering of aviators seated in the mission debrief area at the back of the ready room. Flex, Punk's roommate, the muscle-bound Californian and one of the more senior lieutenants in the squadron, hailed them from across the rows of chairs: "Skipper, you've got to come see this."

Spud, followed by Punk and Einstein, moved to the group reviewing their recent strike: Flex, his pilot and the flight lead, Monster, and the wing crew of Peeler and Elf. Flex yielded his seat to the CO, and as they passed Punk considered the difference in the two men's builds and couldn't decide whether the bulky Flex or skinny Spud was further from the fighter jock stereotype.

Flex stood behind the skipper and set the scene: "We were working with this Special Ops Group FAC north of Kabul," he said. "He had a group of hostiles hiding under a bridge who left their SUV on the bridge, and he wanted to know if we could take them out without knocking down the bridge or damaging the SUV." Flex tapped a finger against his temple. "I figured if I held off firing the laser until late into the bomb's time of fall to shallow out the angle of impact and aimed the crosshairs a little short of the bridge I just might have been able to accommodate the request."

Flex pointed the remote in his hand at a small monitor mounted against the side bulkhead, and the mission tape began to play. As he did in the airplane during a precision-guided bomb delivery, Punk scanned the symbols and digits for the range to the target and the time to bomb impact. He also noted that the laser was not yet firing.

Flex paused the tape and moved to the screen. "This is the bridge, here, and this is the SUV," he said, using a ballpoint pen as a pointer. "It's hard to tell exactly what model it is, but from the size I'd guess it's a Land Cruiser. Word has those as the bad guys' ride of choice."

"Where are they?" Spud asked.

"Under the bridge," Flex explained. "But watch this."

Flex walked back behind the skipper and started the tape again. "Aim point short of the bridge," he narrated. "Laser firing . . . now. And then . . . *pow*."

There was a splash of dirt as the bomb skipped off the earth, and then a ball of smoke and fire belched at light speed from both sides along the axis of the culvert under the bridge.

"Did you see that?" Flex asked.

"Show it in slow motion," Monster said.

Flex stepped around the skipper and retrained his pen on the screen: "Look right here . . . right about now . . . *Wham!* Three or four of them go flying out the back. Did you see it?"

"Show it again," Peeler said.

"I'll pause it this time . . . there." Flex scribed circles with the pen. "That guy's flying off here, and this dude cartwheels off the other way." The tape started moving again, sending the victims to oblivion for the third time this showing. "And when the dust settles, the bridge is still standing." He raised a hand over the other members of his flight. "That's close air *support,* my brothers."

"Play it again in slow motion," Monster said after taking his turn at slapping Flex a high five.

"No," Elf said. "It's best at regular speed."

"It goes too fast that way. You can't see anything."

"Mess with the contrast or the brightness a little bit, see if that makes the picture any better."

"Show it again . . ."

Telephones were everywhere on the Boat, but only a small percentage of them could reach beyond the confines of the hull. One of these was tucked in a secluded corner of the air wing operations office on the operations officer's desk. Punk entered the office and immediately found himself face-to-face with Lieutenant Commander "Igloo" Nanachuk, the air wing operations officer. Igloo, an E-2 pilot, was a massive mocha-skinned human being with a moon-pie face, a terminally cheesy mustache, and a hair-trigger temper. He was also known across the air wing for his malapropisms.

"Can I borrow the phone for a second?" Punk asked, fighting to maintain eye contact, knowing any sign of weakness would cause Igloo to pounce.

"What do you need it for?" Igloo asked.

"Quick call home," Punk mumbled, involuntarily cutting his eyes to the floor.

Punk's countenance must've suggested he needed a morale boost because Igloo uncharacteristically stepped aside and waved him toward the desk. "Be my host," he said. "But make it quick. CAG's cracking down on unofficial calls, and I don't want to throw any steam on that fire." Punk nodded and rushed behind the sheet-metal partition that hid Igloo's desk from the door. He sat and dialed the same sequence of numbers he would've had he been sitting in the *Arrowslingers'* stateside hangar.

Suzanne still hadn't answered by the fifth ring. Punk checked his watch and did the math: The ten-hour difference made it early afternoon in Virginia Beach. That was usually the best time to catch her at home, as it was right around young Jason's naptime. But by the seventh ring he figured her day's normal routine had been modified and she wasn't home.

In the nearly two months he'd been gone, they'd established a pattern of trading daily e-mails, but phone calls had been hard to come by between Igloo's gatekeeping, the time difference, the flight schedule, and the Boat shutting down service for long periods of time because of security concerns. Whatever the means of communication, not enough time had passed for Punk to get used to the fact that his best friend's widow was now his significant other. He'd fantasized about her over the years; any red-blooded male would have after, say, seeing her slink out of the pool. But he had no more planned on this situation than he'd planned on her husband, Lieutenant Cal "Crud" Workman, dying in a midair collision during a training flight the spring before. Now, as he had every day since then, he fought to push the image of the explosion over the swamps of North .Carolina out of his consciousness.

He kept the phone to his head and ignored Igloo's hovering. Ten rings. In his mind's eye he replaced the Tomcats plunging to a fiery demise with Suzanne weighted down with a bundle of laundry, desperately trying to make it to the phone. And it rang. No answering machine clicked in. "I don't want to hear news secondhand," she'd said, an explanation Punk had never really understood.

By the fifteenth ring he was ready to admit defeat. He dropped the receiver from his ear, and as he did, a tiny voice came through the earpiece: "Rick?"

Punk jerked the phone back to his ear: "Suzanne?"

She laughed, and he was grateful to hear it. "I figured it was you," she said. "Nobody else would let the phone ring that many times."

"Where were you? Outside?"

"No, upstairs. Jason needs a nap, but he's been fighting me on it." As if on cue Punk heard a crying child entering the room. "Hold on a sec," she muttered, frustration evident. There was a thud through the receiver as the phone was dropped, and then an exchange from across the room:

"I'm on the phone now, honey; I need you to go lie down."

"No! I'm not tired!"

"Go upstairs and wait for me; I'll be right up."

"No!"

"Go upstairs now!"

"I have a headache!"

"Of course you do. You gave it to yourself by crying so much."

Punk heard the tramping of feet across the hardwood floor in the living room that Crud had been so proud of and then up the stairs, and he figured three-year-old Jason had realized the folly of his fight. Suzanne picked the phone back up about a minute later.

"Sorry about that," she said with a sigh. "Where were we?"

Punk chuckled. "At hello, I think."

"Hello," Suzanne said. "Welcome to a day in my life."

"I'd much rather be there than here."

"I doubt that. It's not very exciting around here."

"Excitement ain't all it's cracked up to be," Punk said. "Plus, I'd make things exciting for you if I were there."

"Oh, really," she purred, readily accepting his abrupt shift in tone. "How would you do that?"

Punk fought to remember where he was as his blood rushed to places it normally did not during visits to the CAG ops office. "Well . . ." A good bout of phone sex would have been just what the doctor ordered. He furtively peered around the partition, half tempted to ask Igloo if he might take a hike for ten minutes or so. "I'm not at liberty to discuss details at this time."

"That's too bad. Maybe I should tell you what I'd do to you, instead."

Punk swallowed hard. "That would be quite acceptable," he returned.

"Let me lie down on the couch first," she said.

He heard Igloo move for the door. "What are you wearing?" he blurted into the mouthpiece in a raspy whisper.

"Just a T-shirt and warm-up pants," she said.

"And under that?"

"Nothing but a bright red thong." Saints be praised. Punk surreptitiously reached down and adjusted his ever-growing self.

"Why don't you take it off?" he asked.

"That sounds like a good—oh, hold on here." Punk heard rustling, followed by the patter of little feet, louder with each step.

From across the room the boy cried, "Mommy, my stomach hurts," and then it sounded as if something was spilled on the hardwood floor.

"Oh, shit," Suzanne exclaimed. "Jason just threw up. I'm sorry. I've got to go. Can you call tomorrow?"

"I don't know," Punk replied, in a daze.

"Well, call if you can. I miss you."

"Miss you, too." And the line went dead.

Punk's understanding of the downside of being the *Arrowslingers'* operations officer was made one data point fuller at just after two o'clock in the morning when Peeler, the schedule writer, plowed through the back door to the ready room and over to the ops desk and announced: "They're changing the air tasking order again. You might as well wipe your ass with that flight schedule in front of you."

"The one we just finished writing an hour ago?" Punk said.

"That's the one. I'm headed down to CAG ops right now to see if Igloo's got a clue about how long we're going to have to wait for the new version."

Punk joined Peeler for the trip back along the main starboard passageway, well traveled and bright during the day shift but vacant and red-lit now. Punk thought about the denizens of the Cheesequarters—all except Peeler, of course—and cursed their naïveté. He saw them around the circle, convincing each other of how screwed up the chain of command above them was. Then they were jumping into their warm bunks to recharge their batteries so they could spend the next day acting as angst ridden as they had the one before. Then he remembered his last deployment a few years back and how he'd been convinced that Beads, the operations officer at that time, had been Soup's no-load toady. Now, as he further considered the man, Punk felt an unsettling sense of kinship that gave him as much pause as the look on the JOs' faces had when he'd entered the Cheesequarters a couple of days before.

They walked into CAG ops and found Igloo with a phone to each ear—one red, one black. He simultaneously hung them up and turned to the new arrivals. "The new ATO is coming through now," he said. "Plan on adding another two-plane event to the end of your current flight schedule."

Peeler let out a sigh of relief. Tacking an event on the tail end of the flight schedule was a relatively easy change to effect, and ten minutes later, after sending the schedule writer to bed, Punk was standing in the skipper's stateroom, dark save for the bluish glow from the laptop on the desk, waiting for Spud to approve the modified plan.

"We've had to add an event," Punk explained in an effort to accelerate the approval process. "Nothing too complicated, really."

"Hold on," Spud said, seated at the desk. "Let me finish up going through my e-mail." He gestured toward the couch, the back of which folded down and doubled as a bed, and Punk sprawled across it, making no secret of his fatigue. Spud appeared unmoved and continued to focus on the computer screen, tapping the keys and offering an occasional hum or chuckle in response to whatever he was reading.

Then Spud emitted an astonished gasp that caused Punk to bolt upright. Spud drew the corners of his mouth down and followed his last noise with a hissing sound as he sharply inhaled across his teeth.

"What is it?" Punk asked.

"Hold on for a sec," Spud said as he waved Punk in place and continued to read, eyes alternating between wide saucers and narrow slits. A minute later he pushed back from the desk. "The cat's out of the bag," he said. "Take a look."

Punk took the skipper's place at the desk and began to read:

Subj: Fwd: Senior Officer Linked to Refugee Bombing
From: doolantz@hq.pntgn.navy.mil
To: CO@vf104.navy.mil

Spud—
This article is making the rounds in the Building. I'm told it hits the streets tomorrow.

Fly safe, Wizard

Subj: Senior Officer Linked to Refugee Bombing
From: CHINFO@hq.pntgn.navy.mil
To: flaglist@hq.pntgn.navy.mil
CC: staffers@hq.pntgn.navy.mil

SENIOR OFFICER LINKED TO REFUGEE BOMBING (From wire reports)—A high-ranking naval aviator has been linked with the accidental bombing in southern Afghanistan that killed an infant and maimed several other Afghan refugees who were fleeing the violence along a desert highway west of Kandahar. Captain Alexander Campbell, who was celebrated as a national hero two years ago after being shot down while patrolling the no-fly zone over Iraq, reportedly was piloting the F-14 Tomcat that dropped a bomb on a civilian pickup during a close air support mission around midday local time yesterday. Campbell is currently serving as the assistant commander for the air wing aboard an aircraft carrier that has planes flying into Afghanistan as part of Operation Enduring Freedom. The carrier has been steaming in the Northern Arabian Sea south of the coast of Pakistan. The incident, along with damaging the tenuous diplomatic relationship between America and the Northern Alliance, the loose arrangement of formerly warring Afghan tribes, has raised the question of whether the pilot had adequate training prior to joining a war in progress.

Captain Campbell is new to his post. Records show that at the time of the 9-11 terrorist attacks, he was assigned to the Pentagon as an advisor to the Joint Chiefs of Staff. While Navy officials declined comment, military experts claim that even if he left that assignment the following week and immediately began retraining as a pilot, there wouldn't have been enough time for Campbell to gain the requisite proficiency in the array of missions that a combat-ready aviator might be asked to perform in wartime.

"Flying skills erode very quickly," said Melvin Bernard, a Haskins Fellow at the Jandow Study, a military think tank and consultant group. "And these days, with multimission airplanes, even a seasoned pilot like this needs time to get back up to speed."

"Do the math," a retired naval pilot who asked to remain anonymous said. "There's no way Captain Campbell went through the proper syllabus before reporting to the carrier. He barely had enough time to get carrier qualified, let alone qualified to drop bombs."

At a press conference earlier today, the Secretary of Defense said that the accidental bombing was "a terrible tragedy" and quickly added, "but in war these things happen. Nobody plans on it, nobody's happy about it, but it's inevitable. That doesn't mean we won't attempt to find out what happened in this case, and if there's negligence we'll take the appropriate action."

Before this event Captain Campbell was generally regarded in Navy circles as a fast-track officer destined to be an admiral. His official biography shows he was previously assigned to both the Blue Angels and Top Gun, plum jobs for a Navy fighter pilot.

But sources close to Campbell said that, in spite of his meteoric rise through the ranks, he can be self-centered and is given to impulsive behavior. In his autobiography, *Flight to Glory,* published after his short POW stint in Iraq, even Campbell admits "I've never been guilty of thinking too much," but he goes on to say, "that's been the secret of my success."

Melvin Bernhard said an investigation into the facts of the accidental bombing will reveal either that Campbell is guilty of bypassing important steps in his zeal to get to the action or that the system pushed him into the war too fast. "In either case," Bernhard concluded, "it's pretty obvious there was no way Captain Campbell was going to let this war happen without him."

"Has Soup seen this?" Punk asked.

"I doubt it," Spud replied. "I'm not sure how Wizard does it, but he always seems to get things way before anyone else." Spud urged his pilot and operations officer out of the chair and retook his place behind the desk.

Punk wandered over to the nearest bulkhead and in the low light studied the lagging around one of the many pipes that ran along the edges of the stateroom. "What do you think he's going to do?"

"What he always does when he gets himself in a jam," the skipper said, pushing his laptop aside. "He'll blame someone else." He tapped a finger against the sheet of paper Punk had laid on the desk a few minutes before. "Now, how about explaining what's going on with this flight schedule . . ."

Toward the end of the four hours of sleep Punk managed before his next brief he was gripped by a vivid dream, one of the few during the deployment that he would remember after he woke up. He found himself perched on a bough just above the reach of a mob on a dusty street below. The crowd was huge, stretching as far as the eye could see. The people's faces were nondescript, for the most part; some wore beards. He could tell they were angry. They shook their fists and threw things at him that he was just able to dodge. He couldn't hear them, but he knew they were yelling words of hate, extolling each other toward violent acts.

Several of them ringed the tree's trunk and attempted to dislodge him. At first their efforts were uncoordinated; they pushed against each other, barely moving the tree. But eventually they synched themselves up, and the branch he was on began to violently twist. He lost his grip and fell past the mob's outstretched arms to the ground, but the ground wasn't solid, rather a dirty cloud that he penetrated for a short time before emerging into the light on the other side.

He continued to fall, accelerating beyond the pull of gravity. Geometric shapes formed before him, and he realized he was now at the controls of a jet. He pulled back on the stick and climbed. Darkness fell. He gazed over his shoulder and watched the earth grow smaller behind him.

"We're in space," he said.

"It's time to drop," Spud said from the backseat. Punk looked in one of his mirrors and noted that his RIO wasn't wearing a helmet.

"What are we aiming at?" Punk asked.

"We don't aim at all," Spud replied. "*They* do."

The radio crackled something unintelligible and prompted Punk to depress the bomb button, and as he did the bomb didn't fall away but instead roared forward like a missile. The weapon traveled away and appeared to hook left, disappearing behind the far side of the planet, leaving behind a wide white plume like the space shuttle did during a launch.

They were in deep space now, weightless and calm.

Punk looked over the canopy rail and watched the bomb as it repeatedly passed through the light while orbiting the globe beneath them.

"Will it ever hit?" he asked.

"They don't tell us," Spud said. "And we shouldn't ask."

CHAPTER FIVE

Punk was tired of numbers: latitudes, longitudes, rendezvous altitudes, bomb configurations, return to force profiles, airspeeds, checklists, and fuel flows, the exactness of it all. He didn't want to write down numbers or punch numbers into keypads or work numbers through his head. He wanted simplicity and the blissful absence of the requirement for accuracy, days when the hardest decision would be what brand of beer to choose from his options along the inside of the refrigerator door.

But for now the war was still on. Punk knew it because the people around him were talking about it at great length. So he dutifully watched the screen in the intelligence center's video teleconference room and thought on how far technology had come since his first days aboard an aircraft carrier and how they'd accepted each exponential leap without question. Now not only did you have to read the words authored by the tasking authority, you also had to hear their voices and see their faces. He considered the movement of an eyebrow beaming in from thousands of miles away and wondered how the military had managed to fight wars before digital science, the same way people wondered how society had survived before electricity and automobiles.

Punk, Spud, and their normal wing crew of Muddy—the lone female pilot in the squadron—and Flex sat on one side of a planning table along with two Hornet pilots—Jocko, a big-armed, barrel-chested workout freak like Flex who fairly rippled under his flight suit, and Melba, a skinny redheaded distance runner with a face full of freckles. They all looked into a small camera perched between two big monitors—one showing the six of them and one that framed whoever was speaking on the other end—as an enlisted technician occasionally adjusted the lights like a studio hand. The tech then returned to his position off camera, ready at a moment's notice to dial down to the communications center in the event of a dropped connection.

"CENTCOM, are you there?" asked the bald Air Force colonel seated in the current operations cell at the Joint Task Force—Southwest Asia. "Rear Admiral Whatley?"

"I'm here, Colonel Pine," said an equally bald but elegantly mustachioed admiral from CENTCOM headquarters as he entered from stage left. As he spoke, the image on all the other screens in the "bridge"—the term for the link between sites—automatically shifted from the VTC facility at Prince Sultan Air Base to the VTC facility at MacDill Air Force Base. Like the colonel, Rear Admiral Whatley was dressed in desert cammies, which Punk found mildly amusing since the admiral wasn't deployed to the Saudi Arabian desert but rather was sitting in a nice air-conditioned room in

Tampa, Florida. "I was on the phone with the general," Whatley said, his shiny head reflecting the studio's lights and framed by the CENTCOM emblem on the wall behind him.

"B-one, are you up?" Colonel Pine asked.

"We're up," said a chubby captain from Sheik Isa Air Base in Bahrain, flanked by the rest of his six-person crew under a banner that read GLOBAL REACH, GLOBAL POWER.

"Navy?"

"We're here," Spud passed, offering a little wave to the camera while fighting the urge to look at himself in the other monitor.

"K-two? Major Bando, is it?"

"Banko, sir," said an Army officer, face eerily lit from below in a way that reminded Punk of his Boy Scout days when he and his friends used to play with flashlights. "I'm here." The quality of the picture was relatively poor compared to the other locations, but he could see in the scant light that the major was sporting the sort of recently acquired scraggly beard that had become de rigueur for the special operations guys in theater. Punk could also make out that the man was wearing a heavy parka with the hood down, and behind him something flapped in the breeze, the door to a tent, perhaps.

"All right. Looks like we're all here," Colonel Pine said. "I don't want to waste any of your valuable time, so I'll get right to it: After weeks of a virtual stalemate it looks like the dam is about to break. Mazar-e-Sharif is on the verge of going down, and once that happens we're certain that Kabul and Kandahar will follow. This is happening none too soon. I don't have to tell you folks that the media and some members of Congress have been questioning whether the Northern Alliance would be able to get the job done. The next number of days is crucial in answering that question. If this next phase doesn't work, we're probably going to have to start putting more American boots on the ground . . ." The admiral's voice trailed off, and he stroked his mustache for a few moments but then briskly rubbed his hands together, snapping himself out of his pensive state. "Major Banko, why don't you review the high points of the mission?"

"Can we bring the chart up, please?" Major Banko said. A high-resolution depiction of the area jumped onto the screen, and the major began scribing electronic white marks on it like an analyst covering a football game. "I'm here at K-two, our base camp." A little circle appeared in the southern extreme of Uzbekistan. "At first light four of us will be carried across the border in a Russian-made Hind helicopter." Banko chuckled. "I never thought I'd be excited to have old Russian technology at my disposal, but this Mi-eight we're using can handle the altitudes we have to deal with as we make our way south through the mountains. We'll make contact with General Wali's Northern Alliance forces . . . here, along this highway. From there we'll start the push north. We expect a fight on the outskirts of Mazar-e-Sharif. That's where we'll need air support. We'll be looking for the B-one to flush the enemy out of where he's dug in, and then we'll call in the close air support assets to clean up what's left as we advance."

"So we think the enemy will be out in the open after the B-one goes through?" Spud asked.

"Most likely," Banko said.

"Sounds like we should load cluster munitions."

"Negative," Rear Admiral Whatley said. "CENT-COM just put a moratorium on cluster weapons.

We've spread so many of those bomblets across the country that it's going to take years to clean them up. Plus, we've had reports of kids blowing themselves up after finding unexpended stuff. I don't think I need to tell the folks on the carrier that we don't need any more bad press like that."

Spud checked the load plan for the day on the table in front of him and saw that some of the jets over Afghanistan at that moment were armed with cluster bombs. He was tempted to ask the admiral when the moratorium had gone into effect but chose not to. "Copy, Admiral," he said. "We'll figure something out."

"I'm sure you will, skipper," the admiral replied. "All right, let's work it around the horn before we go off the air. B-one, final concerns?"

"We need good coordinates and a run-in heading for our drop," the chubby pilot said. "Our stick length from the first to the last bomb is nearly a mile long. That's a can of whoop ass you want to make sure you put in the right place."

"Good point," Rear Admiral Whatley said. "Let's make sure the FACs get the word. Any concerns from the jet guys?"

"Our OP is a good distance from any of the tanker tracks," Spud said, "so our loiter time is at a premium, especially for the two Hornets in our flight. If you need to slide our on-call window to the right, let the AWACS know before we push from the tanker."

"Very good," the admiral said. "Major Banko, anything else?"

"Yeah," Banko said as he scratched through the matted hair that had grown just beyond military standards. "We could use some saddles."

* * *

By his own and oft-repeated assertion, Chief Warrant Officer Mickey Hooter had lived a sailor's life for the bulk of his adult years, which to look at him was a believable claim. The weathered skin on his face and hands told of months spent on the flight deck singed by jet exhaust and peppered by salt spray. His hair was coarse, terminally windblown, and prematurely gray. Both arms were covered with tattoos, and with the slightest provocation he'd work his way up one and down the other, relating the origins of each ink rendering—an exercise the junior officers in the squadron had labeled as "the journey." Punk wasn't sure of his exact age, but as he'd listened to Hooter's sea stories over the weeks on the Boat, he'd come to the conclusion that the man was probably twenty years younger than his appearance suggested. Indeed, time hadn't been kind to him, but he didn't seem too concerned about it.

Hooter, known as "the gunner" like every other ordnance officer in every other squadron around the fleet, ambled into the ready room like an aging cowboy and parked himself on the ottoman at the skipper's feet. He wasn't a fat man, but he had a belly, and as he leaned forward it spilled over his belt, making the front of his red flight deck jersey look like a balloon about to burst. He labored to catch his breath. Punk caught a whiff of cigarette smoke and figured he had been catching a quick nicotine fix between the next launch and recovery.

"The load plan is out of date, Gunner," Spud said. "We can't carry Rockeye. Cluster munitions have been banned from the war."

The gunner rolled his eyes and said, "Skipper, we got that word a few hours ago. All the Rockeye has been struck below."

"Well, shit," Spud returned with disgust. "I guess

I'm the last guy to get the word. So what are we loaded with?"

Hooter produced a wrinkled sheet from his back pocket. "Mark-eighty-threes. Two each."

Punk looked over at Spud and intoned, "We're going after troops in the open with Mark-eighty-threes."

The skipper focused on the gunner and asked, "Can we do something else?"

"Like what, sir?" Hooter returned.

"I don't know," Spud said. "Something to make a standard dumb bomb act like a Rockeye."

"The bombs are already loaded on your jets."

Punk threw his hands up. "Once again, the tail wags the dog around here."

Hooter puffed an exasperated breath and started to get up, but Spud held him in place. "Nobody's blaming you, Gunner," he said. "Is there any way to polish this turd, or not?"

The gunner pinched the bridge of his nose like he was fighting a migraine. "Do you need yolk or shell?"

"What?" the skipper asked with a confused grimace.

"Yolk or shell?" the gunner repeated. "Do you want a lot of shrapnel or a big blast? It sounds to me like you want lots of shrapnel." The two aviators nodded. "Okay, we'll download the eighty-threes and load four eighty-twos instead. And to get them to air burst, I'll stick TDD-thirty-four fuses on the noses. That should give you a nice big frag pattern."

"All right, then," Punk said. "Now we're getting somewhere."

The gunner jabbed a finger at the pilot and said, "We don't like to do business this way, Punk, changing things at the last minute. These are live bombs we're talking about."

Once again the CO worked to calm his ordnance officer. "Do whatever you can, Gunner. Let's go with the Mark-eighty-twos."

Hooter made another whooshing noise and stood before Spud could attempt to restrain him again. "If I'm going to do this, I'd better get to the flight deck," the gunner said. "I'll have to look in the munitions manual in the ordnance shop on the way up there."

"In any case, let's keep it by the book," Spud said.

Hooter pulled the ready room door open and called over his shoulder: "Always."

Punk sheathed the nine-millimeter pistol he'd drawn for the mission into the holster just below his left armpit and looked at his female wingman through the line of flight gear that hung from big hooks throughout the paraloft like sides of beef in a butcher's freezer. "Are you ready for this, Muddy?"

"Why not?" Lieutenant (junior grade) "Muddy" Greenwood replied with a smile. He nodded and, working the zipper on his harness, reflected on how far she'd come since the day just over eight months before when she'd earned her call sign by inadvertently taxiing off the asphalt and burying her jet's right mainmount in the mud of NAS Oceana. She'd been a student in the F-14 training squadron at the time, and Punk had been one of her instructors. In fact, Flex and Spud had also been instructors of hers, and all four of them had been summoned to the Boat in the wake of 9-11. Since they already knew each other and had flown as a section in training, the late *Arrowslinger* skipper, Commander "Smooth" Renforth, had minimized any disruption to his standing tactical organization and crewed them together upon their arrival.

Over the course of their association Punk and

Muddy had connected at some level that he had never been able to completely put his finger on. They were both Naval Academy graduates but beyond the obligatory review of traditions, that alone had had no bearing on their chemistry. There was nothing physical between them, although Muddy was attractive in a tomboy kind of way. The best he could figure was that his affinity for her had to do with her attitude. She'd lost a few battles but she refused to lose the war.

But that didn't mean she didn't tempt failure. For Muddy the basics of tanking off of the KC-135's "wrecking ball" and landing on the Boat were always an adventure. She'd removed one refueling probe already on this cruise before the shooting started, and her landing grades were near if not at the bottom of the heap. But she'd managed those liabilities and further balanced them with guts and a tactical acumen that belied her limited experience. Although few would've predicted it possible during her days as a fledgling fighter pilot, she was now a salty combat veteran, already nominated for a Distinguished Flying Cross and two Air Medals. If she kept from killing herself while trying to land her jet for the balance of the deployment, she'd warrant quite a swagger through the back bar of the NAS Oceana officers club upon their return.

"Skipper, what's this I hear about the gunner changing our bombs?" Flex asked, standing next to Muddy while inventorying the contents of his nav bag.

"Oh, yeah, I meant to talk to you about that," Spud replied from the opposite corner of the paraloft as he wiped the visor on his helmet with a chamois. "I think we're getting poor man's Rockeye. We've got Mark-eighty-twos instead now, and he's doing something with the fusing."

"What about the weaponeering?" Flex asked, referring to the calculations crews did during their mission planning to ensure that the bomb was going to perform correctly.

Spud furrowed his brow. It was a fair question and one that the skipper must've felt a bit guilty for not considering on his own.

"I'll find the gunner and then redo the calculations on the JMEMs computer," Flex said, referring to the weaponeering software program loaded on the operations computer in the back of the ready room. "I'll meet you on the flight deck."

Flex slipped his helmet on and hurriedly threaded his way out the door. The skipper followed him, trailed by Punk and Muddy. They made their way out the side hatch and up two sets of stairs to the flight deck. Punk raised his dark visor and looked at the whitecaps on the sea and up to the cloudy skies and wondered what had happened to the pleasant weather they'd been promised by the forecaster during the brief.

Punk exchanged high fives with Muddy and Flex as the crews split and strode toward their respective Tomcats. Theirs was parked on the starboard side of the fantail and his was across the flight deck just forward of the platform where the landing signal officers stationed themselves during recoveries. Punk followed Spud, picking his way across the grimy arresting wires, noting the activity on and around their jet. The plane captain straddled the pilot's cockpit and wiped the inside of the open canopy while beneath the fighter one of the gunner's teams finished tweaking the Mark-82s—which reminded Punk that they needed to get an update from the gunner on what he'd done to modify the bombs, if anything.

As they reached the grease-obscured centerline they were engulfed by a wave of crew members stretching the full width of the flight deck engaged in the "FOD walkdown," the ritual stroll performed before daylight launches, an elbow-to-elbow human chain that moved from bow to stern in search of small foreign objects that could be sucked into jet engines. Although he was headed perpendicular to their flow, while in their midst Punk made it a point to reach into a padeye and flick at an inconsequential blob of black residue—a symbolic but, to his mind, necessary show of aviator/deckhand solidarity.

Behind the main thrust of the FOD walkdown were a handful of others—the quality-assurance line—and among them Spud and Punk were mildly surprised to see Captain Campbell. The Deputy CAG was focused on the flight deck and continued unawares until the three of them converged on the extreme port side of the landing area.

"Find anything good, Deputy?" Spud asked.

Soup raised his face and offered a meek smile. "No, not really," he replied as he opened a fist and considered the nearly microscopic bits of metal now lodged into the cracks across his palm. "I'm just out here trying to show some support." His voice carried neither regal affectations nor the cutting self-assuredness of the alpha male; in other words, he sounded nothing like himself. "You guys headed over the beach?"

"Yes, sir," Spud said. "Pretty far north this time."

Captain Campbell patted the skipper on the biceps and said, "Well, good luck."

They started to go their separate ways but Soup turned and said, "Spud . . . keep me off . . ." He paused with a wince, as if it pained him to say the words. "Keep me off the flight schedule for a few days." The captain then rendered an informal salute and continued toward the fantail to join the line that had now nearly reached the stern.

Punk and Spud had started their pre-flight walk arounds when Flex came running up waving a scrap of paper. "I figured the weaponeering out after talking to the gunner over by our jet, skipper," he said while holding the paper against the left side of the Tomcat's nose with one hand and tapping it with the index finger of the other. "Here's the gouge."

Punk leveled his jet off at twenty-five thousand feet and cursed the fact that he was still in the clouds. He looked down to the card on his kneeboard to where he'd scrawled the highlights from the weather brief—not ideal bombing weather, certainly, but not bad enough to cancel the mission: "BKN LYRS BTWN 5–15. SCT 15–20. CLR ABOVE 20." *Clear above 20,000 feet, huh?* he thought. *Bullshit.*

"We're overhead Mother, level at twenty-five, Muddy," Punk said on squadron common. "Still in the goo."

"We're still on the S-3," Flex returned. "What do you want to do?"

"Standby. Jocko, are you airborne yet?"

"I am," the Hornet lead replied. "Melba, say your posit."

"I'm on the cat," the first-cruise wingman said.

"Okay," Punk said. "I'm going to press higher and see if we can break out of it. I'll advise once I'm in the clear."

Punk urged the stick back and split his attention between watching the altimeter wind up and looking through the canopy to see if they'd cleared the clouds yet. Twenty-eight thousand feet, thirty thousand feet. The world outside remained a dirty blank canvas.

"We're still in it at thirty-five thousand," Punk passed before shooting a glance at his watch. "We've got to get headed north. Muddy, how's your fighter-to-fighter data link looking?"

"It's tight," Flex said while double-checking the symbols that represented the two fighters on his tactical information display.

"Stay in five-mile trail and level off at thirty-four. Hopefully these clouds will thin out along the way."

"Roger."

"After we finish getting our gas off of the S-3, Hornets will do the same drill at thirty-three and thirty-two," Jocko advised.

"Punk copies."

Spud moved the cursor across his tactical display and hooked the first waypoint of their navigation plan, which caused a steering cue to appear on the outside of the electronic compass rose in Punk's cockpit. "Steering is to the tanker track," Spud advised over the intercom.

"Thanks," Punk replied as he started a shallow turn to the left. "It's getting lighter, right? Is it just me or is it getting lighter?"

Spud let out a sardonic chuckle and keyed the radio: "Seabird six-oh-one, Slinger one-oh-four is checking in, popeye at Angels three-five."

"Seabird copies, Slinger," said the E-2 controller. "Let me see if I can get a pirep from Bossman." "Pirep" was short for "pilot report," an airborne weather observation. After a minute off the air, the controller came back with, "Slinger, check in with Bossman on Red one." Not quite an answer to the weather query, but Spud figured the AWACS would be able to tell them directly.

"Slinger is switching Red one," Spud said. "Flight switch."

"Two," Flex said.

After some radio manipulation and then a few more beats, Spud said, "Punk flight check," on Red one.

"Two," Flex said again, verifying he'd made the frequency switch along with his lead RIO.

"Bossman, Ajax five-three is checking in," Spud said.

"Bossman copies, Ajax," a female voice said, which caused Punk and Spud to wonder whether it belonged to the same female controller who had been part of their last flight over Afghanistan. "Understand your wingmen are with you?"

"Standby, Bossman." Spud keyed squadron common. "Jocko, are you with us?"

"Affirmative. We're back here just having a blast."

"Wingmen are with us, Bossman, in radar trail separated by altitude," Spud explained. "We're proceeding north, currently in the clouds. Do you have a pirep for us?"

"A pirep?"

"What's the weather like north of us?"

"I'm pretty far away from you . . . I'm not sure, really." It *was* the same controller. "I think your first tanker is monitoring this frequency, though. Shell three-zero, are you up?"

"Hello?" said a distinctly French-accented voice. "Who is calling Shell three-zero?"

"Shell, this is Bossman," the controller said, speaking more slowly now, carefully enunciating every word. "How is the weather around your position?"

"Ah . . . some clouds, perhaps."

"Ajax, do you copy?" the AWACS controller asked.

"Copy," Spud replied. "Shell, understand the Gipper track is workable?"

"*Oui* . . . ah, yes. Is workable, mostly."

"Bossman, can you verify Ajax's steer to Shell?" Spud asked.

"Standby . . . three-five-two for one hundred and twenty miles."

"Ajax copies."

"Do you have radar contact on him yet?" Punk asked over the intercom.

"Negative," Spud replied.

"Jocko was right: This *is* a blast."

They drove through the off-white blanket for another five minutes, and Spud wondered aloud whether the clouds would ever break up as they made their way farther north. He keyed the radio tuned to Red one: "Bossman, do you have any word on the weather over our objective?"

"I understand your tanker said it's workable where they are," she returned.

Spud took a deep breath, trying to keep his frustration from showing over the radio. "We copied that," he said. "I'm asking about the area north of that, around the SAR dot." The SAR dot was designed as the reference point for downed airmen and search-and-rescue crews looking for them. Its coordinates put it smack dab in the middle of Afghanistan. "Do you have any aircraft working in country right now that you could ask for a pirep?"

"Uh, standby," she replied.

The frequency went dead. Spud angrily unlatched his oxygen mask from the right side of his helmet and wiped his face with the bandana tied to the D-ring on his harness. "Are these questions unreasonable?" he asked over the intercom.

Punk laughed and started to say something but cut himself off as Red one crackled to life again: "Ajax, Hammer six-three reports clear below twenty-three thousand."

"Copy, Bossman," Spud replied. "Where are they, roughly?"

"Um . . . they're working near point Hartford."

Spud unfolded the chart he'd perched along his right console and scoured it for the point in question. "Dammit," he seethed over the intercom. "Hartford is about one hundred and fifty miles southeast of where we're headed."

"I'd give it up, skipper," Punk advised. "She's barely hanging on to the clue merchant as it is. Let's just press to the tanker and work it from there."

Spud released a long exhale and strapped his mask back across his face. "I've got radar on the tanker," he said over Punk's radio, tuned to the squadron common frequency. "Three-five-five, fifty miles, Angels two-five. Currently headed eastbound."

"Muddy's contact," Flex said.

"Jocko's contact," Jocko said.

"Punk's headed down to the tanker's altitude," Punk said. "Muddy, you level off at twenty-four; Jocko, twenty-three; Melba, twenty-two."

"Muddy copies."

"Jocko."

"Melba."

Punk urged the stick forward and established a moderate rate of descent. "Are we in Afghanistan yet?" he asked over the intercom.

"That's affirmative," Spud said. "We crossed the border about twenty miles back."

"Flying blind over bad-guy country . . ."

The four jets continued to close the first of the three tankers they would rendezvous with during the mission. As the separation walked down to twenty miles Punk descended through thirty thousand feet and advised his RIO, "I'm not going any closer than ten miles if we don't break out."

"No argument here," Spud said.

With that, several quick flashes of brightness hit them as the clouds showed some sign of breaking up, and then the wing Hornet transmitted, "Melba's in the clear at twenty-six." A weight lifted from each of them, like in the old sailing days when the crew heard the cry of "Land ho!"

The flashes intensified around Punk and Spud until suddenly they were clear of the clouds. Punk glanced over his shoulder and saw two of his three wingmen strung out behind him, and as he looked under Jocko he thought he could see Melba's F/A-18—a speck at nearly fifteen miles away, but a beautiful sight nonetheless.

Punk focused through the diamond Spud's radar lock projected against the glass of his HUD, and he got a tally-ho on the French tanker, a KC-135F, just now throwing a wing up as it went into a slow turn at the far western end of the Gipper track. "Punk's tally the tanker," he passed over squadron common.

"Bossman, Ajax flight is clear of the clouds, and we have a visual on Shell," Spud said over Red one. "We'd like to switch the boom frequency."

"Roger," the controller said, relief evident in her voice. "Contact Shell on Maroon five."

"Flight switch Maroon five."

"Two," Flex said.

"Three," Jocko said.

"Four," Melba said.

Punk drove right into the basket, and one by one the three other Navy jets lined themselves down the big airplane's left wing. Although the KC-135 was not the friendliest of the tankers in theater, with its afterthought of a male-to-female rig that had a very hard basket and no take-up reel, it did pump gas at the healthy rate of two thousand pounds per minute. Punk managed the curve in the thick rubber hose until he was topped off and then slid the fighter's probe from the drogue and moved over to the right side of the tanker to wait for the rest of the flight to get their gas.

Spud checked the distance to their orbit point and shot a glance at his watch. "Shell, could we get a drag of about zero-two-zero?" he asked on Maroon five, the tanker's discrete frequency.

"Talking to Shell three-zero, repeat, *si'l vous plaît*."

"Could you pick up a heading toward our destination, please? Zero-two-zero would work fine."

"No," the Frenchman replied curtly. "Is impossible. We must stay on the track."

So they drove to the east while Spud lashed out at those who'd authored the day's air tasking order without assigning a plucky British tanker to their mission. He was just hitting his vituperative stride over the intercom, now cursing all things French, including toast, fries, and braids, when the gaggle inadvertently flew into another cloud bank. Spud silenced himself as the tanker momentarily disappeared and then barely reappeared as a gray silhouette. Instead of peeling off to the right, Punk eased the Tomcat slightly left until the tanker's wingtip was nearly touching his canopy.

"We can't see you," the French pilot said excitedly.

"Stay straight and level," Punk instructed. "We're all still aboard." He keyed the radio on squadron common, remembering that Muddy had already ripped one probe off during her first attempt to tank from a USAF KC-135. She'd successfully tanked from the unforgiving device dozens of times in the weeks since then, but Punk feared the bad weather might conjure up the images of when it had gone very wrong. "Muddy, are you still in the basket?"

"Yes," Muddy replied apprehensively. "I've got three thousand pounds left to take on."

"How are you guys doing on the left wing, Jocko?"

"We're okay," Jocko replied. "This hop just keeps getting better and better, doesn't it?"

"Muddy, do you think you can make it to the right wing once you've got your gas?" Punk asked.

"I don't know."

"Don't press it if you lose sight. Descend and exit to the right. We'll sort it out once you're sure you're clear."

"Okay."

The clouds remained, occasionally growing wispy enough to tease the pilots into believing that they were about to disappear altogether only to thicken up again, at some points enough to obscure the tanker's fuselage completely. Punk fought to stay unmoved, dutifully focusing on the big jet's right anticollision light, watching it jump with the turbulence. At times when the clouds were most dense the red light was his sole reference, and he clung to it like a flood victim to a tree branch.

Punk's inner ear began to play tricks on him. Being positioned slightly beneath the tanker, it looked to him as if they were in a turn. He wanted to sneak a quick look at his attitude indicator but didn't, fearing even the slightest bit of attention away from the wingtip.

"Are we in a turn?" he asked over the intercom.

"Negative," Spud replied. "We're straight and level."

With that input the gyro in Punk's head uncaged completely. "Keep talking to me, skipper," he said. "I've got a bad case of vertigo."

"Still straight and level," Spud intoned before adding a little more data to help his pilot rebuild an accurate mental plot. "Two hundred and fifty knots, twenty-five thousand feet."

"Shell three-zero left turning," the tanker pilot transmitted as they reached the eastern end of the Gipper track. The tanker's right wingtip started to climb away, and Punk worked to stick with it, trying to stay smooth with the controls while simultaneously waging a battle against the sensory cues that told him he was flying inverted.

Spud continued to advise him with a public-radio announcer's meter: "In a turn now, ten degrees left wing down."

"Muddy's topped off," the young female pilot passed over squadron common. "Do you want me to try and make it to the right wing while we're in a turn or wait until we steady up?"

"How's your gas, Jocko?" Punk asked.

"I wouldn't mind getting in the basket before too long," Jocko said. "But whatever Muddy needs—"

They were suddenly clear of the clouds. All they'd needed to do all along was fly a bit more to the north, something they would've discovered a long time before had they been granted the courtesy of a drag toward their orbit point. Spud launched into another diatribe, this time describing in great detail what the French pilots could do with the Eiffel Tower.

Punk used the cloud layer beneath them as a horizon of sorts, and his vertigo vanished. Behind him, with due haste, Muddy retracted her probe and then moved outside of her lead on the tanker's right wing. Both Hornets took on their gas in clear air, and once Melba was in place outside of Jocko Punk started a gradual right-hand turn away from the Gipper track without giving the French pilots his half of the friendly wave normally offered between cockpits following a gas up.

"Bossman, Ajax five-three is first tanking complete," Spud passed on Red one.

"Roger, Ajax," a confident male voice said, surprising those in the flight expecting the same female controller to respond. "You'll be working with Lion one-five on Rose four."

"Copy Lion one-five on Rose four."

"That's affirmative. We need you to buster to station, Ajax. The unit you're fragged to assist has just made an expedite call for close air support."

Spud checked his watch. "Bossman, our vul window isn't supposed to start for another forty-five minutes. What happened?"

"Can you buster or not, Ajax?"

"That'll reduce our on-station time."

"No factor. It looks like you'll be dropping your ordnance on arrival."

"What about the Air Force heavy asset?" Spud asked, referring to the B-1 they were supposed to follow.

"We're already talking to him. He's bustering. Lion one-five will sequence you in behind him."

Spud checked the range to their orbit point: two hundred miles. "What do you think, Punk?" he asked over the intercom.

"We'll be hurting for gas on the back side of this," Punk said.

Spud rekeyed Red one: "Bossman, if we buster to station we'll need Shell to come north and meet us on the way out."

"Roger," the AWACS controller said. "We'll coordinate."

"He didn't seem very interested in deviating from the tanker track earlier," Spud added.

"Let us do our job, and we'll help you do yours, Ajax," the controller said. Punk figured from his tone he was a fairly senior officer, the AWACS squadron commander or even the wing commander.

For a time they sped through clear skies, and Punk looked down at the mountains that reached ever toward the aviators, revealing sharp ridges and sheer faces as the four jets hustled their way slightly west of north. He quickly referenced his chart and noted that some of the peaks slipping under their wings topped out at nearly fourteen thousand feet. He rechecked his altitude, wanting to keep at least a ten-thousand-foot buffer between the airplanes and bad guys with shoulder-fired SAMs. Still, he figured it was highly unlikely that anyone would be able to station himself at those sorts of altitudes for very long except for a specially trained Sherpa, maybe, and he hadn't heard any intelligence reports about any of those among the enemy's ranks.

At fifty miles away from their orbit point the AWACS controller transmitted, "Ajax, contact Lion one-five on Rose four." Spud rogered up and directed the switch while the thought of impending action gave Punk the urge to urinate.

Punk pulled out one of the four piddle packs he'd stuffed into his nav bag and passed, "I'm switching the autopilot on for a sec," over the intercom, a euphemism for the fact his hands were leaving the flight controls temporarily to take care of matters of "pilot comfort." After ensuring he was properly mated with the plastic sponge-filled sack (it wouldn't have been the first time he'd miscalculated and dampened his G suit), he watched the sponge grow and then looked over at Muddy and wondered if she could tell what he was doing. For her own part she'd long since owned up to wearing "protective undergarments" during the strike missions and had taken to referring to exceptionally long hops as "diaper soakers."

He smiled under his mask at the notion of Muddy's self-deprecation—blunt and unapologetic—the underlying secret to her success in the *Arrowslingers*. Hers was a wit as dry and cutting as any among them, and as she displayed it she also exploded their myths and quelled their fears regarding the feminine presence in the boys club that had traditionally been naval aviation. Of the three female aviators in the squadron, she alone had managed the accomplishment. Now if she could just land the jet every time without scaring the LSOs . . .

Punk admired the engorged sponge floating in a thin layer of urine before rolling the piddle pack closed and chucking it against the aft bulkhead along the right side of his ejection seat. "I'm flying again," he said to his RIO.

"I trust your efforts were successful?" Spud quipped.

"Quite. Thanks for asking."

Punk's momentary ebullience was suppressed by the first post-potty break glance through the bulletproof glass in front of him. The skies in line with the velocity vector on his HUD were filled with a solid line of clouds. "I'm easing it downhill," he said over squadron common. "I want to try and stay below this stuff in front of us."

He started a gradual rate of descent but soon increased it after they passed through the outskirts of the cloud layer. They were quickly passing through sixteen thousand feet, and as he looked ahead Punk feared they might have to press even lower to stay in the clear. He glanced through the right side of the canopy, off to the east, and noted several mountains disappearing into the clouds. Never mind a ten-thousand-foot SAM buffer. The bar had been lowered to that of basic terrain avoidance.

"Bone two-three, call your position," the forward air controller ordered on Rose four. His voice was professionally calm, but still retained an immediacy that suggested the situation on the ground was far from resolved. Punk wondered if the FAC was Major Banko, the guy who'd beamed in from K-2 during the VTC.

"Approaching the OP," the B-1 pilot replied. "Understand the original frag is still valid?"

"Negative, negative," said the FAC. "Intel was bad. They're dug in about two clicks south of reports and hitting us pretty hard. Standby for new coordinates."

CHAPTER SIX

Punk listened for the sounds of gunfire around the FAC but heard none. "Bone two-three," the FAC continued, "center the stick at thirty-five forty-two-point-one-five north, sixty-seven zero-nine-point-three-six east. Use a run-in heading of zero-eight-five. How copy?"

"Bone two-three copies. Do you have a time on target for us?"

"ASAP."

"Roger. Are the fighters clear?"

"Ajax, are you up?" the FAC asked.

"That's affirmative. Checking in with a flight of four with four Mark-eighty-twos each."

"Say your posit."

"Twenty miles south of the OP."

"Bone two-three, the fighters are clear," the FAC said.

"Roger. Showing two minutes until bombs away."

Punk started the sweep second hand on his watch and scanned the ridge lines in the far distance, trying to get a general visual fix on the battle they were supporting beneath them. Just over two minutes later his problem was solved when the first bombs of the B-1's string hit and the side of the mountain nearest to the fighters began to come alive in a ripple of rapidly growing blooms in black and brown. They seemed to go on forever, like trees lining a country road.

Once the last in the string of bombs had impacted the ground, Punk peered through a momentary break in the clouds above them, a "sucker hole" in aviation parlance, and saw the B-1 streaking high above, leaving several white contrails across the sky. The destruction against the mountain didn't jibe with the distant and steady profile of the bomber overhead or the quiet over the radio. *At least I don't drop without even seeing the ground,* he thought.

"They're smoked out," the FAC said over the radio, words coming louder and faster now. "Coming down the mountain, charging right at us."

Spud raked the FLIR pod view across the southern face of the mountain just below where the explosions were still dissipating. "I've got them," he passed over the intercom. "Troops on the run and a handful of tanks."

"Jocko, you guys hold at the OP for now," Punk passed over squadron common. "I don't trust that we'll be able to stay in the clear with these clouds all over the place."

"Roger that. Jocko's detaching and picking up a left-hand orbit."

"Muddy, kick it into defensive combat spread," Punk said, pushing the throttles forward as he continued to the north. Muddy showed him the belly of her jet for a few seconds before rolling out just over a half-mile abeam. Punk checked her positioning and then noted his airspeed increasing through four hundred knots. The Tomcats were stepping into the spotlight now. He felt his heartbeat quickening and took several deep breaths to keep it under control.

Spud keyed the rear cockpit radio tuned to Rose four: "Lion, we've split into two flights of two because of the weather. Call tasking for the section."

"Roger, Ajax, I need you to—" The FAC cut himself off and began yelling at someone within earshot on the ground, voice distant but still audible to the aviators. Punk figured the FAC had dropped the headset to his side but kept it keyed, probably unintentionally. "Where the hell are they going?" he shouted. "Sergeant Towers, get those idiots back here!"

An unintelligible voice replied to the FAC, and he shot back, "That's bullshit; stop them," before returning the handset to his head: "Ajax, standby one. One of our flanks has started a charge without the rest of us. We don't want any blue on green here. Stand by."

"Ajax is standing by," Spud said, manipulating the FLIR joystick with his left hand in an attempt to figure out what was going on beneath them as Punk started a tight orbit over the battlefield. The F-14s passed through another thin layer of clouds, and Punk reluctantly urged his fighter yet closer to the ground. The RIO studied the infrared picture now showing enemy tanks rolling down toward the base of the mountain with men in full sprint around them, and then he slewed the pod across the barren plain to the south until movement of another sort came into view.

"Holy shit," Spud said over the intercom. "It's the charge of the light brigade." Punk glanced down at his FLIR screen, a smaller repeat of Spud's FLIR presentation, and saw there at least a dozen horses in full gallop flying headlong toward the advancing forces north of them. The pilot's glance morphed into a stare, and for a time he sat mesmerized by the scene: raw, powerful, classic, and curiously out of place. He'd seen many things through the FLIR, but among those images had never been the rush of cavalry.

"We're awfully low," Flex observed over squadron common, snapping Punk from the distraction Spud had put before him. "Recommend all eyes out of the cockpit looking for shoulder-fired SAMs."

Punk cut his eyes toward his altimeter. Sixteen thousand feet, lower than some of the surrounding terrain now. He tightened his orbit to remain within the plain ringed on all sides by mountains, many of which had their highest peaks currently obscured by the broken layer of clouds, and honored Flex's recommendation.

"The horses are turning around," Spud said, obviously still focused on his screen and not as concerned about the surface-to-air threat as the others in his section. "Let's get ready to drop."

"Is the weaponeering still going to work from this altitude?" Punk asked over the intercom as he continued to scour the ground under them for the telltale plume of a Stinger launch.

"I think so," Spud replied before keying the front seat radio: "Flex, are we still good from here?"

"The last bomb has to come off before eight thousand feet or it won't have time to fuse," Flex said.

"That doesn't give us much tracking time," Punk said. "After we roll in we're—"

Punk silenced himself as the AWACS controller, the same male voice that had passed them off to the FAC, suddenly came up Rose four: "Ajax five-three, this is Bossman; how do you read? I say again: Ajax five-three, this is Bossman; how do you read?"

"Bossman, Ajax has you loud and clear," Spud replied.

"Ajax, a Predator west of you has spotted a high-interest target," the AWACS controller said. "Zeus needs you to investigate."

"How far to the west?" Spud asked.

"Bossman is showing the Predator sixty miles from you at this time."

"Bossman, Lion one-five needs Ajax to stay on station," the FAC said, now accompanied by a burst of small-arms fire. "I'm about to call him in once I get my own forces out of the way."

The AWACS controller didn't respond, so Spud transmitted, "Did you hear that, Bossman?"

"Hear what?"

"Our FAC needs us to stay here. He's currently engaged with the enemy."

The radio was still for a time. Just as Spud was about to ask whether the AWACS had copied his last, the controller said, "Ajax five-three, contact Zeus on Gold one."

"Why?" Spud asked.

"Why?" the controller repeated, obviously taken aback by the CO's response.

"I say again: There's a battle going on right where we are. Lion one-five is in danger of being overrun, and we're about to drop our ordnance to prevent that from happening."

"Ajax, I'm not going to argue with you," the controller said. "Contact Zeus immediately."

"Roger . . ." Spud replied resignedly. "Lion, we'll still be monitoring your freq. Flight leave Rose four in one radio and switch Gold one on the other."

"Muddy's switching Gold one on the front seat radio," Flex said.

"Jocko," the lead Hornet said.

"Melba," the wing Hornet followed.

"What's the frequency for Gold one?" Punk asked over the intercom.

"Hold on. I have to look it up," Spud said as he rifled through the cards tacked to his kneeboard. "Predator, huh?" he mused aloud. "The general's getting too cute with his damn toys. What does a fucking UAV see that's more important than what we're doing right here?" He ran an index finger along the theater frequency codes. "Gold one: three-five-five-point-zero."

"Switching three-five-five-point-zero," Punk said.

Spud continued to question the limits of technology as he watched the digits change in the UHF one readout on his instrument panel, and then he keyed the front-seat radio: "Zeus, Ajax five-three is up."

"Ajax five-three, standby for new tasking," a deep male voice said, sounding quite worthy of the call sign assigned. Spud knew the current ops cell in Saudi Arabia was manned by senior officers and he wondered if the general himself, the Joint Task Force commander, was currently on the other end of the SATCOM–UHF link. "Vector two-seven-four for seventy-two miles. We've got a high-priority target of interest working southbound along the road there."

Punk maintained an orbit over the dusty plain with his wingman in defensive combat spread. They were low enough now that he could see the tanks rumbling southward with his naked eye, low enough that a potshot with a tactical SAM just might find its mark. The tanks seemed to be making good speed. Lion one-five was certainly going to need their help soon.

"Zeus, understand you are aware that Ajax is currently supporting Lion one-five, who is engaged with a large ground force including a number of tanks?" Spud asked.

"I'm aware of everything, thank you," the deep voice of Zeus sardonically returned. "We're reassigning other assets to cover Lion. Again, you're ordered to investigate contact to the west."

"What should I do?" Punk asked over the intercom.

"Keep orbiting." Spud pulled out a copy of the air tasking order and verified what he already knew to be true: The Ajax flight were the only four tactical jets over Afghanistan and would be for the next hour.

"Ajax five-three, this is Lion one-five," the FAC said, transmission punctuated on either end by gunfire. "Ajax five-three, are you up?"

"Go ahead, Lion," Spud replied over the backseat radio.

"Tanks nearing danger close. Are you able to work with me at this time?"

"Standby, Lion."

As Punk looked over to check Muddy's positioning, the two Tomcats entered another cloud bank. Punk bunted the nose over and after several disconcerting seconds was once again beneath the weather. He looked to his right and saw Muddy's jet drop into view and then rechecked the reading on his altimeter: fourteen thousand feet. They were seriously low hanging fruit now.

"Zeus, I recommend you split Ajax into two flights of two," Spud said over Gold one. "Ajax one and two will stay here and support Lion, and Ajax three and four can take up your tasking."

"Understand you have *four* in your flight?" Zeus asked tentatively, voice not quite as deep, as if as he spoke he'd increasingly wished he hadn't keyed the mike.

"He's aware of everything, huh?" Spud quipped over the intercom before keying Gold one: "That's affirmative. Flight of four."

"Copy," Zeus said, authoritative radio demeanor quickly regained. "Ajax one and two kick back to Rose four for Lion one-five control; Ajax three and four, stay with me on this frequency. Your vector now: two-seven-zero for seventy miles."

"Jocko, you're cleared to detach," Punk said on Rose four. "Let's switch squadron common on one radio and separate control freqs in the other."

"Jocko's detaching," the Hornet lead replied. "Switching back to squadron common on UHF one. Melba switch."

"Melba switching."

"Ajax is switching back to Rose one," Spud said, ignoring the fact he'd never left that frequency on UHF two.

"You're cleared to switch. Contact Bossman on Red one once complete."

Punk switched his own radio back to the squadron frequency before reading his fuel gauge. He cross-checked that quantity against the fuel ladder—a gas versus time matrix—he'd come up with during his mission planning. "We have only a thousand pounds to play with," he told Spud.

Spud thought for a second and then keyed the front seat radio: "Jocko, Spud on *Arrowslinger* common."

"Jocko's up, skipper."

"How's your gas?"

"It's going to be tight."

"Keep an eye on it, and watch out for the weather. It looks even nastier to the west of us."

"We noticed," Jocko said. "We're cheating it downhill with the hope that they're sending us after Osama in an SUV."

"I'm *sure* that's it," Spud said wryly. "Be careful. If you're done before we are, work hard with Bossman to get that goddam frog tanker to meet us as far north of the Gipper track as possible. We'll see you there on the way out; and if not, we'll see you back on the Boat."

"Roger. Good hunting, skipper."

"Same to you."

Spud returned his focus to the FLIR display on the ten-inch-square screen in front of him and saw that the enemy tanks and associated foot soldiers had reached the flat land at the base of the northern range and were rapidly bearing down on the road that split the valley. "Lion one-five, are you ready for Ajax?" he asked over Rose four.

"Affirmative. Stand by for tasking." The FAC had obviously been chomping at the bit, and Spud was impressed that he hadn't lost it over the radio already in the face of the current ops cell's distraction. "Are you contact the hardball running east-west in the center of the valley?"

"Contact," Punk said.

"North of that hardball are vehicles, tanks, and troops on the move. Are you contact any of those?"

"We see them."

"Those are your targets. Take as many of them out as you can. Be advised the road is danger close to us."

"Understand cleared hot now?" Spud asked.

"That's affirmative," the FAC replied over the hammering of a machine gun.

Punk threw the stick against his left thigh and then tugged it into his lap. Spud joined him in fighting the crush of Gs while working his way around his switch settings for ordnance delivery: "AWG-fifteen panel is set; I've got Mark-eighty-twos in the weapons window, attack mode is computer pilot, fuse is set to 'VT' like Gunner said, delivery option is set for four bombs at once, and I've got weapons stations three through six selected."

"Muddy, fall into trail," Punk said. "You roll in behind me."

"Roger," Muddy replied. "Are you dropping one at a time?"

"No. I've got a line of tanks I'm putting the full stick of four across. That should slow their drive down."

Punk saw that he was going to overshoot his intended run-in line, so, accompanied by several grunts into his mask that were byproducts of fighting the increased force of gravity on the F-14, he yanked on the stick and raised the G on the fighter just past the NATOPS limit of six. Once convinced he'd salvaged the setup, he rolled the Tomcat onto its back and pulled the nose forty degrees below the horizon.

"Check master arm on," Spud said over the intercom.

"Master arm's on," Punk confirmed. "Good lights up here."

"Looks good back here. We're ready to drop."

"Ajax lead's in hot," Punk said on Rose four.

"Roger," the FAC replied. "Kill them bastards."

Maintaining his dive angle, Punk rolled the F-14 upright and found the bomb button with his right thumb. He looked through his forward windscreen toward the ground while in his head he heard the female reporter with the Southern accent talking after Rear Admiral Dykstra's abruptly terminated press conference: *You can kill anyone at any time with no worries for you.*

"Forty degrees down," Spud chanted. "Four hundred and fifty knots, nine thousand feet . . ."

The pipper walked across the brown desert and over the first tank in a column of four, and as it passed over the second one, Punk depressed the bomb button.

"Pickle, pickle, pickle . . ."

Four rapid thumps nudged the jet and let Punk and Spud know their bombs had come off. Punk puffed a sigh of relief into his mask. He waited a potato and then pulled the stick back to get the fighter climbing.

But the Tomcat didn't respond.

Instead the fighter lurched along a strange axis, like a toy in a child's hand. Punk caught flashes of orange and yellow in his mirrors and an instant later the entire airplane was engulfed in a ball of fire. The jet tucked forward, and his helmet smashed into the top of the canopy. Dazed, he stirred the stick in vain.

The last thing he heard over the radio was Muddy shouting, "Eject!"

"Spud, I don't have the jet," Punk screamed, unsure if the intercom was still working or if his RIO was even alive. "We've got to eject!" There was no response. "Spud! Eject!"

The F-14 tumbled, and Punk was tossed about the cockpit so violently that he couldn't read any of his gauges; the world outside the canopy had transformed to swirls of brown and white. After shouting one more unanswered plea to his RIO, he fished for the lower ejection handle and pulled as hard as he could.

Punk waited for an ejection sequence, but he didn't hear the canopy blow off or Spud fire up the rails, and he didn't feel himself rocket clear of the cockpit.

The fighter simply disintegrated around him, and before he could consider it further he was hurtling through the leaden skies over Afghanistan piloting nothing—a passenger in his own ejection seat.

The seat fell away and the parachute opened with a whiplash jerk of the harness across his collarbones and around his groin. He looked up and saw a full and undamaged canopy blossomed above him and then scoured the sky for Spud but came up empty. He labored to breath and reflexively unhooked his mask.

Punk focused through his feet to the ground, fully expecting to be floating into the middle of a fierce battle, but saw instead that the winds were whisking him westward, out of the plain and into dramatic rises.

For a time he could hear the fighting more clearly with each foot of the descent; the explosions of tank shells were punctuated by the constant staccato hammering of semiautomatic-rifle and machine-gun fire. Lower still he thought he heard men yelling in anger or screaming in pain but, after checking that his helmet was still on, figured he was yet too high for that. He was sure he smelled gunpowder, and something else, dirt maybe. Then he was carried farther to the west, and the sounds of battle faded so that all he could hear was the *crump* of explosions and the occasional crack of gunfire.

Punk attempted to steer his parachute using the risers but realized he was at the mercy of the winds— any efforts to fight them would simply be a waste of energy. He passed through a thin cloud layer and hoped to keep sight of the ground, especially in the terminal phase of his descent. Hitting a mountain face would be bad enough without doing it blind. He heard a single jet roaring above—Muddy and Flex. He thought about reaching for his radio but took another look at the daunting topography underneath him and decided to deal with first things first.

His teeth started to chatter as he looked to the west and attempted to conjure up a mental plot of the terrain he was falling into. He pictured the chart he'd scanned in the air-conditioned comfort of his cockpit not five minutes earlier. How high were the peaks? Twelve thousand feet? And what would the temperature be there? He shivered and pulled the zipper of his flight suit all the way up, pained by a new vision: the brand-new pair of thermal underwear neatly folded in one of the drawers back in his stateroom.

More gunfire in the distance reminded Punk that the cold was probably not his most immediate threat. Fighting the sharp sense that he'd forgotten something, he reached around the left side of his rib cage and found the holster threaded into the webbing of his harness. His nine-millimeter pistol was still there. Then he raised his right knee and felt through the bottom pocket of his G suit for the distinctive shape of the bullet cartridges he'd placed there before leaving the paraloft. He had bullets, too. So . . . now what?

Punk could still hear his wingman overhead but didn't see the other Tomcat and wondered if they could see him. As he looked over his shoulder and beyond the edge of the parachute in an attempt to find them, he was enveloped by another blanket of clouds. This time he didn't immediately break out, and for several minutes he focused intently through his boots, ready to dodge the sharp edges or deep crevasses imminently lurking below. He remembered his last ejection and the sprained ankle he suffered when he hit—and that was on the flat Kuwaiti desert.

He fell clear of the cloud bank and was relieved to see that he was still several hundred feet in the air and tracking much farther down the mountain than his previous extrapolation had suggested he would. But as he studied the steep face rising up to meet him he realized that landing at a lower point didn't make the mountain any less dangerous as a landing site. He widened his scan, desperately seeking a lesser-of-all-evils option in the few seconds he had left to change his descent path.

Punk made out a small plateau in the shadows of one of the many sharp peaks and steered toward it with a host of tugs on the risers. Fifty feet before impact he was reasonably sure that he'd suitcased the approach, but at the last moment a gust of wind pushed him low. He braced for a head-on collision with the sheer face under where he'd meant to land.

Another gust buoyed him slightly and slowed his forward speed enough that his first impact with the mountain didn't break any bones. He turned his head to avoid smashing his face, and when his helmet met the rock his dark visor cracked in two. He bounced off and felt the bottom drop out, and without looking up he knew his chute had collapsed. He plunged for a hundred feet across the nearly sheer face just beyond arms' length. The chute partially filled with the fall, jerking him back into the mountain, and the second time he hit he clawed at the brown rock with his hands and feet to no avail. Through the stars in his eyes he saw he was going over a cliff, and in the time it took to do so he considered whether his chute would continue to reopen or instead be so torn to shreds that it would do nothing but flap tauntingly above him for the rest of his fall.

An uncontrollable scream welled out of Punk's throat as he started what he was sure was his final

descent. As he heard himself he mentally detached
and wondered if those who'd jumped from the World
Trade Center on 9-11 had screamed, and for some
reason that thought caused him to silence himself. The
view over the ledge snapped him back to the present;
he was being cast from a thousand feet up into the
vast expanse above the plain upon which several miles
to the east a battle raged.

And then he jerked to a quick halt, a force nearly
equal to when his chute had opened the first time. He
swung back and forth a few times, afraid to move for
fear that he'd wrench himself free of whatever had
stopped him. Eventually the swinging stopped, except
for what the gusts of wind caused, and he slowly tilted
his head back and saw the shrouds of his parachute
had jammed into a deep crack along the ledge.

Punk hung over the precipice for a time, trying to
gather his wits as he watched the battle in the distance
below with the detachment of a spectator in the cheap
seats of a large stadium. He heard the sound of jet
engines again. He'd nearly forgotten about contacting
his wingman. He removed his helmet and hooked the
chin strap through the D-ring on his harness and carefully pulled his radio out.

"Ajax two, this is Ajax one pilot," Punk beseeched
into the small mouthpiece. He heard the desperation
in his voice and judged it as if someone else were
speaking. He tried to calm down before keying the
small radio again. "Ajax two, how do you read?"

"Is that you, Punk?" Flex returned. "Are you on
the ground?"

"Yeah, it's me," Punk said. "I'm hanging by my
parachute about halfway up one of the mountains to
the west."

"Are you okay?"

"Well . . ." Punk looked up toward the ledge again. "I need some help."

"Standby," Flex said. "I'll relay your situation to Bossman."

The radio went silent. Punk held the radio intently to his ear as he fought off a shiver and panned the vastness before him. He noted a line of dust far away moving north across the steppe, swirling and twisting—a tornado? No, as he judged the speed of it he thought it might be evidence of the cavalry at long last advancing. Across the steppe explosions blossomed around the tanks in greater numbers than before. Then he worked his eyes toward his feet and saw a line of vehicles headed in his direction along the main road through the valley. But whose vehicles were they? Punk wanted Flex to keep talking to him.

"Ajax two, are you there?" he implored.

"Yeah, Punk, er . . . Ajax one pilot," Flex said. "Bossman has fragged us with emergent tasking in support of Lion. Say your position."

Punk had forgotten about the other crucial piece of gear in his survival vest. "Wait one," he said before shoving the radio into one pocket with increasingly shaky hands and digging in the opposite one for the handheld GPS stashed there. He mashed a few buttons, memorized the result, and then carefully and deliberately grabbed the radio again: "From the sardot, two-eight-zero at sixty-two miles."

"Copy," Flex said. "You're out of our way."

Punk was a bit confused by the statement until a Tomcat suddenly roared from behind him, high overhead in a steep dive. Punk could see Muddy had lined up with the road, and he watched a single bomb fall away and hit smack in the middle of the convoy. Two vehicles were consumed by the blast while the remaining half dozen at either end of the train veered in various directions, some of them leaving the road and speeding off across the flat plain.

Muddy continued with three more bomb runs that appeared, from Punk's vantage point anyway, to hit their marks, before going to work on the stragglers with the F-14's nose cannon. During her second strafing run Punk heard the gun spool up but only spit what sounded like half a normal burst of bullets. He instantly knew and feared what had happened.

"The gun jammed," Flex confirmed over the survival frequency.

Punk thought he saw one of the vehicles limping toward the west, toward him. "Is Jocko still around?" he asked.

"Negative. The Hornets are RTB for gas."

"How are you looking?"

"We've probably got about ten minutes left on station, but we're trying to get some gas to us so we can stick around and be the rescue mission coordinator."

"Roger." Rescue mission coordinator? What was there to coordinate? He was almost certain that no American helicopters could fly, not to mention hover, at the altitude at which he was dangling. And friendly forces were miles away engaged in battle.

Punk thought about Muddy and Flex flying away without him and suddenly felt cold and alone. Whether the enemy had radio homing devices or not, he needed to hear American voices. "Did you see what got us?" Punk asked, still trying his best to remain composed over the distress frequency. He was taking his cue from himself and knew that a single crack of the voice could cause his noble house of cards to come crashing down.

"Yeah, I did," Flex said. "I was tracking you with the FLIR pod. Your fourth bomb went high order as soon as it left the rack." He paused for a beat before keying the radio again: "I'm afraid you shot yourself down, Punk."

That wasn't a surprise considering the sequence of events after he'd depressed the bomb button, but hearing Flex say it crystallized the infamy of it all in Punk's mind. In spite of his precarious perch and rapidly deteriorating physical state, he still had enough semblance of an ego to picture himself slinking through the back bar at the officers' club, ignoring the whispers that surrounded him—*that's the guy that, you know* . . . —and then he flashed back to the gunner and the powwow in the ready room about the fusing on the Mark-82s. Almost subconsciously Punk keyed his survival radio again and asked, "Any idea how?"

"We'll figure it out later," Flex replied. "Recommend we stay off the air for now. Save your batteries, Punk."

"Have you heard from Spud?"

"No."

"Did you see his chute?"

"It was cloudy," Flex explained. "I didn't even see *your* chute. Save your batteries, now."

Punk put the radio back in his survival vest but left the pouch unzipped so he could hear if someone was trying to contact him. He hung motionless from the cliff and pictured himself looking into one of the pilot's mirrors at Spud smiling at him down either canopy rail during the hundreds of sorties they'd flown together and then tempered the sorrow by simply refusing to believe their pairing had ended. That refusal turned into anger. There was no way a squadron would lose two commanding officers to freak accidents in a single deployment. No *fucking* way. The law of averages wouldn't support it.

Damn, his legs hurt. Punk pulled up on the risers periodically to relieve the pressure against the back of his upper thighs, but that wasn't enough to keep the pain at bay, so he stopped pulling with the hope his legs would fall asleep. Then he worried about having the circulation cut off for too long and returning to Suzanne as a double amputee.

What would Suzanne do if he didn't come home? She'd suffered enough already, a widow at thirty. But was there a quota on suffering over the course of a lifetime (any more than there was a quota on how many COs a squadron could lose on a deployment)? Maybe it was Suzanne's fate to endure tragedy, like Rose Kennedy, and maybe Punk's role was to be an unrealized dream along the line, like Joe Kennedy— an honorable part, sure, but ultimately a bit player in the story.

With each surge of pain, the supply of adrenaline shot into his veins during the ejection was taxed a bit. With its loss came a chill and a profound sense of despair. Shivers shook his body uncontrollably, and he wondered how long it would take him to pass out— and how soon death would come after that. Was Spud already dead, and if so, would he be there (where was *there*?) to give him the lowdown just as he always had during their days among the living?

Another wave of clouds obscured the steppes below starting to the east, over the skirmish that had by the look and sound of it reached a crescendo a few minutes earlier. It filled Punk with the hope that those under Major Banko's charge could divert their attention toward a search-and-rescue operation. The dirty white clouds continued their trek westward, and soon he could no longer see the remnants of the convoy. Then the weather swallowed him, and he dangled in the mist, more miserable still with the tiny water droplets hitting his face and hands. When the sound of gunfire and shelling stopped altogether, the only thing he could hear, besides the whistling of the wind in his ears, was the lone Tomcat circling high overhead.

"No joy on the gas, Punk," Flex's voice reported over the small speaker on the survival radio. "We have to head back. I'm sure more of our guys will be up here shortly."

"Roger . . ." Punk replied, mind unable to fashion any organized thoughts now.

"Stay tough, Punk," Flex said. "We'll be waiting for you."

Punk didn't speak but simply fumbled with spastic hands for the radio and clicked the transmit button a couple of times in response. As the sound of the Tomcat faded, the clouds thickened around him, acting as a sensory-deprivation chamber of sorts. He wasn't sure if it was the altitude or the lack of circulation, but he began to feel light-headed. His chin drooped to his chest, and it looked to him as though his flight suit and boots had turned different shades of gray. He caught the pallor of his hands, now off-white. Color was being drained from the world.

Slowly the blackness crept in, seeping into the corners of his vision before stealing his sight altogether.

CHAPTER SEVEN

Captain Campbell stood next to the air wing commander outside of the battle group commander's stateroom door, waiting for the admiral to respond to the second series of knocks. While they waited, Soup fought the urge to coach the CAG—technically his boss—on how to deal with Dutch Dykstra, a man he'd known for years. Penguin had screened for major command at sea through the same process every other CAG had gone through. The system worked, right? And that fact should have rendered Soup's concerns moot . . . but it didn't. As he briefly thought about it, he realized he'd seen nothing in Penguin's actions to suggest he was the right man for the task immediately before them. What did a guy who'd spent his aviation life chasing subs and now tanking other jets know about these sorts of crises? And how did an S-3 guy screen for major command at sea, anyway?

Rear Admiral Dykstra opened the door and his expression immediately transformed from curiosity to concern as he recognized the two men standing before him. He hadn't summoned them, and they never stopped by just to chat. Penguin started to speak but Soup's instincts got the best of him and he cut the CAG off, announcing: "We have a jet down in Afghanistan, Admiral."

The admiral didn't flinch. He'd certainly prepped himself for this eventuality before the shooting started. Without a word he opened the door wider and gestured toward the couch in his office. The captains slid through the doorway and sat down.

"What happened?" the admiral asked, taking a seat in one of the two leather chairs in front of his large mahogany desk.

"Word's still coming in," Penguin said, "but initial reports said something about one of their bombs blowing up next to the jet."

"Early burst," Soup added.

"Did they make it out?" Admiral Dykstra asked.

"Yes, sir," Penguin replied before correcting himself. "Well, we know the pilot made it all the way to the ground."

"The wingman couldn't establish comms with the RIO," Soup said.

"RIO? So it was a Tomcat?"

"Yes, sir. A Tomcat."

"Who was it?"

Penguin was completely out of the conversation now. "Lieutenant Commander Reichert with Commander O'Leary in his backseat," Soup said.

"The skipper?"

"Yes, sir."

"What sort of mission were they flying?"

"On-call close air support just south of Mazar-e-Sharif."

Admiral Dykstra's chest heaved as he let out a heavy sigh. "So what are we doing now?"

"We're working with CENTCOM on a search-and-rescue plan."

"What are we doing about the bombs?"

"We've impounded that lot of fuses," Soup explained. "We're also going to avoid dropping more than one bomb at a time until we figure this out."

"CENTCOM's going to love that." The admiral focused on the carpeted floor in front of the two captains, processing the information. After an extended silence he looked up. "What else?"

Penguin looked at Soup, who shrugged. "I think that's it right now, sir," Penguin said. "We'll keep you posted."

Rear Admiral Dykstra's head jerked as an unresolved issue hit him. "What about the press? They'll be all over this, especially with the skipper of the squadron shot down."

"I'm working media issues," Soup said. "I have been since I got aboard."

The admiral cut his eyes toward the CAG and said, "Would you excuse us?"

Penguin appeared confused momentarily but then quickly complied with Rear Admiral Dykstra's request. The instant the door clicked shut the admiral turned to Soup and said, "You know, I just welcomed the team aboard that's conducting the investigation into your training track."

"Yes, sir," Soup returned confidently. "I'm looking forward to working with them."

The admiral banged a fist against the top of his desk and railed, "You've never known when to back down, have you? This is serious shit, Alexander. The board members are going to want to see a bit of contrition from you. And the last thing I need now with a crew on the ground in Afghanistan is my deputy air wing commander pissing off the board that could end his career with the stroke of a pen across a punitive letter of reprimand." He ran a hand across his face a couple of times. "And how do you think you're in any position to work with the press?"

"The board's got nothing on me, Admiral," Soup said boldly. "I checked the blocks that matter on the way out here. Besides, what happened to 'innocent until proven guilty'?"

Rear Admiral Dykstra spat a "pshaw." "Since when has the press played by that rule?"

Soup had dealt with the press enough to know they had one rule over all others: Get the story. And once word of the downed Tomcat reached the press pool aboard the Boat they'd be banging doors down. He wanted to be the man with the message. He *had* to be the man with the message. Who else was going to do it? Penguin? When that guy walked into a room it was like someone interesting had just left. No, this one was going to take a deft touch, the *Soup* touch. Besides, Soup the spokesman, the man exceptionally gifted in transforming complex aviation issues into audience-friendly sound bites, would do much toward making the public and their duly elected representatives in Congress forget about Soup the bomber of innocent civilians.

"You know that I've always had good rapport with the media," the DCAG suggested. "Besides, I have been contrite. I've taken myself out of missions over the beach. I've got to do something to pull my weight around here."

The admiral considered the captain for a time,

freezing him with the same stare he'd employed years before, when they'd served together in a West Coast fighter squadron, days when Dutch had been a fresh-caught lieutenant commander waiting for his chance to take one of the plum department head jobs and Soup had been a nugget pilot. From the beginning Dutch had seen unique traits in the young Campbell, traits not commonly found in junior officers: He was an exceptionally hard worker, and, more importantly, he didn't care if his peers liked him.

"All right, go ahead and work with the bastards, if you have to," Rear Admiral Dykstra said with some resignation. "But be careful."

"Don't worry, sir," Soup said. "I know how to handle the press."

"Fine, fine. But let them come to you. Right now our first priority is to get our boys back. God help them."

The inputs came in snatches. Flashes of color. Cold wind against his face. Thirst. Heavy arms. Punk could move his fingers, feel the texture of his G suit. His fingers informed that he had legs, numbed as they were. He could see color, brighter now, but no form. He wondered if he were dead.

Across his shoulders he felt tugging on his harness, something pulling him upward. His back was raked across the ledge, and then the motion stopped. He feared he might be dragged back over the cliff. He wanted to see—*had* to see—and blinked repeatedly, prodding his eyes to work again. Shadows passed over him. The colors took shape, and soon his mind had cleared enough to label them: a rifle, a beard, a turban. A black turban.

Taliban . . .

Hands swarmed and pinned him to the ground. Out of the corner of his eye he caught a glint off the blade of a dull knife that painfully pulled at his skin as his flight gear was hacked away. The captors responded to his yelps with cackles, hideous laughter.

A blindfold was wrapped across Punk's eyes, and a filthy rag was shoved into his mouth. He was forced to sit up, and his wrists were bound behind him. From off to his left came the sawing of zippers and ripping of Velcro; they were rooting through his survival vest. His survival radio clicked to life. They laughed with each burst of static until one of them yelled sharply, the first words from them—in Pashto?—and the next thing he heard was what sounded like his radio being smashed by a rifle butt.

The cold wind cut through the newly made holes in his flight suit, and Punk started to shiver again as he listened intently to his captors arguing. He felt something running down his arm. Was he bleeding and, if so, how badly? Before he could consider it further, the back of a hand landed on each cheek, and with the second strike he fell onto his side. Before he could gather his wits, he was rousted to his feet as one of them shouted at close range, immersing Punk in a cloud of putrid breath and peppering his face with droplets of saliva.

Punk's numb legs offered no support, and once burdened with his own weight he crumpled to the ground. He tried to curl into a ball as several of them took turns kicking him in the chest and gut, but his efforts did little to stave off the attack. A foot caught Punk square in the stomach, knocking the wind out of him. He drew on the rag for air but got none. The blackness had almost overtaken him again when the rag was plucked from his mouth. He coughed and fought to fill his lungs.

Punk hadn't fully caught his breath when he was hoisted back to his feet, and this time he locked his knees to steady himself. After several seconds he felt he could stay upright. He didn't need any more beatings at the moment. For now they had stopped hitting him; once his breathing became somewhat rhythmic one of them shoved the rag back into his dry mouth.

A hand wrapped around each biceps, urging Punk forward. As they moved they spoke to each other in what he continued to assume was Pashto, an ugly language that sounded like they were gargling instead of conversing. He stepped as tentatively as his handlers' pace would allow, blind and unsure of where the next stride would take him. After a handful of steps the bottom fell out under his right foot. He fell headlong and hit hard against the dirt and loose gravel that lined the steep face and slid headfirst for several hundred feet before coming to rest on what he guessed was another plateau.

The cruel laughter was farther away now. Punk used his momentary solitude to assess how badly he'd been hurt in the fall. He wiggled his fingers and moved his hands along the small of his back as far as his bound wrists would allow and then rolled onto his back and drew each knee up. Nothing broken.

Punk felt blood trickling down a nostril. If his nose clogged he might suffocate; he dropped his face to the dirt and moved his head back and forth until the rag caught on something enough that he was able to spit out the last bit of it. He took deep breaths and tried to think clearly, tried to remember his survival, evasion, resistance, and escape training, although it had been years since he'd gone through the course. Thoughts of the SERE course brought on a brief remembrance of Cal "Crud" Workman, who'd been there for that cold week in the mountains of Maine. The thought of Crud morphed into an image of his widow, Suzanne, that, in turn, caused Punk to wonder whether his late best friend was up there rooting him on or damning him.

Punk was already banged up and still had a long way to go down the mountain. He shuddered with the idea of how much worse things were going to get in the hours ahead. He was scared. If they were going to kill him he hoped they'd do it quickly.

He listened for the sounds of jets. "Where are you bastards?" he slurred to himself, tilting his face to the sky. He was dying of thirst. He opened his mouth and imagined a fire-fighting propeller plane flying over and dropping water into his mouth. He might be able to make it if he could just get some water—some water and a coat.

The Taliban yelled in a clipped singsong as they picked their ways down the face he'd just traveled the hard way. As they closed Punk heard their feet shuffling across the dirt and felt against his face the small rocks they loosed. They surrounded him again and kicked his legs, stomach, and ribs. A blow to the back of his head caused light to shoot in his eyes. He shouted as loud as his parched throat would allow, pleading for them to stop, but the pathetic sound of his voice just seemed to fuel their hostility. They hit him and started to work the rag back into his mouth. They must've seen he couldn't breathe because they immediately pulled it back out and left it out.

The routine was repeated over and over as his captors moved him down the mountain: Punk was hoisted to his feet, guided for a few steps and then allowed to fall. Sometimes they pushed him; sometimes they simply let him go. Either way he'd slide or tumble down the face until stopped by a boulder or a small plateau. And every time they caught up to them they kicked and punched him a few times before hiking him back to his feet and starting the drill all over again.

Punk tried to ignore the pain and the cold and keep going, fearing they might kill him if he came up lame. He was relieved when he took a dozen steps without falling down a ravine, and he hoped that they'd made it down to the steppe. He asked for water but got nothing but a slapped cheek for the request.

They walked across flat terrain for what seemed like several miles before Punk was shoved back to the ground. He braced for more beatings, but this time they didn't come. His blindfold was removed, and as he worked to focus, he could see that it was nearly dark. He furtively studied his surroundings as several of the Taliban gargled a heated debate around him, emphatically thrusting their AK-47s into the air. They were stationed on a narrow dirt road—rock strewn and potholed—that snaked along the narrow valley between nearly vertical rises jutting up on either side. Before taking a slap to the side of the head for doing so, Punk snuck a quick look into the cloudy sky. It would be nearly impossible for any jets passing overhead to spot him.

The roar of engines and the metallic clanking of tank treads intensified, echoing off the walls of rock. The vehicles came into view from around the bend in the road in front of them, kicking up a huge cloud of fine dust in their wake that glowed eerily in the waning light. Punk counted two tanks, Russian T-72s, and three pickups—old Datsuns, he guessed.

Once the convoy got close, the blindfold was
wrapped across his eyes again. He was guided a few
more steps and then thrown into the back of a pickup.
He heard the sound of others boarding. He could tell
by their voices that he was once again surrounded;
even in the open air their collective pungency pierced
his blood-clogged nose and turned his empty gut.

The pickup lurched several times before making its
way through the first of the holes in the road, slam-
ming the passengers into each other. Punk flew up and
then smacked against the bed before one of his captors landed a knee against his groin. He writhed in
even greater pain along the bed of the truck where
he was kicked repeatedly, accompanied by the same
sick laughter that had taunted him during the long trip
down the mountain. He was cracking; he felt himself
pissing on his thigh and was powerless to do anything
about it. The wetness spread across the middle of his
flight suit, and amid the jeering and the raucous laughter Punk's head was swimming, and in his mind he
was suddenly back among the boys in the ready room
telling a story about the time he pissed his pants in
front of the Taliban. A swift kick to the jaw brought
him back to his current miserable state.

The pickup bounced down the pockmarked road,
slowly from the feel of it, and Punk remained prone
along the bed, hitting against feet and ankles and absorbing a few kicks each time he did. In time they
grew either bored or fatigued and ceased the torment
in spite of the fact that he continued to fall against
them. The gargling around him had stopped; one of
them began snoring loudly.

Punk tried to listen beyond the roar of the untuned
engine and the grinding of the gears for the sound of
jets overhead but heard none. Even if they were up

there, would the crews know that he was buried among the legs of the Taliban riding in the convoy, or would he simply be vaporized by some first-tour lieutenant or, worse, an Air Force guy? Punk considered the irony of having his death unknowingly captured on a FLIR tape, and he flashed back to Flex and the others bathing in the glow of the small television in the ready room. For the first time that day, Punk was glad for the cloud cover and that sense, in turn, further deepened his despair.

Some hours later—Punk had long since lost track of time—the bouncing ceased and the pickup's motor shut off. Hands were on him again. He was dragged across the filthy bed and thrown to the dirt behind the truck, an action that brought every bruise across his body alive. Punk moaned, and his captors laughed and brusquely got him to his aching feet. Again, he willed himself to stay upright, although doing that was more difficult now. He fought for balance against fatigue, hunger, thirst, injury, and the thin air at thousands of feet above sea level.

Punk's blindfold was removed as before, and he saw that the sky was now completely dark around them. He wanted to survey the surroundings but knew the consequences if they caught him trying to do so. What he could see in front of him was that the party had arrived at the foot of some sort of camp carved into the face of a mountain. In the dim light he saw dozens of cave openings, darker holes against the dark face of the rock, some punctuated by flickers of orange light—campfires, perhaps. The air was tinged with wood smoke, an inviting scent in other circumstances. Punk yearned for warmth and a drink of water.

The Taliban led Punk toward crudely chiseled stairs, and as they did the high-pitched buzz of an engine grew above them. Punk joined his captors in craning their heads to the sky just in time to see a UAV fly over, underside barely lit by the camp's ambient light. He could make it out well enough to tell it was a Predator, and he considered breaking away from their grasp and running across the flatland with the hope that the controller monitoring the UAV's FLIR image would notice him. He got as far as jerking himself free of the hands around his biceps but was dissuaded from further proceeding with his plan by an AK-47 jabbing into his navel.

Without warning, a ball of fire welled out of one of the caves, and from it emerged a surface-to-air missile that roped across the sky, straight path traced by the glow of the rocket belching from the tail of it. The SAM—a Stinger, most likely—ran the Predator down in short order, catching it just as it reached one of the ridgelines surrounding the camp. The explosion cast a brief light over the land, and its noise echoed loudly off the terrain in waves.

Punk's captors jeered, putting their faces right up to his and boxing his ears. He weathered the abuse with ever-waning resolve and wondered if those watching the images the UAV provided had noticed him before the signal was snuffed out. Probably not. There hadn't been enough time.

Even though the UAV was destroyed, its momentary presence compelled the Taliban to put the blindfold back over Punk's eyes. They grabbed him by both biceps again and dragged and pushed him up the steps, which varied in size and height. He stumbled often, several times nearly landing flat on his face before having his fall barely broken by his handlers.

A musty smell and the distinct reverberation of voices—Punk reasoned that they'd entered the confines of one of the caves. He was pushed off his feet, and as he landed he hit against another human being on his left side.

"No talk!" one of the Taliban barked, the first English Punk had heard from any of them since they'd pulled him from over the cliff. The captors conferred with each other for a short time, and then it sounded as if they had walked out. He sat with his knees drawn up against his chest, wrists still bound behind his back; his shoulder sockets burned, and his hands had long since gone numb. The rest of his body had joined in a massive throbbing bruise.

He wrestled with the pain and whether he should attempt to communicate with the person next to him, presumably another prisoner. He listened a minute for evidence that the two of them were really alone, and once he was convinced, he muttered, "Blindfolded?" in a cracked and barely intelligible voice.

"Yeah," the other returned in a hoarse whisper.

"American?"

"Yeah. You?"

"Yeah," Punk said. "Service?"

"Navy."

The voice had just enough inflection that time for Punk to make a connection. *"Spud?"*

"Punk? Punk, is that you?"

They started to cry out with their joy but quickly silenced themselves and instead celebrated by smashing against each other like schoolchildren. All at once the stress and emotions of the past hours came out. *Spud is alive!* Punk felt the corners of his mouth tug downward and he was sure tears would've streamed down his face if he wasn't so damn dehydrated.

"Are you hurt?" Spud asked once he regained his composure enough to speak.

"Some," Punk croaked. "You?"

"Same. Need water."

"Same here." Punk tried to conjure up some saliva to get his tongue working better. "You know, we shot ourselves down."

"I was afraid of that."

Suddenly someone was on them. Punk was soundly slapped. "Says no talk!" a Taliban yelled before slapping him again.

"Knock it off!" Spud exclaimed, which obviously threw off the captors a bit because nothing happened for a few beats. Then came the sickening sound of fists and feet against flesh.

"Stop the bullshit!" Punk shouted, louder than he would've guessed his present physical state would've allowed, which caused the thugs to refocus their attention on him. They pounded away, and Punk cried out in anger and pain and torqued around the strikes to his body he couldn't see coming. The blackness was descending again; he was losing consciousness. They weren't going to stop this time. They'd keep pummeling him until he was dead. He tried to say something to Spud but couldn't get it out.

"Na! Na!" another, more commanding, voice shouted. *"Hálta laàr shaa kha!"*

The beatings stopped. The new voice exchanged words with the others followed by a shuffling of feet and a flurry of low-level thuds and slaps that sounded like a scuffle to Punk's ringing ears. The sounds moved away and eventually lost their echo as the captors passed to the outdoors through the cave opening.

A single pair of feet methodically clopped back toward Punk and Spud. As they got close Punk braced for another round of beatings. He felt fingers thread under his blindfold. Then he could see again, though not clearly. He blinked repeatedly, attempting to make the shadows and flickers into recognizable objects.

Punk looked over to Spud, who'd also just had his blindfold removed, and then behind him where several knife-wielding Taliban, beards blacker than their turbans, sawed away at the line around Spud's wrists. The same drill was next performed on him, and when the binding fell loose Punk was shocked to discover he couldn't move his fingers. Slowly the blood flowed; after several minutes he was able to open and close a fist.

The cave was lit by a single bulb overhead that buzzed and pulsed with stray voltage. In the bad light Punk looked down at himself and saw his flight suit stained with clotted blood and sand-dried piss. He studied Spud closely. He'd traveled a hard road, too, although he didn't look quite as beat up, probably because he hadn't tumbled down a mountain to get to the camp.

The Taliban with the knives suddenly withdrew. In their place a barrel-chested man dressed in an animal-skin coat, dark green-and-black camouflage fatigues, and black boots appeared. He was bald with a ragged beard like the rest—his starting at each ear and glowing red in the dim light—and as he got closer Punk saw his complexion was lighter than the others and he had no eyebrows.

Without a word the man produced a pistol and slowly trained it on Spud. He held the pose for an agonizingly long time before returning the gun to its holster at the small of his back. He turned to the others and shooed them with a sharp bark.

Once those wearing black turbans left, the man's posture relaxed. He held out two plastic containers of water. Each American seized a bottle and drew lustily from it. The captor let out a belly laugh as if their thirst was the funniest thing he'd ever seen, steam of his breath billowing from his mouth in small mushroom clouds.

"Ho, daa shaa dai," the man said soothingly. "Yes, it is good. *Tsk-al;* drink. And we have food for you, too." From out of nowhere two meals appeared—thin strips of fatty meat and meager portions of rice, but food nonetheless. They ate, cautiously at first, fearing the offer was some sort of trick. Punk hadn't gone so long without eating to ignore the stale aftertaste of the meat—mutton, was it? But he also knew there was no telling when and from where the next meal would come.

"For your treatment by those men I am sorry," the big man said as he took a knee at the aviators' feet. "Of course, they are upset with you. As they come to pick you up the airplanes of your countrymen killed their comrades." He raised a hand in petition. *"Ahk,* think of it: They want to help you, and they are blown up for it. You would be angry too, I think."

The big man's countenance grew suddenly stern; he shifted into a crouch and laced his fingers over his knees. "I am not Taliban," he said. "I am Chechen." He shrugged and waved his hands. "But that does not matter, does it? I go where I am needed."

He wandered around the cave for a time before crouching at the feet of the Americans again, cradling his chin in a palm as he silently considered them. Punk wasn't sure whether to make eye contact, to show strength, or to avert his eyes in the face of the captor's menacing demeanor, his sadist's aura. "Your names?" he asked, to which neither aviator replied. "You can tell me that. Your president has declared *war* on us, no? Geneva Convention is in effect, correct? Name, rank, date of birth? You must follow Geneva Convention." He focused on Punk with cold black eyes, and Punk felt what little adrenaline he had left shoot through his veins. He'd learned firsthand during his POW training that the slow build to torture was in some ways as bad as the torture itself. But even as realistic as that training had been, Punk knew he was on unmapped ground.

He was exhausted. Hungry. Tired. From where would the strength come?

"O'Leary, commander, June 30, 1955," Spud said firmly.

Punk took Spud's words as his cue and followed with: "Reichert, lieutenant commander, August 1, 1970."

"Sha," the man said with a broad smile that fully revealed his stained, crooked teeth. "Cooperation is good. I was afraid we were not going to be friends. This can be very bad if we are not friends." He patted himself on the chest. *"Salam.* My name is hard to say, but since we are friends you can call me Slobo." He grew a wry smile as he stood and produced a long Bowie-style knife from the same general area of his back where he'd holstered his pistol. " 'Slobo the Butcher' I am known in some places." He ran a finger gingerly down the blade, mesmerized by it. He looked back at the Americans and said, "But my friends call me just 'Slobo.' " He returned the knife to the sheath behind his back. "Do you want to hear a funny thing?"

A funny thing? Punk cut his eyes toward Spud and again waited for his cue.

"I first came to this country as *Spetsnatz,*" Slobo explained, now pacing before them, voice intense but conversational. "Have you heard of this? *Spetsnatz*—like your SEALs or Green Berets?" He spread his arms. "Because I am big I am allowed to join. Maybe they did not know I was Muslim. Maybe they do not care."

The light flickered, and Slobo gave the bulb a contemptuous stare before continuing his soliloquy: "So I come to Afghanistan with Soviet invasion. I fight. I fight well. But then things are *naapoh gaam,* how you say . . . *confused*? I see Soviets do not know what they are doing here. I see they are unjust. Soon I feel that my place is not with them. I go with mujahadeen."

Slobo reached behind his back with both hands and withdrew the pistol and the knife. He studied them alternatively, as if weighing his options. *"Ze shaa obakha,"* he said. "I am sorry. I talk too much. Everyone tells me, 'Slobo, you talk too much.' 'I know that,' I say. 'But what do you want me to do about it?' They laugh. I like it when there is laughing. There is not enough laughing in the world now, I think. Do you think I am right?"

The Americans remained nonplussed, each staring at the toes of his boots. "You do not want to talk, I know," Slobo continued. "Your Code of Conduct I have read. How you are trained I know. But the situation you are in here in Afghanistan those who train you do not understand. Their training will hurt you now." He pointed toward the cave entrance. "The rules men here do not play by."

Slobo paused, waiting for some sort of response. He dipped his head to attempt eye contact with each of them, and they impassively accepted the attention. *"Sha,* perhaps it is hard for you to answer my ques-

tions. Maybe you want to ask me something?" Another silent pause. Punk felt the tension growing with
each passing heartbeat. He wished Spud would say
something, anything, to mollify the man. Nothing of
tactical consequence, of course; just the toss of a bone.
He felt himself weakening, willing Slobo to be sincere.
The Chechen was right. What did those guys back in
the States know about the here and now, anyway?
Had any of them ever been where he and Spud were
at the moment?

"I am trying to help you," Slobo explained, eyes
beseeching cooperation.

Punk was about to speak when Spud lifted his head
and asked, "What's going to happen next?"

Slobo's expression brightened. "There. That was not
hard, was it?" His brow furrowed. "But I am not sure
what you mean: 'Next'?"

"Will we stay here or are you going to move us
somewhere else?"

"*Sha,*" Slobo said. "I think we stay here for the
night. After that we probably go somewhere else. We
shot down your airplane without pilots, but your spies
must know we are here now." The big Chechen
mulled over the issue for a time before suddenly
bridging to another subject. "Do you like television?"

The aviators exchanged glances, and Spud allowed
an unenthusiastic nod.

"I do," Slobo said. "America makes the best shows.
My favorite is *Knight Rider.* You know of this one,
the car that talks? David Hasselhoff? He is also a
singer, you know. Did you know this? He is very popular as a singer everywhere but America. That is sad,
don't you think, that his own country does not know
of his talents?" Slobo produced another bottle of

water and took a big slug. "Do you watch the news? I read on the Internet that you watch the news on your ships."

As if on cue a pair of spotlights bounced through the cave entrance, blinding Punk. In the glare he could just make out someone setting up a tripod with a camera perched on top of it.

"Your country does not know where you are," Slobo said. "You saw what happened to the small airplane without pilots. The same thing would happen to any airplanes coming here." He gestured toward the camera. "We will help tell the world you are alive. These are friends from the news. Have you heard of Aljazeera? They make you famous." Punk heard several men laugh, although the lights made him blind to their number.

One of them said something to Slobo, and the big Chechen removed his coat and put it on Punk.

"How were you shot down?" a higher-pitched voice with a distinctly Arab accent asked once Slobo was out of the shot.

The Americans remained silent.

"*Ho*, this is the news," Slobo said. "You must talk to them. They are like CNN."

"Tell us how you fell into Taliban hands," the Arab said.

Neither spoke.

"*Ra-sha*," Slobo said. "Is impolite not to answer simple questions. These reporters have come a very long way to talk to you."

Suddenly the lights went out. The captors and newsmen groaned and milled about in the dark, bumping into each other and fumbling with their equipment. Slobo produced a small flashlight and lit his immediate area as he conferred with one of the news crew.

"Our generator is kaput for now," the Chechen

said, turning the flashlight on the aviators. "We do the interview tomorrow. We wait for daylight." He moved to Punk and pulled his jacket off of him. "*Ta ke-dal.* Sleep. Tomorrow you talk much. Don't worry. I will be here to guard you. Now sleep."

"Midrats," short for midnight rations, was the third meal of the day for most aviators since they normally slept through the breakfast hour. It was a very social time, a time for recounting the day's events or telling "best ever" stories, but this night the mood was somber. Two of their own were missing.

"How the hell does a bomb do that?" Einstein asked Flex from across the table in Wardroom One.

"I don't know," Flex replied. He swallowed a last bite of hamburger—a "slider" in seagoing slang—and pushed his plate aside. "Gunner said he heard of it happening back in the old days but that there's no way it should happen now. A proximity fuse shouldn't fuse on the bomb next to it. Where is Gunner anyway? He never misses midrats."

"He's seriously bumming over this," Einstein said. "I don't think he's left the ordnance shop since he first got word of it."

"Do you think they're captured?" Peeler asked.

"I don't know," Monster said, now the *Arrow-slingers* senior man aboard the Boat. "The CSAR effort is being run from CENTCOM. They haven't exactly been keeping us posted."

Captain Campbell walked up holding a bowl of ice cream—comfort food? "Evening, gentlemen."

"Evening, DCAG," Monster said. "Care to join us?"

"Actually, I just needed to speak with Einstein for a sec."

Without another word the officers excused themselves, scattering like roaches after the lights are turned on and leaving Einstein alone at the previously well-populated table. Soup watched them go and shrugged, saying, "I didn't mean to scare them off."

The deputy air wing commander took a seat in the chair Flex had newly vacated and began spooning ice cream into his mouth. "A UAV might have spotted something," he said. "Unfortunately it made only one pass before it was shot down by a SAM."

"What did it see?" Einstein asked, surprised and flattered that the captain would see fit to share such important news with him.

"I don't know exactly. The intel guys at CENTCOM are being real careful with this one. We're in close comms with them, though. We'll know if anything comes up." He stared blankly at the table just beyond his bowl. "That's not why I wanted to talk to you." His eyes slowly walked up and met the younger officer's. Einstein felt his heart jump to his throat. Soup had never talked just to him before except over the airplane's intercom. Had he fucked something up? His career flashed before his eyes: wings pulled, commission lost, pay docked, sentence awarded, all because he'd done . . . what?

"I don't know if it's this investigation I've got bearing down on my ass, or what," Soup said, "but I feel like I have to bury the hatchet with a few people around here." He pointed an index finger across the table. "You're one of them."

The captain took a deep breath and ran his fingers along the edge of the table. He offered Einstein a pained smile. "I'm not real good at this, so please bear with me." He paused and exhaled again, longer this time. "I'm sorry for getting us shot down a few years ago."

"Captain, this isn't—"

He held a hand up. "No, let me finish. I'm not doing this for you. Trust me." He took another second to organize his thoughts. "Anyway, I was reckless, and . . . and I'm sorry." He paused one more time before performing a drumroll on the table. "That's it."

With that Soup pushed away from the table and walked out.

Punk snapped back to consciousness, exhausted but too miserable to manage sleep. He lay on his side on the cave's hard, dirty floor and tried to ward off the damp cold, jamming his hands deep into his armpits and drawing his knees up as far as his cramping muscles would allow. In the flickering light he studied Spud in repose, a man at peace, and as he pondered the source of such calm one of the skipper's many sayings popped into his head: "Why die all tensed up?" The line's logic was inarguable—boilerplate for a fighter pilot—but as he thought about it now it seemed overly simplistic. It was easy enough to sound cool on the radio as your jet was going down; it was a different matter to outlast the enemy when you were his prisoner. His teeth chattered—cold or nerves, he couldn't say—and he fought to keep his jaw clenched.

Punk slowly rolled over to see who else was with them. Across the cave he saw Slobo bent over a candle, the sole source of light in the place. He was holding something silver over the flame, a spoon. Punk narrowed his eyes with the hope that if Slobo looked over he wouldn't notice he was being watched.

With his other hand the big Chechen put the tip of

a syringe to the spoon. He sat back against the wall and threaded his thumb into the loop at the other end before drawing it back, filling the cylinder with clear liquid. Punk had seen enough cable TV shows to know what was coming next: Slobo set the needle down and wrapped a piece of rubber tubing around his biceps and held it taut with his teeth. He flicked at the vein near the crook of his arm and picked up the syringe again. He slid the needle into his arm without changing his expression and pushed down on the plunger.

Punk heard him let out a long sigh and then he saw his eyes flutter. Once the plunger was fully home he sat still for a time. Finally he dropped the tube from his teeth and pulled the needle from his arm. He murmured to himself, head lolling from side to side, eyes three-quarters shut. Punk had a thought.

He rolled over. "Spud," he whispered. "Spud, wake up."

The skipper's eyes opened. "What?" he replied, startled.

Punk put a finger to his lips. "Slobo's shooting heroin," he quietly explained. "He just gave himself a fix."

Spud sat up and looked past Punk toward the other side of the cave and said, "He looks out of it, all right."

"Should we do something?"

"Something?"

"Make a break for it?"

Spud's brow furrowed as he worked the idea around his head. "How much time until sunrise?"

"I don't know," Punk replied. He focused on Slobo's left wrist. "Let me check his watch."

Punk cautiously crawled across the floor, fearing the

man might emerge from his stupor at any moment. How long did a heroin high last?

"It's ten after four," Punk reported after cocking his head so he could see Slobo's watch right-side up.

"Let's go."

Spud got to his feet and ambled over to the cave entrance with stiff legs, followed by Punk walking with a pronounced limp. Because of the low light in the cave, their eyes were already well adjusted to the night, but it was still pitch-black outside.

"Which way should we go?" Punk asked, peering beyond Spud's shoulder into the abyss.

"East," Spud replied.

"Which way is that?"

Spud pointed off to his left. "That way."

The two Americans hobbled into the night, each fearing that a step taken would be his last. Certainly Slobo wasn't the only guard in the camp. Taliban must have been posted high on the ridges looking down on the valley. They may have been wearing night-vision goggles. But the aviators kept going, slinking down the steps to the plain as fluidly as their conditions would allow and then traipsing along the edge of the road that led away from the camp, slowly at first but quicker with time, emboldened by their success. Muscles were loosening up; blood was pumping. For crissakes, they were making it. They were going to free themselves from their enemy by simply walking away. Again Punk pictured himself surrounded by the boys in the ready room as he related his exploits: *That's right; we just walked away . . .*

Suddenly Punk was doubled over by cramping in his intestines. He bore down, trying to stay quiet while fighting off the first wave, but by the time the second hit half a minute later he knew there would be no stemming of the tide. He shed his torn, filthy flight suit and soiled boxers to his ankles and crouched down, trying his best to get out of the way of himself.

"What the fuck's going on?" Spud hailed over in a loud whisper, cued by the splattering against the hard ground.

"What does it fucking sound like?" Punk seethed in disgust between muffled groans. "I've got the shits. It must've been the meat."

Something sparked the ground between them followed by the clap of a rifle thundering through the valley. A single voice shouted from above quickly joined by a group of voices. Another spark went off near where the first had erupted, trailed a second later by another crack of gunfire, and although they couldn't understand the words thrown down at them, they were sure of their general meaning. Punk continued to yield to his loose bowels while Spud froze in place with his hands raised over his head.

Spud was right. They'd been headed east. Punk knew so because when his blindfold was pulled off he was standing on the flatland near the road, facing into the dawn just cresting above the mountaintop. He glanced up to the sky. The day was as cloudy and raw as the one before, maybe worse. Air support was unlikely. The ceiling was low; some of the peaks were hidden. The wind was already starting to howl.

Punk tried seeing beyond blurry shapes moving in front of him, his bloodshot eyes walking into the distance. How far had they gone down the road? It didn't matter. However far, it hadn't been far enough.

The gray daylight that assaulted Punk's eyes made his already aching head feel like it was now about to split open. His guts burned with a gnawing pain born of stress, dehydration, hypothermia, and hunger. The cuts that laced his body stung; the bruises throbbed. He'd long since shit himself dry, nearly filling the "honey bucket" in the corner of the cave. Torn between a strong desire to either sob or vomit, he did neither. He fought not to feel anything.

Punk had nearly regained his sight when he was roundly slapped. "*Kho*, you make me lose face," Slobo shouted. "In front of my comrades you embarrass me. You try to escape from me. Now you must cooperate. Cooperate or severe punishment will come to you both." He reached for his knife and cut the ropes that had bound the Americans' hands and feet for the last three hours.

The TV crew bustled about, earnestly fiddling with their equipment. The reporter was a well-groomed Arab with a mustache who looked dressed for an up-scale safari, and the other two were darker-skinned versions of any technicians Punk had ever seen: unshaven and sloppily dressed. Around them a large crowd of Taliban fighters looked on, laughing and chatting animatedly. After a few more minutes of running wires and blowing on plugs, one of the techs gave the reporter a thumbs-up. The reporter called for silence and then held a microphone to his mouth and asked, "How were you shot down?"

Neither aviator spoke.

"You must cooperate," Slobo insisted from behind the reporter. "I warn you."

"O'Leary," Spud slurred in a halfhearted monotone. "Commander. June 30, 1955."

"Reichert, lieutenant commander, Aug—"

"*Kho*, you think I joke?" Slobo yelled as he pushed past the reporter, arms flailing. He pointed at the cam-

era and shouted something that caused the cameraman to reach over and click a switch and stand idly
by. Slobo gestured to a group of Taliban who fell in
line behind him as he strode toward the Americans.
"I show you I not joke."

Slobo grabbed a fistful of Spud's flight suit before
throwing the thin-framed RIO on his back. Half of
the Taliban thugs descended on him while the other
half surrounded Punk and gruffly pushed him into position so he could see what was going on with his
skipper. The Chechen stood on Spud's wrist and removed the knife from the sheath on his belt.

Punk was forced to watch as Slobo bent down,
splayed the fingers of Spud's left hand, and began sawing away at the base of his pinkie. Spud's pleas turned
to horrific yelps as Slobo cut through the bone and
then made short work of the remaining flesh under
it. Punk fought in vain against those holding him; he
screamed his protest, but his voice was lost in the
perverse laughter of the Taliban that rang nightmar-
ishly in his ears.

Slobo finished what Punk feared was only the first
phase of his grisly work. The Chechen stood erect and
radiated a broad smile through his red beard, eyes
wild and murderous, blood running down his hand
and wrist as he held Spud's finger aloft. A loud cheer
erupted, drowning out the skipper's moans.

Someone produced a scimitar and handed it to
Slobo. He waved it above his head, whirling it faster
and faster as the throng urged him on. Blood lust had
seized them all, and they weren't going to be satisfied
with a finger or two.

Punk momentarily detached from the insanity before him. He raised unfocused eyes above the melee,
and against the mountains he saw Suzanne's bright

face smiling. The vision gave him an overwhelming urge to live, and he was made even weaker by the despair that accompanied the realization that he had no control over that now. His knees buckled, but those surrounding him held him up.

Slobo returned his attention to Spud, who was no longer moving. Punk figured he'd gone into shock and was glad for nature's mercy. The Chechen lined the curved blade up with the skipper's neck before raising it over his head. Punk tugged and screamed for all he was worth, babbling incoherencies with a mouth that had lost touch with his brain in the face of such horrors.

Slobo arched his back until the blade was parallel to his spine and froze, reveling in the drama of the moment, working the crowd like a circus performer. As the Chechen stood poised to render a deadly blow to Spud's neck, Punk took one more look at Spud's motionless form and, with that, his desperation gave way to peace. They'd kill him next, but in death he wouldn't be cold or hungry and he wouldn't have a splitting headache. No pain. He'd simply cease to be.

What was there to fear in that? *Why die all tensed up?*

Slobo continued to hold the pose, nodding repeatedly across the mob, seeking consensus, and as the cheers reached a crescendo Punk hung his head and muttered, "See you on the other side, Spud."

Something zoomed over their heads, and Punk looked up in time to see a Tomahawk Land Attack Missile hurl past in a steep descent. Two more TLAMs flew over in rapid succession, piercing the dawn with the menacing whine of the god's own blowtorches. All three dove nearly into the mouths of separate caves and exploded in series, spewing fire and shrapnel

across the valley. The third missile hit an ammunition
storage cave, causing the initial blast to be met by
dozens more, and together they heated Punk's face
from half a mile away while the sum of the multiple
concussions nearly knocked him off his feet.

The Taliban scattered in all directions. Punk saw
some of them fall and then noticed bullets stirring the
ground around him. He turned and caught sight of
two U.S. Army AH-64 Apache helicopters just as they
pushed past the ridgeline, banking left and right, guns
ablaze. Behind the Apaches a single CH-47 Chinook
transport helicopter lumbered a more straight-line
path toward the camp. Punk was surprised to see the
helicopters at this altitude but didn't spend time questioning his fortune.

He looked back toward where Slobo had stood, fearing he might not have been distracted from his macabre
deed in time to save Spud's life, but the Chechen was
nowhere to be found. Spud lay motionless on the
ground, left arm extended with a small pool of blood
spreading under his hand. With Taliban falling all
around him, Punk grabbed an AK-47 off the ground
and limped toward his stricken commanding officer.

Punk was almost to him when out of the corner of
his eye he caught a Taliban with his own Kalashnikov
taking a bead. Without pause Punk whirled around,
ignorant of how to operate the rifle other than pointing it and pulling the trigger, and peppered the man's
chest with a full burst of bullets. The man shook like
a rag doll in a dog's mouth and crumpled in a heap.

Punk stared at his victim for a few beats, the man's
lifeless body contorted with arms splayed out and legs
bent at weird angles, and he realized for all the bombs
he'd dropped in anger this was the first time he'd actually seen someone die at his hand. He wasn't quite

sure how to feel about it. More bullets ricocheted at his feet, and before he could contemplate his emotions further he leveled the rifle to his left and cut down two more of them.

Punk dropped the rifle and scooped Spud up with both hands. He threw the skipper across his back and started toward the Chinook, now in what looked to be the final phase of its approach to a landing near the road. After a few steps he went back to make a quick search for Spud's pinkie on the off chance that Slobo had dropped it amid the chaos. Surgeons could still reattach it, right?

Punk did two three-sixties around the patch of blood in the dirt and came up empty. Even if he did find the finger, the effort was probably in vain anyway. From what he could remember from medical shows, he needed to stick the appendage in a cooler full of ice. Maybe there was a medical team aboard the Chinook. Spud's warm blood dripped against his hand, and he realized that getting the bleeding stopped trumped his hunt for the digit. He hoisted the skipper higher up his back and again took off running toward the arriving chopper.

Punk humped his burden across the steppe, picking his way over the crevasses and dodging the bowling ball–sized rocks as he went. His head continued to pound, but he was surprised by his strength in light of his treatment over the last hours. He'd had physical challenges during his adult life—a 10K here, a beach volleyball tournament there, not to mention the act of piloting a jet fighter—but he had never been forced to dig this deep. As the distance to the landing site seemed to grow before his bouncing eyes he wondered how much deeper he'd be digging before he could rest. He had another vision: his rack in his stateroom,

pillow fluffy and soft, sheets clean, taut, and wool
blanket warm.

The Apache attack helicopters continued to make
deliberate attack runs on the camp, mowing down
groups of Taliban and firing rockets into cave openings, as the Chinook's tandem rotors beat the air in
increasingly loud, rapid-fire thumps and stirred up the
fine sand that covered the ground near the road. Punk
wasn't a helicopter pilot, but as he watched the big
transport helicopter approach, he thought it might be
coming down too fast.

The helicopter disappeared into a cloud of dust and
Punk heard the impact, a single crack followed by the
sickening sound of metal twisting beyond its design
limits. He saw the rotor blades arcing out of their
normal horizontal plane as the aircraft rolled rapidly
onto its side after the first bounce. He fell to the
ground with Spud next to him, and the last thing he
saw before burying his face in the dirt was the rotor
blades disintegrating and flying in all directions, as
dangerous as the shrapnel from the TLAMs that had
just wreaked havoc on the Taliban. He waited until
the bits of composite material stopped tapping him on
the back before raising his head.

Fire followed, starting in the engine housing above
the fuselage and quickly traveling to the cabin. Smoke
poured out of the smashed Plexiglas windows. Punk
left Spud on the dirt and ran toward the Chinook's
aft ramp. Two figures emerged from the back of the
helicopter, running madly. One of them collapsed
after a handful of strides. Punk grabbed an arm and
pulled the soldier to safety next to where Spud lay
before running back toward the helicopter, passing the
other survivor along the way.

"How many are left?" Punk asked. The soldier didn't respond. On closer inpsection Punk noted the man's flight helmet and figured he was one of the pilots, or more likely, the crew chief. He wandered robotically, jaw slack.

The Chinook was engulfed in flame by the time Punk reached it. He tried to push toward the ramp, but the heat was too intense. He heard screaming and shouted, "This way!" A second later another soldier appeared, aflame head to toe, running in terror. Punk tackled the man and rolled him on the ground until the flames were doused. Then he ran back to the burning wreckage, so close that his own hair was singed, and continued to call out in the hope that someone else might make it out. No one did. Rounds from the ammo boxes in the cargo bay started to cook off, so reluctantly Punk ducked and backed away.

Punk gingerly cradled the badly burned soldier and moved back near Spud, where the others had gathered. One of the soldiers, a big guy in desert cammies, had his wits about him enough to drop to a knee and exchange fire with the Taliban now rejoined and headed their way. Punk laid down the burned man and searched for the AK-47 but remembered that he'd left it behind when he'd hoisted Spud onto his back.

A SAM streaked over their heads and beelined for one of the Apaches as it labored to maneuver defensively in the thin air. The missile hit the attack chopper square and exploded, blowing off the tail boom and throwing the rest of the craft into one last groaning turn toward the mountainside before it impacted in a fiery mass. The crew never had a chance.

"I need a rifle," Punk yelled at the soldier who continued to squeeze off short bursts from his M-4.

"Use his pistol," the soldier yelled back, pointing to the figure in flight gear seated in the dirt next to Spud. "He won't be able to; he's out of it."

The second Apache made another attack run on the advancing Taliban, spraying bullets and firing two more rockets as it passed overhead. Punk saw the bodies sail through the sky along with pieces of a tank as the ordnance hit, and he raised his fist and cheered, but then he heard a strange string of pops from the helicopter's engine. The Apache had been hit. It disappeared over the ridgeline trailing a thick line of black smoke. He listened for a crash but heard nothing. Maybe the pilot would make a forced landing in the next valley; maybe he'd manage to limp back to base. In any case, it looked like the Americans on the ground were out of air support for now.

Punk reached into the zombie's holster and removed his pistol, a nine-millimeter model he'd fired before. He unlatched the safety and flopped facedown in the prone position with the hope that the small lump of rock in front of him would stop oncoming fire.

"It's just you and me," the soldier said, seemingly excited by the prospect. "Alamo time."

The soldier continued to fire off short bursts, picking off Taliban one at a time as they hit their stride in a banzai charge. Spent magazines were coolly ejected and replaced with full ones from the leg pocket of his desert cammie trousers. Punk extended his arms and squinted down the sight, waiting for the enemy to close to pistol range. *No HUD now,* he thought. *Just a notch in the barrel.*

"I've got a bayonet if things get hairy," the soldier mentioned between shots. "You got a knife or anything?"

"No," Punk replied, wondering what the soldier

considered "hairy." An army of bloodthirsty barbarians bearing down on the two of them from a couple hundred yards away wasn't hairy?

"Don't you pilots carry knives?"

"Yeah, we carry knives; it's just that my stuff was all stolen by those assholes running this way."

The soldier caught Punk's eye and smiled. "Maybe we'll get it back when they get here."

One hundred yards now, Punk figured. Close enough for a pistol. He steadied his hand and lined the barrel up on the middle man among a baker's dozen sprinting down the center of the road, pumping their AK-47s above their heads after each poorly aimed shot at the Americans. As he'd been taught at the Naval Academy during Plebe Summer, Punk applied smooth and steady pressure on the trigger while holding his breath so his hands wouldn't shake.

The pistol went off and Punk was surprised to see three of them fall.

"Behind us," the soldier shouted. "Horses!"

Punk wheeled around to see the plain to the east alive with movement. Riders drove chargers at full gallop, rifles ablaze, robes flowing, earth flying. The ground shook as the lead elements split around the wreckage of the CH-47 and rode past the small band of crash survivors and former POWs without acknowledging them. Punk grimaced through the dust they kicked up and marveled at the boldness of their attack. The Taliban were equally impressed: Punk saw those who remained on their feet running in the other direction as fast as their legs would take them. They were cut down in short order. The horsemen pressed on, dismounting and charging up the stairs toward the caves, firing rifles and rocket-propelled grenades along the way.

A handful or more of the second wave of riders came to a halt in a cloud of fine dust near Punk's group. "Americans?" one of them asked with a distinct Texas drawl.

"Yeah?" Punk returned, half answer, half question.

"Well, hell, son. Get on."

With all due haste Punk tossed Spud over the back of one of the big animals while the able-bodied soldier did the same with the others. Once Punk and the soldiers were all mounted up behind riders, the rescuers prodded their steeds back in the direction from which they'd come, headlong past two advancing tanks and another wave of cavalry.

Punk looked back over his shoulder only once as the battle faded in the distance, and as he did he hoped never again to see the enemy at close range.

CHAPTER EIGHT

"The UAV spotted you right before it got shot down," one of the rescuers said, a tall, well-bearded staff sergeant who introduced himself as "the Waco Kid," or "Waco," for short. His brown hair had grown out enough to curl around the edges of the black knit cap he wore. From the waist down he was dressed like any military man in theater—desert camouflaged fatigue trousers bloused at the bottom of the leg over desert-colored boots—but above that he wore a fleece pullover with a mock-T underneath. "We launched the rescue operation a few hours later."

Across the hut's only room another staff sergeant, "Mighty Og," or "Og," for short, kneeled next to one of the wooden beds and dressed Spud's wounded hand. Og, similarly attired as Waco, was a massive human being with a single thick eyebrow at the base of a protruding forehead, and coal-black hair grown well past military standards. He had the sort of broad chin custom-made for the bushy beard it hosted. "He's still out," he reported in a voice that seemed too meek to have come from him. "It's probably best. He'd be in a lot of pain otherwise. In fact, if he wakes up, I might have to put him out with some morphine."

"Don't waste that shit on these flyboys," Waco said as he leaned an M-4 against four others—salvaged weapons of the dead and wounded—and flashed a smile at Punk. "Just kidding. Green Berets don't need painkillers, anyway. We've been trained to ignore pain. Right, Og?"

"Pain is my friend," Og replied in an unenthusiastic monotone. "You're starting to sound like a Ranger, Waco."

Punk sat on the floor with a sleeping bag draped across his shoulders and cleared his nose of bloody mucous, byproducts of injury and dry air. That task complete, he dug into the main-course pouch of an MRE kit. With the first swallow he waited for the reaction, hoping that his body's last response to solid food was a function of Taliban preparation standards and not some bug he'd picked up. The gurgles in his gut caused him to brace for the worst, but nothing came of them.

"Where are we?" Punk asked after washing down a bit of cold spaghetti with a swallow of bottled water.

"Here?" Waco asked, pointing to the floor under his desert boots. "This is our safe house. The nicest mud hut in all of greater Bamiyan."

Punk narrowed his eyes. "Bamiyan? Where have I heard that before?"

Waco moved to the hut's door with a pair of binoculars in his hand. "Come here, El Cedar," he said, waving his arm at Punk. The two Green Berets had already taken to calling Punk "El Cedar," which was an adaptation of the "LCDR" abbreviation for his rank, not unlike the nom de guerre of "El Tee" given to lieutenants since Vietnam. Punk didn't mind. "El Cedar" struck a fine balance between field informality and military courtesy. It didn't seem right that they would call him "Lieutenant Commander Reichert" any more than they would refer to him as "Punk."

Punk lost the sleeping bag and took the binoculars from Waco in the doorway. "What am I looking at?" Punk asked as he put the glasses to his eyes and adjusted their width.

"Look straight across the flatland there," Waco instructed. "There are two huge cutouts in the face of the cliffs."

Punk panned across the sandstone until he framed something that resembled what Waco seemed to be talking about. "Are those the—"

"Exactly," Waco said without giving Punk the chance to finish the question. "Those are the Buddhist statues that the Taliban blew up a few years back." He took the binoculars back and put them to his own eyes. "Colossi from the second century," he said ethereally, momentarily losing the cattleman's pastiche. "The wonders of the ancient world, a shrine, a stopping-off point for pilgrims from India and China." He dropped the binoculars from his eyes and threw his hands up. "And these dipshits just blow them up."

"I wouldn't just be standing there in the doorway, Waco," Og said as he buttoned up his medical kit. "That's a good way to get picked off."

"That's a good way to get picked off," Waco mocked. "Ain't nobody getting picked off around here, Og." He looked over to Punk and pointed toward the much bigger of the two Green Berets. "Always sweating the small shit."

"It's not small shit, Waco," Og insisted. "We don't own this area yet."

The sound of horses approaching at a rapid clip grew and then died in an arrhythmic coda in front of the hut. Two men dressed in affected mufti—nondescript ball caps, vests like those worn by photojournalists, flannel shirts, and faded jeans—passed through the door, beating the dust from themselves. Each had a pair of space-aged sunglasses dangling from a neoprene lanyard around his neck. As they stepped across the dirty floor Punk noted they were both wearing the half running shoe/half hiking boot footwear that was so popular stateside with the active crowd, and he wondered if the manufacturer knew that its product was being used across the windswept vastness of Afghanistan as well as the wilds of America's theme parks.

"About time you guys got back," Waco said.

"What do you expect without air cover?" the more rugged looking of them said in a deep voice as he stroked his gray beard as if he were petting a dog. As he came closer Punk read in the lines across his tanned, leathery face that he was older than the others. "I warned CENTCOM about our helos operating up here at these altitudes," the man continued.

"That was ugly," the other new arrival said, nearly to himself. Curly black hair cascaded from under his cap like ringlets of steam escaping a covered pot. He wore glasses with round rims that were a size or two too small for his face and gave off an urbane aura that seemed out of place in a war zone. He had to be the brains of the outfit, or if not, the guy who knew how to make the radios work.

"We've got the bodies outside," the rugged elderly one said. "How did your guys do?"

"One of them died on the way over here," Og reported. "Burned too bad. He's wrapped up behind the hut.'' He pointed to the two beds, one holding Spud and the other the soldier Punk had dragged away from the wreckage. ''These two are pretty fucked up. Both of them are out.''

The graybeard looked over at Punk and asked, ''How are you feeling?''

''Fine, I guess,'' Punk replied. ''I feel better now that I had an MRE to eat.''

''You'll be sick of those soon enough.'' The man extended a hand and shaped his beard into a polite smile. Along with the crow's-feet at the corners of his eyes, his avuncular manner evinced that he had at least a decade on the eldest among the rest of them. ''I'm Tim.''

''Rick Reichert,'' Punk said as he shook hands. ''What did you say your name was again?''

''Tim.''

''Tim . . .''

''Just Tim.''

Punk waited a few beats, but Tim stood stone still with a placid smile on his face. He pointed across the room at the other man and said, ''And that's Terry.'' Punk returned a halfhearted wave, noting that Terry was the only one of the rescue team in the room without any facial hair at all.

''It's *just* Tim and *just* Terry,'' Waco said. ''They don't have last names. They lost them once they became 'blue badgers.' ''

Punk looked over at Tim and asked, ''Blue badger?''

''We're not blue badgers, Waco,'' Tim said. ''Blue badgers are the pencil pushers who never leave northern Virginia.''

Punk looked back to Waco, expression petitioning an explanation.

"CIA," Waco said before throwing a hand over his mouth. "Oh, darn it. Was that out loud?"

"Oh, yeah, it's a big secret," Tim said before sticking his head out the door and yelling like a peanut vendor at a baseball game, "We got CIA here. CIA, over *heeere*." He looked back across the small room. "Get over it, Waco. We're all on the same team now. Hell, you might as well be in the CIA."

"I wanted to join; they said I was too smart," Waco replied.

Tim waved his hands in front of him and, shifting his attention back to Punk, said, "Before we get too distracted by Waco's bullshit, I need to file a preliminary POW debrief with our field office." The CIA man opened up a laptop and parked himself on the floor next to Punk. "They'll be chomping at the bit for the gnat's ass details, but we'll just hit the high points; you know: keep it simple." He stopped and waited for Punk to give an indication of some sort. Punk raised his eyebrows and nodded.

"Okay. How were you shot down?"

Punk took a moment to gauge whether or not Tim was pulling his leg. Tim waited him out with the same placid half smile he'd worn before, and with that Punk figured he really wanted an answer.

"My best guess at this point is that we had one of our bombs explode right after it left the jet," Punk said.

"So it wasn't a SAM that got you?"

"I don't think so."

"And you're basing this assessment on . . ."

"The fact that the explosion happened immediately after I hit the Bomb button, and that my wingman later told me he saw the fourth bomb explode."

"How were you able to talk to your wingman?"

"Over my survival radio."

"What time did this happen?"

"Approximately 1300 local time."

"So you ejected?"

"Yes."

Tim's face softened; his eyes narrowed a bit. "What does that feel like?"

"It'll get your attention. I've had to eject twice now."

"Damn . . . Maybe you should think about another line of work." Tim was momentarily lost in thought but quickly regained his game face and continued furiously whacking the keys of his portable computer. "And then you . . . what?"

"My parachute lines got hung up on the ledge of a cliff and I hung there for a few hours."

"Where did your copilot land?"

"My RIO?"

"Whatever." Tim pointed to Spud, who was flaked out on the bed. "Where did he land?"

"I'm not sure."

"How long exactly were you hung up on the ledge of a cliff?"

"I'm not sure about that either. I was unconscious for part of the time."

Tim looked up from the screen with his brow knit. "The guys I'm sending this to expect details."

"I'm telling you everything I can remember."

"Fine, fine. So what's the next thing you remember?"

"I came to while they were pulling me off the cliff."

"Taliban?"

"I assume so. Most of them were wearing black turbans, anyway."

"What time was that?"

"When?"

"When the Taliban pulled you off the cliff."

"I'm not sure. One of the first things they stole was my watch. That's what I get for wearing a Breitling into combat, I guess."

"Give me your best guess."

"It was starting to get dark. Sunset-ish . . ."

"Sunset-ish . . . the spooks are going to love me." Tim was silent for a time as he concentrated on what he was writing. "Did you walk to the camp?"

"No, they threw me in the back of a pickup truck and drove there."

"How long did the drive take?"

Punk winced. "I'm not sure, Tim. I was blindfolded. It seemed like a long time, and it felt like we weren't moving very fast. I do know it was dark when we got to the camp. That was right about the time the UAV flew over."

Tim's eyes brightened. "Good. I'm sure they can figure out exactly what time that was." He typed some more before focusing on Punk again. "Can you describe any of them?"

"The locals all looked pretty much the same to me, you know, bearded and dark skinned," Punk said. "But there was one big white guy, a Chechen who called himself 'Slobo.'"

Tim nodded vigorously. "Slobodon Davarsevok. 'Slobo the Butcher.' We've been tracking him for years. He's a bad man, pretty high on the al Qaeda hit parade."

Punk looked over to Spud. "He's the one who cut the skipper's finger off."

"They're all savages," Tim said, "but Slobo's worse than most."

"He actually gave us the soft sell at first."

"He's psychotic."

"He's also a heroin addict."

Tim raised his eyebrows. "How do you know that?"

"I saw him shoot up."

"He did it right in front of you?"

"He thought I was asleep. He was guarding us."

"Now *that's* intel," Tim said with a nod. His fingers were a flurry for a time. "Did they feed you at all?"

"Yeah, a little rice and some sort of meat, mutton, I think."

"Did you digest it all right?"

"No," Punk said, putting a hand to his stomach. "It gave me the wicked shits."

Tim looked over his shoulder. "You hear that, Waco? That's why we don't want to run out of MREs, no matter how bad they taste."

Og hovered over Tim's feet. "I hate to break up this party, 'just Tim,' but we need to think about getting our sick and dead out of here," the big Green Beret said. "We need to use your bird."

"See what I mean, Waco?" Tim said. "Same team." He pointed to a small rack of communications gear stacked in the corner. "Og's right, Terry. Do your thing."

Terry kneeled in front of the gear and flipped several switches before plucking the handset out of its cradle: "Kilo two actual, this is Tiger base; Kilo two actual, this is Tiger base, over."

A quick burst of static gave the initial reply followed by a voice that sounded like it was coming from deep space: "Tiger base, this is Kilo two. Go ahead."

Punk saw Terry breathe a sigh of relief before putting the handset back to the side of his head: "Kilo two actual, Tiger base. We have six KIAs and two wounded to ex-fill. Need Ivan to make a run."

"Have them bring some more MREs," Waco said in a loud whisper, which made Tim chuckle. Waco glowered at him and explained, "Not because of that. We're running low and now we've got more mouths to feed, for a couple of meals, at least."

Terry focused on the radio's small speaker as the voice on the other end modulated its way through: "Tiger base, Kilo two copies. Understand you need this hit ASAP?"

"That's affirmative."

"It can't wait until dark?"

"Negative." Terry looked over his shoulder to Tim and shook his head.

"Roger. Expect hit at base hour minus four."

Terry checked his watch and then counted on his fingers. "Copy."

"MREs," Waco insisted.

Terry put the handset to his head again. "Oh, and Kilo two, can you bring us an MRE resupply?"

"Will do. Understand mission report is inbound?"

Terry glanced across the room at Tim seated on the floor with his back against the dried mud wall, still whacking feverishly against the keys of the laptop computer balanced across his thighs.

"Misrep inbound," Terry confirmed. "Tiger base, out."

Terry turned the radio off and stood at Tim's feet. "If my math is correct our helicopter should be here in three hours."

"And you guys were giving us grief for having a Russian helicopter," Tim said without looking up from his work. "At least it can fly around here."

"That's a cheap hit, just Tim," Waco said. "Those were brave Americans, our guys, who crashed back there."

Now he looked up. "I know that, Waco. That's not my point."

"Then what *is* your point?"

"Terry, what the hell is wrong with this thing?" Tim asked with his eyes on the thin screen in front of him, abruptly and effectively changing the subject. "I hit Save and the whole picture went black."

"C codes?" Terry asked in return.

Tim punched a few keys and sheepishly said, "That was it. Thanks."

"That's why I'm here, I guess."

Tim stood, holding the laptop out like a platter of food. "The signal strength is no good in here," he said. "I'm going out back to transmit this misrep."

After Tim walked out, Waco focused on the two Army guys in the room, the soldier and the crewman, seated on the floor across the room. The soldier was dressed for desert war except he wore a brown knit hat instead of a helmet. The crewman was still in his flight gear and remained in the grip of some sort of shock-induced catatonia, conscious but by appearances, unaware of anything as he sat with his spine bent, shoulders rolled forward, and legs crossed like a shaman in deep meditation. Punk hadn't bothered to study him previously, but now he thought the crewman looked about fifteen years old. His blank expression featured a weak chin that radiated inexperience even though he sported the requisite accoutrements of an airman associated with special operations: knives strapped to each ankle, flashlights and D-rings at his chest, and the like. The other guy was big, almost as tall as Og, though not quite as massive in build. He had windblown cheeks, blue-gray eyes, and white-blond hair neatly cut around his ears. He was sporting a barely there scraggly beard, a work in progress, most likely, or perhaps he was simply unable to muster up a very good effort in terms of facial hair. His brow was terminally furrowed, and his aura was one of intensity.

"I didn't get your name, Soldier," Waco said.

The soldier stared impassively at the dirty floor just beyond his boots and said, "No, you didn't." He allowed the tension he'd created with Waco to percolate a bit and then said, "I'm Sergeant Nathan Powell of the Tenth Mountain Division."

"Ranger?" Waco asked.

"Yeah," Sergeant Powell replied.

"You go by anything?"

"Just Nathan. Some call me 'Nate,' but I don't care for that."

"Glad to meet you, Nate." Waco pointed to the crewman. "What about him?"

"Not sure of his name, exactly. If I remember right, he called himself 'Boodle.' I just met him before the flight. He's the crew chief."

"Is he going to be all right?"

The Ranger considered the man and shrugged. "He's better off than the others who were in the helo with us."

Waco nodded and asked, "We should get word to your unit. Do you guys have SATCOM capability?"

"HQ does. I'm not sure what the frequency is. I'll bet Boodle has the comm card on him somewhere." Sergeant Powell looked around Waco to the communications suite in the corner. "Did I hear you say there's a chopper inbound?"

"Yeah."

"Where is it going when it leaves here?"

"Back to K-2, our home base."

"Where is that?"

Waco cut his eyes toward Og. "North of here."

"Any way you could drop Boodle and me with our unit on your way back?"

"Where do you need to go?" Waco asked.

The soldier scratched his beard and said, "We did have a staging base east of here, but I'm sure it's not there now."

"So where do you need to go?"

"Pakistan."

Waco's head shook as if the Ranger had hit him with a rock between the eyes. "Pakistan ain't on our way." He ran a hand through his scraggly mop. "This op is already way too complicated," he said. "I need some fresh air, thin as it may be." He ambled out the door. Og followed him seconds later, then Terry.

"Green Beret," Sergeant Powell spat once the last of the others cleared the hut. "They always think they're so laid-back and badass, too cool for school. The only thing they are is damned unprofessional. And I know exactly where their fucking base is."

Spud suddenly let out a bloodcurdling scream and bolted upright on the floor. Punk rushed across the room and tried to calm him, but the skipper's wailing just grew louder with his touch. Og bolted back through the door and went right to his medical kit.

"I was afraid this would happen," Og said as he ripped open a plastic bag that held a fresh needle. He shot an order at Sergeant Powell: "You, get over here and hold his legs down while I get this into him."

Spud continued to struggle as Og slid the needle into his arm and Punk and Sergeant Powell worked to keep him steady. Spud's screams continued, each more gut-wrenching than the last, and Punk willed the morphine to work quickly. Within the minute he saw Spud's eyes roll back and felt his body go limp.

"How long will that last?" Punk asked.

"Varies," Og said. "He should be good until Ivan gets here, anyway."

More horses clopped up. Soon two dark-skinned men in local dress walked in carrying rifles. Punk tensed at first sight but calmed himself when he saw their headgear: *pakols,* the traditional flat wool hats of the northern tribes instead of the black turbans of the Taliban. Punk had received some cursory cultural briefs before his first flight over Afghanistan weeks before, and was pleasantly surprised that even the smallest bit of it was of use. He also noted that they were armed with AK-47s. The lead man—on the chubby side with fat cheeks, squinty eyes, and a Fu Manchu mustache that gave him an almost Asian appearance—looked about expectantly. At his heel was a diminutive, dark-haired boy whose stare methodically swept the room.

Tim, Terry, and Waco rushed in and went right for the boy. "What took you guys so long?" Tim asked.

The boy started to answer but was interrupted by the chubby man who railed at the Americans in his native language, whatever that was. Tim nodded a few times and occasionally narrowed his eyes as he processed the harangue. Tim looked to the boy, and the boy started to translate.

"The general is not happy with the air cover," the boy said in fine English. "He wants to know where the jet bombers were."

Tim pointed up and tried to respond in their tongue: "*Hava* too bad for *tayara. Hava* bad." He quickly grew frustrated as the locals responded with nothing but confused expressions. "My Dari fails me, I'm afraid," he said as he looked at the boy again: "Bad weather. Airplanes must see ground."

Even before the boy finished translating the English the man started his retort, and even before he was finished with it the boy started translating the Dari: "The general has heard of the use of other bombs in the south and the east. Bombs that can be dropped through the clouds."

Tim looked over to Punk. "Do you know what he might be talking about?"

"JDAM, maybe," Punk said.

The man's eyes lit up as he pointed at Punk and said, "JDAM, *bale.*"

The boy nodded at the man and said, "JDAM, yes."

"JDAM?" Tim said with a grimace. "You need GPS coordinates for that, right? That's not a close air support weapon. Things are changing too fast. We'd wind up fragging our own people."

The big Afghan paused long enough to deliver one more Dari rant before taking his leave. "The general wants you to know we lost many more men than we should have today," the boy reported from the spot in the doorway the other had just occupied before disappearing out the door. "He says he is sorry for the loss of the helicopters, but he thinks they would have survived with more air support from the jet bombers. He says we need more than missiles before the attack. He says we need bombs from the jets during the battle. He says that if you cannot support him like you support other generals then he cannot guarantee how well his men will fight."

Tim gestured toward Punk and said, "Tell the general we have a jet bomber pilot with us now. He will work with the other pilots to make sure we get all the best bombs and other weapons. Tell the general we respect him very much."

The boy gave a courteous bow. "I will tell him these things. *Khoda-hafez*." The boy ran to his waiting mount and with a series of kicks galloped after the rest, who were soon nothing more than shrinking clouds of dust on the horizon. Tim, Waco, and Punk stood in the doorway watching the Afghans ride off like a family watching weekend guests drive away.

"We're going to have to show those guys a little love," Waco said, "and quick."

"The general is impossible to please," Tim said. "He always wants more: more money, more equipment, more men, more time . . . There's only so much I can control at my level, goddam it."

"That fat guy was the general, huh?" Sergeant Nathan Powell asked, still seated on the floor.

"*That* wasn't the general," Waco said, gesturing toward the fading dust cloud. "That was Urat, his chief of security."

"General Abdul Haskarim is the leader of the Uzbek elements of the Northern Alliance," Tim explained. "He doesn't come to us. We go to him."

"General Haskarim is the guy we've been hooked up with for the last two weeks," Waco said. "And if he's not happy, we're sucking."

"We're not sucking," Tim said.

"We're *sucking*," Waco insisted. "That guy's our fucking lifeline, just Tim, and now he's pissed. We'd better have somebody plink a JDAM down somewhere fast just to show him we've got the power." The Texan faced Punk. "You know anybody back on your aircraft carrier who might be able to help us out?"

"The kind of jet I fly doesn't carry JDAM," Punk explained. "Plus, we don't decide on our loadouts. CENTCOM does."

"No shit," Waco said. "Like I don't know that. CENTCOM has been giving us the short end of the stick since we snuck into this goddam country. I thought that since we saved your life you might put a good word in with some of your pilot buds at CENT-COM and see if we couldn't get a JDAM mission laid on. You guys all know each other, right? You know, like famous people all know each other?"

Punk looked over at Spud writhing in tortured semi-consciousness on a sleeping bag on the bed and felt his patience waning. He looked past Waco and asked Tim, "What's the game plan once the helo gets here?"

"We'll put the dead and wounded aboard and see how much more weight the pilots can handle after that," Tim said. "Depending on the time, they might be able to make another run today. Otherwise, you guys may be spending the night out here with us and then flying out tomorrow."

"Tomorrow?" Punk said, trying to mute his frustration as much as his fatigue would allow, realizing he'd lost most of his professional etiquette about the time Slobo was ready to chop Spud's head off. "When are my CO and I going to get back to the carrier? And what was this shit about you having a jet bomber pilot with you now?"

Tim shrugged. "I had to calm the Afghans down. Sometimes you have to stretch the truth around here."

Waco appeared over Tim's shoulder. "El Cedar, we'll do everything we can for you, but right now the situation is fluid. Why don't you cozy up on the rack over there and grab a few winks before the helo gets here, huh?"

That struck Punk as a very good idea, and he was asleep nearly before his head nestled against the cold floor. The exhaustion he'd tried to hold at bay over the last hours overtook him, and for a time the sting of his cuts and the cramping in his limbs ceased to register. But his mind didn't rest; rather, in the middle of sleeping more deeply than he would've imagined possible amid his surroundings, it fired with images.

In his dream he saw Suzanne, a vision in white standing at the front door of the suburban home she'd shared for years with Crud. A gentle wind furled her gown and playfully tossed her hair about her angelic face. Punk ached with the need to kiss her, to touch her. He called to her, but she didn't respond and instead hailed her son, Jason. The three-year-old didn't appear. Each of her cries grew more desperate until she was screaming, frantically running around the front lawn in circles. Her cries turned to sobs; tears streamed down her cheeks. From his vantage point in the sky, Punk could see the boy contentedly pushing a toy truck in the backyard. "I see him; he's okay," Punk yelled to her, but Suzanne didn't hear him.

Neighbors streamed from their homes, and as they approached Suzanne blubbered her despair. One among them pointed down the street, and Suzanne took off running. Punk was suddenly bouncing at ground level behind her. "He's not this way!" he shouted. "He's in the backyard." She kept running. Above her head a cloud of dust grew in the distance. He feared the source of the dust like a sailor fearing a hostile sail shape on the horizon. He tried to catch up to her but couldn't; in fact, the harder he tried the heavier his legs became. Then he saw the black turbans, the beards, the wild eyes. Suzanne vaporized.

In an instant Punk was awash in the wave of Taliban. He looked down and saw that a rifle had materialized in his hands. He fired dozens of bullets, but none of the enemy fell.

A menacing face beamed before him, head four times normal human size, floating like a helium balloon above the others. Punk took in the appearance: bald head, red beard, no eyebrows . . . *Slobo*.

"You embarrass me," he shouted at Punk over the caterwauling of the Taliban horde beneath him.

"I didn't say anything," Punk pleaded in return.

Silence. Punk was now in a dark room, cold and shivering violently. A column of light appeared, warm and inviting. He moved for it only to be rocked back on his heels by Slobo, who pushed his head and upper torso into the light. "You embarrass me," he said, calmly this time.

Slobo was wearing a necklace, and Punk wondered why he hadn't noticed it before. The leather strand was threaded through a medallion of some sort, and as Punk studied it more closely he realized the medallion was actually Spud's pinkie. Blood dripped from the amputated digit and streaked down Slobo's naked chest.

Punk jumped back in shock and horror, but his fear quickly turned to anger. He lunged for the necklace. There was still time. The finger could still be reattached.

But Slobo was too quick. He grabbed Punk's wrist and twisted his arm over and over like a rubber band attached to the propeller of a toy airplane. Punk watched in disbelief as his arm knotted. Then the pain hit.

Punk screamed and tried to wrench his arm free of

Slobo's grasp. Waco appeared next to him, and the two of them pulled against the Chechen in a bizarre tug-of-war. "El Cedar," Waco said. "You're okay."

Punk opened his eyes and saw both of the Green Berets standing over him. "That must've been quite a dream," Og said.

"You were jerking and wiggling like my dog does when he's chasing rabbits in his sleep," Waco said.

The rapid beating of rotor blades bounced across the plain and through the hut's open door.

"Here comes Ivan," Tim announced. Those who could pushed through the doorway to watch the helicopter's arrival. Punk moved to follow them, and as he drew his legs back to get off the floor the quadriceps muscle in each of his legs twitched in a hint of a cramp. He stifled a yelp, gingerly straightening his legs again before getting to his feet and moving through the door as if walking on glass, each step deliberate, knees unbending.

The group stood in a small circle scanning the sky for the helicopter. "There it is," Tim said, pointing just above the destroyed colossi across the steppe from them. Once the helicopter cleared the ridgeline the pilot pushed the nose over so radically Punk feared he had lost control, but the aircraft leveled at what looked to be mere inches off the ground and drove straight toward the hut. It flew directly overhead at an impressive clip, clearing them by no more than fifty feet.

"That's the security pass," Waco explained as all eyes followed the helicopter through a steep turn back toward them. "If they're going to get nailed it'll be while they're trying to land . . . or take off . . . or sometimes they get popped while they're just flying around."

Punk noted the chopper was an Mi-8, NATO code

name "Hip," a troop transport built by the former Soviet Union. For all of the threat quizzes he'd taken over the years—slide shows of different aircraft, ships, and SAM systems that he'd been made to correctly identify—he'd never imagined that the first time he'd actually see a Russian helicopter in real life would be as it flew over him while he was standing on the ground in Afghanistan. Paris air show, maybe. Afghanistan, never.

The Hip performed a series of roller-coaster turns until the final approach when it picked up a smooth and steady descent and vanished into a dust ball of rotor wash. Punk compared the landing to the image of the Chinook rolling over that was forever burned into his brain. This time the main rotor slowed, and the dust cloud soon dissipated enough that he could see the oversized tires at the end of the fixed tricycle struts sitting safely against the earth.

"That thing's seen better days," Punk said. "There's hardly any paint left. And look at the size of those dents."

"Classic Russian elegance," Tim said. "They've always been good for vodka, caviar, and helicopters."

"I don't see any insignia. What country did you get it from?"

"I'm not sure it was a *country,* per se. Let's just say we got a good deal on Ivan."

The Hip's side door flopped down and several boxes sailed from the cargo bay and thumped against the ground in small explosions of dust. Behind the boxes came what appeared to be a tightly wrapped bundle of plastic that landed with a resonant slap.

"Grab the body bags, Sergeant," Tim said to Nathan. "They're your guys; I'm afraid you get to head the detail."

"It's the least I can do for them," Sergeant Powell said. "Can I get somebody to help me, though?" He looked at Waco, who didn't respond in any way.

"I'll help you, Nate," Og said. "Let's go." He grabbed the other soldier by the arm and moved toward the Hip.

"Those Rangers are all fucking Boy Scouts," Waco said as he watched Nathan and Og walk away. "They need to take a reality pill."

Two helmeted figures in green flight suits, each carrying a large black duffel bag, approached.

"Hello, boys," Tim said as the pair came near. "What's in the bags?"

"Your future," one of them answered with a wry smile, raising his dark visor as both placed the nylon bags at Tim's feet. The crewman scanned the full length of Punk's tall frame and said, "What the hell happened to you?"

"This is the pilot we rescued," Tim explained. "He had a little run-in with some Taliban knives."

"In that case, you look wonderful," the crewman said as he reached out and shook Punk's hand. "Where are the wounded, Tim? We want to get out of here in a hurry."

"They're in the hut."

"How many are there?"

"Two."

"And how many morts?"

"Six. How many more will you be able to take on this run?"

The man looked to the sky and thought aloud: "Two . . . six . . . four aircrew . . . We won't be able to take any more, Tim. We were at max torque on the way in here as it was. We were barely able to hold our altitude around those peaks by the Shebar Pass."

"Will you be able to make another run today?"

He checked his watch. "Doubtful."

"Tomorrow morning, then?"

The crewman shrugged. "Where are these guys going anyway? Are we taking them to K-2?"

"Do you ever go anywhere but K-2?"

"No, but we could if we had to, I guess."

Tim pointed to Punk. "Okay, he needs to get back to his aircraft carrier." Then he pointed to Nathan lifting the bundle of body bags next to the Hip. "And he needs to get to Pakistan. I'm sure you could make those runs without compromising our mission here."

The two guys in flight suits exchanged shakes of their helmeted heads, and the one who'd spoken before said, "You're a funny guy, Tim. I wish I was going to be around to see what the mission folder in that bag does to that great sense of humor of yours." He cut his eyes toward Punk and back to Tim and changed the subject. "We're going to grab a couple of stretchers and get the wounded loaded."

As the pair walked back toward the helicopter Tim crouched down and pulled the zipper on one of the bags, which allowed half a dozen bundles of money to spill out. Punk picked one of the banded stacks up and studied it. One thousand dollar bills. Nonsequential. The entire duffel bag was full of them.

Punk handed the bills back to Tim, who quickly stuffed them in the bag with the others before pulling the zipper closed again. "How much is in there?" Punk asked, fully expecting that Tim would balk at an answer.

Tim held up the bag. "This is the three-million-dollar size." He hoisted both bags and headed for the hut. Punk followed, marveling at the fact that there was six million dollars in cash right in front of him.

Fuck this war shit. Why didn't they just throw the bags back onto the helo and fly somewhere and live like kings?

"What's the money for, Tim?" Punk asked from behind him.

"The same things we need money for," Tim said. "Uniforms, supplies, equipment . . . influence."

"What did that guy mean when he said your future was in those bags?"

"I guess I'll find out when I read the mission folder." Tim stopped and faced Punk. "That's beyond top secret, by the way, so no more questions right now, okay?"

"Fine," Punk said, trying his best not to seem offended. "Hopefully I won't be around long enough to worry about it anyway. While we're on that topic: I didn't hear that aircrew guy give you a straight answer when you asked about me getting out of here tomorrow. What do you think my chances are?"

"Please, no more questions right now. We've got a few things to figure out and then we can deal with your problem."

By the time they reached the hut, the two guys in flight suits were at their heels, each carrying a stretcher. Punk stepped aside and they barreled past. With stoic efficiency the two teamed up at the head and feet of the wounded and swept them from the beds to the stretchers.

"Can you two give us a hand?" one of them said to Tim and Punk.

Punk moved to the end of the stretcher by Spud's head and one of the aircrew took his feet, and they followed Tim and the other aircrew carrying the wounded soldier out of the hut and across the steppe to the helicopter. Punk focused on the skipper for most of the walk. His eyes were closed, his countenance serene. How would he make it from K-2 back to the Boat? Or would he just fly back to the States instead?

The States. An inviting notion at that moment, and Punk looked up at rusty Ivan and wondered how much damage he could inflict if he slammed the side hatch onto his fingers. They'd have to take him with them, then, wouldn't they?

"Put the stretchers down," one of the aircrew directed. "We've got them from here."

"What's your waist size?" the other one asked Punk.

"What?" Punk said.

"What's your waist size?" the crewman repeated.

"Thirty-six."

"This guy looks like about a thirty-six." He pointed at Punk. "Take off your flight suit."

"What?"

"Take off your flight suit." He motioned toward the helicopter's side hatch. "Benny, go grab a couple of blankets."

As one of them climbed into the Hip the other began removing the wounded soldier's clothing. "You're going to need these more than he does tonight," the crewman explained.

"Will you be able to keep him warm enough?" Punk asked as he started removing his boots and peeling his dirty, shredded flight suit off.

"He'll be fine. We've got blankets for the flight and then we'll hook him up with some gear on the other end."

The crewman's logic was sound, but Punk still felt a bit awkward and guilty as he peeled his dirty, shredded flight suit off and slipped the soldier's pants on.

The pants were a smidge loose in the waist and short in the leg, but they'd work. He put the desert camouflage jacket on—an inch short in the arms—and jammed his boots back onto his feet.

"You're sure he'll be warm enough?" Punk asked again.

"Like a bug in a rug," the crewman said.

"What should I do with the flight suit?"

"Burn it," the crewman said. "Oh, and take these, too." He pulled a pair of wraparound sunglasses with a neoprene strap over the wounded man's head and handed them to Punk. "It may not look like it today, but trust me, you're going to need these when the sun comes back out."

Og and Nathan returned with the last of the filled body bags and laid it next to the other five they'd lined up near the left tire. "You want us to load these?" Og asked.

"Yeah," one of the crewmen said. "Put them all the way in the back of the cargo bay."

Og and Nathan exchanged shrugs and began dutifully carrying out the final phase of their dour task.

Once the dead were loaded, the crewmen hoisted Spud into the cargo bay. Punk reached for his hand and squeezed it, and although the skipper's eyes didn't open and his expression didn't change in any way, Punk could've sworn he felt him squeeze back.

"Have a safe flight, Ralph," Tim hailed through the open window on the left side of the cockpit.

The pilot waved and replied, "Thanks, Tim-o. If the weather's as bad as it was on the way down here, we're in for a real treat."

"So, we'll see you tomorrow, then?" Punk called from across Tim's shoulder, but the pilot had already shut his window and turned his attention to his pre-start routine in the cockpit. Soon the rotors began to turn, and not long after that the Hip lifted off and, after a brief hover check, flew to the northeast, over the vandalized colossi and into the clouds.

"Ever fired an M-4 before?" Waco asked.

"Not an M-4," Punk replied. "I have fired an M-16, but it's been a few years. Why?"

"Because you and me are at the top of the batting order for guard duty tonight. Grab one of those rifles and an MRE and let's get on it."

Punk walked over to the rifles piled in the corner. "Does it matter which one I grab?"

"Well, not the one with the melted stock," Waco said. "The rest of them should all be fine."

They pushed through the door and Punk gazed up into the night, pleasantly surprised to see stars. The breeze had died; the air was still and cool. He scanned the terrain and saw he could make out some of the contours; it wasn't as dark as it had been the night before, or maybe his eyes were just working better now after a few hours of rest.

"Where are we going?" Punk asked as he fell in behind Waco.

"This little hill out that way," Waco said. "It's the highest point around here."

Punk's first steps were a bit sluggish. Although the cuts hadn't completely lost their sting and his body still ached from his fall down the mountain, the eight hundred milligrams of Motrin Og had given him seemed to be working. After walking a few yards he thought he could keep up with Waco's quick pace.

"You an outdoorsman, El Cedar?" Waco asked, deftly stepping over a calf-high rock that Punk didn't notice until he nearly kicked it.

A moment of truth. "Outdoorsman" implied many things to which Punk arguably could not lay claim. The events of his life quickly reeled through his brain, starting with a Cub Scout overnighter and ending with the time he caught a carp using a paper clip and a wad of white bread during Naval Aviation survival training when he was an ensign.

"Sure," Punk said. "I love the outdoors."

"Me too," Waco said. "That's the best part of this job. Could you imagine being in some nine-to-five bullshit buried in one of them cubicles so deep that you don't even know if the sun is shining?"

"That would suck, all right."

"Scares the shit out of me. I'll tell you that. That would be worse than getting shot at on a daily basis."

After trudging up the small hill Punk felt winded, much more so than he figured he should have been considering the short distance he and Waco had traveled. He also began to feel light-headed. It had to have something to do with the altitude, he figured, the altitude and maybe the medicine Og had given him. Those pills *were* Motrin, right?

But just as Punk was about to ask Waco to hold up, Waco leaned his M-4 against a boulder and worked the knapsack off his back. "Come on up here, El Cedar," Waco said. "You ain't gonna see no bad guys from down there."

Punk gathered himself enough to make it the last dozen yards to the top without falling over, and once up there he marveled at how high above the steppe they were for having climbed so little. Something flashed in the far distance.

"You guys must be bombing again," Waco said. "Of

course, that may not help us none, but at least we got something to hope for."

Punk scanned his immediate area and asked, "Where do you want me?"

Waco pointed to the left and right. "Our position isolates the threat to these two quadrants: here . . . and here. That's how we get away with only two guys on patrol at a time. Sit down right over there. You take the west. I'll take the east."

He reached into the sack and pulled out a pair of night-vision binoculars. "We've only got two pairs of these, so be careful. They cost about a million fucking dollars, so if they get broken the supply Nazis back at K-2 are going to be pissed."

Punk delicately took the binoculars from Waco and put them to his eyes. "They're not working."

Waco reached over and flipped a switch on the side of the glasses. "You've got to turn them on, El Cedar," he said. "I thought you pilots understood technology."

Through the lenses Punk was now greeted with a deceptively dimensionless world of greens and blacks, a land of shape without form. "What are we looking for exactly?"

"Movement," Waco said.

"Yeah, I figured that," Punk said. "But how will they come at us? Will they be in pickup trucks or on foot?"

Waco dropped the night-vision devices from his own eyes. "You know, the Taliban forgot to invite me to their last attack-planning meeting. Just look for movement."

"How will we know if they're not our guys?" Punk asked.

"Our guys are all back in the hut asleep."

"No, I mean our Afghan guys."

"They're camped behind us. That's why we're looking out this way."

"I didn't see any of the horses around the hut," Punk observed. "Did the Afghans take them back?"

"Yep. They're very protective of their horses. All we ask is that they don't steal our nice American saddles. Plus, what are we going to feed those beasts, MREs?"

Punk began scanning his half of the steppe stretching out before them. All was still except for occasional flashes on the horizon that reminded him of distant summer thunderstorms. The thought of warm American summers along with the possibility that the flashes were coming from bombs dropped by his squadronmates filled him with the loneliness he'd managed to suppress in the hours since Spud's departure.

"Did we hear if the helicopter made it back to K-2?" Punk asked.

"I didn't. You got to ask Tim."

"Do you know what time the helo's making the run tomorrow?"

"Nope."

Silence followed, and Punk suppressed his desire to chat, figuring that he was violating some sort of special operations etiquette surrounding sentry duty with his questions of Waco. He occupied his mind with the memory of his last night with Suzanne. The towel dropped and with the first touch years of theory became a passionate reality. He wondered if it had been the same for her, or if she was simply caught up in the events of the day combined with his imminent departure.

No, it must've been the same for her. It *had* to be.

Suzanne had never been impulsive. She and Crud had always been kindred spirits in that way, constantly executing the next protracted strategy to completion. Punk wondered how his own often knee-jerk modus operandi would fuse with hers over the long haul. That wasn't important now. Now it was thoughts of her shape, her smell, her taste.

But the memory was fading. Each time he'd conjured it up another detail was lost, so in the current calm of the hills and plains of north central Afghanistan he put his mind to inventing some new ones, yet unrealized circumstances and contortions that could certainly take place upon his return.

"Quiet out here," Waco muttered, importunely shattering Punk's sexual reverie.

"Uh, yeah," Punk returned in an equally quiet voice, reluctant to let go of his thoughts but happy that Waco had initiated conversation.

"You married?"

"No."

"No kids, then?"

"Nope. How about you?"

Waco puffed a barely audible laugh. "Well, I got kids, but to be perfectly honest I'm not sure I'm still married. I haven't heard from my wife since I went into isolation."

"Isolation?"

"We live and train by ourselves for a while before a mission."

"So how soon after nine-eleven did you go into isolation?"

Waco laughed again, louder this time. "I was in isolation last summer," he explained. "I was in Kazakhstan on nine-eleven."

"Damn," Punk intoned, feeling a bit guilty for his

daily e-mail exchanges and occasional phone calls with Suzanne during the last seven weeks. "Isn't there any way to check in with her?"

"No, and that's probably best. Even the new war on terror can't change the fact that she's pretty much had it with my shit by now. She's done with wondering when I'm leaving and how long I'm going to be gone." He paused for a moment. "It's kind of funny. Before I went Green Beret my buds told me the ladies went crazy for them, but I'm sure my wife would be happier if I was a vacuum cleaner salesman."

Punk thought about Jordan, his last girlfriend of any consequence, who'd taken up with an accountant in his absence. He struggled to shake off a full-blown flashback of the moment he was made aware of the fact.

"Where is your family living?" Punk asked.

"Kentucky."

"Kentucky, huh? Horse country."

"That ain't how it is around our place. We live in a typical military town, you know: strip clubs, tattoo parlors, laundromats, and Japanese steak houses. I wanted her to move near my parents in Texas, but she blew me off."

"So they're in Waco?"

"No, they live in Dallas."

"Why do they call you 'Waco,' then?"

"My first outfit already had a 'Dallas' in it when I got there, and that whole thing with that religious cult in Waco was going on in the news at the time, so there you go."

Two more flashes lit up the distance in rapid succession.

"Why do they call you 'Punk'?" Waco asked.

"During my first cruise we were sitting in the eight-man stateroom listening to some tunes, kind of loud, I guess, and the captain of the ship came in and told us to turn down the punk rock. After he left I made the mistake of telling my roommates I wasn't a punk rocker. That was all it took to be known as 'Punk' from then on."

More flashes ignited to the northeast, a flurry of them this time, like the grand finale of a fireworks show. "Somebody's getting pounded but good," Waco said.

"I wonder what they're going after," Punk said. "I can't remember what was on the target list over that way."

"Yeah, you boys love turning mud huts into rubble. A lot of good that does us."

"We've been doing a lot of close air support," Punk said defensively.

"Really? Where were they today?"

"They can't do anything about the weather."

"Could fly under it."

"That's a good way to collide with a mountain," Punk said, "or get shot down."

"Oh, we couldn't have that, could we? We can handle only one of you guys on the ground at a time."

The sound of jets roaring high overhead briefly punctuated the night around them. "There they go," Waco said. "Headed back for their T-bone steaks and a full night's sleep in a nice warm bed."

"I wish," Punk said, as he tilted his head back, searching for the sources of the noise. "More like a bowl of beans and two hours' sleep with airplanes landing on your head."

"If you say so, El Cedar. It doesn't matter, though. I could never live on a ship for weeks at a time." He spread his arms out. "I need the wide open spaces."

Punk continued to sweep the steppe with the binoculars. "Well, you've definitely got those around here."

"Oh, yeah," Waco chuckled.

"So what do you think of Afghanistan so far?"

Waco mulled the question over for a short time. "In some ways it's what I thought it would be, and in some ways it ain't," he said. "There ain't much to the landscape, but at the same time the place's got this strange magic to it. Hard to explain, really."

"What about the locals?"

"The ones we're fighting or the ones on our side?"

"The ones on our side. I've met the ones we're fighting."

Again Waco silently considered the question before offering a response. "I don't think I got an opinion yet, El Cedar. I see good in them, no doubt. At times the general strikes me as a good man, a strong man. The translator boy seems like a good kid. But God help us if the money runs out."

"What? They'll stop being good?"

"Let me just say they ain't got the religion that our president and his boys say they got. The Afghans like the new uniforms and the rifles. They like that we can conjure up jets and blow things up. Hell, who wouldn't? But you can already see in their eyes that they sense at some point we're going to run out of tricks. And after that . . ."

"Yes?"

"Well, I don't know. Hopefully, I'll be long gone by then."

"How long are you going to be over here?"

"I'm not sure. How 'bout you?"

"Well, the carrier's supposed to be home by Christmas."

"Christmas, huh? That sounds good."

"You've got to have a return date, right? Don't you have a relief somewhere?"

Waco puffed a sad laugh. "No. I just might have made myself indispensable when it comes to fighting this here war we've got going on, right down to my knowledge of using pack animals to keep the supply lines going. I updated that manual a year ago. Everybody laughed at me." In the dim light Punk saw the Texan shake his head. "It's funny, all right. Just for a different reason."

"So you came over here without any idea of when you're going back?"

Waco released a long exhale and stirred the ground with the heel of one of his boots as he sat on the dirt with his legs crossed, causing little dust explosions to form, barely visible in the night. "My great granddad was in World War II, fighting in Europe under General Patton—Battle of the Bulge, the whole deal. He told me about a saying they had: 'The way home is through Berlin.'" He placed the binoculars back against his face. "After all these years I finally know what he meant."

Captain Campbell had taken to hanging out in the *Arrowslinger* ready room in Spud's absence, much to the chagrin of Monster and the other lieutenant commanders who chose to view his presence as evidence of a fundamental mistrust in their ability to lead the squadron. For his part, Einstein had never seen Soup spend so much time among his fellow aviators, even during his time as commanding officer on the previous deployment. Then-Commander Campbell had always shown himself to be a loner of sorts, spending the bulk of his nonflying time sequestered in his stateroom.

Soup kicked his legs up on the CO's ottoman fashioned out of an empty hydraulic fluid can covered with Naugahyde and shifted the angle of the faux leather high-backed ready room chair a few more degrees aft and then half as many forward again. Once satisfied with his position, he ran his hands along the smoothness of the armrests and said, "Man, this old chair brings back some memories." Einstein didn't have the heart to tell him that the Boat had replaced all of the ready room chairs during the turnaround between cruises and that his chairful of memories was probably stacked along the wall of a dingy warehouse somewhere in a long-since ignored corner of the naval base back in Norfolk.

"You know, one of my greatest fears is that the best time of my career will ultimately prove to be the days when I was the commanding officer of this fighter squadron," the captain continued. "I'm not sure it gets any better than that."

That notion struck fear in Einstein, as well, as he would never characterize Soup's days at the helm of the *Arrowslingers* as the best of times.

Lieutenant Ronnie Wheedle, the Boat's public affairs officer, pushed his way through the front door and strode purposefully to Captain Campbell's feet. "Captain, CAG Sutcliffe directed me to you," the lanky PAO said. "He said you wanted to handle all of the press queries on behalf of the air wing."

"That's true," Soup confirmed.

"I must say that sort of surprises me, sir, you know, in light of . . ."

The captain fixed his gray eyes on the lieutenant in a manner that suggested he drop his current line of reasoning. Wheedle caught the message and got to the business at hand. "I have a couple of reporters from the embarked media pool out in the passageway," he explained. "They wanted to get a few comments on today's rescue of our downed airmen."

Airmen. That term sounded a bit archaic to Einstein, and in his mind's eye saw a sky filled with B-17s.

"What else do they want to talk about?" Soup asked, eyes narrowed.

"What else?" Wheedle returned. "Nothing else, I don't think. This rescue is big news. It's been dominating the coverage all day. You saw that Aljazeera footage, right, sir?"

"Briefly."

"Very dramatic stuff," Wheedle said. "It's been playing at the top and bottom of the hour on all the twenty-four-hour news networks all day. You know one of the Aljazeera crew was killed in the fighting."

"Breaks my heart," the captain said sardonically.

Lieutenant Wheedle gave the DCAG a derisive stare. "Come on now, Captain. Let's not make news here, all right?"

Soup waved a hand impatiently and twisted his face into a comic scowl, brow furrowed and mouth twisted. "We are deeply saddened by the loss of innocent life," he intoned before relaxing his expression. "I've got it."

"So you're willing to do the interview?" Wheedle asked.

"Why wouldn't I be?"

Wheedle shrugged noncommittally as Soup looked around him and called over to Lieutenant "Cracker" Croiquier, the squadron duty officer for the day: "When's the next brief start?"

Cracker held his copy of the flight schedule closer to his face and replied, "Twenty minutes from now, DCAG."

Soup looked back to Wheedle. "You've got twenty minutes."

Wheedle nodded and hurried back out the door. Almost immediately he reappeared with two civilians in tow: a mousy brunette woman and a man with severe bed head, little round glasses, and bad teeth. Both wore polo shirts and faded jeans.

"Who do you all work for?" the captain asked as he stood and shook hands.

"We're newspaper writers," the man said. "For wire services."

"Ah, very well," Soup replied, as if that information made some sort of difference. "Why don't we sit down in the debriefing area in the back?"

Einstein hovered behind the group as they moved toward the rear of the ready room. He took a seat a few rows in front of the rectangle of chairs that formed the debriefing area and pretended to read a magazine as he eavesdropped on the interview and furtively glanced over his shoulder to pulse the body language and expressions of those involved.

"Now, you are the what?" the woman asked.

"The *what*?" Soup asked in return. "I'm not sure what you're asking."

"What is your position on the aircraft carrier?" the man asked.

"I'm not attached to the aircraft carrier," Soup said.

The reporters exchanged furrowed brows, and Captain Campbell allowed them to stew in their confusion for a few moments before explaining, "I'm the deputy air wing commander. Technically, I'm attached to the air wing, not the ship."

"Isn't the air wing attached to the ship?" the man asked, looking away from Soup toward Lieutenant Wheedle. Wheedle shrugged, obviously uncomfortable with suddenly being in the middle of a semantics debate.

"Just to make sure," the woman said, " 'Campbell' is spelled the regular way?"

"What's the *regular* way?" Soup asked.

"It's spelled the regular way," Lieutenant Wheedle interjected. "We're a bit pressed for time here. Why don't we get to the questions?"

"Fine," the man said. "Captain, when did you first hear about the rescue?"

"Almost as soon as it happened," Soup said. "We're in very close contact with CENTCOM."

"Did you know about the plan before it happened?"

Soup glanced over at Wheedle, who simply raised his eyebrows in response.

"Some of our airplanes were going to be used for close air support during the operation," the captain said. "Unfortunately, the weather precluded their involvement. Naturally, we were part of the planning process, including coordinating the use of TLAMs."

"Where is Commander O'Reilly now?" the woman asked.

"His exact location is classified, but I can say he's safe and being cared for."

"Is it true that he lost a finger during his captivity?"

"I have heard that, but I don't know the details."

"Will he be returning to the aircraft carrier?"

"Yes, I believe so. The best surgeons in this theater are stationed aboard this ship."

"When exactly will he return?"

"As soon as it can be arranged and he's healthy enough to travel."

"Where is Lieutenant Commander Reichert?" the man asked. "And when will he be returning?"

"His location is also classified and—"

"Is he still in Afghanistan?"

"That's not really a question for Captain Campbell," Lieutenant Wheedle said from the chair between the two reporters. "Why don't you ask CENTCOM that one?"

"Fine," the man said without missing a beat or taking his eyes off of Soup. "Do you agree with some that it was foolish to use U.S. Army helicopters in this operation because of the altitude involved?"

Soup looked down at his flight suit. "I'm in the Navy. I don't pretend to be an expert regarding the Army's capabilities."

"Certainly you know something about helicopter performance," the man insisted. "After all, you are a pilot. Your air wing has helicopters."

Captain Campbell crossed his legs and threaded his fingers over his knee. "From what I saw and read I wouldn't say the issue was helicopter capability," he said. "We had two of them shot down by shoulder-fired SAMs and one crash while landing."

"Wouldn't altitude be a big factor there?" the woman asked. "I'm not a pilot, of course, but other sources have said that the lack of maneuverability in the thin air was a big contributor—"

"Or it could have been simple pilot error," Soup said.

Silence followed, and Einstein sensed that, for the briefest second, the reporters didn't know what to make of the statement, that they were distrustful of the offering laid before them. They scribbled furiously on their notepads as the DCAG qualified his intent: "I'm not saying that's what it was; I'm just saying that I'd be careful about defining some sort of inherent performance problem with those helicopters at those altitudes." He looked back to Lieutenant Wheedle. "I just want to make sure we don't send the wrong message about our ability to fight in the mountains. I'm sure I speak for all the services when I say that we'll go wherever we have to go to win the war against terror."

"Captain, you surely heard that one of the Aljazeera cameramen was killed during the rescue operation," the woman said. "Do you have any comment on that?"

Soup didn't immediately respond, but rather sat for a time, focused on a knee as he picked pieces of lint from his flight suit. He looked up and spoke directly to the woman: "I'm not telling you anything when I suggest that being a war correspondent is a dangerous business. That's part of what you sign up for, right?" Both of the reporters nodded. "But that said, I'd agree with what the Secretary of Defense said a few days ago: It's always a tragedy when noncombatants are killed; but, unfortunately, that will always be part of war."

Einstein saw the reporters lunge forward in their seats as they attempted to ask their next questions at the same time, creating a wall of unintelligible crosstalk. After a brief battle between them to seize the floor with the volume of their voices, the woman relented, silencing herself and resignedly flopping back in the chair.

"Captain, speaking about innocent casualties, what about your situation?" the man asked. "What is the status of the investigation into the amount of training you received before you arrived aboard the carrier?"

Soup flinched nearly imperceptibly to the unlearned eye but enough that a student of the man like Einstein knew that the question had taken him aback. The captain wore a placid expression, the picture of peace, and said, "It's not really an investigation; it's more like an audit. In any case, it would be improper for me to comment on the details right now. It's no big deal, really."

"Do you think you had enough training before you got here?" the woman said, quickly jumping back into the discussion.

Soup demurred: "This isn't my first deployment."

"How do you feel about the refugees in the pickup you inadvertently bombed?"

Now the DCAG's head shuddered a bit, and his cheeks flushed near crimson. Einstein willed Lieutenant Wheedle into action—why wasn't he doing anything?—but the PAO sat motionless, apparently unaware or unconcerned that Soup was about to explode. At that moment four *Arrowslingers* burst through the back door to finish the final preparations before staring their brief for their nighttime strike mission over eastern Afghanistan. All of them offered an "Evening, DCAG" as they passed on their way to the first row. Their sudden presence seemed to calm the captain, and Einstein was relieved to see his posture soften with each greeting.

Soup refocused on the reporters. "We're out of time, I'm afraid," he said, "but let me finish with this thought: We've gone to great lengths to avoid civilian casualties and collateral damage. No other nation in the history of warfare has done as much. We're fighting a *precision* war in every sense of the term. But it's still war." He rose out of his chair and started for the back door.

"So will you be allowed to fly bombing missions anytime soon, Captain?" the woman asked.

Captain Campbell stopped and turned back toward her. "Who said I wasn't allowed to fly bombing missions?"

The reporters exchanged another glance. "We heard

you weren't allowed to fly missions over Afghanistan," the man said.

Soup smiled confidently and said, "Newspaper writers should know not to believe everything they hear."

A sharp burst of static sounded the wake-up call for Punk, and in the dim light he instinctively looked at his wrist to check the time, momentarily forgetting that his expensive fighter pilot's watch now graced the wrist of some Taliban thug. Actually, that thug was probably dead and another thug had come into the possession of it, pulling the watch off the first one's arm even before his body grew cold to the touch. Punk wistfully thought about all the places he'd been while wearing that watch. Now it was out there without him, strapped to some uncivilized bastard who surely had no appreciation for the difference between a Timex and a Breitling—hell, he probably couldn't even tell time.

"Waco, are you up?" Punk said to the lump on the floor next to him.

"Sleep is for the weak," Waco slurred, obviously fresh from slumber.

"What time is it?"

An arm snaked out of the bag. "Five twenty," Waco replied.

Punk struggled to remember what time he'd crawled into the sleeping bag, but decided it didn't matter. However much sleep he'd managed, it wasn't enough. The morning air passed cold against his face and made him reluctant to relinquish the warm sanctuary he'd been temporarily afforded. His body ached again; the postrescue adrenaline had worn off.

Punk rolled over and watched Terry adjust the radio controls and put the receiver against his head. "Say again for Tiger zero-one, base," he said.

The response was garbled, but Punk thought he heard the word "sabotage," an ugly word anytime but especially so early on a morning that held such promise.

"I didn't copy, Kilo base," Terry said. "Say again, please."

"Tiger zero-one, this is Kilo base," the voice cracked through the speaker, clearly this time. "Helicopter was sabotaged last night. Ivan is down."

"Have them define 'sabotage,' " Tim said as he strode through the door with rifle in hand, fresh from his four-hour sentry shift that he'd stood with Nathan.

"Kilo base, can you give us a better idea of what you're talking about?" Terry said.

"Somebody tossed a grenade in the gear box," the voice said. "I say again: Ivan isn't flying anywhere for a while."

Tim rushed across the room and took the receiver from Terry. "Say status of next supply run?"

"Unknown."

"Can you procure another asset?"

"That's in the works, but nothing yet."

Tim dropped the receiver to his side and cursed under his breath. He stood for a time, pensively running a finger along his arched brow, and then raised the handset again. "Kilo base, understand most recent tasking is still a go?"

"Affirmative, Tiger one."

"What about the personnel we were going to ex-fill this morning?"

There was no reply. "Kilo base, do you copy the question?" Tim said.

"We copy, Tiger one. Incorporate them until other assets are made available. Are the ex-fills nearby?"

"That's affirmative."

"We've got somebody here who wants to pass a message to one of them."

There was a short pause and then a familiar voice came over the speaker: "Punk, this is Spud."

Punk rolled out of the sleeping bag and hustled to the console. "How are you feeling?"

"I'm going to make it. Keep your eyes open for my pinkie while you're waiting for us to get you out of there."

"I will," Punk said with a chuckle. "Are you headed Stateside?"

"I hope not," Spud said. "I'm trying to get back to the Boat."

"Did you ever think you'd hear yourself say that?"

"I swore I'd quit before I ever said that," Spud chuckled back.

There was a bit of dead air as the aviators simultaneously sensed that the CIA's SATCOM frequency was the wrong place for light banter between squadronmates.

"Keep your head down, buddy," Spud said. "We'll get you out of there as soon as we can."

"Okay, skipper." In spite of his desire to be optimistic, Punk couldn't mute the doubt in his voice.

After another short pause the first voice came back over the net: "Kilo base, out."

Punk wasn't sure how to respond so he simply gave the handset back to Terry, who, in turn, clipped it to the side of the console. Waco looked over at Punk with a wry grin and said, "Welcome to the other side of the war, El Cedar."

CHAPTER NINE

"I really didn't need to baby-sit in the middle of everything else," Tim said, pacing in front of the hut like a caged wolf, kicking up a small dust cloud with each step. "This is enough of a balancing act as it is."

"Give El Cedar a break, just Tim," the Green Beret said, seated among the rest of them, enjoying the light if not the warmth of the midmorning sun as it climbed into a clear blue sky. "Nobody meant for things to happen this way, but here we be."

"Here we be, huh? You know, Waco, sometimes you're so cute I'm torn between whether to give you a big kiss or a punch in the nose." The older man's response surprised Punk as he hadn't seen Tim come anywhere close to losing his temper over the last two days. The latest wrinkle had obviously pushed him near his breaking point.

Waco stood and slapped the dirt from the seat of his pants. "Well, I don't know about the first part—must be a CIA thing—but I'm obliged by law to warn you off trying the second thing. After that, if you want to get your ass kicked it's up to you."

After several tense seconds the CIA man took a few steps away and said, "Look, Waco, I apologize, okay? Lots going on, you know?"

"So what's the plan?" Punk asked once sure the tension had passed.

Tim shrugged and said, "You heard for yourself what happened to Ivan, and I just read in an e-mail that CENTCOM has a moratorium on helicopter ops up here for the time being." He cast an index finger across each of those stranded in their midst. "Our orders are to incorporate you and you and *him*." Tim let out a laugh as he gestured toward Boodle, who Nathan had seated against the wall, a very lifelike mannequin. "What are we supposed to do with him?"

"He'll be fine," Nathan said defensively. "He'll snap out of it anytime now, I'm sure."

"What about you?" Tim asked. "Are you ready for this?"

"Rangers are always ready," Nathan said, preemptively shooting Waco an angry glance as if he expected some sort of jab at his sentiment. Waco just gave him a sly smile.

Tim cut his eyes back to Punk. "What about you, Sky King? Are you ready?"

"For what?" Punk asked back.

"For this."

"What the hell is *this*?" Punk snapped. "I'm still not clear on what the deal is with all this about 'incorporate' and whatever."

"Look, we didn't shoot you down, Commander," Tim returned with a camp counselor's pedagogy. "And we wouldn't keep you here if we didn't have to. But we don't have a choice right now. So, I'll ask you again: Are you ready for this?"

Punk looked over to Boodle. "I'm as ready as he is, I guess."

"This isn't a joke," Tim said. "We're in the middle of a serious situation here, and it's only going to get worse in the next few days."

"Then I'm not ready," Punk said.

"Wrong answer," Tim replied.

Punk silently stared at him through his hand-me-down sunglasses, a silhouette with the bright morning sun cresting in the background.

"What training do you have?" Tim prodded, eyebrows raised above his own shades. "A few days of survival school?"

"Look, Tim," Punk said. "I'm not going to sit here and measure dicks with you, okay? If you can't get me out of this fucking country then that's your problem, not mine."

"My problem, huh? I still don't think you get it." Tim swept his arm across the group. "This is it, right here. This is all the manpower the United States of America is throwing at this problem. There's the four of us, and the two and a half of you. Now I've been to Ranger school, so I know what Nate can do, but I've never been to Navy flight school, so you're going to have to tell me what your skill set is. Have you ever fired a rifle?"

"Yes," Punk replied.

"When?"

"I fired an AK-47 yesterday. Killed two Taliban with it."

Tim's expression softened. "Okay, that's a good start. How about an M-4?"

"No, not an M-4. I did fire an M-16 when I was at the Academy."

"Ever cleaned one?"

"Yeah, the Marines during summer training at Quantico were real pains in the ass about it. It's been a few years, though."

Tim pointed to the weapon Punk had pulled from the pile the evening before. "That's yours. Take care of it. If you can't remember how, Waco will help you." Waco raised his sunglasses and gave Punk a wink.

Tim waved Nathan closer and then spread a chart on the dusty ground at his feet. "All right, men, you're about to be incorporated. The following information is top secret. You got it?" The CIA man made eye contact with both Punk and Nathan, and both nodded in return.

"General Haskarim is moving up the Northern Alliance hit parade," Tim said. "Of those in the mix, intelligence sources give him the best chance of success for this move we're going to make." He ran a finger along the chart. "With our assistance, the general is taking his Uzbek fighters and heading west from here, through the Nil Pass to Nayak. From there we'll leave the road and follow this valley here until we pick up the Harirud River. You see a couple of airfields along the way. We'll be surveying those."

"Surveying?" Punk asked.

Tim raised his face up to Punk. "Yeah. If they're in decent shape we may be able to get a transport in . . . and get you out."

"How far is it to there?" Punk asked.

Tim took a reading with his thumb and forefinger and then placed his rigid hand over the scale at the bottom of the chart. "About eighty miles or so."

"So how long will that take?"

"How much fighting will we have to do between here and there?" Tim asked in return before looking back down at the chart. "We'll pick up the road again in Chaghcharan and stick with it all the way into our ultimate objective: Herat."

"Herat," Punk echoed.

"Yes. Herat."

"What is that, like, seven hundred miles away?"

"No, more like three hundred and fifty."

Punk drew his mouth taut and shook his head. "Three hundred and fifty miles . . ."

"That brings up another good question, just Tim," Waco said, turning to face Punk. "El Cedar, have you ever rode a horse before?"

By its external appearance in the dim light just past sunset, General Abdul Haskarim's safe house wasn't any more impressive than the hut in which the Americans were currently quartered; it was larger, certainly, but had no more curb appeal than any of the rock formations they'd passed during their one-mile hike to the place. In spite of that the interior of the house turned out to be a pleasant surprise.

Escorted by two of the general's men that they'd met along the way, Tim, Waco, and Punk entered, greeted by delightful scents—curry and jasmine and other things Punk couldn't label but that pleased him no less, the most appealing smells to pass through his nostrils in days. The entryway was tiled with what looked to be marble that butted against the finished wood planking of the next room, which was furnished with thick area rugs and gigantic pillows the size of beanbag chairs that ringed a half circle around a decent-sized TV, not wide-screen but not portable, ei-

ther. Lanterns and candles perched in ornate holders
bathed the scene in a series of flickering orange glows.
The small flames dotted the walls between framed
prints of what Punk figured were heroes or deities he
felt woefully ignorant of.

The Americans followed their escorts toward the
dining room as Punk continued to marvel at the ap-
pointments. He would've never thought this sort of
luxury present or even possible in the wilds of central
Afghanistan, and he wondered if the dwelling wasn't
the general's permanent residence rather than some
flophouse he'd been provided or even seized along
his route.

General Abdul Haskarim didn't look like a warlord,
at least not like the image Punk had previously conjured up in his mind when he'd heard the word. There
was nothing menacing about the general, nothing that
suggested iron-fisted demands on those around him.
He sat at the head of the plain wooden banquet table
dressed in a collarless white dress shirt with a brown
woolen shawl draped over his shoulders. He wore his
black hair short and trimmed his gray-flecked beard
closely along the lines of his square jaw. His eyes were
dark and expressive.

The general presided over the proceedings with
calm confidence, listening more than talking as the
food was passed and the conversations in Dari and
English intertwined. Beyond his placid demeanor he
was obviously pleased with the news that the plan now
had him leading the push into Herat; he was further
pleased with the twenty thousand dollars in cash Tim
had handed him over the first course of the meal.

To either side of him sat the pair who'd descended
on the Americans' safe house the day before: the corpulent chief of security and the boy translator—Urat

and Mushkai, respectively. Next to Urat sat Waco, who was, following the guidance he'd offered Punk during the mile hike, at once enthusiastically and selectively picking at the spread, doing his best not to offend while guarding against gastrointestinal distress.

Punk did the same but found himself increasingly less selective as the meal went on. Offerings that would've made his stomach turn with their mere mention a few weeks prior, now danced on his tongue, meats and cheeses from animals not known in America for other than their presence in petting zoos. Plus, the food was warm, an element Punk had already found lacking in MREs. And he washed it all down with a rich tea that flowed from a host of bottomless pitchers around the table.

"El Cedar," Waco said, "we got to get you something else to wear now that you're part of our little team here." He looked over to Mushkai. "Can we get our pilot friend a coat and a hat so that he blends in a little better? He's going to be standing next to me a lot, and I don't want any more fire coming in my direction than otherwise might."

Mushkai barked an order at one of the men lining the wall behind those seated around the table. The man ushered Punk out of his chair and spread his arms for him. After a cursory check of several lengths and circumferences, the man rushed out of the room. Punk stood a bit confused until Mushkai motioned for him to retake his seat.

From the place next to Mushkai, Tim tried to speak to the general in his native tongue but wound up mostly talking to Mushkai instead. Punk wasn't sure how much English the general knew, but he noticed the warlord often began speaking before the boy was finished translating.

"Chetor ziad mard?" Tim asked, again attempting Dari.

General Haskarim winced in confusion and looked at Mushkai, who, in turn, winced and looked back at Tim. "What are you asking?" Mushkai said.

"I wanted to know how many men you were bringing with you," Tim explained a bit sheepishly.

The boy turned back to the general and rephrased the question in proper Dari. The general looked at the CIA man and said, *"Hasht sad."*

"Eight hundred," Mushkai translated.

Waco and Tim momentarily locked eyes, and Punk studied their expressions, wondering whether eight hundred was too many or too few. Neither American allowed much in the way of a reaction.

"Will they be ready to move first thing tomorrow?" Waco asked.

"Bale," the general responded without waiting for Mushkai to finish the translation.

"Yes," the boy said. "They will be ready. Most of the Army is already waiting for us to the west."

"We'll need two of your best men to join us in the scouting party," Tim said, to which the general again replied *bale* without waiting for the translation. Haskarim looked over his right shoulder and coolly aimed a finger at two of his men against the near wall. Both subtly nodded in return.

"And we'll need horses for Nate and El Cedar," Waco said.

"How experienced are the riders?" Mushkai asked.

"You didn't answer me last time, El Cedar," Waco said just before he took another small bite of roasted goat. "Ever rode before?"

Punk's mind flashed with a lifetime of equine memories, which in his case didn't add up to much. He'd feared the animals as a child, something his father, a career Marine, had never let him forget. As a third-year midshipman at the Naval Academy he'd briefly dated a girl whose family owned a farm in the country south of Annapolis and faced his fears on her behalf, cleaning the stalls and occasionally exercising an old mare named Slowpoke.

"I've done some," Punk allowed.

"And the other?" Mushkai asked.

"He's back at our camp," Waco explained. "I'm pretty sure he's rode before."

"How do you know that?" Punk asked.

"He's a Ranger, ain't he? Mr. Can Do?"

"What's that got to do with it?"

Waco was momentarily nonplussed. "Look, El Cedar, if he don't know how to ride he's going to have to learn quick. Otherwise he ain't going to be able to keep up."

"So the general's entire Army is going to be on horseback?"

"No, but *we* will be. Mushkai, two more horses, please."

"Khub," Mushkai said. "We will bring them to you."

The man who'd performed the quick bit of haberdashery on Punk came back into the room holding a bundle of clothing. He whispered something to General Haskarim and placed the clothing in his lap. The general stood and the others around the table followed his lead. He moved over to Punk and placed a woolen coat across his shoulders and then plopped a *pakol* on his head. *"Shoma pushidan garm va solh,"* he said.

"May this clothing bring you warmth and peace," Mushkai translated.

"Garm va solh," the other Afghans in the room echoed in a way that sounded like a toast.

The general sat back down at the head of the table and motioned for the others to take their seats as well. He waited for the group to settle itself, passing his eyes across each of them with an expression that was devoid of intent or meaning. Then he began to speak, and although Punk didn't understand the language, he found the general's tone and meter calming. He spoke for a relatively long time before pausing to allow Mushkai to translate, and Punk was surprised the boy could remember everything that had been said.

"It is poetic that I have been tasked with liberating the city of Herat from the oppression of the Taliban," Mushkai translated. "Herat is my home, and I welcome this gift from God that is the opportunity to return to this place, still wondrous and worthy of love despite its scars. I am happy to have America's help." Punk noticed the general's eyes walk to Tim with that line. "I am thankful for the money donated to our cause. I assure you it will be used toward our swift and ultimate victory. My men need uniforms, equipment, and food. We can obtain all of those things now."

Mushkai looked back to General Haskarim. After another extended soliloquy, this one containing what sounded to Punk's ear as at least one use of the word "pilot," the warlord stopped and the boy picked up the translation without delay.

"I appreciate the skills you bring," Mushkai continued as the general shifted his eyes to Punk, "especially those of your pilots, who can drop bombs exactly where we need them. But I must tell you from the outset of this campaign a few things that I am feeling. I have heard Mr. Tim speak of honesty between us, and I think that is important. So I will tell you that I am not new to war. War has been part of my life since my youth. I am also not new to other nations coming into Afghanistan under the cover of military and humanitarian assistance."

Mushkai stopped; the general spoke for another while, then stopped, and the boy picked it up again: "The Soviets built an air base to the south in 1979 and settled in Herat in large numbers. Many of them brought their families to live with us. Their desire for this was no surprise to us; for centuries Herat had been a cultural center, home to artists and poets. We welcomed the Russians as we have welcomed you. For a time there was harmony. But they abused our courtesy. They showed no respect for Afghanistan. They profaned the Prophet with their actions. The people took it until they could stand no more, and then they rose up. They killed many Russians and some families, which was regrettable, but you must understand their anger." General Haskarim bounced an index finger between Waco and Tim and offered his remarks in a more forceful tone, and this time the boy rendered the translation without waiting for the general to finish speaking: "You should not ignore that anger."

Punk watched the general's eyes grow distant and unfocused as he shifted his gaze to the center of the long table. He had gotten himself fired up, and now spoke in shorter bursts before gesturing subtly toward the boy. "The Soviets responded by bombing the glorious city for days, until it was nothing but fire, and then sent hundreds of tanks to kill any who might have survived. Greater than twenty thousand Heratis perished before the destruction was complete."

Another burst of Dari from Haskarim, this one delivered with a toss of his hands, followed by the translation: "Where was the international outcry?" Mushkai said. "Where was the condemnation?"

"With all due respect, General," Tim said, "we were here. I know *I* was here."

Mushkai seemed a bit surprised that the American had offered a retort of sorts but dutifully delivered the Dari version of Tim's remarks to his boss. The general listened to half of it and started speaking before the boy was through.

"But you didn't stay," Mushkai said, head twisting back and forth like a fan at a tennis match. "Why not?"

Tim briefly stared at a flickering candle against the far wall and then said, "Our war ended when yours did."

Following Mushkai's translation the general's eyes widened and he spoke with great animation, as if lighting on Tim's point. "Our war never ended, and therefore neither did yours," Mushkai said. "You left. For a decade you ignored Afghanistan. Now three thousand Americans have died and that has brought you back. But three thousand dead Afghans will not keep you here."

Punk saw General Haskarim nodding as his chest heaved in a long exhale. "And so it goes," the general said nearly under his breath in perfect English. In the time it took for the Americans to exchange furtive glances of disbelief Haskarim rose from his place and offered a kind smile. *"Shab bakhayr."*

"Shab bakhayr," the boy repeated, following the general to his feet. "Good night."

The sky had a brown tint along the horizon that gave way to a clear blue overhead. The wind was still, which kept it from being uncomfortably cold, but Punk was still miserable.

"This saddle sucks," he said loud enough to be heard over the clopping of hooves around him as he shifted his weight from one ass cheek to the other. "Who the hell ever heard of a wooden saddle?"

"Standard issue," Waco called back from atop the horse a few strides in front of Punk. "The locals been using them for centuries."

"Oh yeah? I noticed you and Tim and Og have nice leather ones."

Waco torqued around in the saddle and from behind his wraparounds gave Punk one of his big smiles: "We're not locals."

"I'm not a local either," Punk said. "Neither is Nathan."

"You're also probably not going to be with us long enough to warrant having a Western saddle dropped in for you."

"Why don't you have a couple dropped in and then you can give them to the locals when Nathan and I leave?"

"Oh, no. That would never work. Who would we give them to?"

"I guess you'd start by giving one to the general."

"No, because then we'd run into another general somewhere and he'd wonder why we gave Haskarim a saddle and not him and pretty soon we'd be supplying the entire Northern Alliance with these nice Western saddles—made in Texas, I might add."

"So, supply the entire Northern Alliance, then," Punk said. "What's the big deal about that? Tim just handed the general twenty thousand dollars last night. Why don't we just get a couple of hundred saddles over here?"

"They've got the money," Waco said. "They can do

whatever they want with it. I doubt they'll be buying saddles."

"They'd better not be buying saddles," Tim said from behind Punk. "Wooden or not, they've got saddles. They'd better be buying uniforms and rifles and boots."

"And trucks," Waco called over Punk's head.

"And trucks," Tim agreed. "You can never have enough trucks over here. Anyway, the general's a smart man. He'll spend the money wisely."

"How do you know?" Punk asked over his shoulder.

"Because he has to," Tim replied.

"Why wouldn't he just take it and run?"

"He knows we'd find him. Besides where would he go?"

"Hell, anywhere; a tropical island somewhere."

"I don't think Haskarim is the tropical island type," Waco said. "And he's got only twenty thousand dollars. That wouldn't get him all that far."

"It's enough to get a pretty good start."

"This may be hard for most Americans to understand," Tim said authoritatively. "General Haskarim doesn't care much about material things."

"What does he care about, then?" Punk asked.

"The general's only interest is to get back to Herat and establish himself as the provincial chief."

"And that's better than living in peace on a tropical island?"

"Power will beat affluence every time in this part of the world."

"And if he's a good boy we might just let the general be powerful," Waco said. "Right, just Tim?"

"That call's above my pay grade," Tim replied.

"No, it ain't," Waco said. "That's the beauty of being us right now."

"Well, as long as I've got this laptop and Terry's got the communications set, somebody else is making those decisions."

"Those are your bosses, just Tim, not mine."

"You might be a Green Beret, Waco, but you're TACCON to us right now," Tim explained. "They're your bosses, too."

"Maybe you should stay off the air for a while, then. Take control of this situation at your level."

"What call are you talking about, Tim?" Punk asked. "Is there some doubt about the end state of this mission?"

Tim surged silently along for a few strides, so long that Punk twisted around in the saddle to see if he'd heard the question. Tim pulled his sunglasses off and fished for a cleaning cloth in one of his vest's many pockets. "Let's just say the situation is fluid," he said while removing the light coating of dust from the glasses. "Tiger zero-one is just one of the missions in play over here. We're Herat bound. We've got others headed for Mazar-e-Sharif, Khost, and Kabul, of course."

"Kabul!" Waco exclaimed. "That's Johnny Mac's boys, nothing but Green Berets on that crew. And Masir is where Major Banko is—never been a big fan of his, though. I mean, he's a good man and all, but he's sort of uptight all the time."

"They're all TACCON to us," Tim said.

"Who's 'us'?" Punk asked. "CIA?"

"Not exactly," Tim replied.

"Then who is it?"

Tim slipped his wraparound sunglasses back on and peered into the lightening sky above the cliffs to the north of the road they were traveling. After a few silent seconds Punk figured no answer would be forthcoming. The pilot was thirsty for information and eager to keep the conversation going, so he changed the subject: "I thought it was pretty gutsy last night when you argued with the general, Tim."

"Argued?" Tim said. "When did I argue?"

"When you told him that our war ended when theirs ended."

"And what was wrong with that?"

Punk shrugged as he urged his horse back to the right side of the dusty road and said, "Nothing, I guess."

"The guy's not an idiot, Punk. And if we kiss his butt too much, he's going to run over us. That little exchange was my way of pushing back a bit, letting him know that he owes us the same respect we're giving him. It wasn't an argument."

"Argument or not," Waco said, "I got a feeling the general speaks plenty good English when he wants to."

All mumbled in agreement and with that the conversation died. Punk turned his thoughts to his own condition. How long had it been now since he'd bathed, four days? He lifted his *pakol* and ran his fingers through his increasingly greasy hair and then scratched at his increasingly itchy beard. He was sure he stunk, although his nose had grown so accustomed to his odor that he wasn't offensive to himself. And his standard for uninterrupted, never mind restful, sleep had rapidly decreased since he'd knocked himself out of the sky, but even by that low standard he had been deficit the night before. He was tired and light-headed and noted that the altitude would be steadily decreasing in the mean as they worked their way west. Perhaps they'd be able to get him out at the first airfield along the route.

Waco suddenly whipped around, face gripped with pain, and barked, "Come here and take the reins." Punk gave his horse a single kick, moved abreast of the Green Beret, and took the leather strands from him; as soon as he did, Waco slid out of the saddle. Clutching at his stomach, he waddled into a large crack between two formations of rock. Seconds later the nature of his distress was known to all within earshot.

"Revenge of the muj, huh, Waco?" Tim cried toward the rock, throwing his head back in a hearty laugh. "I told you to go easy on that chow last night."

"It's not fucking funny," a feeble voice called from the darkness. "This is a darn good way to get dehydrated, you know."

A few minutes later Waco stumbled back into the daylight, looking a bit peaked but putting on a resilient face, obviously trying to keep from giving Tim any more ball-busting fodder. He dug into a saddlebag on the left side of his horse and removed his fanny pack full of field remedies. After washing down a single small white pill with a gulp of water from his canteen, he put everything back in the saddlebag, retrieved the reins from Punk, and climbed back on the horse.

"Am I the only guy with this particular postfeast affliction?" Waco asked as they resumed their steady pace down the road.

"After that Taliban meal I must be immune now," Punk said, emotionally buoyed by the idea of it.

"I didn't eat anything," Tim explained.

"What do you mean you didn't eat anything?"

Waco asked incredulously. "I watched you stuff your face all night."

Tim grew a closed-lip smile and then offered, "It's an old secret they teach us at the Farm. How not to eat while you look like you're eating."

"Cute," Waco said. "Very cute."

"If it's anything like what I had, Waco, it passes pretty quick," Punk offered. "Try eating an MRE. That seemed to help me, too."

"An MRE, huh?" Waco said. "That's probably a good idea. A little solid American food will get me right."

"We're not stopping yet," Tim said. "Whatever you eat you're going to have to eat it in the saddle."

"That's fine," Waco said as he twisted around and reached into the right saddlebag. He immediately set about consuming the contents of an olive green pouch with a plastic spoon while keeping the reins threaded through his fingers. He finished in short order and then returned the empty pouch and the spoon to the saddlebag.

"Feel better?" Punk asked.

Waco patted his stomach and smiled but then as soon as he did the smile turned into a wince.

"Oh, Christ, not again," Waco groaned. "Take the reins, quick."

As the Green Beret disappeared behind another boulder, a cloud of dust grew along the road to the west of them. Tim raised his sunglasses and put his binoculars to his eyes, making sure it was the party he was expecting.

"You'd better hurry up, Waco," Tim called over to the rock. "The list of guys ready to give you grief is about to grow a bit."

Three figures on horseback were headed toward
them at full gallop, and soon Punk could make out
Mushkai, Nathan, and Og prodding their chargers
along like jockeys headed down the final stretch of
the derby. They came in a wall until Og slowed his
horse to a canter a hundred yards away while Mushkai
and Nathan continued barreling toward the others.
Several dozen feet away they simultaneously yanked
hard on the reins and brought their mounts to skid-
ding stops, throwing up a cloud of dust that enveloped
the rest of the party.

As he squinted against the dust, Punk marveled at
the boy's ability to control the large animal. The horse
spiritedly threw its head about, fighting the young
rider, but Mushkai didn't flinch. He deftly transmitted
his demands with coordinated movements of hands
and feet, although his legs were too short to reach the
loops of the stirrups. For his own part, Nathan showed
an impressive saddle-borne prowess as well, obviously
having spent time in the company of horses.

"We got movement on the other side of the pass,"
Nathan announced. Punk saw a newfound confidence
in the Ranger's eyes, as if he'd come to terms with
his new mission and was satisfied, even happy with it.
Punk envied him.

"How many?" Tim asked.

"It's a good-sized group," Og said as he pulled up
next to Mushkai. "I'd estimate three dozen or more,
at least."

"Any sight lines?" Tim asked.

"Yeah. There's a decent overlook north of the
road."

"I will show it to you," Mushkai said.

Nathan noticed Punk was holding an extra horse
and asked, "Where did Waco go?" Punk pointed over

toward the boulder, and after a moment's confusion the Ranger let out a belly laugh and said, "And he was giving me a hard time because I had to stay back last night and help Terry guard the gear."

Waco ambled into sight, adjusting the bottom of his pullover and pretending that all was well. Punk cut his eyes toward Nathan, who looked ready to pounce but surprisingly said nothing more. Waco took another draw on his canteen and unceremoniously climbed back in the saddle.

Up to that point he'd only walked his horse, and Punk felt a bolt of apprehension when Mushkai, Og, and Nathan took off in a gallop. Unsure what exactly to do, Punk laid two kicks into the horse's side and cried, "Yah, Bushwhacker, yah!" To his surprise and relief the horse began to move, just a trot at first but soon fast enough to keep pace with the others in front of him.

Punk had followed the lead of the other Americans who had taken to calling their horses Americanized versions of their Afghan names. Waco had explained that they didn't want to offend their hosts but needed some way to remember the unfamiliar horse names. For instance, Mushkai introduced Punk's horse to him as "Buzkashi," but after the third time he was forced to ask the boy his horse's name, Waco, who'd weeks before summarily changed his steed's name from "Rashka" to "Racecar," christened the horse "Bushwhacker."

They rode along at a breakneck pace, and Punk held the reins with a white-knuckled grip while shoving his feet hard into the stirrups. The pounding against the rudimentary saddle further inflamed his crotch, butt, and inner thighs, but at the same time he was taken with the exhilaration of it all. He tugged the *pakol* tight against his head and leaned into the breeze with his rifle slung around his neck and an irrepressible grin on his face, emboldened with each stride that didn't throw him to the ground.

The lead rider, Mushkai, veered off the road and led the team partway up a shallow embankment. The young Afghan dismounted and silently signaled the others to do the same. Once they were all close enough he spoke to them in conversational tones.

"The overlook is up that way," Mushkai said, gesturing up the narrow path that disappeared around the bend several hundred yards away. He looked to Punk and said, "You must stay behind to hold the horses."

Before Punk could begin to protest, he had six sets of reins threaded through both hands, looking a bit like a balloon vendor at a carnival. He watched the others run up the path until they disappeared, and then he stood alone with the horses, wondering if the fact that the boy immediately handed the reins to him was some sort of high-plains affront to his manhood.

What did you do in the war, Daddy?

Well, son, I was the guy who stayed behind and held the horses . . .

The horses ringed him now, and Punk divided his time between them, giving each a firm series of pats on the side of the neck or a nice stroking along the flat of the muzzle. He considered their size, shape, and where they were in the world and guessed they were all Arabians. Mushkai's horse, Sor'at, was jet-black and nothing but sinew, muscle, and bone, with a pure white blaze on his nose. Racecar was next around the circle, chestnut colored with a mostly white head and ribs springing a bit too far out, giving him a look while still that belied the name Waco had awarded him. Then came Og's horse, Ankle Biter (from his Afghan name "Ankabutai"), dappled gray, a bit smaller than the others and appearing even more so whenever Og was on his back. Tim's horse, Whose Boy, was named after the Pakistani border town of Vus-e Bai. Whose Boy was solid tan in color and looked as powerful as Sor'at, though, by Punk's Academy girlfriend–schooled eye, a hand shorter at the shoulder.

Nathan thought the drill of changing the horses' names silly and rather unprofessional, so he called his white horse with the longest mane and nattiest tail by the same name used by the locals: Abrishom. Completing the circle was Bushwhacker, blacker in color and calmer in disposition than the rest, which didn't trouble Punk as long as the horse kept up when he needed to.

Bushwhacker consistently hung his head lower than the others, either out of deference to the rest of the herd or hunger. Punk gave the reins a tug and Bushwhacker raised his head, and for a moment man and beast stood eye to eye. The man thought he saw something in the horse's expression: loyalty? trust? Had there been things communicated through the reins and saddle that had warmed animal to rider?

Suddenly the crack of a rifle echoed off the walls of stone, causing all six horses to simultaneously rear their heads back, jerking the reins from Punk's hand. For an instant the horses stood in place with their reins dangling, and as Punk reached out to grab them a fusillade erupted from around the bend. With that the horses bolted, rushing down the path and back along the road in the direction from which they'd come.

"Come back, Bushwhacker!" Punk cried as he began sprinting after the herd as if he had some chance of running them down. "Bushwhacker! Come here!" He tried calling to the others among them: "Racecar, come! Here, Whose Boy, here! Ankle Biter . . ." His voice trailed off as the horses disappeared from view, and after a dozen more desperate strides he stood in the middle of the rough road, looking eastward as if there was some hope that the horses might return once they realized they'd left without their riders.

The shots intensified for a time and then ceased before the other five in the scouting party reappeared from around the bend above Punk, running for all they were worth.

"Where are the horses?" Tim shouted, legs kicking like a halfback's, holding his rifle still with one arm while pumping furiously with the other.

"They ran off," Punk called back matter-of-factly, adding an air of incredulity, albeit feigned, to his voice, as if he couldn't believe how impolite the animals were.

"Ran off?" Nathan said. "How the hell did they run off?"

"The shots scared them," Punk said as the five passed in a hurry. "What were you guys shooting at?"

"What do you think?" Waco called over his shoulder. "Not friends, I'll tell you that."

"Taliban?" Punk asked as he picked up into a sprint, joining the others as they continued down the road.

"Tim, you got your phone on you?" Waco asked.

"It's in the saddlebag," the CIA man replied without any attempt to mute his disgust. "Yours?"

"Same."

"Why don't you guys keep those with you?" Nathan asked. "Carry them in your pockets or something."

"That's a great idea, Nate," Waco said sardonically. "If I ever find my horse again, I might just do that."

"I can't believe he let the horses get away," Nathan said to no one in particular before focusing on Punk again. "How did you let them get away?"

"Suck it up and keep running, Ranger," Waco said. "No time for whining right now."

"Mushkai, how far behind us was the general last time you checked?" Tim asked.

"I think about three kilometers," the boy replied between growing huffs of air.

"Well, we just earned ourselves a little exercise, gents."

Nathan let out a sharp snort and shot Punk another comment over his right shoulder: "Good work, El Cedar. I want to thank you for this."

"The shots scared them," Punk offered, sounding as lame to himself as he was sure he did to the others.

After five minutes sprinting and another five jogging, the group slowed to a brisk walk. "Spread out and keep moving," Tim ordered. "Let's split the road; three on each side. We'll walk for a bit and then pick up double time again once everybody has had a chance to get his breath."

Waco led Og and Punk along the right side of the road while Tim led Mushkai and Nathan down the other. Punk was feeling the effects of the altitude; in spite of the rest plan, he couldn't seem to catch his breath. And his saddle-damaged ass made it painful to walk. He wheezed along, a bit embarrassed that he was sucking eggs while Tim, the graybeard senior, was stepping out just fine. More than once Punk made the mistake of looking over at Nathan, and each time the soldier returned a derisive expression from behind his wraparounds and shook his head as if he'd never seen anything as pathetic as the downed pilot.

As Punk blankly stared at Og's back twenty paces in front of him he started to feel sorry for himself. He couldn't help it that the horses had run away. It wasn't like he'd wanted that to happen. Why had Mushkai given him six horses to hold in the first place? Why couldn't he have stayed back and shared the load? There'd been no need for an interpreter at the overlook.

"All right, let's get ready to step it out again," Tim said. "I'm sure the general's only another mile or so up the road."

"Hold on, just Tim," Og said. "Let me grab a sip of water first."

Water. That sounded good. But Punk's canteen was strapped to Bushwhacker's back and was currently wandering around Afghanistan without him, just like his Breitling watch was. He admired the Green Beret as he took a slug and then another.

"Og, can I get a hit from you real quick?" Punk asked, yielding to the impulse. "I promise I'll pay you back once I get my canteen back."

"Sure, El Cedar," Og said as he turned toward Punk with his teeth shining through his black beard. "*If* you ever get your canteen back." He took a step to close the distance between them and when his foot hit the dirt two distinct metallic clicks pierced the air. Og barely had time to say, "Ah, shit," before the earth exploded underneath him.

Punk was blown off his feet and onto his back. His ears rang as the boom echoed off the rock and flecks of dirt landed on his face. For a time he lay there dazed, blankly staring into the clear blue sky, systematically taking stock of his condition and wondering what exactly had just happened.

"Og stepped on a fucking land mine," Waco shouted.

"Everybody stay put," Tim ordered. "Og, can you hear me?"

There was no reply.

"Punk, are you okay?"

Punk sat up slightly, leaned against his elbows, and said, "I don't know," with a quavering voice.

"If you're okay, take a look at Og. You're closest to him. Step lightly along the way."

Punk slowly got to his feet and inspected himself. No bloodstains. Everything seemed to be in place. He put his sunglasses back on from where they'd been slung by the cord around his neck. He took a handful of paces, each more ginger than the one before, and as he leaned over Og's motionless body he could see the Green Beret's left foot was missing and he was bleeding profusely from the stump at the ankle. The sight was grisly and disturbing, more so even than Spud's hacked-up hand had been, and Punk fought to keep a clear head.

Punk probed Og's neck for a pulse and reported, "He's alive."

"How bad is he hurt?" Waco asked.

Punk took several deep breaths before answering: "His left foot is gone. He's losing a lot of blood. I need a belt or something to make a tourniquet with."

"Og's the medic. Check his fanny pack."

"It figures the damn medic would be the one to get smoked," Nathan said.

"He ain't smoked, goddam it," Waco said, aiming a finger at the Ranger.

"There's nothing in the pack to use for a tourniquet," Punk said, frustration evident in his voice. "It's just got pills and syringes and shit in it."

Waco started for his downed comrade. "I've got something that'll work," he said, untying the tribal kerchief around his neck.

"Watch your step!" Tim said.

"I'm all right," Waco responded, cutting an irritated glance toward the CIA man. "I ain't going to just sit there and watch the man bleed to death, I'll tell you that."

Waco wrapped the kerchief around Og's ankle and then pulled his knife from the sheath at his waist and twisted it into the cloth until it was tight enough to stop the flow of blood from the wound. The Texan was double-checking his handiwork when several shots ricocheted off the boulder just to his right.

"Take cover!" Tim shouted, as if the others needed prompting to do so. Concern for land mines now moot, Punk and Waco dragged Og behind the same big rock the bullets had just careened off of while the other three dove behind a formation of sandstone on their side of the road.

While more bullets rained around them, Tim shouted, "Do you see anything, Waco?" from across the road.

"Hell, no," Waco shouted back. "And I ain't sticking my head out for too long to look, neither."

Between the cracks of gunfire from down the road and bullets sparking the ground nearby, Punk heard a now-familiar sound overhead: the buzz of a Predator UAV. He looked up and caught a brief glimpse of it before it disappeared behind the ridgeline above Tim's side of the road.

"I wonder if that thing can see us," Waco said.

He had his answer as an explosion split the road a

quarter mile east of them. It was followed by another several hundred yards closer and then another still closer than that. *Long stick bombing,* Punk thought. *B-52 strike.*

"Get down!" he screamed, and he hugged the back side of the boulder, covering Og as best he could. Waco fell on top of both of them. The bombs continued walking toward them at a rapid clip, each blast more deafening than the last. Punk hoped they were only five hundred pounders, as he feared they wouldn't have a chance with anything bigger than that.

Another bomb hit and the concussion from it lifted the boulder they were behind slightly off the ground. *This is it,* Punk figured as he waited for the next bomb to explode. *This one's got our names on it.* He considered the irony of dying at the hands of American forces and closed his eyes and took back every Air Force joke he'd ever told.

But instead of hitting the adjacent ground, the bomb hit the top of the ridge above them, throwing a large amount of newly made gravel over the road and those hiding to either side of it. Subsequent hits grew more distant, and after a few more tense seconds, Punk felt Waco's weight lift off of his back.

"What the hell happened?" Waco asked. "I thought we were goners, for sure."

Punk stepped to the center of the road and lined up the smoking bomb craters with his arm. "Dumb bombs drop in a straight line," he observed. "That bend in the road right there saved us."

Tim rushed up and said, "Let's get moving while the gomers have their heads down. Those bombs missed us, but I'm pretty sure they also missed them."

"I've got to get Og." Waco started to move toward the boulder.

"Your skinny ass will never be able to carry him, at least not very far," Nathan said. "Throw him on my back."

Waco feinted toward an argument but instead led the Ranger across the road and aided him in placing Og across his shoulders. Nathan gave a single heave accompanied by a grunt and hoisted the wounded man farther up the back of his neck and then was off at a surprisingly fast clip.

"Let me know if you need me to spell you, Nate," Waco said as he took up a close trail.

"I've got him," Nathan replied. "You watch our back. Make sure those Taliban don't run us down."

Punk scoured the ridgelines around them and peered into the sky above them, and as he did he noted the contrails left by the heavy bomber that had just tried to kill them. He pictured the crew crawling from station to station between the cockpit and fuselage, slapping each other high fives over the great mission they'd just flown. He wanted to jump on the radio right then and demand . . . what? An apology?

"Every time I see one of those fucking UAVs something bad happens," Waco said. "Who's flying those things anyway?"

"They're being controlled from Riyadh," Tim said. "It's like fighting a war through a straw."

"You want to know what I think?" Waco said. "I think we're getting too damn cute with all this technology we got. All the higher ups want to do is play with their toys now."

Nathan stumbled and nearly fell, and as he did Og slid off of his shoulders. The Ranger managed to contort his body in a way that kept the big Green Beret from hitting the ground too hard, and Og wound up on his left side with his face against the dirt.

"Let me take a look at him," Waco said as he rolled Og over onto his back. Waco opened each of Og's eyes and then placed a finger against his neck. "Pulse is pretty weak."

Punk moved behind Waco, crouched down, and studied the base of Og's damaged leg. "Bleeding's still stopped."

A gunshot echoed from somewhere to the west. "They're closing again," Tim said. "We'd better get moving."

Nathan started to reach for Og, but Waco stopped him, saying, "I've got him this time."

"I'm fine, Waco," Nathan replied. "I didn't carry him that far."

"Let me carry him," Punk said. "It's only fair. I'm the dumb ass who let the horses go."

"You can try to carry him, El Cedar," Waco said. "But not for that reason."

"Officer or not, it's okay with me if he admits that he messed up," Nathan said, making it a point to look at Waco and not Punk.

"Oh really?" Waco said. "Then why don't you, while we're at it, son?"

"What the hell are you talking about, Wacko?"

"What I'm talking about, Nate, is you blasting away at the enemy before they're in range."

"They were in range," Nathan said, raising the volume of his voice to match Waco's.

"Oh, yeah? I didn't see nobody fall. Plus, what were you shooting for in the first place? We're a scouting party, not the first wave of troops. We're not supposed to let the gomers know we're around."

"Somebody pick Og up and let's get moving," Tim said.

With Waco's help, Punk got Og onto his shoulders.

His knees buckled under the weight of the burden. The Green Beret felt like he was filled with cement. Punk wasn't going to get very far, but he wasn't going to complain, either. He'd earned this Sisyphean fate; he'd simply struggle with each step until he collapsed. With any luck Og would crush him and give him the gift of a quick and painless death.

After a dozen demistrides the thundering of hooves grew around them. The noise echoed in a way that made it hard to tell from which direction it was coming, and all except Punk craned their heads around looking both west and east for the source of the sound. Nathan moved to the near side of the road and, dropping to one knee, trained his rifle to the west, waiting for something, anything, to appear.

"It is General Haskarim," Mushkai announced with as much dread as enthusiasm, pointing to a cloud of dust that was just peeking around the next bend to the east. The cloud grew, and soon Punk could make out twelve horses, half of them without riders. Behind them were two vehicles: an SUV and a pickup truck, both so caked with dust it was impossible to tell what color they were. Closer still Punk was able to identify the general riding tall in the saddle on his sleek charger, by appearances very much the leader. On one side of him was Urat, the fat chief of security riding a proportionally sized horse. The others were Afghans Punk didn't recognize.

General Haskarim and Urat split off from the others and rode directly to Mushkai and started yelling at him even before their horses had slowed from a gallop. The boy stood stooped shouldered, eyes to the ground as the general's tirade continued for some time, aided by the occasional word from Urat. Mushkai didn't respond save twice sheepishly gesturing toward Punk. The pilot wanted to run over and try to take the heat off of the young translator but was unsure of how the general might react, so he stood in place with his human burden across his shoulders, pained and embarrassed by the boy's expression. In turn, Punk looked over at the horses and gave Bushwhacker a scornful stare, projecting some of his discomfiture toward the insolent beast as if that might have some effect on the animal's future behavior.

Tim ran up to the pickup as Terry skidded to a halt and jumped out from behind the wheel. Another Afghan Punk didn't recognize was riding shotgun, and in the center of the cab was Boodle, who didn't seem any more aware of his surroundings than he had been earlier that morning when they'd started heading westward.

"What happened to Og?" Terry asked, pushing the bridge of his glasses back to the top of his nose before helping Punk lay the wounded man on the ground.

"Stepped on a damn land mine," Tim said as he pulled his laptop out of Whose Boy's left saddlebag and then took a seat on the pickup's tailgate. "I need to fire a blast to K-2 to get a line on decent medical help ASAP. Maybe they've even got another helo by now."

"You guys scared the hell out of us," Terry said. "When those horses ran down the road toward us without you guys on their backs I thought you were all dead, no doubt about it."

General Haskarim handed his reins to Urat and climbed out of the saddle. He joined Punk and Terry over Og, accompanied by Mushkai, and began to speak.

"The general knows of a doctor in Bamiyan," Mushkai translated. "We have men who can take him back there."

"We need to get him out of here, Tim," Waco said. "I'm not a medic, but just looking at him tells me he ain't out of the woods by a long sight."

"Of course he ain't out of the woods," Tim said. "His foot's been blown off, for crissakes." The CIA man slapped the side of his laptop and yelled at the screen: "Come on! Answer the damn mail, base." He looked over his shoulder at Terry kneeling in front of the rack of electronic gear pushed up against the front of the pickup's bed. "How's the SATCOM link?"

"Nothing," Terry said. "We must be in a null zone—a tropospheric shadow or trapping layer or something."

"We ain't got time to fiddle around with K-2, Tim," Waco entreated. "We've got to get Og out of here now."

Tim pulled off his ball cap and ran a hand through his thinning gray hair. "Make the call, Tim," Waco prodded.

"All right," Tim snapped as he folded his computer shut and stood up. "We'll let the general's men take him back to Bamiyan." He leveled a finger at Waco. "But somebody's got to go with him."

All wraparound-shielded eyes went to Punk, but Tim mused aloud: "No. If he got smoked it wouldn't look good."

"How about Nate?" Waco asked.

"You'd like that, wouldn't you, Wacko?" Nathan said.

"No, we need Nathan's fighting skills," Tim said.

"Then you can't lose me," Waco said, to which Nathan released a muffled guffaw that Waco chose to ignore.

"Obviously we can't send him anywhere," Tim said, gesturing toward the back of Boodle's head as he sat stone still in the cab. "That leaves you, Terry. What do you think?"

"How long would I be gone?" Terry asked.

Tim shrugged. "Until Og was stabilized, at least."

"How would I get there? Horses?"

"Take the SUV," Tim said, subtly shifting the exchange from theoretical to directive. "Pull the MREs out of the back and put them in the pickup."

At that point they all stood motionless, momentarily paralyzed by the fact they had fashioned a plan and now all Terry had to do was execute it.

"Who's going with me, Mushkai?" Terry asked.

The boy barked an order and two men bedecked in new mostly green camouflaged fatigues and solid green parkas dismounted and jogged over with their rifles slung across their shoulders. On their heads they wore *pakols* like Punk did, except theirs were worn with more panache—canted at jaunty angles and bent with signature folds. Mushkai pointed to the SUV and the men climbed into the vehicle—one in the forward passenger seat, one in back—without another word.

Waco opened the SUV's rear hatch and pulled out a large cardboard box. He set it on the ground and looked inside. "We're running low on MREs," he observed. "We need to coordinate a drop or something pretty soon."

"Or we'll just eat the local fare," Tim returned, curling his lips into a satanic smile.

"I'll leave you ten of them, Terry," Waco said without acknowledging Tim's gibe. After moving out of

the way so Punk and Nathan could get Og off of the
dirt and into the back of the vehicle, Waco replaced
the knife he'd used to tighten the tourniquet with a
foot-long stick he found alongside the road. He
slipped the knife into the sheath at the small of his
back, then stacked ten meal boxes next to the
wounded man and lugged the rest over to the pickup.

"You've got a phone on you, right?" Tim asked.

"Yeah," Terry said. The bespeckled CIA man stuck
his pack in the car and slid behind the wheel. "Take
care of my radios." And then he drove off, cautiously
turning around and then picking his way along the
crater-laced road. Punk watched the SUV grow
smaller and wondered if he'd ever see either of the
Americans again, and as he did, a ton of guilt landed
on his shoulders. If only he hadn't let the horses go.
If only he hadn't asked for a sip of Og's water. If only
he hadn't shot himself down . . .

"Now I work on putting a crimp in the Talibans'
style," Waco said. "Otherwise we all might be needing
a doctor." He leaped into the bed of the pickup.

Shots began to ring out again from the west, and
several of the Afghans began to fire indiscriminately
in return.

"Tell them to wait until they actually see something," Waco shouted to Mushkai before tearing open
the top of an olive drab canvas bag that contained a
UHF radio. Waco twisted a few dials and raised the
handset: "Bossman, this is Tiger one; how do you
read?"

A female voice could barely be heard over a burst
of static: "Tiger one, this is Bossman; read you five
by five. Go ahead."

"Bossman, Tiger one is at thirty-four fifty-nine-
point-nine-five north, sixty-seven twenty-one-point-

one-five east. I'm in the middle of the main road running east-west. Request immediate air support. We have enemy forces just west of our position threatening to overrun us. Can you assist?"

"Standby, Tiger one." Following ten seconds of silence that felt like ten minutes to the men gathered around the bed of the pickup, the female controller came back with, "Tiger one, all assets are tasked at this time."

Waco dropped the handset away from his head and cursed as bullets whizzed by at an ever-increasing rate.

"Tell her you want to speak to the mission commander," Punk suggested from where he'd crouched down behind the tailgate.

"The what?" Waco asked.

"The mission commander, the senior controller in the AWACS. They've got like a million people in that damn thing."

"Got it," Waco said with a grin. "Go over this bitch's head." He lifted the handset again: "Bossman, are you the mission commander?"

There was a slight delay before the female controller passed a curt "No."

"Let me speak to the mission commander."

A forceful male voice immediately jumped on the frequency: "What's the problem, Tiger one?"

"The problem is that we are in company with an indigenous code one whose forces have not constituted yet," Waco explained, frustration growing in his tone with each word. "We are heavily outnumbered right now and are in danger of being overrun."

"Bossman has your request, Tiger one," the mission commander said impassively. "I'll relay."

"He's going to *relay*," Waco said sardonically. "Thank God for that. As long as he *relays* we'll be just fine." He glanced back at Punk who was now crouched so low that all Waco could see was the very top of his *pakol.* "Great idea, El Cedar. I'm sure your buddies are all too busy pulverizing mud huts to help us out."

One of the Afghans began to shout and point excitedly down the road to the west. Punk peered over the tailgate and saw objects growing in the distance, black dots surrounded by clouds of dust. Men? Trucks? Tanks? Whatever they were, Punk figured they couldn't be much more than a mile away.

The shrill sound of something streaking through the sky ripped the thin, crisp air and the road erupted several hundred feet in front of the pickup—a smaller explosion than those from the bombs dropped by the B-52 but of no less concern. Somebody screamed, "Mortars!" General Haskarim, Urat, and the other Afghans fought to stay in their saddles while the horses without riders neighed and bucked. Another shriek announced a second shell that hit closer than the first, and with that the others on foot joined Punk behind the pickup.

"Bossman, we have a visual on the enemy forces now," Waco transmitted as the second blast died away enough for him to hear himself. "I estimate they are less than three thousand meters away from us. They appear to have vehicles and heavy armor, as well. We are also now under mortar attack."

"Bossman copies, Tiger one," the female controller replied, sounding a bit put out by the new developments. "We're working with CENTCOM at this time. Standby."

"What happened to the mission commander?" Waco wondered aloud.

Another shell screamed overhead, and Nathan

shouted, "Incoming!" just like soldiers did in the movies. A half-second later the road spewed shrapnel and dirt from two hundred yards behind them.

"They're bracketing us," Nathan said from his new position over Punk's shoulder. "Getting the range down little by little."

Punk suddenly snapped. He scrambled over the tailgate and into the bed of the pickup, seized the handset from Waco, and tersely transmitted: "Bossman, this is Lieutenant Commander Reichert, United States Navy. I am a downed American pilot who's been incorporated into Tiger one. We need close air support *now*! We are in extremis here."

"All right. Calm down," a new, more authoritative male voice said. "We heard you and have been working as fast as possible. We've redirected a flight of two Hornets to you for your control, call sign Bronx two-five."

Calm down? Easy for that asshole to say sitting in the comfort of the AWACS or, worse, the current operations cell in Riyadh. Punk handed the receiver back to Waco, who shook his head with either respect or disbelief—Punk couldn't tell which.

"Tiger one, Bronx two-five is checking in as fragged by Bossman." The guy had said they were Hornets, right? Punk wondered if they were from his air wing. The voice was indistinct, too laced with static to identify.

"Tiger's got you loud and clear, Bronx," Waco replied. "Say loadout."

"Four five-hundred-pound precision-guided bombs each," the lead pilot replied.

"Copy. Standby for tasking."

"Standing by."

"We've got a couple of cans of whoop ass up there,"

Waco quipped after dropping the handset to his side. "This just might work."

Mushkai pushed his way to the tailgate as General Haskarim and Urat rode closer. "Are you calling for the fighters to drop bombs on the enemy?" Mushkai asked.

"Yeah," Waco said as he pulled a waterproof map of the area out of a side pocket of his cammies.

The boy turned and said something to the general and Haskarim threw a line back. "The general would like to use the radio before you do that," Mushkai said.

"Use the radio?" Waco said, fighting to maintain an appropriate level of respect for the warlord. "What for?"

The boy paused, darting his brown eyes and twitching his barely visible prepubescent mustache as if he sensed the truth was going to be unsatisfactory to the Americans. "Custom," he replied cryptically.

Waco read the general's body language as the warlord handed the reins to Urat, dismounted, and walked to the pickup. As another shell hit closer still the Green Beret whooshed a long exhale and then keyed the radio: "Bronx two-five, Tiger one is going off the freq for a few seconds. Say your posit."

"We're fifty miles away from you," the pilot replied.

"Roger," Waco said. "Once overhead, pick up a holding pattern at those coordinates. I'm going off the frequency momentarily. I'll be right back with you with tasking."

"We understood from Bossman that you were under attack, Tiger one."

"We are. I swear I'll be right back."

Waco passed the general the handset across the side of the pickup bed. Haskarim said something to Mushkai, and the boy reached in and twisted a knob at the top of the radio, presumably switching to another frequency. Mushkai nodded and the general began to shout stridently into the handset. Another voice came back at him and soon it was obvious to all around the pickup that a full-blown argument was going on across the airwaves. At the same time Punk noted that the shelling had stopped.

"Who's he talking to?" Tim asked Mushkai in a loud whisper.

"Taliban," Mushkai replied matter-of-factly, casting an arm down the road to the west while his eyes remained glued on the general. "He's telling them that he's about to order the Americans to drop bombs on their heads." The boy grew a sly smile. "He's showing them his power."

General Haskarim barked something at Waco and thrust the handset in his face. "The Taliban don't believe that we have Americans with us," Mushkai explained. "The general wants you to say something to them."

"What?" Waco said, wincing in confusion and disbelief.

"In English . . ." the boy added.

Waco looked at Tim and shook his head. He raised the handset, transmitted, "Hello. This is a genuine American speaking. Bombs be coming soon," in a mechanical monotone, and handed control of the radio back to the general.

Jet engines roared high overhead as General Haskarim ended the taunt with several tersely delivered sentences. When he was done speaking, he proudly walked off, leaving the handset dangling by its cord over the side of the pickup.

"You may drop the bombs now," Mushkai said. The

boy bailed out of the bed and crouched down behind the pickup.

Radio debate complete, the shelling resumed with the first mortar hitting well down the road. Punk entertained the idea that the argument had thrown the enemy off and forced them to start their targeting from scratch. Perhaps there was a method to the general's madness—a notion muted when the general suddenly wheeled around as if he'd forgotten something. *"Jay-dahm?"* he asked, eyes dancing between Punk and Waco.

"What?" Waco asked.

"The general wants the fighters to drop the JDAM bombs," Mushkai explained over his shoulder. "He has told the Taliban that we have a pilot with us and that he can order the most powerful weapons whenever he needs them. We must show the Taliban this is so."

Waco redialed the close air support control frequency into the radio and pointed to the sky. "These guys aren't carrying JDAM, Mushy."

Mushkai yelled back to the general: *"Jay-dahm, na, sahib."*

General Haskarim muttered something unintelligible back and stormed over and mounted his horse.

"This is most disappointing," the boy intoned toward the bed. "The general is a man of his word with both friend and enemy."

"Well, go tell the general not to ride away just yet," Waco said. "He's going to want to see this." He returned the handset to the side of his head and transmitted, "Bronx two-five, are you still with me?"

There was no reply.

"Bronx two-five, this is Tiger one; are you up?"

Still nothing.

"Where the hell did they go?" Waco asked Punk, who was crouched with his head nearly to the floor of the bed now. Another mortar exploded behind them, and with that Punk jumped over the right side of the bed and sprawled on his chest across the ground. He peered under the front bumper and saw the enemy bearing down on them, figures distorted by the dust but growing by the second. He reached for his rifle and then realized in his frightened haste he'd left it in the bed of the pickup. He wanted to grab it, but with the bullets hitting all around him he couldn't convince his body to move.

"Tiger one, this is Bossman," the radio crackled. "How do you read?"

"Tiger has you loud and clear, Bossman," Waco eagerly replied. "What happened to our jets?"

"We've been calling you for the last two minutes but couldn't get an answer," the controller said. "Zeus redirected the assets we'd fragged for you. We're working on getting you some new help at this time."

Waco dropped the handset and asked, "Who the hell is Zeus?"

"That's the general himself at the Joint Task Force in Riyadh," Punk shouted with a cheek against the dirt.

"The general himself, huh? Well, that makes my epitaph easy enough: *Thanks for nothing, General.*" And then the Green Beret sought out the Afghan boy, whose thick black hair crested above the lowered tailgate. "Mushy, remind me to thank General Haskarim for this, too."

The sarcasm was lost on the young interpreter: "I think there is no need for the thanks."

Nathan, still kneeled next to the pickup's left rear wheel, squeezed off a handful of semiautomatic shots and cut his eyes across the stock of his M-4. "You guys want to knock off the bullshit and start helping us kill some of these fuckers?"

Tim calmly retook his seat on the tailgate and focused on his computer screen. "I'm sending an e-mail straight to the director," he reported. "We'll see if we can't up the ante on CENTCOM here."

"Nate's right," Waco shouted over his shoulder as he crawled forward and laid his rifle on the roof of the cab. "We ain't got time for that. Put down the laptop and pick up a gun." With that the Green Beret began firing. Punk saw the lead elements were running, a banzai charge with more than twenty abreast and several ranks deep. Even as many among them fell, those who remained continued their manic sprint without any sign of slowing. He could hear their battle cries now, a chilling chorus of shrill wails. He cursed himself for being unarmed, for being paralyzed with fear.

"Done," Tim announced proudly. "If that doesn't get us air support nothing will." He slid the laptop against the side of the pickup's bed and took station on the ground outside of Punk.

"You got a knife, El Cedar?" Waco asked as he slammed a fresh magazine into the bottom of his rifle.

"Why?" Punk shot nervously back.

Waco didn't have time to answer. In what seemed to Punk as too few strides, the enemy reached them. The first one came over the hood only to be greeted by Waco's knife in his chest once he got to the cab. Punk saw a leg and the flash of a black turban around the front of the pickup, and before he could get off a shot he was blinded by something hitting the dirt in front of his face and throwing sand into his eyes. He raised his fists to his face and heard Tim fire a handful of shots next to him. Something warm splattered against Punk's forehead, followed immediately by a body dropping across his back.

He twisted his hands against his eye sockets, desperately trying to regain his sight while torquing around in an attempt to throw the dead man off of him. He could see shadows—legs and feet kicking up more dust—and could hear Tim above him engaged in hand-to-hand combat. He heard the dull resonance of a fist against a face and then the *pfftt* of a knife into flesh. Another body fell to the ground at Punk's feet.

"Are you all right?" Tim asked.

"I can't see," Punk replied. "I've got dirt in my eyes."

Tim fired several shots directly over Punk's head now, and the resultant screams sounded like they were mere feet away. He felt the bodies thump against the ground as they hit. There were more shots and cries of agony from beyond the left side of the pickup along with frightened whinnies from the horses. Bullets against the truck's front windshield ticked out an arrhythmic beat. *What about Boodle?* Punk wanted to see if he'd had the wherewithal to duck down in the cab but at the same time figured if the aircrewman was hit there was little that could be done for him right away.

After another bloodcurdling cry courtesy of Waco's knife, the Texan said, "That takes care of the first wave. What say we take down the next one before they get to us?"

A transmission buzzed over the radio.

"Can somebody answer that?" Waco asked between rifle shots.

Punk's eyes had cleared enough that he could make out colors and shapes, and he mustered enough bravery to crawl his way up the side of the pickup and over to the radio. He lay on his back in the bed and keyed the mike. "Go ahead for Tiger one," he cried into the handset, voice carrying the stress of the moment.

"Tiger one, this is Brooklyn three-five," a voice returned. "We're a flight of two Tomcats reassigned to you by Bossman. Say tasking."

Tomcats! Who was it? "Did Bossman relay our position?" Punk asked.

"That's affirmative, Tiger one."

"We're still there, in the middle of the main road running east-west. How copy?"

"Brooklyn copies."

"We just fought off the first wave of the enemy. Second line is threatening. Need you to take out any vehicles you see west of us. What's your loadout?"

"Two one thousand pounders each, one dumb, one guided."

"Tell them danger close is approved," Waco instructed.

"Are you sure you want that?" Punk returned.

"We ain't got time to argue, El Cedar! They got to take out the vehicles and the tank or we're done for."

Punk rekeyed the handset: "Danger close is approved. You're cleared hot at this time."

"Roger," the RIO replied. "We've got FLIR on vehicles heading down the road west of your posit. Looks like a tank and a couple of personnel carriers. We're moving into position for initial bomb release."

"Need you to expedite, Brooklyn." Punk suppressed the desire to identify himself. The aircrews didn't need any distractions at that moment. Hopefully they could all catch up after the job was done.

Punk tried to keep the fighters in sight between

dodging the bullets ticking off the hood of the pickup
and wildly squeezing off shots. He saw bodies fall but
wasn't sure they were from his bullets. Above the fray
the jets were flying in a lazy arc, which caused him to
think they were going to drop their precision-guided
bombs first. That instinct was validated as the first two
bombs hit, no more than a half mile away. Punk saw
the tank's turret fly across the sky highlighted against
the orange flames of the initial blast. The shock wave
rippled across the road, shaking the pickup and blowing the horses' manes back. The air was momentarily
warmed. Punk's *pakol* nearly came off and he was
struck by how much louder and more powerful a one-
thousand pounder was than a five-hundred pounder.
He cast his eyes back to the Tomcats and imagined
the crews coolly monitoring their FLIR screens, not
hearing the noise or feeling the blast or heat of their
bombs.

Without warning General Haskarim and his five
men galloped toward the foe's next line. The general
led the charge with the reins free, rifle in one hand,
pistol in the other. The others flanked him, firing their
rifles from the hip as they rode. One of them fell and
tumbled across the ground for a few turns before coming to rest, motionless, presumably dead, while his
horse continued full-bore alongside the others.

"That's either the bravest or dumbest thing I've
ever seen," Tim said as he watched the general continue his charge.

"We'll see," Waco added.

The F-14s rolled in again, more aggressively this
time. One after the other they dove, the lead from the
east, out of the still-rising sun, and, a few seconds
later, the wing from the north. The visibility was good
enough for Punk to follow the unguided bombs for the

duration of their fall. They hit and exploded, throwing another vehicle and many more bodies into the air. Punk watched the flash and braced for the shock. He saw the general's line of horses pull up short and feared they may have been hit by the shrapnel, and even though he expected it, the effects of the bombings still caught him off guard.

An eerie silence followed, and for a few seconds Punk thought he might have gone deaf with the last explosion. He looked through the dissipating clouds of dirt and ash to the west and saw no movement of any sort. Had the general and his men been taken out, as well?

"Bronx two-five is complete," the lead RIO transmitted. "We're switching back to Bossman."

"Tiger one copies," Waco replied after relieving the dazed pilot of the handset. "Good shooting, Bronx. Looks like you've stopped them dead in their tracks."

"Glad we could help. Flight switch Bossman."

"Two," the wing RIO said.

Punk reached back for the radio but the Tomcat crews had already jumped to the next frequency, certainly talking to the AWACS as they headed for another rendezvous with a heavy tanker. He watched them disappear over the peaks several miles to the south and felt like Gilligan on his island watching ships pass on the horizon—so close yet so far. They didn't even know he was down there. Would they ever know?

Suddenly General Haskarim and his four remaining men emerged from the dissipating clouds of smoke and ash, trailing the extra horse. Mushkai ran out to greet them, arms waving about the air like a civilian greeting a liberating force. He led the general's horse to the pickup. As they neared Punk noticed those on horseback appeared to be smoldering; ringlets of gray smoke rose from each shoulder and *pakol*. They all wore broad smiles in spite of the near miss and the loss of a compatriot.

"The general is pleased that the aircraft were able to drop the JDAM bombs," the boy said. "He says that their precision is quite impressive and that the message will not be lost on the enemy for many days to come."

Waco, still buzzing with adrenaline from the attack, shook his head and shot back, "Those weren't JDAMs, fer crissakes, Mushy. Look, you tell the general that—" He stopped himself with several cleansing breaths. He removed his sunglasses and let them dangle around his neck and shifted his eyes to Haskarim.

"Anytime, General," the Green Beret said with a bow. "Anytime."

The sound of whimpering was heard, and following a moment's confusion, Punk realized it was coming from the cab of the pickup. He rushed over to the driver's-side door and looked in to see Boodle sprawled across the bench seat, facedown with his body shuddering in slight waves.

Punk opened the door and helped the man sit upright. He had dark circles under his bloodshot eyes that made him look nearly his age, and he wore a vacant stare. The tears had smeared the dirt across his smooth cheeks.

"Boodle? Boodle, can you hear me?" Punk asked, gently shaking the aircrewman.

Boodle didn't respond at first but slowly the corners of his mouth jerked downward and before too long the tears started flowing again. He worked to speak, but nothing came out. Punk continued his attempts to calm him, and after a few more false starts Boodle was able to utter a single question:

"Where the fuck am I?"

CHAPTER TEN

Einstein looked up from the piece of paper on his stateroom desk and asked, "Where did you find this, Peeler?"

"I pulled it off of the Internet," Peeler replied. "I thought you'd be interested."

"What site?"

"Early Bird," the nugget pilot replied, referring to the electronic news clipping service run by the Department of Defense that compiled newspaper, magazine, and Internet articles that might be of interest to the military. It was generally the first stop of the morning for those working in the Pentagon, and any article that landed on the site, regardless of whether it originally appeared in the *New York Times* or at globalsecurity.org, was sure to be seen by every high-ranking military officer, staffer, and political appointee.

Einstein put his elbows against the desk and cradled his head in his palms while he read the article again, more carefully this time:

EXPERTS SAY RESCUE MISSION FLAWED
Navy's Controversial Captain Points to Army
Pilots for Afghan Mountain Mishap

(From wire services)—Pilot error and not high altitude may have been the main contributor behind
the disastrous mission to rescue two downed airmen held by Taliban forces, according to Navy
Captain Alexander Campbell, renowned fighter
pilot currently serving as the assistant air wing
commander aboard an aircraft carrier patrolling
the waters of the Northern Arabian Gulf. The mission, codenamed "Operation Python," claimed
three helicopters and the lives of seven soldiers
and a cameraman for the Qatar-based Aljazeera
network. While the captured Navy airmen were ultimately rescued, the conduct of the mission has
brought into question the United States military's
ability to fight in Afghanistan's hostile terrain.

"I wouldn't say the issue was helicopter capability," Campbell said during a recent interview
aboard the carrier. "You had two [helicopters] shot
down by shoulder-fired SAMs and one crash while
landing. It could have been simple pilot error."

On paper Operation Python was a trademark
special operations effort, designed to quickly extract
the captives before the enemy could react. An official
involved in the planning for the rescue mission said
the original plan was for the downed aviators to be
loaded into a CH-47 Chinook troop transport helicopter while two AH-64 Apache helicopter gun-
ships provided air cover overhead. While the
accident investigation is ongoing, it has been
widely circulated that just before touchdown the

Chinook pilots experienced a loss of visual reference caused by blowing sand from the helicopter's down wash—a condition known as "brown out." The Chinook hit the ground hard and burst into flames, killing all but three of those aboard. The Army has not released the names of the dead or the disposition of the survivors pending notification of next of kin.

The downed Navy crew, identified by the Pentagon as Commander Sean O'Leary and Lieutenant Commander Richard Reichert, were taken out of the area by Northern Alliance forces on horseback. Commander O'Leary was wounded during the rescue and is expected to return to the aircraft carrier for medical treatment in the next few days. His wounds were described as "not life threatening" by Lieutenant Ronnie Wheedle, a Navy spokesman on the carrier. Military sources said Lieutenant Commander Reichert was alive and well but would not confirm his whereabouts.

"This type of operation is inherently risky," said Dr. Reno Marcello of the Bunting Corporation, a security firm that specializes in special operations. "You have to go when you have good intelligence, but when you speed up the time line, some things are bound to go wrong."

"Pilot error or not, I remain unconvinced that military planners fully considered the effect altitude has on helicopters," said Victor Fiche, a retired army colonel who served several tours in Vietnam.

Captain Campbell balked at the idea that the American military might have trouble flying helicopters in northern Afghanistan. "I'd be careful about defining some sort of inherent performance problem with those helicopters at those altitudes," he said. "We shouldn't send the wrong message about our ability to fight in the mountains. We'll go wherever we have to."

Military expert Melvin Bernard agreed that helicopter performance wasn't to blame for the disaster. "I doubt the pilots involved in the mission received adequate training," he said from his office at the Jandow Study, a military think tank and consultant group.

The subject of adequate training has recently plagued Captain Campbell, as well, following a mission where he inadvertently dropped a bomb on a truckload of refugees, killing one and injuring several others. After a series of news reports on the incident the Senate Armed Services Committee launched an official investigation into whether or not Campbell intentionally bypassed some critical parts of his training in order to arrive on scene while the war was still in full gear. That investigation is ongoing.

The accidental bombing has tainted the reputation of an officer who was previously considered one of the Navy's brightest stars. As a fighter pilot Campbell has held many prized positions, including stints as a member of the venerated Blue Angel flight demonstration team and Top Gun instructor. Just over two years ago he was celebrated as a national hero after being shot down by a surface-to-air missile while patrolling the no-fly zone over southern Iraq. He spent five days in a Baghdad prison before the U.N. brokered his release.

But Campbell remains sanguine in the face of controversy. "It's no big deal, really," he said about the investigation. The captain went on to say

that he regretted the loss of innocent life but that
unintended deaths "will always be a part of war."

Peeler saw Einstein lean back in his chair and asked,
"What do you think?"
Einstein raised an eyebrow and shrugged.
"Do you think DCAG really said all those things?"
"Yeah," Einstein replied. "But I'm pretty sure he
didn't realize they'd look like this on paper."

Several mules took the place of the pickup once they
left the road at Nayak. With loading techniques little
changed since the days of Genghis Khan, the state-of-
the-art communications equipment was strapped to the
scrappy animals' backs. Punk studied their faces, eyes
droopy and mouths slack, and saw in them a working-
class resignation, unhappy with their station in this life
but compliantly accepting it, nonetheless.
Once the mules were loaded, the party mounted
their horses and started up the impossibly narrow trail
that snaked along the side of the mountain. Punk
urged Bushwhacker to stay close behind Sor'at, Mushkai's horse, relinquishing himself of the responsibility
of guiding his mount, hoping that Bushwhacker would
simply place his feet where Sor'at did. Farther up the
mountain Punk let the reins go slack and held on to
the front of the saddle with a white-knuckled grip. He
thought he'd grown accustomed to the wooden saddle,
his prehistoric perch, but the steep angles they were
now working threw him against it in new and painful
ways. He cursed Waco under his breath for conducting
a coin toss for Og's Western saddle instead of giving
it to him outright. Had rank lost all of its privilege?
And he cursed Nathan under his breath for calling
"heads" first and for flashing his toothy grin through

his beard when the quarter came to rest. "Fair is fair," Waco had said paternally.

Each one of the horse's missteps, each rumble of falling rock set Punk's heart racing. He focused on Bushwhacker's mane as a way to keep himself from looking down over the thousands of feet he was sure he and his horse would be falling at anytime now.

Would the fear ever end? He was tired of it. He considered a pilot's fear—episodic, predictable, manageable, the fear of night traps and in-flight emergencies, stuff he'd trained for. You didn't always know when it was coming, but when it did you were generally ready for it. And even if you weren't ready for it, like when the bomb went off next to his jet, it was over pretty quickly.

But since he'd landed on the ground he'd been in the grips of a constant, gnawing sense of fear, even when he slept, although the fitful periods of rest he'd managed over the last days could hardly be labeled as sleep. He glanced over his shoulder at Waco aboard Racecar and beyond him at Nathan on Abrishom and saw serenity in the men's countenances, a truly remarkable state. From where did it come? They certainly hadn't spent years traveling harrowing mountain trails any more than they'd passed much time in the company of Afghan warlords prior to this operation. And yet, levels of intensity notwithstanding, both of them seemed so comfortable, even happy at times, reveling in the austerity, the uncertainty, the savagery. Punk tried to picture each one of them in his backseat, strapped in and breathing into an oxygen mask as they pulled six-and-a-half Gs and accelerated to nearly twice the speed of sound. What would they feel during the flight? Fear?

Punk snuck another look behind him, this one

toward Boodle perched on the back of a mule led by
Nathan. The youthful aircrewman remained garbed in
his flight suit but had camouflaged himself somewhat
by drawing a shawl Mushkai had obtained for him
around his shoulders. Boodle wore a dour expression
at the moment, one markedly less confident than those
of the other two soldiers in front of him. He'd been
talkative for the first few hours after emerging from
his crash-induced haze, a phenomenon Dr. Waco labeled as "Post Coma Oral Diarrhea." In short order
the others were made aware of everything from Boodle's squadron, the *Nightporters,* to his ex-fiancée's zo-
diac sign to the details of his father's suicide attempt.
But once he was ushered out of the pickup and onto
the back of a mule his chattiness vanished. Since
they'd started up the mountain he'd uttered only a
single line: "The rest of my crew is dead."

Higher still the trail disappeared and their progress
slowed to a crawl. Near the first peak General Haskarim, who was in the lead, dismounted, and the others followed suit. They picked their ways past the
rocks and over the crevasses, carefully considering
each of their steps as well as those of their animals.

At the top Punk took in the view, an amazing vista.
The wind whipped at his face, and he felt like he could
actually feel the planet spinning through space. He
looked to the west; how far could he see? Herat?
Iran? His eyes panned above the tapestry of brown
and tan that was the land under them and into the
sky, nearly purple at that altitude. West was the way
home, the way to Suzanne.

What would she think if she could see him leading
a horse across the top of the world? He wondered
what she'd been told, if anything, about his situation.
Their relationship, if a single intimate liaison, dozens

of e-mails, and a handful of phone calls could be called a relationship, had not been made public. Not even Spud knew about it, and therefore his wife, Carla, was ignorant on the matter, as well. No, the only evidence Suzanne would have was that Punk's daily e-mail posting had been missing for the last few days. What conclusions would she draw from that? He was suddenly paralyzed by the desire to speak to her—a single sentence, a word—just to let her know he was alive. He wanted to grab the SATCOM off of one of the pack mules and get her on the line. He fought the impulse off with a series of even deeper breaths of the ever-thinning air and trudged along with the rest of the train to the other side of the mountain.

The slope gradually grew shallower on the western face, and once a trail reappeared they climbed back into their saddles. The general picked up the pace, and soon they were working across the steppe between the peaks just shy of a trot. The mules brayed and stiffened their legs against the rate of progress, digging their hooves into the dirt until a series of healthy whacks from the handler's stick coaxed them on.

"We should be reaching that first airfield pretty soon, right, Tim?" Punk called over the horse in front of him.

The graybeard turned halfway around in his saddle and replied, "You mean Lal? Yeah, we've scheduled an airdrop there for about this time tomorrow."

"Airdrop?" Punk asked.

"We're running low on MREs."

"So I guess there's no helicopter coming to get me there . . ."

"No. CENTCOM ruled an attempt to get you out would still be too risky."

"When did you find this out?"

"A few hours ago."

"Were you ever going to tell me?"

"I wanted to wait until we were off the first mountain."

"When am I flying out?"

"I think they're working on a plan to get you out farther down the road."

"Where?"

"Farther west."

No shit, Punk thought.

"Cheer up." Tim turned even farther around, working to see around Mushkai and make eye contact with Punk. "We've got a special surprise for you."

"What?"

"Ah, ah . . . let's not ruin it."

Punk let out an exasperated guffaw. "Hell, who cares about getting back to my squadron? I'm getting a *surprise!*" In spite of his sarcasm the pilot couldn't deny that Tim's teaser had piqued his interest, perhaps even buoyed his spirits. A surprise? What was it?

Halfway across the plain toward the next rise the party crossed a road running north-south ("Too bad we're not going north or south," Waco said), and just beyond that they found themselves tilling through a field of ratty-looking plants, long brown stems punctuated by the occasional serrated leaf and capped with a large orb of a bulb.

"Are these poppies?" Punk asked the boy ahead of him.

"Yes, they are poppies," Mushkai replied. He gestured to his right, toward a low-slung earthen building Punk hadn't noticed previously. "That is the factory where they make the heroin."

An image of Slobo hunkered over the candle in the

cave flashed into Punk's mind even as he was taken aback by the boy's matter-of-fact approach to the topic. "Is that well known?"

Mushkai considered the question and then nodded. "I think so, yes."

"And it's legal?"

"No, very illegal."

"So why is it here?"

"Officially it is not here. And as long as it remains a profitable business that will be so."

In Punk's silence Mushkai heard the American's confusion. "Even the Taliban are not total fools, *Ah See-dah*," the boy continued, giving a local twist to the soldiers' label. "There is one thing you must know about Afghanistan. It is a harsh place, a place at war for many years." He pulled his horse up short, allowing Punk to move astride, and locked eyes with Punk, showing a wisdom well beyond his years. "But some good comes of war: In time it removes the fools."

The poppy field flowed on seemingly without end, and as the train waded through it Punk looked down and watched the bulbs hit against Bushwhacker's fore-legs, each collision releasing a puff of cream-colored dust. Suddenly he sensed the air filled with poppy dust; with each breath he took more in.

"You can't get high from this, can you?" Punk asked back to Waco.

"Unfortunately not," Waco returned. "I could use a good buzz about now."

But still Punk could have sworn the browns were growing browner; the sky was a more vivid shade of blue. The wind was howling in his ears now, delivering messages in strange tongues. The population of poppies grew less dense and eventually ended altogether.

Punk cast his eyes into the distance, where he caught a glint of sunlight off the ground, and as he studied it he had a vision. He saw a large silver box, unattended, eerily out of place in the middle of nowhere, as if it had fallen to earth from outer space. Closer, Punk could see it wasn't a vision but a shipping container, and with that realization he heaved a sigh of relief that he wasn't in the grips of a bad trip after all. He searched for markings on the container that might indicate its origin but found none.

The Afghans among them became quite agitated in the presence of the container, and Punk looked for Mushkai, as had become his instinct, but the boy was too far away and too deeply embroiled in the discussion to bother with an explanation now. In spite of the box's nondescript appearance, Punk's concern grew with the intensity of the argument. He moved his hand over his rifle until he found the trigger, eyes darting about the scene, nervously waiting for something to happen. He wasn't alone with his anxiety.

"What the hell's their problem, Tim?" Waco asked.

"I hope this isn't what I think it is," Tim replied. He got off of Whose Boy and strode into the middle of the Afghan debate.

"What do you think, Waco?" Punk said quietly. "Ambush?"

"I don't think so," Waco replied. "But keep your eyes open."

Punk watched as General Haskarim and Urat stridently spoke to the CIA man, gesturing emphatically toward the container. With some reluctance Urat finally poured his corpulent self out of the saddle and, after one more heated exchange with the general, worked the handle and pried open one of the container doors.

The door was barely ajar before several bodies hit the dirt with hollow thuds at the security chief's feet. The corpses were contorted at macabre angles, stiff with rigor mortis and streaked black in a way that reminded Punk of pictures he'd seen of coal miners emerging from a day's work deep beneath the surface of the earth. The first body came to rest facing Punk, face gripped in a grimace that defined agony, teeth white against the cooked skin.

As the door opened fully Punk could see the container was full of bodies in a similar state. Clothing was scattered about, including many black turbans. The stench of decaying flesh, of death, wafted over the living, gagging all as it reached them.

Mushkai steered his horse to the Americans and simply said, "Tajik justice," before circling back to the general.

Fighting nausea, Punk turned to Waco and asked, "What the hell does he mean?"

"I heard rumors of this," Waco replied, "but I never believed them."

"What?" Punk prodded.

"They stick their prisoners in the container and let them die a slow death, either from suffocation or from the heat."

"The heat?" Punk questioned. "It can't be more than forty-five degrees right now."

Waco pointed at the ball of the sun high overhead and then to the container. "You add that to that and you got yourself a convection oven, even in this cold."

"Who did this?"

"You heard the boy; the Tajiks did it."

"Tajiks? Aren't they with *us?*"

"Last I heard, yeah."

Punk sat up in the saddle and swung an arm toward the container. "And they're—"

"This is local business," Waco interrupted. "Been going on like this for years."

"So you're okay with it?"

"I didn't say that," Waco returned, more sharply than he probably intended.

"What do you care, El Cedar?" Nathan asked from beyond Waco. "They're Taliban. Let them all rot in hell."

"This here ain't about us," Waco said before he paused, eyes dropping to the dirt beneath his horse, as if trying to sort it out for himself. He suddenly snapped his head back up. "We all got to keep our eyes on the prize, El Cedar. Keep our eyes on the prize."

The balance of their force was camped on the plateau and visible to them once they crested the westernmost peak of the mountain range. General Haskarim spotted their ranks and, with the whoop of a war cry, charged headlong down the face, followed obediently by his inner circle, including Mushkai. Through force of will the handlers even convinced the mules to join the charge. Punk watched with amazement, certain one of the Afghans would be launched between the ears of his horse at any moment or that the communications gear would be strewn across the slope.

After crossing two mountains and countless miles Bushwhacker now needed more prodding to carry out Punk's directions. The other horses had grown equally cantankerous, and as they picked their way down the

final length of the downslope their neighs of protest
and head shakes evinced that all of the animals were
ready for a break. Punk felt the same way; it had
been a long day, and he was ready for a meal and
some sleep.

By the time the Americans made it to the flatland
the Afghan army was a series of long shadows
stretched before the setting sun. Tents dotted the horizon, Punk would've guessed by the hundreds. Happy-
sounding voices carried far across the steppe and
would have given the impression to any casual ob-
server that a festival was in progress.

Mushkai rode up and announced, "We are meeting
in the *chaikhana*. The general has asked for you to
come immediately."

The Americans tied their horses to a hitching post
just like cowboys in a Western movie and ambled into
the *chaikhana,* a structure indistinguishable from the
safe houses or even the heroin factory on the outside.
The warmth was inviting as they entered, and Punk
was pleased to see a ski lodge–sized fire raging in the
hearth against the far wall. The same smells that had
graced General Haskarim's dinner the night before
permeated the air. Steam gently wafted through a
beaded curtain adjacent to the hearth, and Punk had
an image of a cook busily preparing food for his
guests. The place was nearly empty in spite of more
than a dozen large round tables within. The *chaikhana*
must've been the general's exclusive domain, off-limits
to the six hundred strong scattered about the plain
outside.

Haskarim, Urat, and Mushkai sat among a few
other Afghans chatting amicably and sipping tea. Next
to the general was an imposing man with a long beard,
prominent nose, and wild eyes that pierced though his

dark, weathered skin. He wore a plain white tunic covered with a black vest and a black-and-white checked kerchief around his neck, more traditional Muslim dress to Punk's eye than what General Haskarim and his men favored.

"This is General Hussan," Mushkai announced as the Americans drew near the table. "He is the leader of the Tajik forces who have joined us to capture Herat."

Punk looked into his eyes as they shook hands, and in them he saw a man who had lived the fighting life, his prewar conception of a warlord. He exuded the ominous aura of a man capable of meting out "Tajik justice," as Mushkai had put it, unspeakable punishments to his enemies—slow cooking them in shipping containers, for instance.

Punk studied General Hussan as the introductions continued and wondered if the warlord was ever haunted by the tortured expressions of his victims. But the six-inch scar behind the Tajik's right ear gave the pilot pause, and he took his seat struck by the notion that his revulsion with the charred Taliban bodies might be more a function of his cushy American middle-class rearing than the warlord's ruthlessness. Hell, Punk had been forced into only one real fight growing up, and he'd wound up getting his ass kicked. So how could he judge a culture hewn by centuries of conflict? What did he know about survival in such a land? He'd been on the ground for only four days now.

Punk was surprised to see there was in fact a cook working behind the beaded curtain. The man burst through the beads and set a cup before each new arrival and filled it with tea. He rushed back into the kitchen and another cook appeared, this one leading a goat. He looked at Punk and smiled.

"Are you American?" the second cook asked in plain English.

"Yes," Punk replied.

"My brother, he goes to UCLA."

Punk was about to say something in response when the cook produced a knife and summarily slit the goat's throat. The Afghans clapped enthusiastically, and the cook dragged the dead animal back through the beaded curtain, leaving behind a trail of smeared blood along the dirt floor as he went.

"You will like the goat," Mushkai said to the Americans. "It is very fresh."

Without warning the two generals rose and started out of the *chaikhana*. Urat called to General Haskarim, presumably asking him where he was headed. The general answered in a word and exited with his Tajik counterpart.

"They want to have a look at the Army before it is too dark," Mushkai explained.

"In that case," Waco said, "how about a movie for the rest of us while we wait for our goat burgers? We might be in the middle of nowhere, but that don't mean we got to be uncivilized, do it?" He reached into his backpack and produced a device that resembled a portable compact disc player, only bigger. "What suits everyone's fancy? Comedy? Drama? Horror?"

Tim scanned the Afghans, who leaned over the table curiously eyeing the silver machine and said, "Be careful, Waco. We don't want to offend our hosts here."

"Don't worry, just Tim. I don't got nothing worse than PG-13 here." He pulled a small black case out of the backpack and flipped through it. "Here we go. A little something for everybody. There's even a camel for you, Mushy."

"What is it?" Tim asked.

"An oldie but goodie: *Cheers for Reggie*."

"Cheers for Reggie?" Punk said excitedly. "That's my skipper's favorite flick."

"So you've seen it?" Waco said.

"About a million times."

"It sucks," Nathan said. "It's not even funny."

"I agree," added Boodle, seated next to the Ranger.

The Green Beret dropped the disc into the player and closed the top. "This here's the director's cut, the twenty-fifth anniversary wide-screen edition."

"What's it about?" Tim asked.

"A teenager losing his virginity to a whore," Punk said.

Tim furrowed his brow at Waco. "We're not showing a movie about—"

"Now, just Tim, calm down," Waco said with a wave of his hand. "It ain't as bad as El Cedar makes it sound. This here's art." He petitioned the Afghans: "You guys want to watch it?"

Mushkai offered a quick translation and they all smiled and nodded.

With that Waco worked his way through the matrix of options to get the movie started. An expectant hush fell over the crowd as the credits rolled. With the first images on the small screen the security chief began to titter nervously, big belly shuddering, while the boy sat stone still. Punk furtively watched Mushkai, and in the screen's glow he could see the young translator appeared hypnotized by the show; his eyes were wide and unblinking.

But as the movie continued the boy could not suppress his curiosity. He saddled up to Punk and whispered questions into his ear. Why was that man angry? Why was the girl kissing more than one man? What made that man vomit?

The pilot attempted answers, but the boy's twisted mouth and knit brow only suggested greater confusion. As they reached the famed ice-cold pool scene Punk shared Tim's concern that the movie could inflame Islamic sensibilities or, in Mushkai's case, damage the fragile psyche of a teenager working his way through the teen years without prurient Western influences. The boy knew plenty about Kalashnikovs but nothing about women, at least not those who spent the bulk of their days in bikinis. As Punk thought about it he realized he hadn't seen a single female since he'd landed on the ground.

Mercifully, the food arrived from the kitchen, and Waco complied with Tim's request that the movie be stopped during the meal. The plates of steaming goat were laid before the Americans and they exchanged looks, apprehensive of the effects the meal might have on them but at the same time tempted by the warmth of the plates and the heady blend of spices that filled their nostrils. Waco suggested that their supply of MREs was dwindling and they should take advantage of any opportunity to eat a local meal that seemed reasonably well prepared. With the first bite Punk focused on the CIA man, watching to see how he pulled off his eat-without-eating trick like an audience member studying a magician from the front row.

"Where did you learn to speak English, Mushkai?" Punk asked as he cut into meat that was more tender than he would've expected it to be.

"America," Mushkai replied.

Punk cocked his head. "America?"

"Yes. I lived there until I was eleven."

"How did you get over here?"

"My father brought me. He was called back in 1997 to lead the Uzbeks against the Taliban."

"Lead the Uzbeks? What about General Haskarim?"

"General Haskarim was my father's deputy."

Punk cut himself another piece of goat and processed the information. "What happened to your father?" he asked innocently enough.

"He was assassinated by al Qaeda three months ago."

Punk's head snapped with the boy's answer. "Assassinated? How?"

"Two of them posed as a news crew wanting an interview with him," Mushkai replied. "They had a bomb in their camera."

Punk studied the boy's stoic demeanor, not quite sure of what to say next. "I'm sorry."

With that the boy allowed a hint of emotion, straddling his plate with his elbows and cradling his head in his hands. After a time he looked up, composure apparently regained.

"Where's your mother?" Punk asked.

"Still in America."

"Why don't you go back there?"

The boy vigorously shook his head. "No. This is where I am needed now. My future is here, with General Haskarim. He will be governor of the province once we return to Herat."

"Will you ever go back?"

Mushkai was silent for a time; his eyes walked to the low ceiling and then locked on Waco's portable DVD player. He started to speak but cut himself off as the two generals reappeared in the *chaikhana*'s main doorway.

The warlords threaded their way by the tables and chairs that fouled the direct route to where the others sat over their meals. Mushkai stood as they approached, cuing the others to do the same. The generals moved right to Tim, and once they reached him Haskarim shot a couple of sentences at the boy.

"The generals have agreed that the Army cannot proceed without more money," Mushkai translated. "And tomorrow he wants you to drop the JDAM again."

Soup walked into Flag Briefing and Analysis, hoping that his face belied how rapidly his heart was beating. The admirals—two one stars and a two star—sat along the far end of the situation table that took up most of the space, dressed in gabardine khakis, rows of ribbons, and a gold warfare pin over each left pocket. Soup wore working khakis, freshly pressed but still a less formal uniform than what the others in the room were wearing, and he wondered how he'd failed to get the word.

Their poker faces were glued on him as he made his way to the lone chair across from them. He felt gawky moving across the room and desperately tried to conjure up some semblance of his swagger, nothing overtly cocky, just a signal that he wouldn't sacrifice his dignity without a struggle. But the swagger wouldn't come.

"Thank you for coming, Captain Campbell," the two star with thick-framed glasses and a severe comb-over said as Soup took his seat. "Let me start by introducing the investigation board to you." He splayed a hand across his sternum. "I am Rear Admiral Denny Blackstone . . ."

Soup nodded as if that information was news to him, as if he hadn't talked to Rear Admiral Dykstra or hadn't performed an Internet search on the board members or hadn't hit up all of his best Pentagon contacts via e-mails and phone calls, gathering useful tidbits while fashioning his defense strategy. One look at Blackstone's bio a few days earlier had revealed the secret behind his professional success, and it had little to do with his chosen warfare specialty of driving ships: He'd spent nearly all of his shore tours in the Office of Legislative Affairs, the Navy's lobbying arm on Capitol Hill. A military man who'd repeatedly gravitated to the congressional arena was one of two things: a glutton for punishment or extremely well connected. Based on the fact he was wearing two stars Soup guessed it was the latter, and that had played heavily in his strategy. Officers with big-league political instincts were chess players. They knew the impact of every action, and how and with whom it would resonate. Gut players were anathema to them. Soup knew he had to avoid coming off as rash or impulsive to Blackstone. In the course of his research he'd also learned that Admiral Blackstone's eldest daughter was a lesbian who'd gone through rehab a handful of times. Soup wasn't quite sure how to incorporate that information into his game plan except that he decided it was best that he not come off as too judgmental.

Rear Admiral Blackstone gestured to the one star on his left: "This is Rear Admiral Peter Zorhanski . . ."

The Zorhanski file had been tough to build because although the newly pinned one star was technically a line officer—he wore a surface warfare pin—for the last decade he'd worked in naval intelligence, which meant he was in the business of controlling the flow of information, including that on himself. His bio was sketchy at best, and none of Soup's Pentagon contacts had even heard of him. As he studied him now Captain Campbell found the admiral pale, delicate, and weak, like many of those who took to hanging out in dark rooms analyzing data, and figured the man had issues with bullies and other tough guys.

Soup softened his posture ever so slightly.

"And to my right is Rear Admiral Harold Hansen . . ." Of course, the token pilot on the board. Soup had known Harold Hollings Hansen for years, and while he'd always found him more of a pretty boy than a golden boy, damned if "Triple H" hadn't been selected for admiral two years ahead of his peers. His had been a simple accession strategy, really, as far as Soup could tell: Be white, handsome, and silent.

But chinks in the Triple H armor had been rumored of late; more than one source had hinted about recent cosmetic surgeries. The DCAG considered him now, convinced that the bridge of his nose was sharper than before and that the mounds of his cleft chin had grown. And there was no way that surfer boy blond was still his natural color. Absent the dye job Soup figured his hair would have been solid gray if not totally white.

Flattery would be the way to his heart.

"We've been anxious to get to the bottom of this situation and get the whole thing behind us, as I'm sure you have," Blackstone said. "But we have some additional issues we'd like to clear up before we reach a finding. Would that be all right with you, Captain?"

Soup counted to three one thousand in his head and then replied, "Yes, Admiral. That would be fine."

Rear Admiral Blackstone opened the top file of

those stacked in front of him and ran a finger along the first page. "How long had it been between your last flight as commanding officer and your first flight in training to come out here?"

One one thousand, two one thousand, three one thousand . . . "Just over two years, Admiral."

"That's a long time when you're talking about tactical jet currency, don't you think?" Rear Admiral Hansen asked. "Systems change, software is upgraded, tactics are modified."

"You're right, Admiral," Soup said. "Our business is very dynamic in that way. That's one of the things I love about it, and I'm sure you do, too. But to answer your question, sir, I have to say I felt very comfortable with my currency and tactical understanding by the time I was on my way over here."

"We've compared the standard training track for a pilot of your seniority to the training you accomplished before reporting aboard," Blackstone said, raising his face from where he'd buried it in the page. "We found significant discrepancies."

"For instance, you flew only three bombing flights," Admiral Hansen said, seamlessly seizing the floor without so much as a raise of an eyebrow from Admiral Blackstone. A thought dropped into Soup's head: *They've practiced this.* "The standard syllabus calls for eight hops. What happened to the other five?"

One one thousand, two one thousand, three one thousand . . . "You're an experienced pilot, Admiral," Captain Campbell said to Admiral Hansen, engaging him with a "been there, done that" smile. "You've probably gone through more training pipelines than I have over the years. I'm not telling you anything new when I say that phase leaders at the training squadron will work with a pilot to adjust the syllabus to his ability and needs."

"Were the five missing flights about your ability or your needs?" Rear Admiral Zorhanski asked with a wry smile. The other two admirals nodded and smiled along with him.

Soup's first instinct was to grab Admiral Zorhanski around his pencil-thin neck, but instead he smiled back and silently counted to three one thousand again. "I didn't really *miss* the flights, Admiral. They simply looked at my log book and decided three flights would be enough."

Rear Admiral Hansen pounced: "So what Lieutenant Simpson told us isn't true?"

Soup narrowed his eyes and asked, "Who's Lieutenant Simpson?"

"He's the bombing phase leader at the squadron. He said you laughed at his recommendation for the number of flights you should have and then ordered him to give you only three to qualify you for that phase."

So they've been talking to lieutenants, huh? Soup's mind flashed back to that day in the phase leader's office. He saw Simpson, respectful but unyielding. Who'd given these young guys their balls? This is what happens when you have all that mandatory touchy-feely training. Everybody becomes a zealot, a rules Nazi. Nobody respects rank anymore or good old-fashioned leadership. *One one thousand, two one thousand, three one thousand . . .* "I'm not sure it's accurate to say I ordered the lieutenant to do anything, Admiral," Soup said. "As I suggested before, finding the appropriate number of flights is somewhat a collaborative process. There's some haggling involved, if you will." *Haggling?* Not the kind of word Blackstone was comfortable with, certainly—too much ad-libbing going on when you were haggling. Soup felt the first bead of sweat trickle from his underarm across the side of his rib cage. Not a good sign.

"Lieutenant Simpson wasn't alone with his impression, either, Captain," Admiral Blackstone added. "Almost every other phase leader felt like you'd pressured them in the same way. Some even suggested you'd threatened them."

"Threatened?" Soup shot back. "Sir, I assure you I never threatened anyone." A forceful counteroffer was a threat? These youngsters *were* soft. Another bead of sweat flowed. Soon his shirt would be soaked, he feared.

"Lieutenant Murphy, the officer in charge of the carrier qualification phase, said you hit him," Admiral Hansen said.

One one thousand, two one thou—oh, fuck it. "I never hit anyone," Soup insisted. "Not on purpose, anyway. He may have walked into me when—"

"All right," Admiral Blackstone said. "I think we've heard enough."

"No!" Captain Campbell snapped, surprising himself, not to mention the three flag officers across the situation table from him. He took a deep breath. "I mean, I'd like a chance to sum this whole situation up, if I may."

Admiral Blackstone appeared taken aback, and Soup chided himself for the outburst. The board chairman silently polled the members to either side of him and, seeing nothing but shrugs in return, turned to the captain and said, "Go ahead."

So much for a strategy. That was out the window. Suddenly it was fourth and long with only a couple of seconds left on the clock. All he could do now was throw the long bomb.

Soup took a few more deep breaths before he started speaking again. "This air wing suffered a terrible blow when CAG Bernard and Skipper Renforth were killed. Yeah, I'll be honest with you: I'd been chomping at the bit since nine-eleven, trying to figure out a way to get into the action. But when those two great men, leaders and friends of mine, died, I knew my place was here.

"So, I fought hard to get out here; maybe I even went overboard a little bit. And, okay, I admit it: Sometimes I'm a little self-centered. But that's not my crime." He ran his gray eyes across each of them, swagger now fully engaged. "My crime is that I give a damn. I've spent twenty-two years of my life flying jets, most of the time off of aircraft carriers, and when I thought my nation needed me—dare I say, when I answered the call of duty—I took pointed steps to get out here. My goal wasn't to cut corners. It certainly wasn't to hazard my squadronmates or innocents." He focused on Rear Admiral Blackstone. "My goal, sir, was to serve."

Silence followed, a silence that went on for too long. Soup considered their faces, tacitly petitioning them for a response to his impassioned aside, but they yielded nothing. Were these men before him or robots? He fought the urge to cry, "Speak, damn you, speak!"

Admiral Blackstone finally accommodated him: "An officer should be careful not to cloak himself in lofty terms, Captain. Words like 'duty' and 'service' need to resonate within our ranks, and without sound actions around them they lose their meaning. It is clear to this board that you abused your rank to speed your training up enough that you would be eligible to take the deputy air wing commander billet."

Each word chopped away at him, and he sensed the deathblow was imminent. In a second his career flashed before his eyes: the day of his winging, walking through an arch of swords with the brand-new Mrs. Campbell, flying his shiny Hornet in a diamond with the rest of the Blue Angels, reading his name among those selected for major command at sea. The memories would all fade with a few dark words from Rear Admiral Blackstone's lips.

"But this board also finds that that abuse, while notable, was relatively minor and without malice," the admiral continued. "And we're certainly not going to let the press decide anything for us." He paused, brow knit and mouth pursed, momentarily miles away. A second later his refocused eyes evinced that he was back. "So, we're recommending that this matter be dropped and that you be allowed to continue in your present billet with all rights and responsibilities reinstated." He looked once more to the admirals next to him and then lowered a fist to the table like a gavel. "These proceedings are closed."

Soup got to his feet and stood at rigid attention, a bit stunned and unsure exactly of how to make a graceful exit. He thought about shaking their hands, but, seeing no movement on their parts, he simply muttered, "Thank you" and spun on his heel. One thought rose above the myriad thoughts in his head as he hit the door: *I've got to find Lieutenant Ronnie Wheedle.*

CHAPTER ELEVEN

Lal wasn't an airfield in the traditional sense of the word in that there was no way even the most rugged transport plane could have landed there. The long strip of dirt that an anthropologist would have labeled a runway after a great deal of analysis was pockmarked with bomb craters and littered with earthen debris. There were no hangars, control towers, or terminals, and there were no signs that there ever had been any about the field. The scene was ghostly still. The only movements of any kind save that of the Army gathered along the perimeter behind them to the east were from several camels casually traipsing across the flatness in front of them nearly a half mile away.

Punk scanned from horizon to horizon and felt naive for the mental images he'd allowed himself to conjure up since the first time he'd heard Tim speak of the place. In his mind Lal had been a dusty but functional version of any desert facility he'd flown into in the States, airfields in Nevada like Fallon Naval Air

Station or Nellis Air Force Base. He imagined it might be abandoned but never saw it as nonexistent.

"Did they ever actually do flight ops out of this field?" Punk asked whoever among the group standing nearby might care to answer him.

"Not since the early nineties," Tim replied.

"I'm sure we'll get it fixed up in no time," Waco said. "Hell, we'll all be flying back into Lal International for our big reunion with General Haskarim and the gang in a few years. I can even see El Cedar boring the guests at the cocktail party: 'I can remember when there was absolutely *nothing* around here . . .' "

They heard the drone of turboprops approaching in the distance, and Punk looked up and saw the silhouette of a C-130 Hercules cargo plane against the solid layer of gray clouds high overhead.

"You gave them good coordinates, right?" Waco asked Tim.

"Yes, I gave them good coordinates," Tim said, obviously a bit offended by the assertion surrounding the question.

"I'm just asking because I've seen that screwed up before."

"Not with me, you haven't."

"Well, we've never had anything dropped in before, either."

"Okay, then why would you automatically assume I'd screwed it up?"

"It was just a question."

"No, it wasn't just a question."

Nathan pointed straight up and said, "Load's away!"

Punk craned his head back again and saw two large objects drop from the rear of the C-130. A parachute blossomed almost immediately over the first load, but the other one continued to free-fall.

"Streamer!" Nathan cried.

A few seconds later Punk could make out the unfilled chute flapping like a flag above the cube screaming toward the ground. "It doesn't look like it's going to open," Punk observed.

"No, it doesn't," Tim agreed resignedly.

"What's in that box?"

Tim didn't have time to answer, although his answer would have been a guess since he had no idea which of the boxes was which. Two hundred yards away the first palletized load hit with a loud crack and burst, filling the air with paper that showered them like oversized confetti while olive drab MRE bags and splinters of wood scattered across the ground in concentric rings.

"There's your answer," Tim said. "Mail and MREs."

Tim and Waco chased down the pieces of paper with the same intensity they would've employed had one of the duffel bags full of money exploded. Mail, timeless manna to the warrior, was even more cherished by those who received it on an episodic and uncertain basis. Punk, Nathan, and even Mushkai joined in, caught up by the others' enthusiasm and the sport of it all. Between picking letters up Punk peered back into the sky and watched the second box float gently down and hit the dirt without breaking apart. He also noticed that Waco appeared more concerned with the state of the MREs than the mail, although the Green Beret seemed to have weathered the previous night's goat dinner without any personal discomfort.

"Bring everything to me," Tim ordered once it appeared they'd collected the last of the loose bits.

"Don't read anything. Just bring it all to me. This is no joke. Some of this mail may be for my eyes only." The others converged on him and reluctantly handed over their parts of the collection. Punk focused on the pile between the CIA man's palms and estimated it to be about thirty envelopes' high.

Tim rifled through the stack, nodding and humming and stuffing nearly every other envelope into the waistband of his jeans. Once he'd gone through the remaining letters a second time, he bounced them against his knee and announced: "Mail call."

Punk cued up at Tim's feet, hoping for a vicarious morale boost. Waco gave a running commentary as Tim handed him envelopes: "Bill, bill, Mom, brother, bill, junk mail . . . hey, one from my wife. I guess I'm still married after all. Or maybe this is the letter in which she finally tells me she wants that divorce . . ."

"Well, I'll be damned," Tim said with a sly smile. "The U.S. military may not be able to get you two guys out, but they can get your mail in." With that he handed a pair of letters each to Nathan and Punk. Tim looked down at the Afghan boy who was standing by with a wide grin, reveling in the Americans' infectious glee. "Sorry, Mushkai. I don't have any mail for you."

"Here, Mushy," Waco said. "You can have this one. In fact, once you're done reading it, why don't you take it to the general? I'm sure he wouldn't mind paying my credit card bill with a couple of thousand out of the millions just Tim has given him."

After eagerly snatching the two letters out of Tim's hand, Punk noted the return addresses: one from "the boys in the ready room" and the other from Suzanne. He also noted that on the envelope from the States his shipboard address had been lined out and next to it someone had handwritten *Status 1 Kilo*. The letter from the ship was simply labeled *LCDR Reichert, Afghanistan,* which struck Punk as poetically accurate in its vagueness.

Punk followed the others in taking a few steps away, carving a bit of personal space, bathing in the joy of the moment. This was the best he'd felt in days; he wrestled with which letter to open first, milking the emotion for all it was worth. He tore the end off of the top envelope and started to read:

Dear Punk,

One of the loser commanders from the admiral's staff came by the ready room and told us that they might be able to get a letter to you, so we took a vote and, after two ties and a miscount, decided to drop you a line.

First, the news: Peeler's rash is improving. It's taking him three days to go through the tubes of cream Doc gives him instead of two. Elf got an e-mail from his wife informing him she's pregnant. He's done the math several times and is pretty sure he's the father. And Yoda finally benched 100 pounds.

Spud made it back last night with a big bandage on his left hand and immediately demanded a viewing of *Cheers for Reggie*. We're balancing our hatred for that movie with our happiness that the skipper's return may mean that the DCAG is done hanging out in our ready room all the time. Oh, by the way, early word has it the investigation found him innocent of any wrongdoing, so

we're sure this means more pain for Einstein over Afghanistan now.

Speaking of Afghanistan, the skipper
hasn't said much, but we're all just happy
to hear you're with friendlies. Cracker
thought he heard your voice on the radio
yesterday while he was flying a CAS mission
west of where you went down, but he
wasn't sure.

This is kind of a weird letter to be writing,
but hopefully the info the staffer gave us
was right and this will get to you. We miss
you, buddy. We'll be overhead until you
get out of there. See you back on the Boat
soon.

V/R, the Boys

P.S. Peeler says you're still not allowed to
hang out in the Cheesequarters. He says
sorry, but rules are rules, even during
wartime.

Punk smiled as he refolded the letter and stuck it
in a pant leg pocket. He studied the second letter,
focusing on Suzanne's delicate cursive handwriting before noting the postmark: six days old, before he'd
shot himself down. This wouldn't be news, most
likely, since he'd received an e-mail just before
briefing for his fateful mission, but that didn't make
the letter any less welcome considering his current
surroundings. He brought the envelope to his nose—
his custom when receiving mail from significant others over the years—and was pleased that her signature scent lingered on the paper. He opened the
letter more carefully than he had the first and de-
voured the words within:

Dear Rick,

I know we e-mail each other every day, and although I love keeping in touch that way, I felt like writing you a letter. It's late at night and Jason is in bed and for some reason a letter seems more appropriate for my mood right now. Call me old-fashioned.

Nights are still the hardest time for me, as I've told you before. I've almost come to dread them. The noise of the TV just irritates me, so I wind up turning on the radio and listening to classical music. You know I've never been a big fan of classical music, but I guess it reminds me of Cal. You remember what a snob he was when it came to the arts. In any case, it seems to calm me down enough that I can go to sleep, that and a few glasses of wine and maybe a shot of Jack Daniel's now and again.

But I'm not writing this to talk about the past or my budding alcoholism. I'm writing this to tell you how much I miss you. This is a very strange path that has brought us together and certainly not one of our choosing. But that's life, I guess. At least, that's what I've come to believe life is. We kid ourselves into thinking we have control over things when really we should just learn to accept what actually happens to us. In any case, as horrible as this last year has been, as much as I wouldn't ever want to relive it, I'm at peace with things and grateful to God for bringing us together. Our future gives me hope, and I'm living for the day you return.

Take care of yourself out there and dream,

as I do, about the next moments we're
alone together.
  Love, Suzanne

Punk reread the letter and allowed himself to dream
as she'd suggested until he feared the lump in his cammies might make the nature of his dreams known to
the others. He sniffed the envelope one more time
before adding the letter to the leg pocket, steeled by
his desire to survive his present circumstance. Again
he wondered what she knew about his whereabouts.
Maybe it was better that she was out of the wives club
loop. And what, if anything, had been on the news?

"Hey, what about that other box?" Waco asked,
snapping the others out of their mental excursions,
pleasant or otherwise.

"Oh yeah," Tim said. "I was so distracted by the
fact my son made the honor roll that I almost forgot
about it."

They ambled over and pulled the parachute off of
the wooden box and took to the top of it with their
knives. In short order Waco and Tim managed to pry
enough planks off to see what was inside.

"It's the surprise," Tim announced. "Come see,
Punk."

Punk stepped up and looked into the box and
winced in confusion. "Hay?" he asked.

"That's just packing material," Tim explained, "although the horses will love it, I'm sure. Look under
that."

The fighter pilot tilled through the box until he
came to something smooth, brown, and beautiful—a
wonderful surprise, indeed.

"Is this mine?" Punk asked, like a kid who couldn't believe what he'd received for his birthday.

"Sure is," Tim said, beaming like the proud papa who'd dug a bit deeper into his wallet for the special day and was now happy for it. "Break it out and show everybody."

Punk reached elbow deep into the hay and with a grunt straightened up, cradling a brand-new Western saddle in his arms. The others cooed their approval and clapped at the beauty of it.

"We couldn't get you a helicopter, so we figured this was the next best thing," Tim said.

"I don't know what to say," Punk said, wearing an irrepressible grin. "My aching ass thanks you, I guess."

As Waco helped Punk replace the wooden saddle on Bushwhacker with the leather one, Mushkai mentioned that some of the Afghans didn't have a saddle at all and would gladly take the wooden one off their hands, which made Punk feel a bit guilty for complaining about how uncomfortable it had been. He thought back to something his father used to say whenever the Reichert boys started moaning about their meager possessions: "I complained I had no shoes until I met a man with no feet," and that, in turn, made him wonder about Og, and he felt even more guilty for not wondering about him earlier.

"Have we heard from Terry, Tim?" Punk asked as he climbed into the saddle that couldn't have soothed him more had it been marshmallows.

The pilot's question caused some pent-up emotions to erupt from the CIA man: "Kilo base wasn't happy with my decision, but that's tough. Unlike those fools back at base, I've spent years in this country and I know if there's one thing Afghan doctors are good at,

it's an operation involving wounds from land mines.
That's a sad commentary on Afghanistan, I guess, but
that's the way it is. He may not have survived if we'd
kept him with us."

Punk waited for the rest of the answer, but it didn't
come, so he prodded Bushwhacker over to where
Waco was stuffing MREs into a bag slung across a
mule's back.

"You look like you're in the tall cotton now," the
lean Texan said.

"Worlds better," Punk replied. "Now I don't feel
like somebody's wailing on my backside with a two-
by-four."

Waco chuckled and said, "That's good, because I
don't think they'd go to the effort of getting you one
if they didn't think you'd be here for a spell. Hell, El
Cedar, you might even be with us long enough to
break it in."

How long did it take to break a saddle in? Punk
looked down at the shiny leather between his legs and
suddenly yearned for the comfort of his padded ejection seat.

Lieutenant Ronnie Wheedle had come to hate going
to the space the ship had provided for the press corps.
Like squatters they'd taken over, slowly creating their
own world within a world, one with wholly less strin-
gent standards of discipline and cleanliness than the
rest of the ship. Word of this unruly caste had filtered
to the highest levels after the executive officer fielded
complaints from the enlisted men responsible for emp-
tying the space's trash cans. Shortly thereafter the
ship's captain had charged the PAO with keeping the
reporters in line. Wheedle had tried being nice, but
that hadn't worked, so he tried being a hard-ass, which

worked even less. The reporters, made inconsiderate by the nature of their profession if not by nature, had stopped being polite once they'd figured out how to get from their staterooms to the wardroom by themselves. At that point Wheedle had become nothing more than an impediment to them, somebody trying to obfuscate the facts and hide the people's truth, the one they were duty bound to write about.

Lieutenant Wheedle knocked on the door and listened closely to the noises within: the clinking of glasses and the shuffling of papers. Furniture scraped across the floor. "Who is it?" one of them asked.

"Lieutenant Wheedle."

"All right, Lieutenant. Be right there."

Another minute passed without any of the reporters answering the door, so Wheedle knocked again. "May I come in for a second?" he asked. "I've got some news for you."

"Be right there," the same voice repeated, accompanied by several blasts from an aerosol can. Fifteen seconds later the door barely cracked enough for an eye to peek out. "What do you got?"

Wheedle caught a whiff of cigarettes. "You guys aren't smoking in there, are you?"

"Ah, no. No, we're not smoking."

"I've told you before this space is not an authorized smoking area."

"Yeah, yeah. We've got it. Look, we're kind of busy in here, you know, trying to file our stories for the next editions and everything. What can we do for you?"

"The board has found Captain Campbell innocent of any wrongdoing."

"What?"

"Captain Campbell didn't skip any of his training before coming out here. He's been cleared."

The door shut again. Wheedle put an ear against it, trying to hear the conversation on the other side. He thought he heard muffled laughter. The door cracked open again and the eye reappeared. "So, what do you want from us?"

"I thought you might want to report the news."

"What news are you talking about again?"

"Captain Campbell has been cleared," Wheedle shot back, patience waning. "So, are you going to write a story about it or not?"

"You know what our editors would do to us if we tried to pitch that fart in the gale as breaking news? Give us a call when we win the war. On second thought, let us tell *you* when we win the war."

With that the door shut for good.

General Haskarim's augmented Army had rejoined the road just west of Lal and continued westward at a steady pace, through Dowlat Yar, where a mysterious river meandered across the steppe before plunging straight down, seemingly flowing to the center of the Earth, to Chaghcharan, home of an airfield with a hard surface runway that Punk thought was in great shape but CENTCOM claimed was unusable. The following day their progress was slowed by twenty-five miles of a mountain range west of Alandar but once through Owbeh the land began to flatten out. The weather was warmer at the lower altitudes, warm enough for Punk to shed his animal-skin coat. He sat atop Bushwhacker, who'd long since stopped acting up, and realized he'd lost track of how many days he'd been on the ground. He figured that was a sign he'd either become acclimated or had lost his mind.

The Harirud River met the north side of the road just shy of Marwah, and many of the Afghan soldiers stripped down to the long underwear bottoms the Americans had supplied and thrashed around knee-deep in the water. Those mounted allowed their horses' heads to dip, and as they drank, Punk watched the soldiers splash each other and laugh with the innocence of children.

The water was clear and inviting, flowing down from the mountains untouched by man. "I wouldn't mind a dip, Waco," Punk said. "What do you think?"

Waco looked past the river to the north, to the gently rolling foothills that were a welcome sight after days of negotiating the rugged mountains. "Who's watching that flank, Mushy?" he asked.

"General Hussan's forces are over there," the boy replied. "The Tajiks were very insistent on that position. They crossed the river some time ago."

The Green Beret looked to the CIA man on the other side of him. "Just Tim?"

"Go ahead," Tim said with a reluctant sigh. "But just for a bit."

"Tie the horses to the trucks, then, boys. It's swim call!"

The Green Beret bailed out of his saddle and lashed the reins to the nearest bumper before shedding his clothes down to his Skivvies. "No skinny-dipping," he counseled as he peeled off his second boot. "Don't want to offend the locals."

Boodle came riding up on "Pedro," the mule he'd refused to relinquish even after he was offered a place in the cab of one of the vehicles that had appeared out of nowhere once the army got back on the road. "Thank God; bath time," he shouted.

"That reminds me," Waco said, splashing his way back out of the river toward Racecar. "I got a bar of soap in one of these saddlebags."

Punk paused at the bank and gingerly draped several toes in the water. It was cold. Nathan saw him recoil and whacked a wave toward him in jest. "Come on, El Cedar," the Ranger said, river lapping against his chin. "It's *refreshing*."

Punk dodged Nathan's shower and slowly picked his way across the smooth rocks until the water was deep enough for him to dive in. The temperature of the river made his lungs tighten and heart race, but he stayed under the surface for a long time, pulling himself along with languid movements of his arms and legs. He exhaled in metered bursts, loving the feel of the bubbles around his neck and head, and imagined that if he swam far enough without coming up he might surface in a different world, one closer to home and at peace.

He broke the surface to Nathan yelling, "Wacko, how 'bout throwing me the soap?"

"I didn't know you Rangers used the stuff," Waco said as he chucked the bar over.

Nathan lathered up as Punk swam back to where it was shallow enough for him to stand. "Let me see that when you're done," he said to the Ranger.

Nathan complied, and Punk ran the bar across his body like a man possessed. "No shoving the bar down the crack of your ass, El Cedar," Waco said. "That's a party foul."

"I didn't," Punk returned defensively.

"I just saw you do it."

"I was washing the inside of my boxers."

"Sure. Boodle, make sure you rinse that bar extra good before you use it."

"No lie," the aircrewman said as he plucked the soap from where it bobbed across the wavelets like he was picking up a turd.

"Fuck you guys," Punk said and pushed off the bottom and floated on his back. He did the elementary backstroke for a time, staring up at the empty sky and wondering where the jets were, and once he got deep enough, treaded water while facing back toward the others near the shore.

"I am cleansed," Boodle proclaimed, arms spread out across the surface of the river. "I am born anew. Damn, this feels goo—"

The aircrewman's words were broken by a sound Punk had come to know too well: the slap of lead against meat and bone. In the blink of an eye Boodle's forehead grew a red dot and the back of his skull exploded. As he crumpled into the water the report from the shooter's rifle caught up to those left alive in and around the river.

"Take cover!" Tim shouted, jumping off Whose Boy and running behind one of the trucks.

Punk paddled for shore for all he was worth and helped Waco drag Boodle's limp body out of the river and over to where Tim had taken cover. The bullets were hitting all around them now. There was obviously more than one shooter.

"What the hell is this, Mushy?" Waco asked the boy sprawled across the ground at his feet. "I thought you said General Hussan's men were covering us over there."

"I was afraid of this," Mushkai replied dejectedly. "Those *are* General Hussan's men."

"What?" Tim asked, mouth agape with disbelief.

"I'm afraid their allegiance is for sale."

"I just gave them forty thousand dollars."

"I think the Taliban outbid you," Waco opined. "El Cedar, see if Boodle's got a pulse."

Punk ran a finger along the man's neck. The body

was already cold, but at first the pilot wasn't sure if that was due to death or simply the water temperature. He found no pulse.

"He's gone," Punk announced.

An RPG hit a nearby truck and exploded, throwing several bodies into the air. From the base of the foothills the tip of a tank's barrel flashed. Several seconds later the shell blew up harmlessly behind them. "We won't be so lucky with the next one," Waco said.

General Haskarim and Urat rode up with several others, each fighting his horse's fear as another shell landed down the line. The general's face was beet red and contorted in apoplectic rage. Although Punk could make out only *jay-dahm* as the warlord shouted his anger and cast both arms to the north, there was no need for Mushkai to translate the rest.

Immediately after the next explosion, this one in the center of the river, Waco, still garbed only in his Skivvies like the other swimmers, jumped into the adjacent pickup's bed and brought the UHF radio alive: "Bossman, this is Tiger one; Bossman, this is Tiger one. How do you read?"

"Bossman has you loud and clear, Tiger one," a female voice replied. Punk did a quick mental inventory of the AWACS controllers he'd worked with during his time in theater, and it struck him that there'd been an equal split between men and women, and he wondered, in turn, if there were really that many women in the squadron or he'd just happened to wind up with a large proportion of them on the other end of the line by sheer chance. "Go ahead."

"Tiger one is under attack; request close air support on forces north of our position. Do you have assets available?"

"That's affirmative, Tiger one; we're complying with

your earlier request for support. We have two Tom-cats coming to you from Bengals."

Waco winced and keyed the radio again: "What earlier request are you talking about, Bossman? This is the first time I've talked to you." The riverbank in front of the pickup erupted, showering them with rock, sand, and hot shrapnel.

"Bossman, this is the Tiger one," a new voice said. Punk tried to place the accent—Middle Eastern or Cajun? It was impossible to tell through the static. "I need a strike at thirty-four twenty-five-point-two-five north, sixty-two fifty-seven-point-three-nine east. There are troops and vehicles along the dirt road. Anything south of the river is hostile."

Waco eyed his handheld GPS and scratched his beard. "The fucking Tajiks are calling in an air strike on us!" He jerked the handset to his head and transmitted: "Bossman, disregard the previous call. There's an intruder on the net."

"Bossman, disregard that call," the other voice said. "Need immediate air support on the coordinates I just passed."

"Air support is inbound as per your request, Tiger one," the female controller said. "Newark three-five should be coming up your frequency anytime now."

"Negative, negative," Waco shouted into the handset. "I say again, we have an intruder on the net."

"That's impossible," the controller stated. "These radios are encrypted and the communications plan is secret. How would the enemy get hold of the frequencies and the equipment?"

"That's correct," the other voice said. "It is impossible. Standing by for requested air support. Please hurry."

"We gave them the stuff, Bossman," Waco tried to

explain without altogether losing his temper. "Part of our force has turned on us. Disregard the tasking you were given. They're trying to get you to drop on us."

Dead air followed for a few seconds. "I'm confused, Tiger one," the controller said.

"Join the club," Waco seethed. "For now, nobody drops any bombs, Bossman."

"Roger. Newark three-five, are you up this freq?"

"That's affirmative, Bossman," the lead RIO passed, again frustrating Punk with the fact that he couldn't identify the voice through the static. "Newark's a flight of two Tomcats with two GBU-12s each."

"Did he say GBUs?" Tim asked, suddenly peeking up from behind the truck.

"Yeah," Waco shouted over to him. "Two each."

"I've got an idea: Let's use the MULE."

Waco jabbed a finger back at the CIA man. "Now, that's a great idea."

Tim rolled across the ground from the truck to behind the pickup while Waco fished around the equipment strewn about the bed until he found the AN/PAQ-3 Modular Universal Laser Emitter, an olive drab-colored monocular attached to a folded tripod. Tim grabbed the MULE from the Green Beret and crouched by the right front tire where he had a direct line of sight on their new foe.

"Newark three-five, do you copy your mission?" the accented voice asked.

"Newark, ignore that call!" Waco ordered once the blast from another shell hitting nearby quieted a bit. "This freq is compromised. You are to drop on sparkle."

"Newark copies sparkle," the RIO said. "Standing by."

"Newark, you are not cleared hot," the controller

said. "We're trying to clear the situation up with Zeus. They want to redirect a UAV to get a look."

"Jeezus!" Punk spat. He scrambled over to the pickup and took the handset from Waco. "*Arrow-slinger* crew, this is Punk. I say again: This is Punk. I authenticate the tasking. Drop on sparkle!"

"Punk, this is Monster and Elf. It's great to hear your voice. We've got you covered."

Punk passed the handset back to Waco, who said, "Do your thing, just Tim," across the right side of the bed.

"Roger that," Tim replied. "Tell them they should have a designation on the tank north of the river."

"Sparkle on tank north of river," Waco passed over the radio before the other side had a chance to cut him off or further confuse the issue.

"Good sparkle," Elf said. "First bomb's away."

"They're bailing out of the tank," Nathan said, binoculars against his face.

"Of course they are," Waco said. "They can hear the radio, too. Tim, you got that thing blazing?"

"Laser's on and firing," Tim replied, shining the laser energy onto the tank several thousand yards across the barren land, giving the bomb a goal. "Crosshairs rock steady."

Punk saw the GBU explode to the north. "Direct hit," Nathan reported. "That one's dedicated to you, El Cedar." The Ranger dropped the binoculars and looked over his shoulder at the Green Beret. "I guess he's not useless, after all."

"Guess not," Waco agreed, matching the other soldier's smile.

"Newark sees good hit," Elf said over the radio. "We've got three bombs left."

"There's an SUV to the left of the tank," Nathan

said after working the binoculars horizontally a few times.

"I've got it," Tim said. "Not a very cost-effective use of a precision-guided munition, but what the hell."

"Newark's got the sparkle. Second bomb's away."

Twenty-three seconds later the dusty Toyota Land Cruiser disintegrated. When the second cloud of flame and black smoke fully blossomed Nathan proclaimed, "We're out of targets, as far as I can see, unless you want to start dropping on troops in the open."

"Are they in the open?" Waco asked.

"No, not really."

"That would probably be a waste of bombs, then, especially smart bombs."

"Both jets have nose guns," Punk offered. "They could make a few strafing runs."

Waco nodded and keyed the mike: "Newark three-five, Tiger one requests strafing runs on any movement you see near the base of the hills north of the river."

"Newark three-five, this is Punk," the other voice said. "Do not strafe north of the river."

"I didn't say that!" Punk exclaimed from behind the tailgate as if there was some doubt among those gathered around the pickup.

"Disregard that, Newark," Waco transmitted. "That wasn't him. The real Punk is south of the river with Tiger one."

"Newark three-five, this is Zeus," a reedy male voice informed. "You are directed to exit the area immediately. We have a UAV inbound to sort the situation out. Do you copy?"

"Newark copies," Elf returned, resignation poorly masked.

General Hussan and several of his men rode up, and immediately the two warlords entered into an ar-

gument. Each general alternately gestured toward the
other and the foothills, as the discussion grew ever
heated. After a minute's debate, General Haskarim
reached over and pushed General Hussan nearly out
of his saddle and then rode into the narrow river followed by scores of his men.

"There they go again," Waco observed.

"I wish they'd quit doing that," Tim said. "It's hard
to coordinate a war when you've got half of your force
on its own program."

"Or fighting against you," Punk added.

The Afghans cleared the river on the other side and
galloped with their rifles blazing. Many of them fell
as they pressed northward across the flats, but the
general continued his charge undaunted by his losses
along the way.

The radio suddenly crackled with, "Sorry we
couldn't finish the job, Punk."

Punk leaned across the bed and took the handset
from Waco. "No, you did good, fellas. You helped
turn the tide. Thanks."

"What's it like down there?"

Punk paused, grasping for the right words. How
could he possibly condense his experiences over the
last days into a single transmission? He took in the
scene before him at the moment—Afghans charging
and dying, turncoats both surging toward them and
running the other way, trucks burning, an American
serviceman lying dead at his feet, the noises, the
smells, the feelings: hunger, fatigue, pain . . .

"Newark three-five, contact Lion one on Rose
four," the AWACS controller said. "We have additional tasking for you to the northeast."

"Roger, Bossman," Elf transmitted. "We're switching. See you, Punk. Take care of yourself."

"Okay," Punk returned, voice catching slightly. And before he could say anything more the fighters were gone. He returned his attention to the skirmish going on across the river, and through the binoculars he saw the horses running and flashes of gunfire among the foothills. Within minutes the flashes ceased, and not too long after that Punk could see that the horses were headed back toward the river.

As the horses splashed through the shallows of the southern side of the river, Punk noticed that a handful of them had bodies strapped across their backs just behind the riders. Closer still he saw that the bodies weren't dead.

"We have prisoners," Mushkai announced as General Haskarim rode near. They circled the horses and brusquely lowered their prisoners to their feet. There were five of them, four dark-skinned Tajiks and a big white man, bald and red bearded. As Punk recognized the man he remembered him waving a sword above a crazed mob.

"That's Slobo," Punk stammered. The Chechen had survived yet another battle. Punk realized he'd never flee but rather keep coming back until all the people he hated were dead or, at least, defeated.

"Which guy are you talking about?" Tim asked.

"Who else? The white guy."

The Americans were surprised to see the Afghans cutting the bindings from around the hands and feet of the prisoners. "What are you doing?" Tim asked as he stepped closer to the growing knot of activity.

"All of these men have brothers here," Mushkai said. "We must treat them with proper respect, even though they have done wrong. It is the Afghan way."

Arguments broke out all around. The two generals exchanged terse words, presumably over how to handle the prisoners. Brother descended on brother, and the Tajik prisoners tried to ward off slaps from their siblings. Punk kept an eye on Slobo: The Chechen stood boldly among the activity, amused by the chaos. Others joined the clutch, kicking up dust as they shuffled their feet in heated debate, and soon it was hard to tell captive from captor.

Tim raised his M-4 and fired a single shot, which stilled the mob. "All right. Knock it off. Mushkai, tell the generals we'd like to interrogate the prisoners away from the others for a few minutes."

The boy turned and addressed his boss and then looked back to Tim. "You can question the prisoners, but other family members must be with them."

Tim shook his head. "No, no, Mushkai. We need to speak to the prisoners alone, just for a few minutes."

"Kafi na ast," General Haskarim said to the CIA man.

"It is not possible," Mushkai translated. Punk noted how the boy's accent grew thicker any time the discussion turned even the slightest bit confrontational. "Brother must stay in the custody of brother until justice is served. It is the Afghan way."

Tim cursed under his breath and said, "Okay, the brothers can come along, but have them mind their rifles. Let's get everybody over behind the pickup truck."

Mushkai relayed the guidance, and a dozen of them, including Slobo, began a slow shuffle over to the vehicles.

"I don't get it," Nathan said, rifle trained at the feet of the group of prisoners and their relatives. "One minute they're ready to kill each other and the next they're family again. I don't like it."

"I agree," Waco said, M-4 raised with the Ranger's.

"Stay cool," Tim said, "but keep your eyes open."

Punk unslung his rifle from his right shoulder and held it at his hip. He focused on the group of Afghans and one Chechen moving slowly in front of him, trying to keep tabs on the ones without rifles. The cavalier attitude of all of them was unnerving; the situation presently had a dangerous lack of definition.

Tim obviously felt the same way. "I want everybody to spread out," he ordered, which Mushkai relayed in the native tongue.

"Have these men been searched, Mushy?" Waco asked.

The boy shrugged.

"Waco, you take those three, and I'll take the other two," Tim said. "Nate, you guard Waco's guys while he's doing the searches, and El Cedar, you watch mine."

Without any more discussion the Americans went to work, and as Tim started to pat down one of the Tajiks, Punk suddenly found himself squared off with Slobo. The Chechen's brow knit as he studied the American across from him, and then his face brightened.

"American *pee-lot*," Slobo said, broad smile creasing his beard. "We meet again. *Salam.*"

"Shut up, Slobo," Punk directed, sounding less resolute than he'd intended.

"I am surprised to see you in Afghanistan still. Where is your friend, the one who is now missing a finger?" A belly laugh roared out of him.

"Shut up," Punk repeated. "And don't move."

"*Kho,* come now," Slobo said, not at all intimidated by the rifle Punk had aimed at his chest. "Don't you think this is funny that I am now your prisoner after you were my prisoner?"

Punk saw the Chechen's left arm disappear behind him. "This is funny, yes?" Slobo said between laughs.

"I said shut up and don't move!"

Slobo's arm reappeared from behind his back, a blur of motion. Punk caught a glimpse of something black, and by the time he realized it was a gun, the Chechen nearly had the pistol trained on him. Punk started to raise his rifle, but all he could think was it was too late.

A shot rang out and the back of Slobo's skull exploded. For a second the big man teetered in place as if only dazed by the bullet, but then he crumpled where he stood. At the far end of the line one of the prisoners reached for the rifle of the inattentive Afghan behind him, but before he could grab it Waco punched him in the face, knocking him flat onto his back, unconscious.

Waco stepped in front of the line and passed the end of his barrel across all the prisoners who remained standing as well as their adjacent brothers. "Now, nobody move, goddam it! We'll smoke all of you if you do." The prisoners froze with no translation required.

"What the hell were you waiting for, El Cedar?" Nathan asked, smoking rifle still pointed at Slobo's body sprawled across the dirt.

There was no good answer to that question, so Punk stood mute. He wondered what he could've done differently short of shooting Slobo the moment he recognized him.

"So much for an interrogation," Tim said. "*Afghan way,* huh, Mushkai?"

The boy took a few defiant steps across the dirt and pointed down at Slobo's dead body. "This man was not an Afghan."

CHAPTER TWELVE

Spud found it strange that in the heart of the dinner hour the only people in the Flag Mess were Rear Admiral Dykstra, Captain Campbell, and he, but then he looked at his watch and realized it was nearly midnight. Where had the evening gone? For that matter, where had the day gone? He reflected on this phenomenon, this inability to sense the passage of time, that had plagued him since his return to the Boat and wondered if the drugs Doc had given him for the pain were slowly and irreparably killing his brain.

Was Soup staring at his hand? He dropped his arm to the table and the DCAG's eyes followed it. He *was* staring.

No surprise, really. Soup had been obsessed with the missing finger since his first visit to Spud's bedside in the ward on the second deck. He'd stayed to watch the corpsman change the bandage and focused unblinking at the stub while the antibiotic ointment was being spread over the tip of it. And along with the obligatory questions about whether or not it still felt like his pinkie were there, Soup probed for dark details surrounding the event: Had he caught the Chechen's expression as the man was mutilating him? How intense had the pain been before he'd passed out?

For his part, while he was able to walk a listener through the ordeal, Spud hadn't yet figured out how exactly he felt about the loss of his finger. He wasn't happy about it, of course, but neither was he despondent. In the quiet moments when the ward was dark and the other patients were asleep, he'd peel the bandage back and look at his wound with a strange detachment, as if he were looking at someone else's hand and this other person had lost a pinkie but had survived to tell about it. He considered things he might not be able to do with his left hand now, but that list was short and, for the most part, inconsequential. An old grade-school joke kept popping into his head:

> *Doctor, will I be able to play piano after the operation?*
> *Why, yes.*
> *That's great; I never played before.*

One of the wardroom attendants placed a tray of cookies in front of the admiral. "What kind are these?" the admiral asked.

"Chocolate chip," the freckle-faced enlisted man wearing a plain white dress shirt and black slacks replied.

Admiral Dykstra pointed at the tray. "Those aren't chocolate chips."

"They're M&Ms, sir," the attendant mumbled.

"Aha." The admiral looked at the other two officers

at the table. "M&Ms are not chocolate chips, wouldn't you agree?"

Soup shrugged and gave a nod.

"They *are* chocolate," Spud observed.

"Yes, but not chocolate chips," the admiral countered, making a dramatic arch out of one of his bushy white eyebrows. "Or is that a trivial difference?"

This was it: the first crossroads of the second half of Spud's career. He read the admiral's eyes. Did the battle group commander favor the fussbudget who was inclined to split hairs at every turn? Or did he want his leaders to be above those sorts of frays and focused on the big picture? The seconds ticked by. Rear Admiral Dykstra waited patiently for an answer, eyes unblinking.

"Are they warm?" Spud asked.

The admiral's face brightened. "Yes, they are. We serve only fresh-baked in this mess, right Smitty?"

"Yes, sir," the attendant said.

"Could a guy get a glass of ice-cold milk with that?" the admiral asked.

"Yes, sir. Coming right up."

For a time the three senior officers were lost in the sugary delights. Each gobbled his fair share washed down with fresh milk. The admiral pointed out that the milk had been brought aboard that very day, unlike the packaged milk, what Punk called "nuclear milk," a chalky liquid designed to survive months on a shelf, served in Wardroom One since they'd entered the Gulf. In no time the cookies were transformed into a small gathering of crumbs.

"Your boy is approaching Herat," Rear Admiral Dykstra said to Spud, pushing away from the end of the table and leaning back in his chair.

"My boy?" Spud said. "Lieutenant Commander Reichert, you mean, sir?"

"You have another boy on the ground in Afghanistan?"

Spud wrestled with whether to remain silent and accept the tidbit of information the admiral had just given him. But as he thought of Punk on the ground with the likes of Slobo, he decided to risk angering the admiral. He had to know more.

"How and when is he getting out of there?"

"I guess that depends on how quickly the situation is stabilized. Once that happens he'll be gone pretty quick."

Spud snorted a sardonic guffaw. "Very respectfully, Admiral, we're way past 'pretty quick.' "

An awkward silence followed punctuated only by several sharp clicking sounds made by the admiral's tongue against the back of his teeth. As Spud kept his eyes glued to the admiral he sensed Soup's cold stare against the side of his head.

"I'm sorry, Commander," Admiral Dykstra said. "I'm not sure I understand what you're saying."

Spud forced himself not to break eye contact. "It just doesn't seem like we've tried as hard as we could have to get Lieutenant Commander Reichert out of there."

"And who's 'we'?"

Spud finished a last bite of cookie and thought about his answer before speaking again. "We . . . the Navy; we . . . CENTCOM; we . . . the United States of America—"

"So you don't mean 'we' as in 'me'?"

"No, sir. I just mean 'we' as in 'we.' "

"Because I'm satisfied that the appropriate effort

was made every step of the way. Would you not agree with that, Commander?"

Again Spud sat silently, considering his response. "Look, we're all fighter guys here, right?" the admiral continued, leaning forward and throwing his big forearms across the table before Spud managed to fashion an answer. "Let's not bullshit each other." He pointed at the commander. "Remind me how you two wound up on the ground?"

Spud stiffened a bit and said, "We had one bomb fuse on another and explode right as it left the airplane."

"No, no," Admiral Dykstra returned. "You're leaving out some important details. Let's back up to the planning phase of the mission. You did some last-minute weaponeering, right?"

Spud took a deep breath. The tenor of the casual get-together had suddenly shifted away from casual. "We adjusted our bomb load so that we could do the mission in spite of the CENTCOM moratorium on Rockeye. We modified our weaponeering appropriately. I'm sure you've seen the mishap report, sir. The investigators found a problem with that lot of TDD-34 fuses, not with our weaponeering."

"Yeah, I read it," the admiral said. "But I'm not sure I buy it."

"Buy what—"

Soup raised a hand and silenced Spud. "Admiral, certainly you're not blaming the crew for what happened with their bombs?"

The admiral looked away from Soup and back to Spud. "How many times have you had to eject?"

"Four," Spud intoned.

"Four times!" the admiral shot back. "And how about your pilot Lieutenant Commander Reichert?"

"Twice."

Rear Admiral Dykstra threw his head back and laughed. "I've got more flight hours than the both of you combined, but I've never had to eject. Now, why is that? Am I just lucky?"

Yeah, you're just lucky, Spud thought as his blood started to boil. He bit his lip and reflected on what he knew about Dutch Dykstra's career: He'd been too young for Vietnam and too old for any of the more recent shooting wars. While those facts would certainly mitigate the admiral's bravado, there was no bringing them up in the current forum.

"A rescue attempt was made and it went very poorly," the admiral said after nurturing the stillness that followed his last rhetorical question. "Beyond that, I repeat: I'm satisfied that appropriate steps were taken to ensure Lieutenant Commander Reichert's well-being."

One of the Flag Staff Watch officers poked his head through the side door to the mess and said, "Admiral, your presence is requested in the command center for a moment. We need you to advise on the surface picture."

Rear Admiral Dykstra got up from the table and stepped directly to the door, but he paused before passing through it and looked back at the two officers now on their feet. "I care about each one of my people, skipper, but you can't expect us to celebrate dubious events," he said. Then he pointed toward Captain Campbell and chuckled. "Hell, as big a joke as his being a hero was, even he didn't shoot himself down."

Admiral Dykstra slipped out, leaving Soup and Spud alone in the Flag Mess. Spud wanted to say something witty to clear the air, but nothing came to him. In the silence he furtively glanced across the table at Soup standing with his shoulders rolled forward, staring blankly at the back of the door. Spud wasn't sure what he saw in the captain's expression—hurt, frustration, or ire—but for the first time he could remember, he actually felt a bit sorry for the man.

The sky had grown overcast during the night and the temperature had dropped to the point that Punk didn't shed his jacket after waking. The wind kicked up the sand, creating a dirty blanket across the earth and limiting visibility to no more than a few miles for most of the morning. By the time they lunched on the last of the MREs, the breeze had died enough that they could just make out the skyline of Herat, defined by a line of ancient minarets and the spires of the city's mosques.

Punk twisted in the saddle and considered the men, beasts, and machinery stretched all around him and thought it an impressive sight. General Haskarim was out front with General Hussan to his right in slight trail. Punk wondered how they'd worked out the little tear in the fabric of unity that was yesterday's Tajik uprising. The shift in allegiances had cost Boodle his life, but it seemed there was nothing more to work out beyond accepting the quirks of the Afghan way.

The generals seemed simpatico enough now, anyway. Both rode proudly, backs ramrod straight atop their mounts. They seemed eager for the fight that was surely coming, but at the same time the pace at which they led the force was deliberate, perhaps even tentative. Punk sensed the first shell was already on its way toward them; someone was about to step on a land mine. The stillness taunted him; his heart raced, and in spite of constantly drawing from his canteen, his mouth was dry. He tried to spit but could only muster up a few white flecks of saliva that disappeared before they hit the dirt.

Punk wasn't alone among the Americans with his apprehension. "What do you think, Waco?" Nathan asked over his left shoulder.

"About what?" the Green Beret returned.

"When's the shooting going to start?"

Waco shrugged. "Maybe it won't. Maybe the Taliban heard we were coming and ran off."

"I hate this."

"What?"

"This waiting. It drives me crazy. I wish they'd just get on with it."

"Just relax, Nate. No reason to die all tensed up."

"You guys say that too, huh?" Punk said.

"What?"

" 'No reason to die all tensed up.' That's an aviator's saying."

"That's bullshit. That ain't no flyboy saying; it's Green Beret, tried and true."

"No, I don't think so, Waco. I've heard that since I was in flight school."

Waco gave Racecar a single kick and moved astride the pilot. "Look, let's get one thing straight: We ain't never copped nothing off you all. Nothing. You guys talking about dying? When's the last time you took off knowing you were going to get shot at? Really shot at? And being really shot at don't mean flying around a million miles overhead looking at a damn screen like some video game, neither."

A dot shrouded in a cloud of dust grew to the west. A lone rider approached. General Haskarim shouted an order and raised an arm. "Hold your fire," Mushkai relayed.

The rider tugged his horse to an abrupt halt directly

before the generals, gesturing wildly as he shouted his news. The two generals raised their arms jubilantly and without explanation continued for the city in a full gallop. Their cue rippled down the line, and one by one the riders matched the warlords' pace.

"This can mean only one thing," Mushkai shouted as he kicked Sor'at. "The Taliban have gone. Herat is ours!"

"I told you," Waco yelled over to Nathan.

"We're not there yet, Wacko," Nathan yelled back. "And I haven't seen anything since I've been here that's filled me with trust."

Cheers and celebratory gunfire echoed about the approaching army as the word spread of their apparent victory. "The people will be greeting us with open arms," Mushkai called over with his jacket flapping and his face beaming as he urged his horse on. "All the bounty of Herat will be at our disposal."

The road was more defined at the city's approach and lined with the skeletons of tall trees that Punk guessed were once lush evergreens. General Haskarim slowed the pace to a walk and ordered everyone to form some semblance of ranks behind him.

"He wants the people to properly see their liberators," Mushkai explained. "It is a great day for the people."

"How long has it been since you were last in Herat, Mushy?" Waco asked.

"I have never been here," the boy said. "But the stories I have heard from my father and General Haskarim make it feel like home."

Punk watched Urat rush up and down the line, barking orders and directing stragglers into the line. In time they were as organized as the ragtag bunch was ever going to be.

Past the verdant entry, the colors were more in concert with the city's high desert locale: all of the structures regardless of size were a narrow range of tan that matched the color of the roads. The only brilliant hues to be found were in the spires of the mosques that had beckoned to them from the distance, ornate ceramic inlays in greens and blues.

"It's Mos Eisley," Nathan said. "We're in the middle of a fucking *Star Wars* movie."

"Now that you mention it," Waco said, "it does kind of remind me of that. So what does that make us? The rebels or the evil empire?"

"Easy with the chatter," Tim said. "Keep your eyes on the rooftops. I still don't believe we're just going to walk into the city without a fight."

The procession wound its way through the outskirts and onto the narrow streets of the city. Around each bend Punk expected to see a cheering throng like those that greeted the allies toward the end of World War II, but the few people reservedly staring out from the doorways and windows all wore the expressions of those who'd seen too many changes of the guard over the years. No flowers were thrown; no music played. The better parts of some blocks had been leveled; some of them still smoldered.

"There's your answer to where the Taliban went, Waco," Punk said. "Air strikes did them in."

"I wonder if this is what they meant to hit," Waco returned. "Why bomb the middle of a neighborhood?"

"A lot of times the bad guys hide their command-and-control headquarters among civilian facilities. The beauty of precision weapons is we can get them anyway."

"Thank God for that," Waco cracked, pointing

toward a twisted strip of shiny red metal and a tiny spoked wheel between some rubble. "Osama won't be doing any damage with that tricycle anytime soon."

Past the confined passages of the residential district they came upon a large square framed at the far end by what appeared to Punk to be a mosque crossed with a fort. Around either side of it a handful of locals moved toward them, including women dressed in light blue burqas, the fundamentalist Islamic clothing that covered them from head to toe with only a narrow slit for the eyes, which made the scene even more surreal. These were the first females Punk had seen in Afghanistan. The handful quickly multiplied into a crowd that grew until the far end of the square was teeming with people. The human sea washed toward them in strange silence while the army fanned out to either side of the warlords.

In the middle of the square General Haskarim reached across the back of his saddle for his rifle, and as he did the Americans found their triggers, as well. The crowd saw the general had drawn his weapon and stopped its advance. For a time the two parties remained frozen several hundred yards apart.

The general put his rifle to his shoulder and, after passing the barrel over the heads of the throng, took aim directly to his left. Punk followed the line of the rifle and saw he was aimed at a large portrait that dominated the front of the largest building on the western side of the square. The subject in the portrait wore a long black beard and a black turban—a Taliban principal, no doubt. The general squeezed off two shots, one at either of the upper corners, and the portrait swung once and then fell, hitting the square and shattering the frame with a loud bang.

With that the crowd erupted in one massive roar and

surged in all directions like water bursting through a dam. Punk couldn't figure out if they were pleased or distressed by the general's action until he saw a group of them descend on the fallen portrait and systematically tear it to bits. Others swarmed around the two generals' horses, chanting something in unison with their fists in the air. General Haskarim clasped General Hussan's hand, and together they raised their arms in a gesture that generated another loud cheer from the gathering.

Music now blared from a rooftop, a frantic tune that sounded like someone bearing down on a melodic duck while accompanied by a tambourine. People began to dance, bumping together in a Middle Eastern version of the mosh pit. Nearby a young girl was caught up in the joy enough to pull off the hood of her burqa.

The two generals were lifted off of their horses and hoisted onto the shoulders of several in the crowd. They flowed atop a sea of adulation, smiles as wide as the distance they'd traveled to get there. Punk looked over to Mushkai and saw there were tears streaming down the boy's face.

Waco saw it too. He prodded Racecar a few steps, careful not to trample anyone, and leaned over to offer the boy a comforting pat on the back. Mushkai stiffened with his touch, and a scowl came over his face. "You must go now," he said and turned with a fist in the air and joined his countrymen in a chant.

The Green Beret sat back in his saddle, confused and hurt by the boy's response. Waco tried to say something back to the young translator, but Tim stopped him and then signaled the other Americans to recede from the celebration. They formed their horses at the south end of the square and watched the crowd start a fire with the frame of the big portrait.

"So that's it, huh?" Waco asked, pulling his shades

off in disgust. "Not so much as a handshake, not to mention a thank-you."

"The Taliban are gone," Tim said. "What did you want beyond that?"

"Hell, a little appreciation might be nice."

"Yeah," Nathan agreed. "What about all the guys we lost?"

"The general lost a few, too," Tim said. "Come on. Let's go."

"Where?" Waco asked.

Tim held his satellite phone up and smiled. "The next bunch of ingrates is waiting for us."

After handing his reins to the CIA man, Waco commandeered the pickup with the comms gear in the back of it and fell in behind the horses as Tim led them out of the square and back down the narrow streets. The city seemed deserted. Word of the celebration had quickly spread.

Tim said that in their last e-mail Kilo base had ordered Tiger one to proceed to the airport south of the city. He worked to decipher street signs as Waco and Nathan looked at city maps and agreed that as long as they kept heading south they would be all right.

They rounded corner after corner until they came upon a marketplace. Waco parked the truck and got out while the others dismounted for a closer look. The stalls were unattended save one surrounded by tables piled high with small rugs and bolts of cotton and silk. Beyond that were stacks of clothing, and as Punk examined them he was surprised to see replica jerseys of American sports heroes: Manning, Iverson, Jordan, Robinson, and others in both home and away colors.

"Where the hell did these come from?" Punk wondered aloud, running his fingers along the emblem stitching.

"Black market," Tim replied. "No way these are

authorized brands, in any case. No such thing as copyright laws in this part of the world."

The vendor, a fat man with a silver beard and round eyes, snapped his head around and glared at Tim. "I beg your pardon, chap," he said with a British accent. "These are licensed products. I am the sole supplier in all of Afghanistan."

The Americans shuffled about awkwardly, taken aback by the man's English and slightly embarrassed by Tim's assertion.

"Are these popular around here?" Punk asked.

"Quite," the man replied. "Even the Taliban teens bought them; why, I'm not sure. I never saw any of them actually wear them." He threw his hands up. "But that's not my concern is it?"

The man moved to another table with the aid of a crutch, and Punk could see that one of his legs was missing below the knee. He wanted to ask him how it happened, to ask him how he'd learned to speak English, to ask him what he thought about their recent liberation, but instead he reached into the adjacent stack and pulled out a plain white T-shirt with HERAT across the front of it in plain block letters.

"How much for this one?" Punk said.

"American dollars?" the man asked back.

"Yeah."

"Twenty."

"Twenty? In the middle of Afghanistan?"

The man shrugged.

Punk turned to the CIA man and asked, "Can I borrow twenty bucks?"

Tim let out a heavy sigh and said, "You know I only have thousand dollar bills."

"We could buy fifty of them," Nathan said. "They'd make great Christmas gifts."

"Here, I got you covered, El Cedar," Waco said and turned toward the hefty Afghan. "I'll take these two."

The man seized the two bills from Waco's hand and said, "Thank you."

"Thank you for what?" Waco returned.

"For buying the shirts," the man said.

"And what else?"

The Afghan stood mute, eyes searching the Green Beret's expression for an answer.

"Ah, forget it," Waco said, throwing one of the shirts at Punk. "Here, you can leave Afghanistan now; you got the T-shirt."

Punk started to move toward Bushwhacker, and as he did he caught his reflection in a mirror tacked to a post that held up one corner of the clothier's booth. At first he didn't recognize himself. Who was this fellow in the *pakol* with the days-old growth of beard and the dark circles under his eyes? And how did he differ from the one who'd floated to earth nearly a week earlier?

They left the market and eventually came to a rusty iron fence that led to a gate, slightly ajar and gripped by tangles of brown vines. Above the gate was a sign adorned with Cyrillic scribbles and below it a single English word: ZOO.

"The zoo, huh?" Waco said with his head craned out the door of the pickup.

"According to this map if we go through the zoo we'll pick up the road to the airport on the other side," Nathan reported.

"After shooting our way across Afghanistan we could probably use a day at the zoo," Tim said. "Maybe we can even get some cotton candy along the way."

They pulled away some of the vines and opened the

gate wide enough for the vehicle to pass through. Just inside they had to dismount and lug a trunk out of the concrete path in order for Waco to drive on, and at that point they decided to walk with the horses in tow. It felt good to walk.

Past the decrepit latticework arch of the entryway was a small building with a square cut out of the face of it. The building's paint was peeling in long strips that split poorly drawn Walt Disney characters whose colors had long since faded from their burnished beginnings. Along the bottom edge of the cutout was a ledge.

Closer Punk saw the back wall of the building was painted to look like the skyline of Herat. There were the minarets, the spires at the end of the square they'd just been in, and the line of trees along the eastern approach, only flourishing here, full and green—faded green but green nonetheless. He imagined the puppet show being staged to the delight of the youngsters seated before the small stage. He saw their smiles and heard their laughter. A chill came over him. How long had it been since joy had visited the very place he stood? How many small souls had been taken since then? Would General Haskarim see to it that the shows started up again soon?

Behind the puppet theater rose the chain-link dome of an aviary that had long since lost its birds through gaping holes in the top of it. Across the path from the damaged aviary was a cinder-block structure with a sign over the door that read MONKEY HOUSE.

"Let's give it a look," Tim said.

"What? Terrorist monkeys?" Waco joked.

"Could be a weapons storage area . . . anything."

"All right," Waco said. "I'll go first since I'm trained for this sort of shit."

They tied the horses to the pickup and made for the entrance in spite of the growing pungency as they approached. Waco opened the door with the tip of his rifle barrel and moved inside, then waved the rest of them in behind him.

Inside they found a single filthy, emaciated simian sitting listlessly on a ledge near the bars that made up the roof, unconcerned about the humans pressing against the cage. Around the monkey were the bones of his former cell mates as well as several partially decomposed carcasses. Their eyes watered and their noses burned with the overpowering stench of urine. Nathan was the first to gag and run out, with the others in close trail.

Back in the open they gulped the air, and once they got their legs back they untied the reins from the pickup and continued for the zoo's southern end. Next to a dilapidated arcade a miniature Ferris wheel had rolled off of its mount and collapsed, bringing the cars to rest in a manner that resembled a multivehicle pileup. A dozen steps later they came upon one final cage labeled: LION, KING OF BEAST.

The cage was littered with RPG fins, spent bullet casings, and grenade fragments. Halfway across the width of it the big cat was stretched along a plateau of smooth rock. At the foot of the rock was a stagnant pond capped with a film of scum. The lion's ribs poked through his sallow coat; his mane was matted and the scalp showed in places where the hair had either fallen out from disease or been shot away. A closer look at his face showed several old wounds: Part of his jaw was missing, along with one of his eyes. Just outside the reach of the lion's forepaws rested a long bone, and a few feet away from that was a human skull lying on its side, half buried in a patch of dried mud.

The strange silence was suddenly shattered as three pairs of all-terrain vehicles came roaring through the zoo's southern gate. Waco and Nathan raised their rifles but quickly pointed them elsewhere as they noted the riders' uniforms and black crash helmets.

The convoy came to a halt in a series of skids, and as soon as it did the lead rider popped off his ATV and raised his goggles. "Damn, that lion's fucked up," he said without identifying himself or offering a greeting.

"Who are you?" Tim asked.

"You Lieutenant Commander Reichert?" the rider asked back.

"No, he is."

The rider looked at Punk and, with a jerk of his thumb over his shoulder, said, "Let's go."

"Where?" Punk asked.

"We've got a C-17 at the airport, waiting to take you to Pakistan."

"Pakistan?"

"Yeah, and then one of your planes is going to take you back to your aircraft carrier." The rider tapped his big black watch. "These pilots aren't going to wait forever. They're not too happy about the security situation here. Let's go."

Punk looked at Tim.

"Well," the CIA man said with a shrug, "you'd better get going, then."

"What about you guys?" Punk asked.

"We've got our orders. We'll be flying out to K-2 this afternoon."

"Is Ivan fixed?"

Tim put a finger to his lips. "I've said too much already." He extended his hand. "Good luck."

"I'm not sure what to say," Punk said, pumping

Tim's arm. "Without you guys I wouldn't be going home."

"You're not there yet. Don't jinx it."

Punk looked at Nathan and asked, "Isn't your unit in Pakistan?"

"I don't know," the Ranger mumbled back, averting his eyes. "If it's okay with these guys, I think I'll just hang out with them for a bit and see what happens."

Down the line Punk considered Waco's steel-blue eyes and figured the Texan wasn't much for emotional good-byes, so he shook his hand and simply said, "Good-bye . . . and thanks."

Waco allowed a crooked half-mouthed smile and returned, "Try not to shoot yourself down again."

Punk smiled and said, "Can I get any word home for you or anything like that?"

"Naw."

"Because we've got a phone on the carrier that can call right to your house."

Waco pointed to Tim's right hand and said, "So do we. Of course, we don't use it for that, but just knowing we could is enough for me."

Punk and Waco stood, nodding at each other, unsure of what else to say, until the lead rider cranked his ATV back up. With that Punk turned and said, "Take me home, boys," and he climbed on the back of the first four-wheeler with his Herat T-shirt shoved down the front of his animal-skin coat.

They'd just started moving when Punk said something into the ear of his driver. The convoy stopped in a chain reaction, and the pilot bailed off and returned to the three he'd just left. "I need a pen and a piece of paper," he said.

"What for?" Waco asked, fishing into a pocket of

his fleece and producing a small wire-bound notebook with a pen attached to it.

Punk took the pen and scribbled four digits on the top sheet of paper. "This is my squadron's base frequency," he explained. "Anytime you guys aren't getting the air support you need, you call for an *Arrowslinger*. We'll be there."

Waco took the paper and pen back and said, "I had a girlfriend say something like that to me a few years back right before she ran off with a biker."

"I'm serious, Waco. Make the call."

"Sure, sure. You'd better get on your bad motor scooter there. Those D-boys look like they're getting antsy."

On his way back to the line of ATVs Punk stopped to pat Bushwhacker on the nose. "Take care of my horse," he called over his shoulder. "And my saddle."

"You got it, El Cedar," Waco yelled back.

Two by two the ATVs raced back through the gate, and Punk wrapped his fingers around the cargo rack to keep from tumbling off while he held his *pakol* tight against his head. As they sped around the first corner, Punk twisted his head to get one more look at the men who had shepherded him across Afghanistan, but they'd disappeared in the convoy's cloud of dust.

CHAPTER THIRTEEN

Awaking, Punk struggled to figure out where he was. He'd slept very deeply, hours unpunctuated by sudden wake-ups or recallable dreams, and now his eyes were slow to focus. He saw movement: a man across from him, he thought, thin with blond hair.

"Waco?" he uttered in a voice that told he had not yet regained dominion over his mouth and tongue.

"Oh, good, you're up," the man said, coming closer, close enough that, even with blurred vision, Punk could see he was very young. "You've been out for over ten hours, sir."

Punk blinked until the red blob on the bulkhead across from where he lay sharpened into a cross, and then it all came back to him: He was back aboard the Boat, in the sick bay.

"Your timing's perfect, sir," the young man said. "I just went and got breakfast for you. I hope you like scrambled eggs and bacon."

"I do, thanks," Punk replied as he started to sit up.

"I'm Hospitalman Second Class Shepard, but every-

body calls me 'Shep,' so please, sir, call me 'Shep.' "
Punk studied the petty officer's face as he spoke, marveling at how young he looked. "I'll be your go-to guy during day shift, so if you need anything—aspirin, water, a magazine, whatever—just let me know."

"How old are you?" Punk asked just before shoving a forkful of egg into his mouth.

"Me?"

"Yeah, if you don't mind my asking."

"Oh, no, sir. I get that question all the time. I'm twenty-two. I know I don't look it, but I really am. I'm constantly getting carded in bars, you know, which is a real drag. But my mom tells me I'll appreciate it later in life when everybody else looks older than they really are and I don't. I guess that's true, but for right now I'm kind of sick of people always . . ."

Christ, a talker. Punk really didn't feel like chatting at the moment, and he felt like listening to a bedside stream of consciousness even less. ". . . and these guys are like, 'Go for it, dude,' and I was thinking, 'No way,' but it turns out she wanted to dance with me because I was young looking and she thought I'd snuck into the club or used a fake ID or something, and I was wondering if she really had a thing for young-looking guys or she was just using me to keep other guys away or she thought I was harmless. It's hard to tell, you know? So, anyway I—"

"Can I get something to drink, Shep?"

"Oh, yes, sir. I'm sorry. I should have thought of that. I'll be right back. Is ice water okay?"

"That would be great."

As he watched Shep rush away Punk spotted a sheet of paper at the foot of his bed. He moved his plate aside and grabbed it, and saw it was a printout of an article posted on the Internet. The headline read

DOWNED FLYER RETURNS TO SHIP. In the center of the layout was a picture of Spud greeting him on the flight deck as he stepped off the COD's ramp, jubilance beaming from both of their faces. He began to read while crunching down on what remained of the bacon on his plate.

"Here you go, sir," Shep said, hustling around the corner with a tall glass of ice water. He saw Punk's hands were full. "I'll just set it down over here. I see you found the news article I printed out for you. You're quite the celebrity, sir. That's not the only newspaper that ran pictures of you, either. And you were on TV. Are you married, sir?"

"No."

"Then I'd pay good money to be in your shoes once we get back Stateside. You're going to be like a rock star. It'll be nothing but late nights and limos for you, sir. I'll tell you what. Have you ever ridden in a limo? Me and a buddy got together for our senior prom and rented one, thinking our dates would be big-time impressed, you know? But my date's dad saw us drive up and said no way was she going out with me in that thing, like I had nothing but bad things in mind or something, which I did, but that's another story. Of course, if you want anyone to recognize you you're going to have to keep the beard, which you obviously can't because you're in the Navy. I heard that back in the eighties you could grow a beard in the Navy. Is that true? I wonder why they changed that. I think that should be allowed, don't you? I mean, what's the big deal about a beard, sort of like, what's the big deal about long hair? I'd grow one, if they'd let me, although I can barely grow a mustache and I doubt a full beard would come in any better. You know in the Civil War they—"

"Can you do me another favor, Shep?" Punk asked, scratching at the dense hair across his face. "Can you get me a razor and some shaving cream?"

"Certainly, sir." Shep pointed to Punk's breakfast plate. "Are you done with that?"

"Yes, I am. Thanks. It was quite good."

"Yeah, they do a good job in the aft galley. It's generally much better than the forward galley, but sometimes the line is too long and I don't have much time so I just wind up going wherever I can, you know. It's not that the forward galley is that bad, but it just seems like the food is always hotter and there's more variety in the aft galley."

Punk silenced the corpsman by handing him the plate, and Shep nodded and dutifully started on his mission to find a razor and shaving cream. As he turned the corner he was replaced by another figure coming the other way: Captain "Soup" Campbell.

Soup grinned widely as he caught sight of Punk and cracked, "Look at the bearded wonder."

"Good morning, DCAG."

"I'm glad you're awake." The captain pulled a chair across the shiny linoleum-tiled floor and sat next to Punk's bunk. "I called down a couple of times this morning and they said you were out cold. They asked if I wanted them to wake you up, but I told them that wasn't necessary."

"I appreciate that, sir. It felt good to get some sleep."

"I'll bet it did. I haven't had enough sleep since I got out here." Soup noticed the article next to Punk's leg. He picked it up and studied it for a few seconds, making a series of humming sounds as he did. "Too bad they didn't use the picture with you and me in it, instead," he said. "Not just because I was in it, but the angle was better." He tossed the paper aside. "So, tell me, what was it like?"

Punk rearranged himself so that his legs were hanging off the side of the bunk. During the airplane rides back he'd given some thought to how he was going to answer questions like the one the DCAG had just asked him. He'd decided to keep it simple and upbeat. "It was a real eye-opener," he said. "I earned a lot of respect for those guys on the ground, I'll tell you that."

"Did they give you a weapon?"

"Yeah, I had an M-4 they let me use."

"Did you shoot anybody?"

"Yeah . . ."

"Did you kill them?"

"I'm pretty sure—"

"Wow," Soup said as his eyes went to the pipes overhead and stayed there for a time. "That's got to be amazing, huh?"

"I'm not sure I'd put it that way, to be honest."

"What, don't tell me you've got the guilts or something. You're not suffering from that post-traumatic stress thing, are you? It's a war, for crying out loud. Am I right? Huh, am I right?"

Punk raised his eyebrows and offered a slight nod, hoping the captain would change the subject or simply go away.

"Hey, I tell you what," Soup continued. "Once you get Doc's blessing and through your back-in-the-saddle hops, I'll let you lead me on your first flight back into Afghanistan. How does that sound?"

"Fine, sir."

"You know Doc just gave Spud an up chit. Turns out you don't need a pinkie to fly. Weird, huh? I'm sure you heard I'm flying missions over the beach again, right?"

"I did hear that, yes, sir."

"The whole scandal, if that's what you want to call it, was a joke. One hotline call and a lot of reporters with nothing better to write about."

Shep walked up behind Captain Campbell, proudly holding a can of shaving cream in one hand and a razor in the other. "Here you go, sir," he said after excusing himself around Soup. "I apologize, though. All we have are single-blade razors."

"I'm sure it'll work fine, Shep," Punk said as he took the items from the corpsman. "Thank you."

Captain Campbell checked his watch and then patted Punk's forearm. "I'll let you get to it. I've got to get up to the admiral's morning meeting."

"Okay, DCAG," Punk returned. "Thanks for coming by."

"I'm serious about that first flight offer. Hell, we'll get with Wheedle, the PAO, see if he wants to make a big deal out of it in the press." Soup stood and moved hands as if he were arranging the words on a movie marquee. " 'American pilot settles a personal score.' No, how about, 'American pilot takes fight from the air to the ground and back to the air again'? No, that has too many words in it. Whatever; we'll figure something out." He leaned over and patted Punk's forearm again. "For now you just get healthy."

"I feel fine, actually."

"Doc says you're malnourished and exhausted."

"Who isn't?"

Soup chuckled. "I'll see you later."

The moment they heard the door to the ward close

behind Captain Campbell, Shep turned to Punk and said, "He seems like a very nice man."

Punk offered a noncommittal grunt in response.

"A lot of times officers come down here and they won't give us the time of day, you know?" Shep said. "It's like we're their servants or something. So, where's the job satisfaction in that? I didn't join the Navy to be a servant, I'll tell you that. Just because I didn't go to college yet doesn't mean I don't want to do something with my life. If my recruiter had said something about—"

"I need to get this beard shaved off before I get any more high-ranking visitors, Shep," Punk said as he slid out of his rack and got to his feet.

"Oh . . . okay. You let me know if you need anything, sir."

"I will."

"Even if you just need somebody to talk to, you know? That's part of our job, too. People forget that sometimes patients just need to get things off their chests. It's not all about operations and shots and stuff—"

"I'll let you know, Shep. I'm going to go shave now."

"Okay, sir. I'll be around."

Punk pushed through the door to the small bathroom adjacent to the sick bay and stood at the sink, staring into the mirror. He squirted some shaving cream into his palm but couldn't bring himself to spread it across his face. He'd earned this beard, dammit.

But as he listened to the voice of the bosun's mate of the watch over the ship's intercom, ordering sweepers to man their brooms, he realized, for all of his desire to preserve his link to the wonder and challenges of the past week, he was back in an environment where standards of grooming weren't so relaxed. He slathered the white foam along his jawline and was hit by an idea: He could compromise. A mustache would be his badge of honor, his link to the recent past.

After dinner in bed, Punk took advantage of the fact that the night-shift orderly was not as attentive as Shep. Dressed in gym shorts, Herat T-shirt, and flip-flops, the convalescing pilot quietly slipped out of sick bay and made his way up to the 0-3 level. Opening the front door to the *Arrowslinger* ready room, he was pleased to find the space a bustle of activity, exactly the therapy required after a day of listening to nothing but Shep's well-meaning but inane prattling.

His presence was barely noticed and those who did see him greeted him with nothing more enthusiastic than a handshake or a slap on the back. Any displays beyond that would have been redundant, as yesterday they'd all released their joy while welcoming him back on the flight deck, forming a raucous human tunnel behind the COD. Now he appreciated their calm. At the moment, he didn't want to conjure up emotions or recount his tale; he just wanted to soak in the squadron atmosphere. He eavesdropped on the last fifteen minutes of the brief for the last event of the night and then walked back to the debrief area where a half-dozen aviators had gathered around the monitor.

"How long do we want this thing to be?" Peeler asked as he reached over and punched a button on the tape player.

"I don't know," Cracker replied. "No more than five minutes, I guess."

"Yeah," Elf agreed. "Five minutes max. After that people start to get bored."

"You know the best one of these gets shown at the Fighter Fling," Yoda said.

"Any gouge on our competition?" Peeler asked.

"I heard the *Deviljaws* have a pretty good one," Elf said.

"Have you seen it?" Elf asked.

"No."

"Do you think you could get your hands on it?"

"I can try, I guess."

A scene from one of the mission tapes flashed on the screen, a black-and-white FLIR picture that showed the crosshairs of a FLIR pod superimposed on a bridge. "This one rocks," Peeler said. "A truck goes across the bridge right . . . now. *Boom!* That's awesome."

"And we've got to use that one from Monster's flight a few days back where he hit that building and had those mad secondary explosions. That's a sick visual."

"Oh, yeah. I know the one you're talking about. Who's got a copy of that?"

"I can get it."

Punk found it impossible to remain in quiet observation. He took a few steps forward and asked, "Have you guys ever been close to a bomb when it hit?"

The semicircle of lieutenants turned and silently stared at him, expressions striking the fine balance between disinterest and politeness, the same face they might have made reacting to the pronouncements of a visiting politician.

"It's loud," Punk continued, "really loud. And it's violent. Even if it's the enemy who's getting their shit handed to them, when you see the results, there's nothing cool about it."

Most of them ignored him. A few of the more polite

lieutenants nodded, indulging the insanity he'd most
likely developed during his time on the ground. Punk
stood over them until it became obvious that no one
was terribly interested in further exploring the topic.
After a few more awkward seconds he muttered, "I'll
check you guys later."

"Later," Peeler said.

"Nice face, by the way, Punk," Elf said. "What did
you shave with today, a machete?"

Punk lightly ran his fingertips across the series of
pinhead-sized scabs dotting his cheeks and explained,
"All they had down in sick bay were single-bladed
razors."

"The mustache looks good, though," Yoda added,
followed by a muted snicker.

"It's a work in progress," Punk said defensively.
"Give me a week or so."

"If you say so, Peppe—I mean, Punk."

Punk shuffled though the back exit, and before the
door closed behind him, he caught the first part of the
JOs' discussion over whether the music for the video's
soundtrack should be heavy metal or rap.

Gunner Hooter stood attendant as Punk and Spud
worked their way around the Tomcat parked on the
extreme starboard corner of the fantail. The aviators
were quick and methodical, tapping on panels to see
if any fasteners were loose, checking hydraulic fluid
levels, and shaking the ordnance to make sure it was
properly hung on the aircraft.

"Those are good bombs," Hooter said as Punk
stood upright next to the left intake after crouching
down and inspecting the two GBU-12s attached to the
fighter's belly.

Punk did a couple of deep knee bends while cinching his harness tight around his chest and upper thighs and said, "As opposed to what, Gunner?"

Hooter's head jerked a little, and his mouth twisted as his mind spun in neutral. He pulled his cranial onto his head and repeated, "Those are good bombs," before walking off to see to the well-being of the rest of his charges for the upcoming launch.

"No complaints about the weather," Spud said, hooking a boot heel on the ladder that unfolded from the left side of the F-14's nose.

Punk cued up at the base of the ladder, waiting to follow his RIO onto the top of the jet for the final portion of their preflight walkarounds, and gazed under the left wing at the glassy surface of the Northern Arabian Sea and up to the clear blue sky above. "No complaints," he agreed.

Twenty minutes later Punk peered through the cloud of steam that billowed from the catapult track and steered the Tomcat with his feet in synch with the taxi director's signals. Once he'd managed to straddle the slippery, grease-smeared track with his nose wheels, he spread the wings, lowered the flaps, and compressed the nose strut in a series of fluid motions about the cockpit.

After his extended period out of the airplane, the mechanics of aviating were starting to feel like second nature again. The week of being poked and prodded by flight surgeons, debriefed by intelligence officers, and informed of every detail of Shep's young life certainly hadn't helped preserve his flying skills. Once Punk had been blessed to crawl back into the cockpit, he'd flown a mini refresher syllabus Peeler had designed for him, including three flights where he dropped inert practice bombs on the carrier's wake.

But on this hop he was finally headed back over the beach.

Punk and Spud held their hands above the canopy rail as the ordnance team scrambled around the jet, pulling the arming pins from the bombs and missiles. Punk paid closer attention to the process than he had before the mishap. He focused on the two ordies as they reappeared from under the jet, sprinting past the foul line with red-flagged arming pins threaded through one hand and signaling a thumbs-up with the other.

With the director's signal, Punk pushed the throttles to full military power and wiped out the controls, moving the stick forward, aft, left, and right, then booting the rudder pedals left and right while checking over his shoulders and in the mirrors to ensure the spoilers and rudders were deflecting properly. After a quick scan of his gauges and warning light panels, he asked Spud if he was ready and saluted the catapult officer.

Just over two seconds later they were airborne and climbing away from the smooth sea. Punk took his left hand and raised the gear and flaps while simultaneously using his right hand to urge the Tomcat into a shallow turn away from the airplanes zooming off the bow. He leveled off at five hundred feet and watched the airspeed grow above three hundred knots. Ten miles in front of the Boat he pulled the stick back and started a steep climb.

"Punk's headed for the S-3," Spud reported over squadron common.

"Roger," Einstein replied. "Soup's plugged and receiving at this time."

Punk followed the diamond Spud's radar lock projected on the heads-up display until he spotted the S-3

tanker orbiting overhead the carrier with their wingman in close trail, taking on the first two thousand
pounds of the more than thirty thousand pounds of
additional gas they'd need to stay aloft for the duration of the seven-hour mission. Punk attached himself
to the tanker's left wing and waited for the hose to
come open. As soon as the S-3 pilot noticed he had
both Tomcats aboard, he stopped orbiting and steadied the flight on a northern course.

Once Soup was gassed up he slid out of the basket,
retracted his probe, and moved to the tanker's right
wing. In turn, Punk inched the throttles back and got
the jet situated for a run at the drogue. He'd been
tanking from the air wing's S-3s over the last days, so
there was nothing much to be concerned about. The
heavy tanker they were scheduled to plug over Afghanistan might be a different story, although if the
air tasking order was accurate they'd be tanking from
a British KC-10 with its docile rig and plucky crew.

They took their gas in short order, and then Punk
positioned the lead Tomcat to the right of his wingman on the S-3 right wing. Spud keyed his radio,
tuned to the carrier's main control frequency: "Strike,
Slinger flight is initial tanking complete."

"Roger, Slinger," the controller replied. "Contact
Seahawk six-oh-five on Button five for en route
advisories."

"Switching." Spud exchanged thumbs with Einstein
and then again after allowing the junior RIO a few
seconds to twist the channel knob from one to five.
"Seahawk six-oh-five, Slinger one-zero-two is north-
bound."

"Seahawk copies, Slinger. Proceed. Air picture
clear."

"Clear?" Spud said over the intercom, feigning surprise. "What happened to all the Taliban MiGs we were supposed to go against today?"

"For years historians will be recounting the swirling dogfights over Afghanistan," Punk said.

"Yeah, but now they'll only be talking about your rendezvous technique in the tanker pattern."

"You're pretty funny for a crippled guy."

"I use humor to hide my pain."

"Slinger, contact Bossman on Rose one," the controller said. "I think they've got a modification to your original tasking."

"Oh, boy, a modification," Spud opined over the intercom as he flashed Einstein another thumbs-up. He keyed the backseat radio and began using their ATO-assigned call sign: "Bossman, Brooklyn four-one is checking in as a flight of two."

"Brooklyn four-one, Bossman has you five by five," the controller said in a deep, authoritative voice. By now the Navy crews going over the beach had become familiar with the Air Force controllers' voices, and Punk had taken the extra step of conjuring up a mental image to go with each. He pictured this guy as a balding major with thick eyebrows and a terminal five o'clock shadow. "You were originally fragged to take your first mission gas at Gipper, right?"

"That's affirmative, Bossman," Spud replied. "We're scheduled for gas from London seven-three."

"And where were you supposed to go after that?" Papers could be heard shuffling behind the controller's voice.

"Tasking calls for us to hold at Chargers for follow-on close air support tasking."

"Negative, Brooklyn four-one. Standby for new tasking: Proceed to Bradley track for initial mission gas and then hold at Falcons for on-call frag. Follow-on gas will be available from Paris seven-one at the Sijan track."

"That's no modification," Spud said to his pilot. "That's a whole new fucking mission. And Paris? I'll bet you money that's the goddam French KC-135 again."

"Why do we even brief these things?" Punk asked.

"Initial steer to Bradley is zero-one-five," the AWACS controller passed.

"Brooklyn copies," Spud transmitted in return. "Coming right to zero-one-five."

"Pass no closer to Karachi than fifty miles."

"Copy," Spud said before keying the intercom: "Got to love our friends the Pakistanis, too."

The tan hue in the distance slowly shaped into the coastline of Pakistan, and as it did Punk fought off a sense of foreboding. He clicked on the autopilot and unfolded his chart. The Falcons area was in the extreme eastern end of Afghanistan, just south of the Hindu Kush mountain range. He'd prepped himself for a flight over the flatlands west of Kandahar, where friendlies were trying to put the final stake in the Talibans' collective heart on the southern front. Now they were headed back over the mountains, only this time they topped out at more than twenty thousand feet.

"Did you guys copy all of that?" Soup asked over squadron common.

"We got it, DCAG," Spud replied. "Semper Gumby, as usual."

"I don't care if they Gumby us all over the country," Soup said, "as long as we don't bring our bombs back."

As long as we don't bring our bombs back. That had been Captain Campbell's refrain from the moment he walked into the ready room for the flight brief. And on the way to the flight deck he'd stopped to address the handful of reporters Lieutenant Wheedle had mustered in the passageway. "This is poetry of sorts, ladies and gentlemen," he'd said, pointing to Punk. "We don't like to make the fight personal, but sometimes it gets that way."

"Bossman, say the call sign of the tanker at the Bradley track," Spud requested.

"Thames seven-three is holding at Bradley, Angels two-five."

"Brooklyn's got him on radar. Confirm zero-one-five at sixty-two miles from us."

"That's affirmative. Contact Thames now on Gold three."

"Switching."

"Thames?" Punk mused over the intercom. "That sounds like a nice British name."

Spud slewed the FLIR pod to the radar line of sight and confirmed that the tanker they were presently headed for was, in fact, an RAF KC-10. *One bullet dodged,* Punk thought.

"Where are we headed, lads?" the pilot asked over Gold three once both jets were aboard his left wing.

"North," Spud replied.

"North it is, then."

Both Tomcats topped off, and as they separated from the British tanker the pilot said, "Give them a bit of hell for us, then, mates."

With that the AWACS controller jumped back onto the frequency: "Brooklyn four-one, understand you're complete with your tanking?"

"That's affirmative," Spud replied.

"Zeus, do you copy?"

"Zeus copies," a deeper, more commanding voice than the AWACS controller's said. "Brooklyn four-one, how do you read Zeus?"

"Loud and clear, Zeus," Spud transmitted.

"Roger, have you the same. Standby for tasking from Zeus."

"Who's Zeus again?" Soup asked Einstein over the intercom.

"One of the generals in Riyadh," Einstein said.

"Damn, this should be good, then."

"Brooklyn four-one, this is Zeus. One of our Predators has located a high-interest contact along the road south of Gardez. Need you to find it, and when you do, need you to take it out."

"Roger," Spud said.

"Also need you to expedite. We don't want to lose this one."

"Expediting, sir."

Punk selected minimum afterburner until their airspeed nibbled at Mach one and then pulled the throttles back to military power, quickly establishing the Tomcat at a reasonable compromise between speed and endurance. He was eager to accommodate the general's directions but remained unclear with the tanker plan to the north, and was therefore reluctant to wantonly burn all the gas out of his tanks. Soup lagged his lead's acceleration at first, but soon caught up by holding his jet in afterburner a little longer.

After twenty minutes of high-speed cruising, Punk could see the mountains. Even from a great distance the sharpness of their peaks was evident. Survival following a parachute ride into them would be unlikely. He looked down at his navigation display and checked the range to the Gardez waypoint that Spud had dropped into the system: Eighty miles. They'd crossed into Afghanistan. After two and a half weeks, he was back.

"I'm tally the road," Captain Campbell said over squadron common.

"Zeus, do you want us to contact a ground unit on another frequency for this?" Spud asked.

"Negative, Brooklyn four-one. Stick with me."

"Can you give us a more detailed description of the contact of interest?"

"Light-colored SUV. Current position is thirty-three degrees twenty-eight-point-five-seven minutes north, sixty-nine-point-zero-zero degrees east."

"Understand we're cleared hot once we spot it?"

"I need you to confirm the coordinates first. I'll clear you hot after that."

"Is the UAV still in the area?"

"Affirmative."

"What altitude?"

"The Predator will be working at or below ten thousand feet."

Spud plugged the general's coordinates into his nav system and cued the FLIR pod to that new waypoint. He clicked the pod's magnification to its highest level.

"I don't see anything at those coordinates, Punk," Spud said.

"Recommend working the crosshairs southbound along the road," Punk replied. "Even with this supposed 'real-time' information flow the data lags enough to throw us off."

"I'll slew the pod to the south."

Punk watched the FLIR picture jump around and then checked his fuel gauge. "What's the range to the Sijan tanker track, Spud?"

There was a slight pause as the RIO punched up the data: "One hundred and eighty-two miles."

"We're going to have to head that way in about ten minutes."

"Roger." Spud keyed the radio: "Zeus, Brooklyn

flight has only ten more minutes of loiter time before we depart Falcons for the Sijan track."

"What?" the general shot back. "Ten minutes?"

"That's affirmative. We'll be back after we refuel, though."

"We can't afford any gaps in coverage right now. Standby." The radio went silent for a time and then the general jumped back up the freq with, "We're going to try and get the tanker to come west closer to you. Continue your search until further notice."

Spud didn't answer but came over the intercom instead: "He's going to get the French guys to leave their tanker station? Good luck. Even a general doesn't have the power to move those stubborn sons of bitches."

"I'm going to cheat it east in about five minutes," Punk replied. "Anything on the pod yet?"

"Negative."

"Einstein, you guys got anything on your FLIR?"

"No," the junior RIO replied. "Hold on, now. I've got a single vehicle headed south along the road. It's not light-colored though, and it looks more like a pickup than an SUV."

"Be careful with pickups," Soup advised.

Spud followed the road with his pod until the crosshairs passed over something moving. "Zeus, Brooklyn's got a dark-colored vehicle, southbound. Looks like a pickup."

"Say latitude and longitude," the general ordered.

Spud leaned into his straps and squinted at the upper left-hand corner of the FLIR presentation. "Thirty-three twenty-five-point-six-three degrees north, sixty-eight fifty-eight-point-three-one degrees east."

"Negative," the general said, frustration rapidly growing in his voice. "Contact of interest is now passing thirty-three thirteen-point-five-one north, sixty-eight fifty-point-two-five east."

"What the hell?" Spud asked over the intercom. "How does an SUV jump fifteen miles or more in less than two minutes?"

"This is bullshit," Punk added.

"Let's hustle south," Soup said on squadron common. "I don't want to bring these bombs back."

Punk eyed his fuel gauge again. "We've got enough gas for one short trip down the road, and then we're heading for the tanker."

Both RIOs worked their left thumbs across their FLIR control sticks to scour the winding road out of Gardez, although in some places it seemed to disappear. Punk split his attention between his FLIR screen—a smaller version of Spud's presentation—and the fuel gauge. What he did manage to make out on the screen reminded him of the area around Nayak where they'd loaded the donkeys and left the road. He wanted to tell Spud about the death-defying passage along narrow trails where a single misstep by Bushwhacker would have caused him to plunge thousands of feet to his death, but there was no time for stories now. Maybe once they were done tanking the next time.

"Anybody see anything?" Punk asked on squadron common.

Before either of the RIOs could answer, the general frantically transmitted, "Zeus just lost the picture! Zeus is blind!"

"What the hell is he talking about?" Soup asked Einstein.

"The Predator must have a bad FLIR pod or something," Einstein said.

"Brooklyn four-one, do you have contact on the vehicle?" the general asked.

"Negative," Spud said. "Zeus, Brooklyn shows a fork in the road just south of the last position you passed. Do you know if the vehicle continued south or turned west?"

The radio was silent.

"Bossman, are you up this freq?" Spud asked.

"That's affirmative," the controller replied.

"Say range from us to Paris seven-one."

There was a short delay before the controller came back with, "Two hundred and ten miles."

"Jeezus," Punk said. "We've got to get going toward them."

"I knew those Frogs weren't going to budge," Spud said before keying the radio: "Brooklyn four-one flight is heading for the Sijan track at this time."

A handset keyed on the other end but no words were transmitted. Someone spat "Damn" away from the mouthpiece. A second later the general dejectedly asked, "How long will you be gone?"

Spud did a quick time/distance calculation in his head and then added some more time for the tanking itself. "Approximately an hour and fifteen minutes, Zeus."

"An hour and fifteen minutes?" the general returned. "I can't have that kind of gap in coverage right now."

"Are there any other assets in the area, sir?" Spud asked and immediately wished he hadn't. *Let the general run the war, dipshit,* he thought to himself. *You just worry about not flaming out.*

"All other assets are engaged at this time," the AWACS controller said, joining the exchange like the general's administrative assistant.

"With all due respect," Spud said, "we have to go get gas now." As the radio fell silent again, Punk thought about the freedom the phrase "with all due respect" provided: *With all due respect, General, we'd like you to go fuck yourself.*

"Be careful, Spud," Soup advised on squadron common.

"I hear you, DCAG," Spud replied, "but we're below our fuel ladder as it is. We can't help it if they blew our opportunity window with a twenty-mile navigational error."

"All the same . . ."

The two Tomcats flew toward the French tanker in silence. Twenty-five-thousand feet above the border between Afghanistan and Pakistan, Punk dipped his left wing and looked down at the landscape. As he considered the curved mountain range that defined the line he could've sworn he saw legions of the enemy flowing freely eastward.

"Brooklyn four-one is contact zero-eight-seven at fifty-two miles, Angels two-five," Spud reported.

"That's your tanker, Brooklyn," the AWACS controller replied. "Contact Paris seven-one on their boom freq: Yellow five."

"Switching Yellow five; flight switch."

While moving his eyes across the instrument panel to read the fuel gauge Punk noted the shape of a KC-135 on the FLIR screen. Damn. That was one element of the mission he'd let slip from his consciousness in the course of dealing with all the changes thrown at them. But then he chastised himself for allowing even the slightest hint of failure to creep into his psyche. *Stop acting like a damn first-cruise nugget*, he thought. *You've done this a million times before.*

Spud had no desire to talk to the French crew, so, without any radio chatter, the two Tomcats parked themselves on the KC-135's left wing and waited until they saw the boom cycle in and out. At that point Punk extended his probe and slid into position behind the "wrecking ball," the nickname Navy crews had awarded the KC-135's unforgiving rig—the result of changing an Air Force configuration into a Navy one by simply sticking an additional length of hose on the end of it and capping it with a basket made of iron. Punk took a few breaths into his oxygen mask and adjusted his grip on the stick.

"You okay?" Spud asked.

"Yeah," Punk replied, trying his best to sound unconcerned. "I'm just getting the jet trimmed up."

Images of jousting matches between jets and tankers filled his mind until he forced himself to advance the throttles and close on the basket. Just before the fighter's probe was about to pierce the plane of the drogue's lip, Punk sensed he was going to miss, and he jerked the stick too far to the left and sent the basket sailing away. He feared it might come back and hit the canopy, so he pushed the Tomcat's nose over to get out of the way.

"Whoa!" Spud exclaimed. "Easy with it."

"I'm all right," Punk said, again feigning calm. "I just overdid it in close."

"Is your airplane okay back there?"—*bock zere*—the French pilot asked.

"Yeah, yeah, we're fine," Spud replied. "Hey, once we're plugged in, can we get a drag to the west?"

"No, no. We must stay on the track."

Spud laughed over the intercom and said, "Have I ever told you how much I love those guys?"

Punk offered a chuckle in return and waited for the refueling hose to stop oscillating. He relaxed his grip on the stick and throttle and puffed a long breath into his mask. *Stop this right now. Don't make it any harder than it is.*

In spite of Punk's best efforts to screw it up, the second attempt to mate probe with drogue was successful. He flew tight formation on the "knuckle," the portion of the refueling device where the metal boom became a thick rubber hose, as the Tomcat took on gas at the rate of two thousand pounds a minute. Just under four minutes later they were topped off.

Soup maneuvered his F-14 into the basket just as the KC-135 reached the northeastern end of the Sijan track, and the two fighters stuck with the big jet as it lumbered around in a left turn to a southwesterly heading. Twelve miles along that leg, Soup and Einstein's jet was full of gas, as well, and the two Tomcats detached from the tanker's right wing without so much as a wave from the Frenchmen.

"Bossman, Brooklyn four-one is tanking complete," Spud transmitted on Red one as they drove westward back to the Falcons holding zone.

"Zeus, do you copy?" the AWACS controller asked without acknowledging Spud.

"Zeus copies," the general replied. "Brooklyn four-one, how do you read?"

"Loud and clear, sir," Spud said.

"Okay, this is the deal. The UAV is working again, but we haven't relocated the contact of interest. We need you guys to augment the search. We've positioned the Predator south of the fork in the road; you work the west."

"Roger."

"What the hell are we doing?" Soup asked over squadron common.

"We're looking for a missing SUV."

"You know I—"

"Got it, DCAG. All we have to do is find this car."

Punk led the flight along the axis of the road until they'd gone nearly all the way to Kandahar, well beyond where the SUV could have traveled in an hour and a half, although the vehicle had made one supersonic leap before. The F-14s doubled back and combed the road in the opposite direction. Besides a handful of destroyed hulks, objects blown up beyond immediate recognition, the road was deserted.

Punk looked at the fuel gauge and the clock, and both suggested it was time for them to head south to hit the RAF tanker one more time and then continue to the sea for their recovery aboard the Boat. "Our wingman isn't going to like this, skipper," Punk said, "but we need to be getting back."

"I guess you're saying I need to tell him?" Spud asked.

"Rank has its responsibility, sir."

Spud heaved an exaggerated exhale and keyed the radio tuned to squadron common: "We're RTB."

"Returning to base?" Soup said. "Already?"

"It's time, sir. We've still got to hit the Brit tanker at Bradley and the S-3 once we get feet wet, and the Boat is one hundred miles beyond that. We drew the short straw today, that's all."

"What a waste."

Spud wasn't sure what to say in return, so he keyed the other radio and passed, "Zeus, Brooklyn four-one flight is RTB."

Again the radio keyed on the other end and there were several seconds of dead air before the general passed a simple "Copy" in a voice that captured his dejection. Punk felt a bit sorry for the man as well as guilty that they'd been unable to find the SUV. He looked at his watch. They'd been airborne nearly five hours and had at least two more to go before the flight was over. Soup was right; this had been a waste.

"Bossman, do you copy Brooklyn is RTB?" Spud asked.

"Copy," the controller said. "Initial steer for the Bradley track is one-eight-four for one hundred and seventy miles."

"Roger. Brooklyn flight is coming south at this time."

Punk occupied his mind during the transit by selecting an obscure detail off the chart and then trying to find the corresponding feature on the ground below. By this time on a deployment there was no challenge to picking out road intersections or specific peaks, so he chose small wadis barely wide enough to be colored blue on the chart and villages with names that hadn't earned a circle next to them. His searches were aided by shadows that were longer than they'd been during the F-14s' ingress, the combination of browns and blacks now defining the topography in a way that made obtaining a visual fix easy.

Punk peered over the left canopy rail and noted that they'd crossed the southern border of Afghanistan. "Seems sort of anticlimactic," he opined over the intercom.

Spud offered one of his chestnuts in return: "Sometimes chicken, sometimes feathers."

"Brooklyn four-one, Thames seven-three now bears one-eight-one at forty miles, currently on a southwesterly heading. Do you have radar?"

"Brooklyn's got him on radar," Spud confirmed.

"Contact Thames on Gold three."

"Switching."

As Spud switched his UHF radio to the new frequency, Punk heard a syncopated crackle on squadron common, metered bursts of static. Although the transmission was unintelligible, he put his Tomcat into a shallow left bank.

"Where are we going?" Spud asked.

Punk didn't answer his RIO but instead keyed his own UHF radio: "Calling on Arrowslinger common, say again, please."

Another few bursts of static followed. "We've got to check this out," Punk said.

"Check *what* out?" Spud returned.

"Are you up Gold three?"

"Yes."

"Ask the Brit tanker if they can bring it north. That'll buy us some time."

"Time for what?"

"Just ask them if they can bring it north . . . please, Spud . . . skipper."

"Where are we going?" Soup asked on squadron common.

"Brooklyn four-one, this is Bossman on Gold three," the AWACS controller said. "I show you northbound again. Say intentions."

"Standby, Bossman," Spud replied before addressing his pilot over the intercom: "You're freaking a lot of people out here."

Punk ignored everything except the static on squadron common. He made another petition to the distant source that beckoned him: "Calling Arrowslinger base, you're coming in weak and unreadable. Please say again."

The reply came back static-laced but clear enough to make out: "Arrowslinger, this is Tiger One. El Cedar, how do you read?"

"Waco? Waco, is that you?" Punk shot excitedly back.

"It is. We're in a jam down here. Any way you can help?"

"Where are you?"

"At the base of the mountains east of the airfield at Mukur," Waco said, voice coming in more clearly with each mile the Tomcats flew farther north. "We're pinned down."

"Where is Mukur, Spud?" Punk asked over the intercom.

"I'm checking," the RIO returned. "Who are you talking to?"

"That's Waco, dammit. Tiger one is the team that saved our ass."

"You're going to get us in a shitload of trouble here."

"For what? Helping a unit in trouble? Frankly, this is the first fight we've been asked to join that makes any sense to me."

Spud muttered an extended "Fuck" into his mask and keyed Gold three: "Thames seven-one, this is Brooklyn four-one. Can we get you to drag it about fifty miles north or so?"

"Certainly, mates," one of the British pilots said. "Be glad to."

"Where the hell are we going?" Soup asked again. "And who is that on the radio?"

"Tiger one is the team of guys who saved us and then got me out of the country, DCAG," Punk explained over squadron common.

"We can't just go off on our own program here."

"Tiger one's got tasking for us, sir. I guarantee you we'll get rid of our bombs if we can find where they are."

"I told you we're at Mukur, El Cedar," Waco transmitted over the crack of a rifle. "And we got targets, all right. How many bombs you boys carrying?"

"Four total between the two of us. Precision guided. Can you sparkle?"

"Negative. The battery to the MULE died an hour ago. We can try to talk you on, though."

"Roger. Hold on." Punk toggled the intercom on and asked, "Did you find Mukur yet, Spud?"

"I'm dropping a waypoint in right now. Mukur bears three-five-four for sixty-three miles."

They were close! "We're on our way, Waco," Punk said. "Give us seven minutes or so."

Waco keyed the handset, but a nearby explosion cut off his words. "I'm not sure we got seven minutes," he said as the blast died off enough for him to hear himself talk. "They're hammering us up here."

"Brooklyn four-one, this is Bossman. Say your intentions."

"If we're going to do this, you'd better get Bossman to agree with the plan," Soup said on squadron common.

"Bossman, Brooklyn four-one is circling back real quick to assist Tiger one," Spud said.

"What?" the AWACS controller said. "How are you talking to Tiger one?"

"They called us on our squadron common frequency."

Dead air followed for a few seconds and then the controller transmitted, "Standby, Brooklyn."

"Spud, we don't have time to wait for any chain-of-command horseshit and neither does Waco," Punk said over the intercom.

"Agreed," Spud returned before keying squadron common: "Tiger one, Brooklyn four-one is ready to copy your talk on instructions."

"Okay, you got four bombs, right?" Waco said.

"Affirmative."

"Well, I got a lot more than four targets down here . . . All right, do you have the runway in sight?"

"We've got it on our FLIR," Spud explained.

"Close enough." Gunfire echoed in the distance. "The runway is one unit of measure. Go two units of measure due west of the runway until you come to a road."

Spud commanded the pod accordingly and said, "Contact the road."

"Roger. Now follow the road to the southwest until it makes a sharp turn to the south."

"Contact."

"Due west of that work your way up the face of the mountain until the color of it changes from dark brown to tan."

"Contact."

"There's an artillery piece at that point."

Spud increased the magnification of his FLIR pod, and, after closer scrutiny of the grainy black-and-white image on his screen, picked out the barrel of the piece sticking out of a crevasse.

"Contact. Standby."

"My switches are set, Spud," Punk said.

"Mission tape is on and running," Spud replied. "I've got station two selected. Target is designated. Three seconds to pickle . . . two . . . one . . ."

Punk depressed the bomb button and said, "Pickle, pickle, pickle."

Both of them couldn't help but grimace as they felt the bomb leave the rack. They waited several long seconds for the bomb to fall well clear of the Tomcat. Punk held the stick with a featherlight touch, waiting for any indication that part of the jet had been blown away. No indication came.

"Laser's on and firing," Spud reported with what Punk was sure was a sigh of relief. "Fourteen seconds to impact."

Punk put the F-14 into a slight angle of bank to keep the fuselage from masking the pod mounted to the right weapons rail and intently stared at the screen behind his control stick. The bomb hit and exploded, belching fire and bits of steel into the sky and down the mountain.

"Beautiful, El Cedar," Waco passed. "I got big eyes on that sucker. Direct hit. Ready for the next one?"

"DCAG, you want this one?" Punk asked.

"What happened to Bossman?" Soup asked in return.

"Tiger one, go ahead with the next target," Punk said.

"Next one's easy," Waco said. "We got two tanks rolling eastbound at the southwest end of the runway."

Spud worked the pod from the road back to the runway and passed, "Contact the tanks."

"You're cleared hot on the tanks, Brooklyn."

With that, Soup's concern for the command-and-control structure faded. "They're too far apart to get with a single bomb," the captain said. "Soup's taking the southern tank."

"Roger," Punk followed, smiling under his mask. "El Cedar's got the northern one."

The two Tomcats released their bombs nearly simultaneously, and several dozen seconds later the two tanks disintegrated in rapid succession.

"You guys are all right," Waco said. The cheers of the men around him rang over the frequency, an infectious joy. Fifteen thousand feet above them Punk felt goose bumps grow on his forearms. Bossman was going to tell them that this wasn't the right mission?

"One bomb left, right?" Waco asked.

"Affirmative, Tiger one," Spud replied.

"Last target is the tower midway up the runway on the western side. They've been running in and out of that thing all day. I think they're using it as a command center or something."

"Contact the tower," Spud replied. "Lead jet is out of bombs. Einstein, you got it?"

"Contact," Einstein said.

"Watch out, though," Waco warned. "They've been shooting Stingers out of there at our air support all day, too."

"Copy. We'll keep our eyes open."

"Soup, you've got the lead," Punk said.

"Soup has the lead," Captain Campbell returned.

Punk flew loose formation on the other Tomcat as the captain worked his jet into position for the final bomb delivery. Several seconds later the bomb came off, and as it fell Punk split his attention between the FLIR presentation and his wingman. Just before the bomb hit he noticed a figure run out of the base of the tower and fire a shoulder-fired SAM into the air, leaving behind a plume of white smoke.

"SAM in the air," Punk called over the radio, which cued both pilots to hit the buttons on their sticks that commanded flares to shoot out of the dispensers under the jets. They were flying too high to worry about Stingers, anyway, and from the arc the missile scribed the crews could tell that it wasn't tracking.

The enemy soldier who'd fired the SAM ran back to the tower and opened the door just as the bomb hit. The explosion blossomed and the tower toppled over. The adjacent hangar went up in a series of secondary explosions, which, in turn, set off the next hangar down the line.

"That'll be a good one for Peeler's video," Punk said over the intercom.

"What?" Spud asked back.

"Never mind."

"That's got it, boys," Waco crowed on squadron common. "We're off to take the runway. No sleep 'til Kandahar, you know."

"Are you with General Haskarim?" Punk asked.

"No. It's the same circus but different clowns. Oh, before you go: Nate wanted me to tell you he never really thought you were useless."

"Tell him I appreciate that. While you're at it, say hello to just Tim for me."

"Will do. Thanks for the help, El Cedar."

"Anytime, Waco. Anytime."

"Tiger one, out."

Soup passed the lead back to Punk, and the junior pilot lifted the nose and turned back to the south. Spud cleared his throat and keyed the radio: "Bossman, Brooklyn four-one is mission complete. We're headed for home, and this time we really mean it."

"Standby, Brooklyn four-one," the controller said. "We're still trying to figure this out."

"We're standing by."

"We just saved the day and they're still trying to figure it out," Soup said over squadron common. Obviously, he was pleased with how things had turned out.

As Punk continued to steer the flight to the south he noticed that Spud had framed the FLIR picture around the horses storming westward across the steppe, bearing down on the runway complex. He stared at the screen, mesmerized by the sight of men on horseback, three score across and a dozen deep, hurtling headlong into battle armed with only rifles and knives. Their courage moved him now as it had when he was among them. The rifles blazed as they reached the edge of the runway. Across the tarmac dark figures retreated, many falling as they ran. It looked as if they'd won another battle, but when would this war be over for men like Waco? When would they be going home?

He focused on the screen a bit more and then peered along the left canopy rail to the ground east of them. He watched the cloud of dust the advancing Army created, clearly visible even from his lofty perch, until the battle disappeared under his airplane. Then, leaving his former comrades to their victory, Punk turned his Tomcat south, toward the tanker, and beyond that the Arabian Sea and home to the Boat.

ACKNOWLEDGMENTS

I owe thanks to a number of people for their assistance and support over the months I wrote *Punk's Fight*. Tom Ricks, *Washington Post* staff writer and novelist, selflessly provided details that brought this particular stage to life. Chase Brandon of the CIA gave me insights on his business that were crucial in setting the tone for Punk's time on the ground. Commander "Sprout" Proano, USN, came through again with recollections of his missions over Afghanistan. Steve Morse taught me grace in the blinding light. Dan Slater's deft touch raised the bar, as it always does. Ethan Ellenberg, my agent and friend, was there when I needed him—and I needed him a lot. Giles Roblyer continued to be the path to my voice—half literary mentor, half psychologist—and I remain lucky that he knows Punk as well as I do.

Several books provided background for the novel (thanks to Tom Ricks for recommending the first two): Peter Hopkirk, *The Great Game* (1992); Joseph Kessel, *The Horsemen* (1968); Bob Woodward, *Bush at*

War (2002); Robin Moore, *The Hunt for Bin Laden* (2003) (accuracy controversy notwithstanding); and Ahmed Rashid, *Taliban* (2000).

And finally, I thank my sons, Hunton and Reid, for their honesty and respect, and my wife, Carrie, for her love and friendship.